Mind Games:
Memento Mori

Mind Games
Memento Mori

Debrah Martin

Published by IM Books

www.debrahmartin.co.uk

MIND GAMES: MEMENTO MORI

ISBN 978-1-9160886-2-7

*"The mind is its own place and in itself,
can make a Heaven of Hell,
a Hell of Heaven"*

– John Milton

Chapter 1

He's going to tell me why he's done it. He's calling my name to get my attention and his mouth is opening and …

And nothing.

I open my eyes and the blank ceiling is staring back down at me, a single exploded paint bubble mimicking Dada's mouth – open but wordless. Just the dream again. And I haven't had it in ages.

'Damn!'

I say it softly to the smoothness of the freshly painted ceiling and the open-mouthed paint bubble. It merely pouts back at me, a soft 'oooh' like that last, lingering breath before death. Why today, of all days? I close my eyes, and wait for the unease to dissipate, but it lingers until I slam the alarm off just as it starts to buzz. The timebomb of a new day can't be avoided even if the dream can. And today is *the* day.

I sit upright, impatiently kicking the drift of bedclothes onto the floor and looking along the line of my body. Me. Long, lean, languorous – but now also with that creeping sense of bewilderment the dream always brings with it. Outside the hum of rush-hour traffic has already started and I'm conscious of the need to go with it. Come on, I mentally chastise myself. Not the same old dream and the same old bewilderment today. That is all behind you. Today is your fresh start so move it, baby, or you'll be late and then what will they make of the new girl? And you ought to check your notes again before you leave. Be on top of things – a *real* professional for your patients, not a facsimile of one. Correction, *clients*. They don't use *patients* at Ethos. No one is sick at Ethos, only *seeking assistance*.

That does it. I cannot linger in the past when the present is so much more pertinent. I roll out of bed and dig my toes into the luxury of new carpet. Everything new today, including me. The smell of new wool is overlaid by the smell of fresh paint. I'm not sure which is the less attractive – or the most abrasive. Both odours will dissipate in time, of

1

course. Everything does, even uncertainty. Who said that? I shrug. Me possibly – in a whimsical moment. I laugh at the thought and stretch. The tightness in my neck reminds me of Romaine's concern yesterday as I left.

'You're going to be entirely on your own there. Are you sure ...'

'I'll be fine. I'll be busy. And you could visit? There's a spare room, you know.'

'I know. I will. But you'll still be on your own until then. What if ...'

'That hasn't happened in ages now.'

'I know,' and then that moment's hesitation. *'But promise me you won't dwell on it nevertheless.'*

'I won't dwell on it.'

But here I am, dwelling on it. Both of us dwelling on it. Secretly. Reluctantly. Guiltily.

No! I breathe in and out slowly and do some stretches. The tension in my neck releases a little as the mental notes start forming to be successfully ticked off. Shower, dress, check the Ethos notes. I pad into the bathroom, avoiding the bathroom cabinet. I don't need what's in there any more, even though I keep it there to remind me. I step into the shower, turning it on full force and it hammers on my skull before shattering into droplets over my skin. I can see a shadowy reflection of myself in the shiny new shower screen until it mists over. Blonde hair plastered to my head and face like a tarnished gold swimming cap, full lips partly open, tongue catching the water droplets as I had as a child when it rained. Blue-grey eyes observe a partial me as I'm gradually engulfed by the steam. Now I see me, now I'm gone. Maybe there'll be a different me in my place when the steam clears? I play the game I always play at times like this. Which me shall it be? I run my hands over my body since I can no longer see anything in the clouded bathroom. I close my eyes and *feel*, skimming the curves, lightly touching the curling down between my legs and then letting my hands slip to my sides as the water purges me. It's good to have a sense of yourself. That's what I've had drummed into me from infancy, all the way through university and on to training afterwards. *Know who you are. Accept who you are. Act on who you are. Unless you do that, you will always be weak, at everyone's whim.*

Dada wasn't weak, he was strong, but still he ...

I shake the thought away.

'I know who I am,' I say decisively to the hazy form in the shower screen. Despite the damn dream, I swear I have moved on – so far, I can barely even see where I was anymore. 'I am a shooting star,' I tell the blurry impression of me. Director Anhelm called me a shooting star, when he read my CV. Didn't that confirm it? 'And I will be fine,' I add on the tail end of that thought, although whether I'm reassuring me or the image of me, I'm not sure.

Dressed and groomed, I head to the kitchen. Everything in here is as new and shiny as in the bedroom and bathroom. The brand-new coffee machine is the first thing I spot. I need coffee the most this morning. A prompt, not a crutch. I set my laptop up on the breakfast bar and log in, then head back to the coffee machine. The laptop screen flickers into life behind me but I am too busy fiddling with the coffee machine's switches and dials to bother with the news headlines for the moment. I select what looks to be the programme for a latte, one cup. I load the coffee capsule into the top, fill the water container at the back and slide a mug in place to catch the coffee. The machine hisses and spurts into the mug but doesn't stop when it reaches the top. It overflows onto the counter and dribbles onto the floor.

'Shit!' I say, searching for something to mop up with as the jaunty ring of a Skype call chooses precisely the same moment to come through. I'm about to ignore it when a glance at the screen changes my mind. It is Director Anhelm. 'Oh God – now?' I sigh and leave the overflowing coffee to talk to my new boss.

'Dr McCray – Gaby!' He is moonfaced-happy, grinning expansively at me.

'Hi,' I say, trying to emulate his grin. His eyes flick from my face to the coffee lake behind me. 'Everything OK?'

'Yes, oh yes,' I say breathlessly, the smile now slipping into the right place on my face. 'It's fine. Everything's fine. Really great.'

'Good.' He sounds like he's praising a small child. 'Had the place completely refurbed for you so I'm glad about that.' I don't miss the hint of gentle admonishment in his tone – *so don't mess it up...* He hesitates – fractionally – but enough for something to stir in my stomach. 'Look, Gaby, I'm ringing with my apologies. I'm afraid I'm not going to be there to greet you today after all. In fact, none of us will – apart from Jenny. She'll be able to help you.'

'Jenny?'

'My PA. Probably knows more than me anyway – or so she tells me.' He laughs at his own joke, but I take note anyway. *Jenny.* 'It's this conference. Didn't expect it to go quite so well for us, but hell, when you're the talk of the town ... Anyway, it means we're all staying on for the rest of this week to capitalise on it. There's a lot of money riding on this so I know you'll understand. I've uprated your status to compensate. And you will be great, of course.' He's nodding and smiling at me and I know from the way he's smiling that I'm meant to wholeheartedly agree.

'Of course,' I repeat, without being entirely sure what I'm agreeing with. My stomach is starting to dip and wheel now, like it used to.

'Good.' The same unctuous smile. 'We'll be back next week, so do whatever you feel comfortable with in the meantime. I've told Jenny you only need tackle what you fancy to begin with, so it'll be a gentle lead in for you, even without us there. I've emailed you the basics. Keep an open mind and your opinions to yourself and we'll talk strategy next week.' He casts a glance over his shoulder at a distant knock on the door. 'Oh, must go; breakfast calling. The full English here is to die for.'

The call ends but a little letter icon flickers at me on the top menu of the screen. The Director's email no doubt. Great. I can't help it, but already I don't like him. Who abandons their new member of staff on their first day? *A man expecting their new member of staff to be able to cope*, is the wry accusation in my head. OK, I will – even if my rapidly beating heart suggests otherwise.

I read the email from the Director as I sip too-hot coffee and try to force down a piece of dry toast. Initially it's pretty much a repeat of what he's just said, but the killer is in the second paragraph – literally.

"So sorry I'm not going to be there for your first day, Gaby. It's crazy here – apologies for the pun – since yesterday's presentation. Need to keep our cohort at the conference to capitalise on it now, but I'm afraid that leaves you holding the fort. Just play the official representative for Ethos – you're a much prettier face than me, anyway!

At Ethos we seek the unique solution for the unique client, so always keep deniability in mind and you'll be fine. That said, there are two clients to avoid; Morgan and Client X. Sorry to bring your father into this, but I know he would want me to steer you away from these two. Foul play and suicide are never a good mix. And best to avoid muddying waters from the past.

By the way, enjoy the little bonus for the inconvenience and enjoy your first week at Ethos.

MIND GAMES: MEMENTO MORI

Robert Anhelm
Director, Ethos Consultants
'Finding ethical solutions.'

I linger over the organisation's tagline before going back and re-reading the second paragraph. So he knew Dada – or was it he knew *of* Dada? Correction. Everyone who was anyone in the world of experimental psychology knew *of* Dada, but Dr Anhelm's mention implied a more personal knowledge. He hadn't mentioned him at interview though, and surely he would have? There is an attachment too, but it is brief and useless. It simply lists various patients' names, their next appointment times – the first ones seemingly not until tomorrow – and the secretary's phone number. I go back to the body of the email and hang over it. '*... and best to avoid muddying waters from the past...*' What muddy waters? And why mention Dada? What had they to do with Dada? The hairs on the back of my neck bristle with sudden concern. I got this job so easily, so quickly. Too easily, maybe? I should have asked more about it first, and how I came to be approached when I have no experience to speak of yet. Ethos: not treatment but solutions. Not illnesses but issues. Not patients but clients – and two already specifically forbidden me; that Dada would have specifically forbidden me if he'd been around to do so. The implication is that Director Anhelm must have known my father rather well, given his claim that Dada would have wanted him to intervene.

I take the laptop with its open email into the bedroom, to the chest of drawers near the window. It is still bare other than for the photograph lying flat on its back because the stand broke when I'd unpacked it last night. Man, woman and child smile up at me as if there have never been any questions to answer, or any explanations to seek. Me, Romaine and Dada. I brush the glass with my fingertips. Truth be told, Dada is the sole reason I've ended up here, trying to figure out the sicknesses that made people do things so unlike themselves they defy explanation. To mend the broken, understand the inexplicable. But Dada wasn't sick; couldn't have been sick. He'd been the one who'd cured the sick, restored the damaged soul, healed the broken mind. He couldn't have been broken himself. I had never believed that, whatever they'd said. Neither had Romaine, whether she admitted it or not. So why? That day is lodged in my memory, even if my memory won't release it from the fissure it has become wedged in. And I have dwelled on it every minute of every day between then and now – wedged it in tighter, more inaccessible, safer. My eyes blur with tears as I try to concentrate on the photograph and I admit now I haven't moved on. I have never moved on from that day my father voluntarily left the world – and me – with no explanation why. I push the photo away and hold my head in my hands, one elbow resting on the laptop and the other on the photo, as the tears flow. They slow only when the wild scrolling of my laptop screen breaks through the haze of misery. Beyond the sign-off on the Director's email, there is a single sentence making up a message below what the Director has sent – one that looks more like a note than a message, and some of it deleted. I read and re-read it trying to comprehend.

"Steer her away. A would have insisted. Chiaro-"

I read it several times more before it shoots a hole as clear as the hole in Dada's skull through what little composure I have left. The Director's email to me has effectively forwarded another, surely not intended for me. I am amazed at the negligence – and yet Director Anhelm can't be so stupid or careless as to have overlooked it. He wouldn't be Director of the most sought after psychological treatment centre in London if he was. This must have been deliberate. Suddenly I have the sense of having walked into a lion's den, with me abandoned to the prowling lions and what else?

I decide there and then how I'm going to tackle this. There are things here that affect me; issues that affect me and I'm not going to tuck them away into fissures or crevices and pretend they don't exist. At least one of these forbiddens has brushed with suicide so they must *know*. Potentially they have the understanding that I have always been denied. Is it that? And what would Dada say if he *had* spoken in the dream? Something tells me that Director Anhelm might even know what that would be, but he is deliberately and frustratingly absent for the next week, so it is in my hands now to find out. They shall be mine, these forbidden ones. Then Dada will tell me why, and I will break my dream. And I will prove to Director Anhelm and everyone else that I am my father's daughter and I *am* a shooting star, just like him: but one that isn't going to fall from the heavens.

Chapter 2

The journey into London from my Putney flat is disconcerting to say the least. The London tube is as busy and crowded as I remember it from the visit here to be interviewed and I am too used to open fields and rolling hills. I need to adjust fast. I squeeze in between a lout with headphones engulfing his head like a prosthesis and a businessman spreading his newspaper into my personal space as well as that of the woman on the other side of him. Around the edge of it, and beyond the Monday morning summary of a bull market despite the difficult political climate, my opposite numbers stare back at me. The elderly man diagonally opposite smiles at me and I smile back until I realise he is fumbling under his mac and his smile isn't a smile, but a leer. I switch my gaze hurriedly to the woman directly opposite, trying to control her unruly brood. The boy, about seven, is kicking the underneath of the seat and his drumming resonates in time with the rocking of the train. He is staring at me too, that baleful-eyed stare of the young and bored. In between him and the woman is what I assume to be his sister. She is grizzling. Her voice has the high-pitched whine of the spoilt. Briefly, I feel sorry for the woman – pinch-faced and harried – then I remind myself that all early behaviour is the product of parental input. Role models. Rosenstock, Bandura, Katz, Kahn – even Freud to some extent – would agree. She should have done better. She is feeding sweets to the girl when she should be setting boundaries. I can feel my lips pursing with censure. The boy is still staring at me and the old man is still fondling himself and leering at my legs so I focus on the girl and the mother and try to tuck my legs as far out of sight as the solid seat base will allow.

The girl is tugging at the woman's bag, whining. The high pitch grates on me, winding into my brain like an earworm. I break – censorious as I am – or something inside me does. *For God's sake! Social learning theory be damned! Just give it to her – whatever it is – and give me some peace while I get my head together for today!* Immediately I am ashamed. Call myself a psychologist? What is the matter with me? Nerves. That's it. Nerves. This is my fresh start and it have to make it work but already I am ragged like a piece of torn cloth over what lies ahead of me. Get a grip, Gab! I would have had more coffee before I left, if it hadn't been for that damned machine.

The mother must have read my mind. She opens her bag and hands over the object of the girl's pestering. A doll.

'Abigail ...' the girl cries and hugs the doll to her. I jolt out of my irritation. The same name as the doll I adored as a child, with her ringlet curls and wide blue eyes that said mischief above all else. Amazingly, this one is almost identical – same golden curls, pouting mouth, eyes that follow you everywhere and you just know she would know what to do, in any situation, if she were real. My head spins at the name and the similarity – and the almost lost memory. A long-ago childhood trip to London with Dada to Harrods. A treat. And there was Abigail. Of course, she didn't come into my life then – not until later – but I knew as soon as I saw her that she would, whatever became of her latterly. And what had become of her latterly? I haven't thought about her for years. How could that be? How could I have forgotten about Abigail?

The girl is staring at me now, and I realise I have been staring at her too. She slowly and deliberately pokes her tongue out at me and I colour and look away, yet the memory of Abigail and her supercilious smile is still with me as I enter the main reception and check in with the bored receptionist.

Red nails, perfect hair and make-up, too perfect to be real; she could be another Abigail, except that no one could even come close. The receptionist is a plastic imitation. She does succeed in making the more average of us feel inadequate, though.

'Ethos?' I ask, showing the ID card I'd been sent. She glances at it and her disdain is immediately obvious. She waves me dismissively towards the lift.

'Second floor.' I stare at her in amazement. Receptionists received, not dismissed. 'Second floor,' she repeats slowly and loudly, as if I'm an imbecile. I still stare. My legs have a long-ago lethargy, reminiscent of another time and another place when I was similarly disdained, but I can't remember when. She sighs and abandons her station to wiggle across to the lifts, beckoning for me to come with her.

'Main reception is for clients. You should come in the back. Staff entrance.' She presses the lift call button and it arrives like a well-trained dog. 'Your Director thinks it's more professional that way.' She gives me a look which condemns me as the antithesis of professional, but unexpectedly, I still have Abigail in my head. I am about to reply – cutting and to the point just as she would have to this kind of behaviour, when I remember this is my fresh start. The day the shooting star's trajectory heads towards mid-heaven, not crashes and burns over some ignorant receptionist's lack of reception. Instead, I thank her coolly and step into the lift. She reaches past me and presses the floor button, like she's pressing the activation button on a waste disposal machine. I watch her through the closing lift doors with something approaching loathing, but I must let it pass. I turn to appraising myself in the mirrored glass walls of the lift to deflect the inclination to dwell on her. I will do. I am brains without beauty. Not ugly, or even plain, but sleek, neat, business-like. Doctor McCray. The title fits the appearance. I know who I am. I can do this.

I practise my freshly acquired, cool, confident smile but am jolted into my new world before it is fully honed when the lift stops suddenly at the first floor. I stab the button labelled two. The lift goes nowhere. I try it again. Nothing. My armpits prickle. Please don't let me get trapped in the lift on my first day. I stab the 'open door' button and still nothing happens. My breath comes out ragged and hot. I push the button again, persistently – a salesman on a doorbell – and this time the doors judder open. A small dark-haired woman is standing in front of them, forehead creased at the buttons flashing on and off on the call panel.

'The lift,' I explain breathily. 'It's stuck. I want the second floor – Ethos.'

'Dr McCray?' she replies, the frown lifting.

'Yes?' I deplore the note of surprise in my voice which makes it high-pitched and girlish.

'I'm Jenny, and this *is* Ethos.'

Jenny. I straighten up.

'The receptionist said second floor.'

I can feel Jenny's frown now playing out on my own forehead and consciously attempt to smooth it. She smiles, but her expression remains a question mark.

'Blonde hair, pink nails, red lips?'

'Yes.'

'She would. It's deliberate. I think she must have had a bad experience with a shrink once and this is her way of getting payback.'

'But that's so inappropriate! She's a receptionist. It's her job to be helpful.'

'And her answer would be she's not here for your benefit, but for our clients'.' Jenny shrugs and the question mark disappears. 'She has a point. It all depends on the perspective you take with anything, doesn't it?'

'Not really,' I reply. 'Courtesy is courtesy, whoever it is applied to. So is ignorance.'

'Well,' she hesitates. *Too much. Too soon. Tone it down.* 'She did ring me to say you were on your way up, and she did send you to the *first* floor so ... Anyway, you're here now, and welcome. Let me show you around so you don't have to suffer her again in the future.' The teasing twist to her lips isn't lost on me and I'm back to childhood and the child who never quite got it right and had to ask and ask and ... She ushers me out of the lift and I follow her neatly arranged back view across the hall and towards the door marked 'Ethos'. She presses an assortment of buttons on the call panel and door swings open.

'Open sesame!' she laughs. 'Abandon all hope, etc.' I get the joke but I'm back to dwelling on the receptionist. She catches my look and straightens her face. 'Well, come on in anyway.' She allows me to walk past her and I can feel her appraising me as I do so. Fair enough. I am appraising her too. She gestures to an open door on our left. 'This is me. Gatepost, gateway, and gate itself. No one comes in or out without me knowing.' She stops and turns to me and I almost catapult into her. 'Security.' She is small, inches shorter than me. And slight.

'Nice to know I'm so safe.' The little pinprick of irony doesn't even draw blood.

'Well, I'm not your bouncer, but I am your early warning system at least.' She laughs deprecatorily, and I might have liked her then – but for that earlier tease. 'Along here are the Director himself, next to me, then your colleagues, and you're right in the middle.'

We have reached the bend in the corridor – plush, pastel and chic – having passed a number of closed doors with brass nameplates before it turns the corner. We are outside a door where the name plate says, 'Dr McCray'.

'Mine?'

I can see she is tempted to say something smart Alec in reply, but she pulls herself back in time and merely agrees. She opens the door and lets it swing wide so I can survey my new kingdom. At first all I can do is stare. The door starts its return trip and she catches it before it slams in our faces. As it comes back towards us, the closing door also announces I am Assistant Director.

'Oh!'

Her eyes follow mine and then we eye each other. Her expression is unreadable.

'Shall we?' she suggests, pushing the door wide again and stepping inside. I follow, suddenly dwarfed by the enormity of what I am becoming today. A shooting star, maybe, but in a wholly unknown universe.

'It's huge,' I say involuntarily. I go back to the door and open it again to look at the name plate. So this was what the Director had meant about uprated status and bonuses. Now I understand the challenge I have sensed from Jenny too. Until now she has been Queen Bee, but another Queen Bee has just infiltrated the nest.

'Didn't you know?' she asks, carefully neutral. 'Robert has been full of it for days. So convenient with the conference coming up ...'

I take stock of that. So it wasn't simply because of an unexpectedly successful presentation – on what topic? This had been planned. The sense of being tested – or maybe manoeuvred – intensifies and the old need to prove myself makes my shoulders straighten and my jaw clamp.

'Oh, of course,' I nod. 'Just taking it all in.'

She continues to scrutinise me. 'We must have a Director or an Assistant Director in situ at all times, so of course, with you ...'

I don't understand her persistence with the subject ... and then I get it. She's warning me. All the shooting star stuff and the references to Dada in the email; my pedigree has gone before me, not my CV. I watch the realisation she's said too much form and make her nibble her bottom lip as if she wished she could bite the words back. So am I being used or employed. Tested or examined? Inwardly I fume. Outwardly I smile politely.

'I see,' I say.

Jenny is waiting for me to enlarge on my polite comment. When I don't she simply nods and crosses the room to stand by the desk – a monstrosity of ice white, highly polished, and reflecting back the blinding light of office walls seemingly made entirely of glass – three walls anyway. In fact, the whole room stands proud of the main building itself, balanced on concrete pillared stilts over the front entrance.

'Well, anyway...' Jenny is indicating the complicated conglomeration of PC and phone equipment. 'This is your phone system and computer combined.' The desk and the phone system hover synergistically in front of the bookcase like a steely silver and white edifice, broken only by a cascade of dirty brown manila folders in the centre of it. I nod and wait. I can see she's feeling uncomfortable but that's fine. We're negotiating terms here, and I'm on the winning side currently because she doesn't yet know what to make of me. She continues, 'it's pretty self-explanatory once you get started, but I can give you a demo if you're not adept with computers.'

In front of the desk, the only other furniture in the room – two leather chairs - float in the middle of a sea blue rug. It's minimalist, and yet surprisingly feminine in a cool, uncomfortable way. I survey it all, slowly and minutely, ending up looking back at Jenny. She is still watching me carefully.

'OK,' I say.

'Do you like it?'

I walk over to the central window-wall and look down into the car park below. Even the floor beneath me seems to be suspended in thin air. My head spins with vertigo. I turn away from the window but either side of me is merely more glass. I head back to the centre of the room and retreat to behind the desk. At least the bookcase behind it is solid and I can't fall through it, like Alice into a rabbit hole.

'Not really.' It comes out, woefully unedited and I too, now wish I'd bitten my tongue first before I allowed it to utter.

'It's one of the best rooms in the suite,' she says, expression indecipherable, but the censure is implicit.

'It's just it's a bit of fishbowl,' I say to soften the criticism. 'A glasshouse.'

'Better not throw any stones, then,' she quips, and waits, but this time I do bite on my tongue. 'Well,' she adds when she doesn't get a response, straightening the already straight phone receiver, 'the rest of the office is this section in reverse, minus the awesome office. The kitchen is round the corner, as are the toilets. Would you like me to show you the rest of your domain?'

There's a gleam of something in her eyes. I wonder if it's mischief. I am not going to achieve Queen Bee in her eyes, whatever, I suspect.

'Thanks, but I expect I can find them myself. I am Assistant Director, after all.' This time the pinprick does draw blood. I can see it in the twist of the lips that isn't quite smile. Touché. We appreciate each other for the briefest of moments and then she moves swiftly on.

'OK.' She moves away from the desk. 'And the phone system?'

'Just tell me how to dial in and out on it?'

'Zero zero one for me, zero zero two for the Director, and so on for everyone else. To dial out, it's nine then the number you want, but all outgoing calls are tracked. I've left a list of passwords for the computer in your top drawer, together with the entry code to the main door. Are you OK with seeing clients straight away, if need be? The Director said – '

'That's fine,' I cut in. 'I'll see whoever needs seeing – oh, and in fact there are a couple you should allocate to me specifically too.' She raises her eyebrows. 'Client X and someone with the surname of Morgan.'

She pauses. 'Oh, but they're the Director's clients …'

'Who isn't here all week.'

'Right.' The hesitation is fractional. 'Well, if you're sure, I'll allocate them to you straightaway.' She eyes me again and her look is even less readable now. I could have done with an ally here, but I'm not sure it's going to be Jenny. 'I've left the files for the clients already allocated on your desk. None too tricky. Myers – she's merely a toxic relationship addict, but…' she pauses. 'Well, Morgan, she's a control freak and Client X, he's –'

Her expression completes the uncompleted sentence and I can't help but take her down.

'Isn't that a bit judgemental?'

She returns my challenge with a small smile. 'Don't we all judge people, even when we claim not to? Is there anything you *would* like me to help with right now?'

'Thanks – I'll let you know when I've had a look around.'

Much as I would have liked to pump her – about the Director, my colleagues, the routine – for now I just want her to go so I can regain equilibrium. New job is one thing. New job where I'm almost the boss and there are reasons still to work out why is quite another. And then there are the forbiddens… She walks over to the door and is about to leave but hesitates again.

'I assume the Director *has* already given you the spiel about always letting them talk the talk so you don't have to walk the walk?'

'I'm sorry?

'Don't be tempted to interact. Too much risk of accountability.'

'I really don't think I need telling how to conduct myself with my patients.' I can feel the hairs on the back of my neck rising. If I were a dog, the ridge would stretch all the way down to my tail. Jenny pulls the door open and slides behind it so only half her body remains showing. Maybe animal instincts remain in us despite our millions of years of evolution since we were apes. 'No offence intended,' I add belatedly. I may not have an ally, but nor do I want an outright enemy in Jenny either.

'Clients,' she reminds me gently. 'And no offence taken,' she adds. 'It's just that we operate slightly differently to the norm here. Just in case.'

'Just in case?'

'Of what it might lead to. You know where I am, and if you really don't like the room, I'll tell the Director when he comes back.'

The door swishes into place and seals her out. I am left staring at it with a mixture of exasperation, irritation and amusement. Part of me actively dislikes her. Another senses a sharp mind and an even sharper understanding that I might want to befriend, but like hell will I let her make comment on my liking or disliking of the office I've been allocated. That will be my prerogative. If I am Assistant Director in recompense for being abandoned and manoeuvred this week, I'm going to make the most of it, whatever the Director has planned.

'Droit de seigneur,' I say to myself as I dump my bag on the desk. It feels like I'm settling myself in for a siege, with my bag as barricade on one side and the complicated phone and computer system on the other. In front of me are the advancing forces – my prospective patients; behind me the wall of weighty tomes that are my defences against mental illness. But first ... I dither – so which to tackle as a priority? The computer maybe? See where the passwords lead me?

I switch on the beast and it purrs at me, the screensaver the Ethos logo – a triangle that isn't quite a triangle – open at the top, a little like an inverted funnel. It hovers in front of me and I study it before moving on. Why a triangle? Or rather, why not a completed triangle? I shrug. Who cares. Every business has a logo these days – an identity. This is the Ethos identity; a triangle with wiggle room – the deniability element, perhaps? I click on the screen and a welcome message pops up, requesting my ID and password. Obediently I enter the details Jenny has left and there she is again.

'Hello, Dr McCray. I am your office support. Can I help you? Anything you need. Please call extension 001 or email me at officemanager.' It's a recorded message of Jenny's smiling image, gloating at me, next to the on-screen missive that I don't seem to be able to shift. I click the screen to move past the message but nothing happens.

Five further attempts merely bring up another message. 'Your log-ins and searches are recorded for data protection purposes. Please call extension 001 or email officemanager for assistance.' I press tab, escape, shift, and eventually give in.

'Yeah, right,' I say to her and turn the computer off again. 'You win this time.' I have my laptop in my bag. I decide there and then that unless I need to access Ethos' records, I'll do my own unrecorded searches – without Jenny's 'assistance'. I sigh, a heavy puff of hot air, like a crusty retired subaltern would have made back in the day, and then laugh at myself. You are the Assistant Director and she is the PA. Remember that. I pull the patient folders towards me instead. The top one is for Candy Myers – the toxic relationship addict. I open it and browse. Not a lot in it. A couple of meeting transcripts, with a lot of woe is me from Candy and not much from her consultant at Ethos. I decipher the signature at the end of the first transcript. R-o-b-e... Robert Anhelm. A patient of the Director? He hadn't mentioned her as a leave-alone – in fact, I don't think she is even on the list he provided of today's appointments. I attack the transcript with more interest. Not much of a challenge, but something to cut my teeth on at least – and right in the spotlight for him to monitor my efficacy. OK, I will show him... but, I still don't remember the name on the authorised list of my patients. I drag my laptop out of my bag and find his email from this morning. It confirms my suspicions. There is no Candy Myers on his list. I turn the pages in the folder back over and end up the topmost one – the appointment record – and a bolt of shock runs through me, ending in my stomach.

Shit! I stare at the appointment sheet. She's due in at ten and it's now nine fifty. I haven't even begun to get to grips with her past history, and apart from that, why hasn't Jenny told me about the appointment? I look at the sheet of paper attached to the list of passwords Jenny's given me and see that, contrary to my assumptions, she has. Or rather, it confirms she hasn't, but the Director has – after a fashion.

'Gaby,' the Director has scrawled across it – now I've seen his signature, I can recognise his hand. 'Ten am, Monday: Candy Myers – folder herewith. Sorry to hand you a pup, but this one needs constant TLC, so has to be seen even though she's not down on your list. She's a private client of mine, so this is a favour to me. Just listen and sympathise – there's a good girl. She doesn't really need anything else.'

The cheek! I'm about to tangle with the phone system and dial the much-vaunted 001 extension but Jenny herself pre-empts me.

'Dr McCray, your ten o'clock client is just arriving. I'll bring her straight down to you, shall I?'

Time to make my fresh start happen in earnest.

'Yes. And Jenny?'

'Yes?'

'I think we need to go over the appointment system later. I don't think it's quite working.'

'Oh?'

'Yes. Like when there's a ten o'clock appointment I don't have listed.'

I hope I sound unfazed and business-like, but there's laughter in her voice.

'Really? Who?'

'This one.'

'Ah! But ... By all means. Anything you want to know – fount of all knowledge, me!'

'Yes,' I say to the receiver as I put it down. 'So you say. Even on diagnoses.'

Forty minutes later, I have to eat my words.

Chapter 3

Candy Myers is chic, sophisticated and expensive – and pathetic. I can see it a mile off even as she enters the room. One of the Director's private clients? How many other 'private clients' does he have? Her limp fingers leave mine feeling like they've been oiled with self-pity, even though hers are dripping with rings. She totters over to the consulting room chairs and perches on the edge of one like it might engulf her if she dropped her guard. Her legs are slim and pretty and she sits like a model – arranging her body so it is on best display. Private client, my ass!

'How can I help you today?'

'How can anyone?' she shrugs pathetically and smooths a non-existent crease from her cream leather coat. Her hair is platinum blonde too – almost cream. As light as mine – very like mine, in fact. She matches the consulting room chair. She could merge with it if it wasn't for the red silk blouse peeking out from the collar of the coat. 'Ronnie is still being such a b – even after what Robert suggested I did last time.'

I sit opposite her and arrange my encouraging look across my face. We hone them – looks – as psychologists. We hone whole personas too sometimes – when they're needed. Who is the more confused? The psychologist or their patient? I try not to laugh at that. It's the kind of thing Dada would have thrown at his students just to provoke them. That's why he was so brilliant. We take on a persona to encourage rapport – to achieve a connection, even where there wouldn't normally be one. We are paid to connect to patients – to create a lifeline between psychosis and health. I learnt that the hard way. Without Dada.

'Ronnie? Your partner?'

'Yes.' Her bottom lip trembles. I settle back for the monologue. At the end of it I am feeling complacent. My brief and hurried assessment of her from the transcripts I skimmed was right. Pathetic. Classic victim mentality, not toxic relationship addict as Jenny had dubbed her. I smile inwardly and swing into victim defusing.

'Relationships work on give and take, not all one way. If it's all give in one direction, that's why it doesn't feel like it's working for you. Why don't you try doing something *you* want to do instead of what they want to do all the time? Think of something you used to do that made you happy before Ronnie, or Ted, or Martin or … I struggle to remember the rest of the men on her list.

'Greg.'

'Greg.' Oh yes – number one on the list.

'But I didn't.'

In the practice runs we did for these kinds of cases there was always progress at this point. Not regression. She starts to cry and I'm fumbling for a tissue or something to offer her. Normally I've been in an office with all the right accoutrements – coffee, tea, tissues. Here, all there is are the giant desk, the monstrous phone and computer system and the glass walls. I eventually find a clean pack of tissues in my own bag and give her one.

I try again.

'You know it doesn't need to be this way for you. We are all entitled to choose what happens in our lives. We make our own destiny.'

She looks doubtfully at me and I smile encouragingly back. Chalk up one to me, nil to the Director and Jenny if she responds positively.

'Maybe you do, Dr McCray. But you're not a mess like me.' She dabs daintily at her nose and eyes, then scrutinises herself in her compact mirror. I'm about to reply but she cuts across me. 'Do I look alright?' she enquires as she peers mouse-like at me from behind it. 'Ronnie's picking me up in ten minutes. He's so sweet like that.'

'You look fine,' I assure her, wondering why the floods of tears haven't ravaged the perfect make-up. She merely looks more natural now. If it had been me, it would have been as if the Aswan Dam had crumbled and carried away all traces of facial structure. And yet, I try to push the thought away uncomfortably; there *is* something of me in her. The hair, and the regularity of the features perhaps. The repeating patterns … Not like Abigail… Oh God, why am I thinking about Abigail again?

'Good,' she gets up and smooths the leather coat again. She is a pale streak of non-colour with a gashed red throat. I adjust my own red shirt collar so it sits differently to hers. 'I feel so much better for our little chat, Dr McCray. It really helps to let off steam, doesn't it? Shall I make another appointment for next week?'

I'd like to sigh with the frustration of it all, but that won't help. I keep the sympathetic smile tacked in place instead – the persona Candy Myers thinks has helped her let off steam in case she decides to come back and give me another shot at beating the Director.

'Of course.'

She twists her lips into a pout, as she considers. 'Or maybe I'll make two appointments,' she giggles. 'You *and* Robert. Double release!'

She's at the door before I can contain my surprise, then I get it. She actually *is* what Jenny said she is. In fact, both Jenny's snap judgement and the Director's advice were sound. They say that successful treatment is one-part diagnosis and two-parts acceptance. I feel a little like a deflated balloon now, having to accept – so, is this all I'm going to have to do here? Accept the role of listener without being able to do anything with what I'm told? I can do that half-asleep and reading a book. I'd hoped for something to make a difference with, finally, after the humdrum of all my archetypal research subjects … But hey – I'm being paid, I'm the Assistant Director, and this is only the start of my blazing star trail. And there are others that are clearly more taxing than the Candy Myers of this world. Morgan and Client X for a start. If I see Candy Myers again I will push the boundaries with her until she sees the pattern for herself too. Patience and persistence; the tools of the successful psychologist. I shake her hand politely, still smiling, and she equally politely refuses my escort back to reception.

'Just in case you're seen with me. You even look like a shrink. He thinks I'm getting my paperwork sorted out. Business accounts.'

'Oh,' again I'm surprised. 'What do you do?' I ask, thinking here might be my way forward with her the next time if she does make a repeat appointment with me.

'I'm an escort, Dr McCray. Not much fun, but it pays well. I suppose I get what I deserve. It comes with the territory. Such a relief you're here to provide the solution to the pointlessness of it all.'

She wafts back down the corridor, leaving me yet again rapidly reassessing her, Ethos and what I am doing here. The unique solution, huh? Something tells me uniqueness has more to do with money and power than ethics and principles for Ethos. I'm going to have to adapt – rapidly – if that's the case.

I wait until Candy Myers has disappeared round the corner at the end of the corridor and the sounds of polite goodbyes and the entrance door opening and closing indicating Jenny has escorted her through the entrance door, then I duck back into my room. I need coffee. The overflowing mess from the coffee machine in my kitchen at breakfast has long since worn off. I need the loo too. Something in my gut isn't quite how it should be. Protesting – nerves probably – but that isn't quite it. I feel out of alignment. Rearranged. More than both of those, I need to get the real measure of Ethos, and how these muddy waters clients fit into it. There's only one person – apart from Director Anhelm, I now suspect – who might know that. Jenny. *Probably knows more than me anyway – or so she tells me.*

I return to the desk-edifice and pull the bottom drawer fully open. I had hastily hidden my bag in there in preparation for Candy Myer's visit although now it is half-exposed and ransacked in the search for tissues. I retrieve it and am about to go in search of the fabled kitchen and ladies' toilets when the phone buzzes at me. The computer screen lights up too, even though I'd turned the damn thing off. Jenny's face appears on it – but in stasis – whilst her voice emanates from the computer's inbuilt loudspeakers.

'Your eleven thirty will be here soon, Dr McCray. She's usually early.'

'My eleven thirty? But I don't have an eleven thirty appointment on the list.' I slam my bag down on the desk and the pen and pad I'd found to use for Candy Myers appointment go flying. 'Jenny, we need to talk about this. I can't keep having patients foisted on me when I don't...'

'Clients,' she interrupts me.

'Clients, patients; they are one and the same. And I don't need the PA to correct me, thank you – especially when she can't even keep track of my appointments!' Damn! I didn't mean to say that. I reel myself in. Cool, calm Gaby. 'I'm sorry, I meant there's a system here that can't keep track of my appointments, not necessarily you...'

Surprisingly, she doesn't sound upset. 'But I have. I gave you all today's appointment this morning as I knew them to be, but there's also a list in your client folder on the computer, updated as they're made, or cases are reallocated.'

'The computer that won't let me past the welcome screen.'

'I did offer to show you how it worked ...'

'I know how a computer works. And I can read files. But what you're telling me and what the list says don't tally.'

'Well, you have rather changed things from what Robert set up.' Her voice is bitter-lemon sweet now. 'You've changed patient allocations. I can't help it if you do that and end up with more than you expected.' I can feel my teeth grinding as the acid burns her victory onto my psyche. And I'm angry with myself too. This is one I should have nailed, but Jenny is good. They don't warn you in research that the biggest mind-fuckers will possibly be your own colleagues in the real world. She waits just long enough for the ire to bite, then adds – on-beat, 'Shall I bring her straight down or do you want me to stall her to give you time to get on top of things?'

'Yes, no, – wait.' I concede – this time, but this is only round one. I know how to deal with smart-asses like Jenny – I've been trained in mind games, after all. I just don't have the time to play them right now. 'Who is she, anyway?'

'Jessica Morgan. You specifically asked for her to be allocated to you, remember? I can give you my ...' I can hear the deliberate pause in her delivery as I imagine the small smile that will be accompanying it. '... assessment of her, if that would help?'

Morgan; control freak, she'd said. Morgan, muddy waters, the Director had said. Whose muddy waters though? And was she the one who knew about suicide, or about foul play?

'No thanks,' I reply as coolly as I can. 'I'll make my own assessment.' I can feel my jaw snapping shut as I complete the sentence, but it seems she's still waiting for instructions. Do I let Jenny bring her down, or stall her so I can get on top of things? I can hear the anticipation Jenny's end, and I'm surprised she's offered me a get-out at all, given our sparring so far. Then it all starts to make sense. Jenny hasn't been playing me, she's been testing me too. I take a deep breath whilst I consider how Dada would have dealt with this? 'Actually, the Director said you are wonderful at dodging bullets for us, so I'll let you do that right now. Can you tell her I'm busy at the moment – unexpected emergency – but I can fit her in this afternoon?'

There is a moment's hush on the other end of the phone, and I imagine Jenny's neat features creasing as she evaluates my response, then spreading into a grin. All we really want is recognition. If I am right, I have played the right mind game. If I am wrong, I may as well go home now.

'A girl after the Director's heart,' she congratulates me. 'I'll re-arrange it.' Her voice cuts off before I can reply but the silent computer screen still bears her image, smiling approvingly at me, with an automated reminder that the notes for the Candy Myers appointment should be filed before my next appointment arrives to avoid them being diluted or contaminated by other unrelated issues. I click it off and toss my bag back in the bottom drawer. I'd still like coffee but the urgency for the loo has gone off, whereas the urgency to get to grips with this brave new world has just racked up a notch. Coffee may have to wait.

I pull the pen and pad towards me – still blank despite having already seen one patient this morning – and prepare to dispose of Candy Myers so I can concentrate on bigger fish. What can I say about Candy Myers other than that Ethos is providing the solution she wants? But Jessica Morgan? The name rings a bell, but why eludes me other than being one of the forbiddens in Director Anhelm's email. I should place it for another reason though. A muddy waters reason, perhaps? I frown with the effort of remembering, but it still eludes me. Jenny's smile – too bright, too big, too artificial – when she eventually ushers in my second patient of the day later that afternoon tells me I should have tried harder. Muddy waters indeed.

Chapter 4

After three false starts, I decide I do need that coffee before I tackle writing up Candy Myers' notes. Even more, I need out of this office for a while. The feeling of continuously being tested and judged as I swim around and around trying to get to grips with my strange new environment, like a goldfish endlessly circumnavigating its bowl, is already getting to me. I feel exposed – both professionally and personally. All my shortcomings under the microscope – even though it's only Jenny and me examining them at the moment. I walk over to the window and stare out over the tarmacked carpark, to the road beyond. It's dotted with trees, gently waving their still greeneried branches in the soft September breeze. The yearning for home is suddenly as strong as the desire to escape. But I can't. How would I explain leaving right now to Jenny? I have said I'm busy, and I have set her the task of fending of Jessica Morgan until later. In setting things onto my terms, I have achieved a modicum of respect from her – that much was clear in the comment about being a girl after the Director's heart – but I also have to be consistent. No, I can't escape outside so I will have to find my escape within – like Dada always told me I could. I place both hands palm to window and try to imagine being the other side of the plate glass, walking away, leaving my fears and anxieties behind me. I close my eyes and trace my steps, out of the building, onto the road, walking far into the distance, back to home, back to the hall, by the study door and the sound of the chiming clock and the raised voices and …

No!

I open my eyes to dispel the memory. I don't want to walk back to that day – haven't for such a long time; why today? I turn my back on the fishbowl window and face into the room itself. And Ethos. What do I know about it, really know about it? It's prestigious, but reclusive, with a reputation synonymous with wealth and power. Not what I envisaged myself being – one the well-paid elitists – but there are certain advantages that go with that, like having backing to publish Dada's book.

Something catches my eye as I scan the room. I cannot place it until I realise it must be emanating from the computer. I leave the window and cross to the console, slipping into my seat behind the desk far easier than I have slipped into the role of its occupant so far. It is a message, demanding to be opened. I click the screen and the message unfolds. It is from 'officemanager'. Jenny. A peace offering, I think – a list of all the local delis, with a star rating against each. Lunch. She's telling me where I can get lunch – and it's getting on for mid-day now. With that I realise the need for coffee and the strange feeling in my gut are most probably symptomatic of the need to eat too, and nothing worse. The dry toast I'd attempted for breakfast still lay as much in ruins in my brand-new Putney apartment kitchen as the abortive coffee. Well, if Jenny was prompting me, I really *could* escape – on the pretext of getting lunch. At least I'd be able to relax and breathe out without feeling like the prime specimen in a glass menagerie for a while too.

I shut down the message and log out of the computer, having first noted the nearest deli to the office, then collect my coat and exit my power-base with a sense of escaping a prison cell. I have all my excuses and expressions of gratitude ready for Jenny – not too much, but enough – but they all prove to be unnecessary. Her own office door is shut, and a note is stuck to it. 'Back for 1pm.' Well, now I really am vindicated. A very long lunch for her then. *While the cat's away...* That's what Abigail would say. I smile wryly. Yes, I still have a long way to go before Jenny acknowledges me as her superior, regardless of the small victory over Jessica Morgan. But she will, if I hold my nerve.

I locate the door to the back exit and make my way down the stairwell leading to it. It is painted stark white and the floor covering is equally sterile. My footsteps echo as I descend, hollow and eerie, into the unlit depths. Good job it's painted white, not black. There are no lights – or no working lights. That is one for Health and Safety. I'm surprised Jenny hasn't flagged it up. At least the door at the bottom is glass-paned and letting in sufficient light to see the re-entry door code re-iterated on the notice just inside. Two-seven-six-one-nine-nine-zero. I read it off and memorise it. It sticks immediately, and I am not usually good with numbers. We either have a number or an images brain. Mine is images. That's why I have that image over and over again of Dada ... I shake it away and concentrate on the numbers again. Then I realise why they appeal to me. They're my date of birth. How weird. I stop and stare at the numbers, making sure I have actually got them right. I have. Romaine would say it's a sign, but I prefer to deal in facts. I shrug and open the door, and the smog-laden air of central London is like breathing in Eden

I follow the pathway round to the front of the building and checking the location of the deli I've chosen on my phone, veer off to the right when I've crossed the half-empty car park. The street comprises a long line of discrete offices masquerading as private residences. The tell-tale that gives the game away is the amount of parking they carefully provide to the front or rear. Almost at the end of the street is a small side road and it is down there I find the deli, thriving, by the look of it, on the business of the discreet offices masquerading as private residences. I am tenth in line and shuffle obediently towards gratification inside the little shop, bulging with people and bread rolls and graciously sharing it's fresh-baked goodness with us as we wait, stomachs gurgling and mouths watering. I idle in the queue, enjoying the very ordinariness of the human condition – that we need to eat, and we need to rest. The girl in front of me is overweight, but jolly. She grins engagingly me when she swings round to pity the ones further back than us.

'Pastrami and coleslaw is best,' she tells me.

'Oh, thanks.' I smile my appreciation.

'Welcome,' she says. 'I shouldn't eat it really. Need to lose weight, but hell – what's life without enjoyment?' Indeed. This is what psychology is really all about. Knowing yourself – and accepting what you know. I nod vigorously until she has to move forward with the peristalsis of the queue. I shuffle forward too, checking how many more are patiently waiting behind me, and it's then I see him. Or think I see him. Someone watching me, turning away quickly as I lazily survey my surroundings, but watching me nevertheless. I know that sensation and it's not paranoia. It's real. You know when you're being watched. I've been studied all my life, without knowing it, I now know, and that feeling is as much a part of my make-up as breathing. The queue shuffles forward another one and the old man behind me nudges me.

'You'll lose your place,' he warns.

'Oh,' I swing round to re-orient myself and when I look back, my observer has gone. But I am not wrong. I was being watched. Intently.

I keep checking until I'm squeezed into the deli and back out again like a sausage through a machine, bearing my prize aloft; a pastrami and coleslaw – that I lose all appetite for immediately after the first bite because as I look the length of the side road, my observer is there again, at the end of it. Waiting for me.

I hesitate. I am being stupid. Why would anyone be looking out for me, let alone stalking me? Barely anyone even knows I'm here. I'm an anonymous face on an insignificant London street. And yet I know it is me he's watching and waiting for. That same shiver of suspense that lifts the hairs on the back of your neck as the climax to the horror film approaches is lifting the hairs on my neck. The elderly man who'd been behind me in the queue brushes past me. He half turns.

'You OK, doll?' he asks. His face is kindly. Laughter lines creasing around his eyes and caressing his mouth.

'My first day in London,' I say, eyeing the figure still lingering at the end of the road. 'I'm a bit disorientated.'

'Where you trying to get back to?' His voice has a cockney twang, more emphatic the softer it is.

'Wellington Road. Number thirty.'

'Oh, that's easy. It's the bottom of this one and along a bit. You ain't gone far out of your way. I'm going back along there. Wanna follow me?'

'Yes, thank you.'

I swing into step alongside him, marvelling at why I feel safer walking along with a stranger than I do on my own. Ahead of me, I keep my eyes fixed on the wavering figure at the end of the road, answering my walking companion's questions mindlessly. As we near enough the corner of the road for me to see more detail, the waiting figure slips away, ducking round the buildings hugging the end of the road. His disappearance suddenly emboldens me. We are in full daylight, after all, and I have a good Samaritan here to help me. I quicken my step in the hope of catching up with my stalker.

'Coo, you late back?' my companion asks, puffing as he attempts to match my pace.

'Oh, no. Sorry. I thought there was someone I knew there – at the corner of the road. I wondered if I might catch them up.'

'That's alright, gel. You plough on then.' He falls back to his previous rhythm and I am already two paces ahead of him before my courage falters. We reach the corner and now I have no choice, especially as my stalker is not far ahead of me. Not close enough to see clearly but close enough to catch up with if I break into a run, yet I hesitate. 'Naw, you go on. You know yer way from 'ere,' he urges. 'See you there another time.'

'OK, thanks,' I call over my shoulder. I break into a trot but the man ahead of me trots too. I am no closer. Holding onto the pastrami sandwich feels like it's hampering me so I dump it in the next bin I pass and really take to my heels. My stalker glances over his shoulder and follows suit. There is something familiar about him now – his gait or maybe his posture – I'm not sure which, but maybe I *have* seen him before. He picks up speed and I struggle to match it but the pavement is rutted and my heels are too high to really sprint in. My ankle caves in and I curse as the stinging pain brings me to a stumbling halt. My stalker races on, not even looking back.

'Wait,' I call to my stalker's dwindling silhouette. He skips in front of a line of traffic, as if he doesn't care if he is mown down, and his trajectory through it is that of a dancer, swift and slight of foot, even though he isn't slight at all. The car nearest hoots at me as I hobble off the kerb to follow.

'Get outta the road,' the driver calls out of his window. He revs his engine and I jump back. Further down there are pedestrian lights, on red. My stalker is now approaching them on the other side of the road, at a more leisurely pace. I totter on towards them and wait for them to change and the 'green walk' sign to pop up. Maybe now he's slowed I might catch him up, but by the time the green light appears, my stalker is far, far down the road – almost out of sight. I hesitate, unsure now what to do. Follow stealthily and maybe I'll catch up with him a few blocks further on – or go back to the office? Caution beats adventure in the end. I don't know London, I don't know what I might encounter if I do catch up with him, nor why he would be spying on me anyway. In fact, I reason as I watch the distant figure disappear from view, I don't even know if he was watching me at all – or someone else in the queue outside the deli. Maybe he is a private detective watching an unfaithful husband or wife, or a pickpocket, lining up his next victim. I laugh, suddenly and uncontrollably, at my ridiculousness. Thank God Jenny hasn't witnessed it – or any of my patients. No, I correct myself; clients!

I retrace my steps as far as number thirty and follow the path round to the back entrance. Now I am hungry again and feeling foolish. It's probably another withdrawal symptom, this feeling of being watched. The literature did warn of withdrawal symptoms, without being too specific. Romaine would know more but I can't tell her. I can't tell anyone. For the first time since I arrived, I wish my fresh start hadn't appeared like a beacon out of the blue. I wish the letter from Ethos inviting me to apply for the position of consultant had never dropped onto the mat, or my PhD been so spectacularly convincing. But it had, and like it or not, this is my fresh start. My only fresh start. The ache of misery makes my throat stiff and intractable. I stab the numbers into the keypad and the staff door swings open. I step back into the silence of the cold white stairwell and its unwelcoming ambience. It is a vacuum lock, this back way in – a capsule devoid of atmosphere other than what I put into it. My heart is still pounding from the unexpected exercise and my armpits are sticky. My fringe is plastered to my forehead and I need to cool and calm down. I must present an unedifying picture – not at all what you would expect your psychologist to look like. I need to gather myself and my thoughts together before I present myself to the world beyond this vacuum again … I close my eyes and think myself back into place; back into Abigail. I open my eyes with surprise at that. I hadn't realised Abigail occupied so much space in my unconscious mind, but maybe that is good. She was cool and calm and in control, just how I need to be … I play the shower game without the benefit of the shower and by the time I reach Jenny's door – now open – I am Dr Gaby McCray, Assistant Director, again.

'Oh, hello,' she calls to me as I attempt to pass it without stopping.

I stop.

'Thank you for the list of delis,' I say politely.

'Oh, no problem. Thought it might help a little, Assistant Director or not.'

'It did.' Warmth floods through me. Yes, it had – despite the strange stalker who'd run away.

'Good, but it wasn't that I wanted to catch you about. I've had a specific request for you.'

'Candy Myers?'

'No. She hasn't even re-booked yet. She's like that. Just expects Robert to be available … No, it's Mr Thierone.'

'Mr Thierone?'

'Georges Thierone. Works in something a bit hush-hush.'

'Oh, OK.' The way she says it makes it feel like a compliment that he's asked for me.

'He said you looked nice. Approachable. From a distance.'

'Oh.' My mouth stops working but my brain shoots on. My stalker? 'What kind of hush-hush?'

'An organisation called Chiaroscuro.' She avoids my eyes, fiddling with her pad and pen. I watch her doodle develop. C-h-i-a-r-o -. Then she crosses it through. 'And Jessica Morgan's at one-thirty now. I hope that's OK?'

'Yes, yes.' As I walk away I realise I would have I would have liked to have asked her to elaborate on Jessica Morgan. Even more so, I would have liked Jenny's assessment of Georges Thierone, even though I cannot ask for it – and why he should have asked specifically for me. C-h-i-a-r-o. The half-deleted word in the message the Director had forwarded to me...

Chapter 5

Jessica is nervous and restless, clearly on the spectrum and far too high-functioning to be unaware of it. She is affected too; very full of herself. She sells shoes, she says. A shoe-shop girl. I express amusement – more because it's expected than because I feel it. She smiles complacently, mouth twisting at her joke. I don't know her though. Or at least, I don't think I do so the muddy waters run clear for now. A snatched glance at her minimalist file before she arrived told me she is the CEO of a well-known retail outlet. I know the brand but not the woman behind it.

She is an odd collection of qualities, and she is immaculately made up and turned out, yet her own shoes are worn brown brogues with the toes turning up from over-use. She sees me looking at them with curiosity – not very professional, but I am still off-balance from the escapade at lunchtime and little details keep catching my eye and trapping me in faux pas I would normally avoid with a lightness of touch that would indeed make me a chip off Dada's block. I try to look away before it is something for her to remark on, but I am too slow. First day nerves and hormones, I put it down to. My period is due and imminently threatening too.

'Yes,' she says dryly. 'Ugly aren't they? They're my penance.'

'Your penance?'

'Self-imposed. For my sins.' She says it with a trill in her voice, like it's amusing, but her expression is far from amused now, mouth turning down at the corners. A sad marionette.

'What are your sins?'

'I thought you knew? Aren't they all in there?' She waves languidly at the buff folder, labelled Morgan, J.

I shake my head because they aren't. Neither folder for the two clients I have encountered so far have anything like enough detail in them – not that I've had much time to take in much of either of them. Name, address, social and business background but no information regarding their *issues*.

30

'It would help if you felt able to tell me,' I suggest, cautious because her left leg is crossed over her right and swinging far too fast to be an idle fidget. Manic rather than control freak, I would say at this stage.

'So you can record them? I don't need to, though?' She looks pointedly at the folder on my lap.

'Of course not. We don't record anything unless you are in agreement with us doing so,' I agree, mindful of what Jenny told me this morning and what Dr Anhelm had written in his email. The normal patient–doctor rules don't seem to apply here, but I'm not sure what applies in their place. Clients! Dammit, I need to get that right by the time I go home tonight. Tomorrow won't be my first day and there will be *no* excuse then.

'But I will. I do it because,' she pauses, staring at the folder on my lap, 'I don't know I'm doing it, and then I'm so angry with myself when I notice, I don't know what to do about it. Annoying there's nothing there ...'

I wait, uncomprehending at first. Then I realise she isn't commenting on the fact that there are no case notes about her issues and under Dr Anhelm's rules – apparently – there is no requirement for it either. Indeed, no. She is commenting on her issue itself.

'I steal,' she adds, in case I am in any doubt. 'I stole these shoes, disgusting though they are. I stole them from a back doorstep. They were still warm when I took them. Moist with sweat. The person who'd been wearing them can have only just taken them off. Disgusting! So why did I take them? And why did I leave my own shoes there in their place? I don't know.' She leans forward in her overstuffed patient's seat and hisses at me. 'Am I going mad, Doctor?'

I study the intelligent aquiline face and immaculate two-piece suit. The two pinch lines just above the bridge of her nose made her look cross. The imp in me lingers on the word 'pinch'. No, *Abigail* lingers on 'pinch'. Pinch, nick, filch... I squash the smirk and rage at myself. What has got into me today? Hardly the way to make my mark on my first day, playing control games with the PA and laughing at my patients.

'No,' I assure her, turning the smirk into a gently reassuring smile. 'It is merely an issue that we are going to tackle together – remember what our aim is here? *Ethical solutions for the unethical.'* Nicely done, Gab, but I don't like myself for it nevertheless. She isn't mad. Not even manic. She does have a genuine problem though. 'But do you really not remember?'

Her eyes narrow and she stares at me, birdlike and hesitant. 'No,' she says eventually. I'm not sure whether it's a lie or not.

'Then we need to work out the reason for you taking them and how you can deal with it.'

'And an ethical solution? What ethical solution is there for stealing?' She sighs, and I suddenly feel sorry for her. She is a pathetic figure too – as pathetic as Candy Myers but in a different way; at the whim of her psychosis, but maybe this one I can fix.

'There's always a solution.'

'I should atone. Thou shalt not steal.' She sounds despairing and I am surprised, then concerned. We'll get nowhere if she despairs of treatment. I need to make her feel better before she makes herself worse.

'Have you ever tried CBT? Cognitive Behavioural Therapy?'

'So you do think I'm mad.'

'No, no,' I laugh. 'CBT helps you identify and manage negative thoughts and behaviour so you can change them to something that is helpful to you instead. Let's try an example. What did you think about when you saw those shoes?'

'I wanted them. It was almost physical.'

'Were there any other feelings involved, like why you wanted them?'

'I wanted them because someone else had been using them – they were almost alive to the touch. If I was wearing them, some of that sense of immediacy of use, of activity, aliveness would be mine too.'

'So, they represented something vital to you – that maybe you don't feel in your own life?'

'Maybe,' she is cautious – seeing where I am going first before replying.

'Can you put your finger on what you feel you are missing from your life?'

'I'm not missing anything from my life, Dr McCray.' She is sharp, angry. 'I just wanted to have what someone else was enjoying. Why shouldn't I? Then I feel guilty when I've taken them – even though I still want them. And now they're mine,' she pauses, 'I want to get rid of them – and the guilt, because I don't want them anymore. I want your shoes now, in fact.' And she is actually looking covetously at my feet.

'I think there are two things here.' I tuck my feet under my chair. They feel vulnerable with Jessica's hot stare on them. 'The first is your desire for something someone else has. The second is how you feel when you have it. Control and guilt. Which feels worse to you?'

'Guilt,' she says decisively, eyes finally leaving my feet and finding my face again. 'I hate feeling guilty. Why the fuck should I?' I wish her eyes were still on my feet now. They are hot and heavy, brimstones set deep into a pasty-pink, cosmetically perfect wasteland.

'Shall we tackle that first then? If you have a strategy for dealing with your guilt, you'll feel much more able to tackle the underlying reason for causing the guilt.'

'Yes,' she agrees. She looks interested – enthusiastic even. 'So, what do you suggest?'

'Well, the most obvious first.' I am in the swing now. CBT in reverse, but hell – at least she is responding. 'You could put those shoes back if you could remember where you took them from? With a note thanking the owner for the use of them, and a new pair to replace them. You could afford to do that couldn't you?'

'Of course, I could. Theoretically. But I don't deal in monstrosities like these. I deal in works of art. Glass slippers to carry a princess to a ball. Red shoes to take girls' imaginations travelling far into never-never-land. Fantasy shoes.'

'Then leave them a fantasy. Leave a pair of beautiful shoes in their size for them to fulfil a fantasy with. You wanted to atone. Would that not count as atoning?'

'Would it?' She pauses, and that hawk-eyed look of careful consideration is back. 'Yes, it would, actually.' Jessica is now bright and cheery. 'Is atoning that easy? I always thought it would be painful and dull. I've never gone in for all that say three Hail Marys and you're forgiven stuff. My parents were full of it when I was a kid and it turned me right off it, but if my therapist is saying much the same thing – hey, who am I to disagree? Just leave someone what you took and a bit more to compensate; perfect! I would have done it years ago if I'd known.' She stands up and balances on her tiptoes, the puckered and curling toes of the brogues seeming to grin at me as they fold in on themselves. 'So that's sorted.'

'Well, I –' I wonder now if I've been too glib, offering this woman atonement when I have yet to really delve into what induces her to steal and want to scourge herself later for what is – in real terms – such a trivial sin. Is stealing wrong? Yes, with some exceptions that are redeeming features, but I have just suggested someone clearly rich and pampered can simply demand that same redemption by effectively paying their victim off. Christ! Now I'm condoning what I would normally be insisting is morally wrong. I return myself to basics. This real-life stuff isn't as easy as I thought it would be. CBT doesn't work in reverse. It should start with the underlying issue and work up from that. Maybe I should have stuck with research? Too late now, though… 'It would be a start,' I add carefully, trying not to openly backtrack. Stealing *is* morally wrong, with or without the moral excuse of poverty or desperation. This woman is neither; poor, nor despairing, and I dislike that her issue has put my own morals in question. 'But there's more to it than making amends. There's the question of why you do it. Wouldn't you rather solve the problem than keep having to make amends? We only sort out problems when we're honest with ourselves – work out our motivations and do something about them if they're inappropriate.'

'No. Not really,' Jessica picks up her neat cream bag with the gleaming interlaced CG logo. 'I just wanted you to fix my problem. And you have.'

'But I can't just fix it for you, like that. You have to fix it for you – by acknowledging the truth about yourself. If that includes elements that are unpalatable, then you can change them and the truth will change to something better too, then. That's how CBT works.'

'Oh, what a darling idea! You are so young and optimistic, aren't you? So, what's the truth about you, Dr McCray? Have you any unpalatable elements or are you perfect?'

'No one is perfect.' I smile – deprecatorily, I hope. This woman needs slapping down whilst still being encouraged to continue if I'm not going to lose her straight away. Whatever other mistakes I make today with Jenny or the tricky computer system, losing a client the Director has warned me off shouldn't be one of them. However, once again, Jenny is right. Control is at the heart of her issue and she needs to know I am the authority for her whilst she's here, not her for me, or I stand no chance of treating her. 'We all have things to deal with. I hope we are going to deal with yours together. Tomorrow, same time?' She stares at me and the brimstones are back. This is becoming confrontational and I'm not sure quite when or how that happened. 'Finding solutions means fixing any underlying issues first, for everyone, including me at times,' I add, trying to sound encouraging, not conciliatory.

She hitches the bag over her shoulder and continues to consider me, thoughtfully.

'Well, you're good. You're very good. Better even than your father, perhaps. Maybe I *will* let you figure things out for me. But I'll decide when my next appointment will be, thanks. And whether I'll tell you about my underlying issues, and *especially* what I'll do about them. But you can deal with my atonements.' She laughs abruptly at my expression. I am flailing around and I know it. 'And you're so much more approachable than him. He could be an ogre at times. He wanted me to actually *repent*!'

'He? My father?'

'Your predecessor.'

Somehow, I'd got the impression my predecessor must have been female, from the décor of the office suite.

'I'm not sure I understand – my father or my predecessor?'

Jessica hasn't heard me, or doesn't want to, apparently too busy with retrieving her phone from her bag and listening to her messages. I repeat the question. Finally, she gives me her attention, and a small satisfied smile, and then I suspect that she hadn't been so engrossed in finding her phone after all. She puts the phone back in her bag and it promptly buzzes again. She ignores it and strolls towards the door, where she turns, hand on door handle, and delivers her parting shot.

'You should know. You knew him well enough. I'll come back tomorrow, sometime,' she adds, as if it's her idea now, not mine.

I knew him well enough? Speechless, I watch the door glide shut behind her.

'Wait…'

I wrench the door open and am about to go scuttling after her when I realise that's exactly what she wants me to do. I let the door float shut again on its soft-close hinges, fuming. Oh no. I am *not* going to rise to the bait and I will not be merely an easy way of getting her conscience off the hook like with Candy Myers. I decide there and then that whether she knew my father or not, I'm going to refuse to treat Jessica Morgan unless she agrees to address her underlying issues and actively undertake treatment for them. Candy Myers was one thing, but this woman isn't weak. She's strong, and I am not going to be anyone's patsy. The decision comforts me, until the nagging questions logjam behind it – but who was the predecessor I knew so well? What connection had she had with Dada? And what waters might they have jointly moved through that could be muddied so badly I needed to be headed away from disturbing them? Then the need to release the logjam, whether it muddies the waters or not, supersedes everything.

Chapter 6

Jenny, and another of her unannounced arrivals into my space via the phone-cum-computer system pre-empts me ringing her about Jessica Morgan. Georges Thierone – my mystery stalker and final patient of the day – has cancelled.

'Is there a reason?'

'There's never a reason with Mr Thierone. He's a bit of a law unto himself.' *Aren't they all?* I want to say. 'He'll probably want to turn up tomorrow, same time. That seems to be his practice generally, so we'll leave your diary clear for then in case.'

'OK.' I have to admit I'm relieved – and exhausted. 'And who else is in my diary for tomorrow now?'

'Client X late morning, and maybe Miss Morgan – like you arranged. She has yet to confirm, though.' She sounds surprised I don't know. I frown. But I haven't arranged anything – yet – for either of them. 'But not until late morning, if she does,' Jenny adds.

'OK; but put a hold on Jessica Morgan for the moment.' I pause. Maybe I'll consider what to do about Jessica Morgan a little longer before I risk sounding Jenny out about her. 'And you *are* sure that is accurate for tomorrow?'

I wish I hadn't asked a second after I've asked it. I am at everyone's whim, I suspect, through my own lack of experience so I need Jenny as my first wall of defence – gatepost, gateway, and gate itself, as she'd put it. And I could do with more Abigail in my life too – more fuck you. Maybe I will put it there. Maybe my fresh start starts tomorrow in reality, knowing now some of what I'm going to have to deal with. I shall be telling Jessica my terms then, if she appears for another appointment, and demanding explanations, for certain, even though I may not like what I hear. But the other two? I don't know about them. The possibilities fill me with anxiety and my stomach grumbles again.

'Absolutely.'

Her tone and expression suggest she hasn't taken offence and the call ends amicably enough. I am relieved. Assistant Director or not, I'm starting to see how important it is to have allies, not enemies. And maybe some exploration is now due? And coffee definitely – at last!

I leave my bell jar of an office and take myself off display to the world. The kitchen for staff to make coffee or microwave ready-meal lunches is small and stifling, but it's a welcome haven for me. A culinary cocoon where I instead make myself a decaf with one of the sachets I've brought from home in an effort to educate myself into better habits than drinking endless cups of Americano and suffering palpitations for my sins. On exploring the contents of the cupboards, I find a packet of crisps someone has long forgotten. At least I assume they must have forgotten them. They went out of date a week ago. I think of Jessica and her stealing. Does stealing matter that much? Do possessions really matter that much to their owners? Isn't it richness of the spirit that is more important? Here – here's something that doesn't matter to its owner. I could eat these crisps, or throw them away, without anyone caring. It's a cross between stealing and clearing up. I do neither. The need to release the frustrations of the day overtakes any mindful act and instead I thump the bag with my fist so it is completely flattened – cannot ever be reclaimed and the act of stealing therefore negated. It bursts, scattering particles of pulverised crisps across the worktop and onto the floor.

'Helps sometimes, I know.' I spin round and Jenny is standing in the doorway. She's surveying me, the crisp crumbs, the crushed packet and the open cupboard door. 'There's a dustpan and brush in the cupboard at the end nearest the fridge.' She edges past me – which is difficult because there is barely room to swing a cat – and pulls open the base unit door next to the fridge. 'I would probably have transgressed my diet with those if I'd found them before you, so you've saved my soul, if not my hunger pangs,' she adds conversationally.

'Oh, I'm so sorry. They were out of date and I –'

'It's fine,' she shakes her head and smiles sympathetically at me. 'Is it not going so well today?' She reaches into the cupboard for the dustpan and brush without waiting for my answer and I feel small and embarrassed as she scrabbles on the floor, sweeping up the remains of the crisps. She stands and whisks the crumpled packet and the spillage on the worktop into the dustpan with an easy, confident movement before dumping the debris in the swing bin under the window. It's the first time I've really taken stock of her without feeling the need to counter animosity, real or imagined. She may be shorter than me, but she has presence. Dark-haired, about forty. Not glamorous, but gracious. Her eyes are doe-brown and kind but she's also business-like. Simultaneously pragmatic and empathetic. I could like her but for barrier of the inherent cross-antagonism that has been the third wheel in our working relationship so far. *And to be honest, you'd already dismissed her anyway,* the Abigail voice taunts me. *She's only a PA and you're the Assistant Director. You're such a snob!* I reel at the self-denouncement. I'm not like that – not at all, I want to protest aloud – almost do, in fact, before pulling myself together.

'Oh, oh no! It's just a habit from childhood. A bad habit – but I'm so sorry if they were your crisps.'

'No, they weren't mine,' she replies, laughing. 'I was just going to requisition them in their owner's absence! I could always replace them if someone wanted to claim them later. Look, I have more background on your clients if you'd like to see it? The Director has this rule about forming a direct opinion before being influenced by third party information, so I was instructed not to show you the guts of your client's files until later, but would you like me to drop them in to you ready for tomorrow? You'll have time to have a look through them before your next appointments that way. You have already seen two of them now, anyway.'

Once again, I am spinning on the spot in my head. The Director actually told her to withhold information from me? I am speechless. Eventually I manage to force out, 'Mr Thierone and Client X as well? Or do I have to suffer them first?'

She hesitates for a fraction of a second and I guess it's over my choice of the word suffer. Then she laughs, wholeheartedly and companionably.

'I think I should break the rule where they're concerned, don't you? As long as you don't tell. Mr Thierone's so unpredictable, who knows how long it will take for him to actually make a first appointment, and with Client X – well, what the Director often overlooks is that sometimes it's better to be forewarned than open-minded.' She waits for my reaction. This time I'm not going to disagree. I'm starting to see that Jenny *is* more than just a PA, and what she proclaims to the Director about herself is probably quite accurate! I nod, appreciatively. 'OK, I'll drop them by once you've made your coffee.' Her parting smile is warm and – to me, finally – non-judgemental.

So, now I have an admission that the Director has been manipulating me throughout, even though he's not been here. But maybe Jenny hasn't? More than anything I wish I could talk to Romaine right now. Or Dada. Even adults need their parents at times. Jenny's gone by the time I remember I wanted to ask her about my predecessor. Oh, well. Next time. I'm not seeing Jessica Morgan until tomorrow, so I still have time to gather more intel. Maybe there will be some in the files and I won't need to prematurely expose my anxieties to Jenny.

Jenny is as good as her word, but I'm too tired to bother with reading files and patient histories by the time she arrives. Nor have I had the stomach to explore further – even my office. Instinctively it is not a place I want to become intimately acquainted with although I know I will have to, but there is always tomorrow, and the next day, and the one after. The thought depresses me, and it is only day one here. I sigh. It is gone five and I've worked without a break writing up the notes of my meetings today. Tomorrow can wait. The old need to hide away is stronger than the need for explanations for the moment. It has a decade long hold on me and I'm psychologist enough to know I am not going to break that hold when I am tired and demoralised. Sufficient unto the day are the evils thereof ...

Chapter 7

Day two. Another fresh start, but unfortunately not a fresher me. An evening away from the office and exploring the vagaries of my new home, still heavy with the smell of paint has left with me with a dull headache and a sense of foreboding. At least I have no appointments booked first thing. I have time to fire myself up. I pull the files Jenny left me last night out of my locked top drawer and begin to browse, but what I'm reading doesn't seem to go anywhere – what little there is, that is. All the files contain bare bones, not just Candy Myers' and Jessica Morgans'. Maybe the Director has stripped them all as a precaution – just in case Jenny or I went against his instructions. There is enough in Client X's to send the jitters through me at the prospect of treating him. I am just pondering that, and the nature of my employer when the computer screen lights up.

'Morning!' Jenny's face greets me, bright and fresh, contrasting with how jaded I feel. 'Ready for round two? Your Client X has called in. Can he come in early? I've currently got him on hold on the other line. Your diary *is* free …'

Determination battles exhaustion. He is the one involved in suicide, according to the Director's notes. Suspiciously and muddily. A suicide with the possibility of foul play attached. I understand now why Dada would have forbidden him me – except Dada wouldn't have known him, surely. The suspicious death is recent. I know I shouldn't assume; assuming is the curse of the curer, but '…*a suspicious death he claims was a suicide…*' must mean he's Special Forces or similar and made a mistake. Got trigger happy and thoughtlessly blew some innocent away, so now there is a cover-up. Secrets and guilt; two things I'm instinctively au fait with. Either that or he really has looked into the eyes of a suicide and seen what is there, but without stopping them. That makes him my main target. That should have me excited and buzzing. Instead it brings all the old haziness back to the surface, and with it, all the old insecurities. If only I could remember clearly – beyond that sound that reverberates in my ears like a death knell. The gun shot, they said – probably. I don't even want to try to work out if they were right. But what can I say? My diary is no longer free. Client X is filling it.

But Client X isn't what I'd expected at all. His eyes are doe-brown, just like Jenny's, and his face kind. Yes, of course, suspecting what he is, I can detect the hard body under the soft clothes, but in the street? I would pass him by in the street with perhaps only a briefest of second glances because of that gentle air of self-possession he has about him. Do all killers look like this, then? What an odd situation if they do. You could be walking past assassins all the time without knowing – but then, you probably were, given the human predisposition to destroy and then self-destruct. Oddly, this man even makes me feel comfortable – as if I know him.

I relax a little and drag the consummate professional out from under the flagging second-day-but-still-new-girl to smile reassuringly at him, even though he doesn't seem to need reassurance. It comes with the job. Payment for positivity. And I am a professional. I offer my hand.

'I'm Dr McCray. The Director has asked me to assume responsibility for your treatment in his absence.'

He takes my hand and his grip is warm and welcoming. My palm tingles. 'Has he now? And on almost your first day too.'

I hesitate. Surely Jenny hasn't told him that? I decide to shrug dismissively and let his hand drop. We are potentially both liars so fair's fair. 'First day, hundredth day. This is my job.'

He pushes the chair intended for the patient sideways so he's surveying the whole room, his back to my desk, then sits, apparently completely relaxed, one leg crossed over the other, ankle resting on the knee of the leg touching the floor – as men do when they lounge in order to display their masculinity. If this man is anxious, I am a little green alien. An alpha male, with that body posture, so that definitely fits the profession I imagine he's in. The face and expression are so at odds, though. I settle into the counsellor's chair after also adjusting position so I'm opposite him, keeping the smile in place. Don't let it waver or his opening ploy might give him the upper hand. He's smart as well as sharp. He acknowledges the smile with one of his own. His eyes are examining me – every plane of me – without doing so. Oh, he is good. I was wrong. He is every inch the wolf in the sheep's clothing. And I'll admit that's exciting.

He gestures – a small token of thanks. 'But nevertheless, not what you might have expected to happen as soon as you arrive.'

'Well,' I feel my palms beginning to sweat. 'No, not what I'd expected to happen, but there it is. As I said, it's my job. How would you like to start this session? I believe Dr Anhelm usually suggests that initially we talk generally about some of the issues that are troubling you and see if there are some specifics that it would be productive to examine further.'

'Robert,' he says.

'Robert?' It takes me a moment to connect the two. 'The Director? Yes.'

'Robert,' he repeats. 'And you are?'

'Dr McCray.'

'Yes, I know you're Dr McCray, but you are also – who? What's your Christian name?'

'I don't usually go by first name terms with my patients.' I bite my lip for using the wrong term but it's already too late. Clients, I chide myself. Not patients. Clients.

'Oh.' One eyebrow rises quizzically. 'Robert has a somewhat more relaxed regime with his... patients – as no doubt he would have told you if he'd been here to greet you. So, I am, who – to you?'

'Well,' I gesture to the buff brown folder with its distinctive X on the cover. X marks the spot, sign by the X, X-ray vision. 'X,' I laugh, but it sounds false.

'X. Yes. I see. The man of mystery.' He laughs. 'Very dramatic. No wonder you don't want to tell me *your* name. I should have called myself John Smith, or,' he cocks his head to one side, 'what do you think I should be called?'

'I don't know. Do you really need a pseudonym?'

'For the moment.'

'Oh.' His expression makes me nervous. 'Alright. So, what would you like to be called? It seems you have free rein.' I laugh but the nerves are butterflies in my chest, fluttering helplessly against my ribs. It doesn't help that those doe-brown eyes are gently dissecting me even as they're appreciating me. I feel like I'm under the microscope in all ways today. New girl, and in an office made almost entirely of glass. Our respective chairs are marooned in a sea of blue carpet, and only he has the security of the one solid section to the room – the bookcase crammed full of books I haven't had time to examine – behind him.

'Hmm, good idea. Would make me more normal, wouldn't it? But how about you go first?' His look is amused, almost teasing.

'I, er ...'

'I'll tell you if you tell me,' he continues.

'Like I said, it's not the way I'm used to working.' I sound too stiff, too formal, but I know his sort. They warned us about them from the word go; the first patient–psychologist encounter; the ones who are too healthy to be sick. Or too sick to be healthy.

'Alright. Since we're both uncomfortable with using our real names, what say you – in the spirit of Robert's regime – we *both* choose first names to use? I'll be Xander – short for AleXander.' He drawls the ex in the middle and nods towards the folder. 'X has to stand for something. I've always fancied a somewhat more extravagant name than the one I have.'

'Xander?' I can't help the little bubble of mirth that wants to escape from the turbulence the butterflies are producing with all their frantic fluttering. I can feel my lips trying to twitch. He's watching them. He grins.

'Why not? It's a ridiculous situation, this – having a codename – so let's make it a ridiculous codename. Xxxanderrr.' He ends it in laughter that is infectious, and I can't help but join in at the preposterous name. 'You can have a codename too.' He adds. 'Who have you always wanted to be?' This time his eyes are smiling too. I forget myself for a moment and bask in the warmth.

'Abigail,' I say. It just pops out. Perfect. Dada specifically chose her for me. Romaine told me that when I was older. He said she was perfect too. Like I never was.

'Abigail,' Xander laughs. 'I like it – A and X. Almost Alpha and Omega – but not quite.' He's still smiling, trying to engage me. Jenny's warning floats back to me. Just in case... I curse myself for losing my grip. I should have avoided engagement. I need to be the professional. Take control again.

'Well,' I smile coolly. 'Joking apart, back to where we were. Shall we begin in earnest now?' The butterflies settle, perching on my internal organs. Folding their wings cautiously. I haven't ever experienced this kind of thing with a patient before. It marks him as someone to be wary of and makes my job doubly hard. We need the connection for the therapy to work, but the connection on my part is undeniable, even now – something a professional would never allow, but I still desperately want to know –

what did he say in those eyes, as they pulled the trigger…

'Of course,' he agrees, making a mock-serious face.

'Right.' I mentally straighten my thoughts and find I am straightening my shoulders too. I count myself in. One-two-three… and launch… 'Is there any one thing that you would like to focus on to begin with?'

'Well – ' His phone rings and he fumbles in his pocket. 'Oh, sorry. I should have turned it off, but technically I'm still on call.' He goes over to the window and turns his back to me. I can only see his outline, his silhouette against the gapingly blank windows. I concentrate on disconnecting, observing only. He finishes the call and turns to face me, stuffing the phone back in his pocket. The amusement that had been there earlier has completely gone and briefly he looks intimidating, but the expression flickers back to good humour so quickly I might have mistaken the change merely for the shifting light from the window. 'Really,' he resumes, 'I wanted to talk about morals, and how we square them with our actions.'

I wait. It's a leading statement and we both know it. I am not going to push it too far yet. *Keep an open mind and your opinions to yourself*, the Director had said. The silence lengthens so I am forced into prompting.

'*Your* morals?' A roundabout route to a form of confession, perhaps? Fast, but not unheard of if the connection is good between patient and psychologist… client…

'Anyone's I suppose. Do we *all* have them?' He is still smiling, and his eyes are back to gently probing me.

'Of course, we all have them.' I smile in return, but his fades as mine begins. 'Don't you think you do?' I add gently.

'I don't know. That's the problem. Maybe I don't.'

'Because of the type of work you do?'

He hesitates. I've touched a nerve. That was clumsy.

'That, and other things,' he says eventually.

'Other things? Like?' I shouldn't push too hard but I can't help it. He is teetering on the edge and I so want a victory on my second day – to wave like a flag at the Director's abandonment of me, at my fellow colleagues' – admittedly imagined – jaundiced disgruntlement that an interloper was appointed Assistant Director, and not them. To prove I am that shooting star… Despite myself, my body wants to express a reaction. The bit is between my teeth. My adrenalin is rising. I can feel it in my shortened breath and edginess. I stifle the inclination to lean forward and instead force my spine against the overstuffed chair back. Bad for your spine, these consulting room chairs, but the interior designers never learn. Make the patient comfortable and then they'll relax and open up but give the therapist years of back problems. Correction. Client.

'Everyday things. Life things.'

'Can you give me an example?'

He purses his lips and the thoughtful look gives him a child-like appeal. If he'd been a boy-doll, he would have been the perfect companion for Abigail – in ringleted angel mode, of course. He sighs.

'Morals can be so adaptable, can't they. So synergistic.' I must look bemused. He continues with a rueful smile. 'Sorry. Getting on my philosophical high horse. I mean, sometimes what's right can be wrong and vice versa, without even intending it to be so, can't it? So how do you decide? How do you decide if what you're doing is right or wrong?'

'Your morals tell you,' I say, nodding encouragingly – hoping it also conveys my empathy, my wish to understand his problem. Keep the connection flowing without it becoming too personal.

'But which morals? What if I'm unsure what they are? I...' He breaks off and gestures despondently. 'I have to go, I'm afraid. That was work. Could I come back later? I know it's not the way things are normally done, but ...'

His expression is glum. He is for all the world the disappointed child, the lost boy, and instinctively I need to help. I think of the appointment times in the Word doc Jenny has posted in my folder. In theory, this afternoon has only one other appointment – Georges Thierone – but given what Jenny said about him, who knows whether he'll show up or not. Whatever – sod it! I'm going on what seems right to me and it seems right to have time free for this man; this 'client' who actually seems to want to address his problems, unlike the Jessica Morgans and Candy Myers of this world.

'Later should be fine, but I only have a finite window until another appointment later on this afternoon.'

'Great!' He beams at me and I am glad I've made this possible. 'This shouldn't take long. I'll be back in about half an hour – if that be OK's even though it may encroach your lunch time? I've got a lot to talk about now I've finally got someone to talk to!'

I nod, the euphoria of success making my head spin a little. The first patient – and a forbidden one – who is keen to actually seek help! At the door, he shakes my hand. The grip is still firm; strong and powerful. Inside I feel strong and powerful too. He pauses before leaving.

'Thank you,' he says as he slowly releases my hand and my fingers slip unhurriedly from his grasp. Then that teasing smile again, 'Abigail... We are possibly so alike, you know.'

I watch him go, swift and light-footed, despite his size, along the corridor and around the corner, the confusion spreading all the way across my face and into my scalp. I sneak to the corner and watch him the rest of the way to the main door. There's a familiarity to him ... I shake my head. No, but there can't be. I don't know him at all, so aside from the suicide issue, why would Dada have forbidden him?

He doesn't stop at Jenny's office and there is no movement from there either. His gait reminds me of something. I can't think what. Oh, yes, I can – it is the stealth of someone used to travelling at speed, with precision and purpose, but in secret. Yes, my first assumptions must be right. He is definitely Special Forces! Like my stalker yesterday – in fact. That's probably what I recognise in him; that stance and gait. Maybe. That pulls me up. Or more? What more do I recognise in him that he also recognises in me? God, I wish I hadn't come out with Abigail now. This man isn't a Candy Myers – or even a Jessica Morgan. He is potentially far more tricky.

Chapter 8

I fill in the half hour until Xander's prospective return with cursory examination of my consulting room, having fought shy of it yesterday. There's little else I can do in the time, anyway. The room itself, I dispose of swiftly. I still don't like it. It *is* a goldfish bowl and I am the fish swimming round it in circles. I particularly dislike the windows and the sense of being suspended in mid-air away from the building that they give. It adds to my second day nerves, but I remind myself that I was a hit with Xander to counter them. He is keen to work with me. I am a professional – a shooting star professional. I straighten my shoulders, trying not to dwell on his teasing eyes and knowing smile. I wish again I hadn't played the pretend name game with him – but it's a persona; a role only. I am on target at last – a practising psychologist, and a hit with her patient. I straighten what little there is on my desk – a pen and a notepad and the Client X file that Jenny gave me on arrival, which has nothing in it except his client name and next appointment time. Since I've made a fuss about accuracy, I should really tell Jenny about the extra appointment, but can't bring myself to tackle the aggressive looking phone system so instead I go on a recce to find her. Jenny's room does indeed control the exit and entrance. All non-staff arrivals have to press the entrance button to be allowed access and she is the one who answers.

She isn't in her office when I end up there on my circuit, but she can't be far away because her handbag is by the side of her desk, conspicuously vulnerable to anyone passing. Of course, she will know we have no patients currently – shit, no! Clients! She will know we have no clients in at the moment because she controls the appointment diary too, and she would still have had to release the door for Xander to leave so she will know he has already gone. I loiter just inside the door, enjoying the sense of containment her room has – four solid walls and only one window, not three window walls and only one solid one – but time is marching on. It is now eleven fifty and I really need to pee before Xander returns. I leave her a scribbled note explaining that Xander – Client X – will be back in later, between midday and one, and am about to go in search of the loo when she returns from wherever she's been.

'Oh, hi. I was just leaving you a note.'

'Oh? Going for lunch already?' She manages to make it both a question and a comment simultaneously. I take time to assess her again – with the gloss of potential friendship. She is smarter and more attractive than me. My blonde hair hangs lank, if silken. Hers has the gloss of innate health to it. Her figure is neat but curved in the right places. Mine is as long and lank as my hair. My saving grace – my grey-green eyes and full lips – only vie with hers for supremacy. She is attractive – chic, even. I am merely presentable; if cool and professional. I have to consciously stop myself from smoothing hair and skirt to reaffirm that.

'No, my pa-client, Client X – he's coming back in about half an hour's time for another consultation.'

'So quickly?' Her face is expressionless, but her words aren't.

'Well, he had to leave before we'd finished. Work.' I curse myself for rushing to explain. She is the PA, not the Director.

'Oh, I see.' She brushes past me and goes over to the desk. The faintest trace of delicate floral notes follow her – all femininity and subtle control. She picks up the note I've written, reads it and then tosses it in the waste paper bin. 'So, how's it gone today?'

'Fine. Absolutely fine... thanks.' She reminds me of Romaine, sympathising with me over early academic disasters. I sound too stiff, too formal. Even a layman would be able to tell I'm being defensive.

'That's good. Bit of a baptism of fire for you, though – especially with him.' There is a question in those eyes though. *Why? Why did you want one of the most difficult clients?* She smiles, and her eyes are kind. My porcupine spines bristle less.

'Baptism of fire? Why?'

'What did Robert tell you about him?'

'Robert?'

'The Director. Director Anhelm.'

'Oh, yes. Of course – well, what he's here for … because of …' I grimace. I can't say it but she nods.

'Then you'll know what I mean.'

'Well ...' I linger by the door. Her knowing smile and arch manner get the better of me. 'Is there something else I should know about him?' It's out before I can stop it.

'Only what Robert told you.' There is mischief in her eyes this time. 'I'll add him to your appointments list for this afternoon. You only have one other.' She slides in behind her desk and logs into her PC. The keyboard makes little clicking noises as she enters – presumably – Xander's extra appointment.

'Jessica Morgan?'

'No Jessica Morgan, yet.'

'Oh, good.'

She catches the swiftness of my response but says nothing. I linger. Now I am sweating, anxious about what she knows but I don't – maybe. She focusses back on her PC screen and waits. She is confident I won't go until I know. After a moment or two she looks up and smiles.

'Do you want me to tell you anyway – what Robert was going to tell you? I know what is in all the client's notes. I have to. I'm the one who enters the details after the consultations.'

Ridiculously, now I don't want to know. I am cross with her – no, with me – for being so lacking in self-belief.

'The Director has already told me what I need to know. I already said that.'

I can't read her expression. It's not deliberately opaque but it is indefinable.

'OK. But you know where I am if you need anything. Robert calls me the office oracle – all-seeing and all-knowing. If you need to know, I'm the one to ask.'

'Thanks,' I shrug.

I leave with as much dignity and self-assurance as I can muster and head for the ladies' loo, collecting my handbag en route, annoyed that we seem to be back to square one. My stomach is grumbling uncomfortably again too, but it's not hunger that is causing it. At least I still have a few minutes before Xander is due back. I pee and find myself back in front of the mirror, wringing my hands with soap and water as I try to see what Jenny saw in me a few minutes ago. Inexperience? Naivety? Weakness? I dry my hands and toss the hand towel in the empty swing bin. The lid flips to and fro, like my stomach is doing. With no Jenny to watch, I smooth my hair and powder my nose. I look fine. Attractive even, in a cool, ice-maiden way. I straighten my shoulders and practise looking stern. I sigh and powder my nose again because the perspiration sheen won't go.

'You're just winding yourself up because you're the new girl. You look the part. Candy Myers even said so. Just be it.'

My reflection's lips repeat it back at me, but I have yet to believe it.

Back in my room, I tuck my bag in the bottom drawer of the desk and wait. The minutes tick by. My stomach grumbles again. Perhaps it is hunger, after all. It's gone twelve now and I would normally be thinking about eating. But I can't. I agreed to this extra appointment even though it straddled lunch. No one arrives. I go to stand at the window, surveying the parking area it looks out onto. There are a handful of cars scattered around it. I have travelled in by tube, since we are in central London, but some have clearly driven in as they are much the same cars as were here when I arrived first thing. My hands are still sticky. I wipe both palms against my skirt. I feel like I'm on a date, waiting for them to arrive. It is now twelve forty. He is late. Maybe he isn't going to come back after all? Whatever was going to be quick, hasn't been. The idea brings a lurch of disappointment, simultaneous with a sense of relief. I try to examine the feeling but am interrupted by a peremptory rap on the door. I swing round, just as I catch sight of a car that hadn't been there earlier – a long, low, sleek beast of a car; bright red. It lodges in the periphery of my vision like a beacon – an alert. The door opens before I can respond with an invitation to enter and Xander is standing on the threshold, saying,

'Now is still alright, isn't it?'

'Yes, of course,' I cross to greet him with something akin to joy in my throat. 'Absolutely fine,' even though I know that his delayed return means time will be tight for me. I may not have time for lunch at all if he stays any length of time. My next – and final appointment of the day – is at two; the potential stalker – Georges Thierone.

'Good.' He looks as pleased as me. 'Shall I sit here again?' He indicates the same chair as he sat in to begin with. I haven't moved them. The scene looks like it has just been waiting for us to repopulate it.

'Yes, that will be fine.'

He sits, smiling, and I notice how white his teeth are against his skin, how deep and mesmeric his eyes, how curved his lips. He raises his eyebrows, asking a silent question. I realise I am just gazing at him, stupidly. Admiringly. It throws me. The confidence of our earlier meeting oozes away from me. For God's sake, woman, get a grip! Why are you mooning over him? Why so anxious and shy? Then I get it. It's the smile and the eyes in combination. They remind me of someone and I don't want to acknowledge it because then I will be a gangly schoolgirl again, the awkward child, the ignoramus too young to understand.

His smile and eyes remind me of Dada.

'Shall I pick up where I left off then?' he's saying. I nod, over-enthusiastically, but I already know this isn't going to go well.

'OK, morals. A simple right or wrong to start with. How about this. Is stealing right or wrong?'

Stealing? Like Jessica Morgan? Not suspicious death? OK, let's start obscure and work up.

'Well, wrong, although there are extenuating circumstances that might make it not so intrinsically wrong. Poverty, starvation – that sort of thing.' Good. Back on track. I am Dr McCray again, not the adoring child hanging on her father's words.

'Yes,' he nods. 'You're right. Nothing is simply black or white.' I feel better. A small portion of my tension eases. He doesn't sound like Dada. And he's asking my opinions, agreeing with me too. The earlier connection is still there. The failing is purely in my head – my lack of self-assurance in a new role I am formally qualified for, but barely experienced enough to handle yet. He doesn't know that, though. I consciously uncurl my fists. 'But beyond that is the whole notion of the word "stealing",' he continues. 'Where does that come from?'

'The word "stealing"?' I wonder where this is going. It's certainly strayed a long way from murder – or suicide – already. 'Well, I'm no linguist but it obviously derives from describing the action – taking something that's not yours.'

'Yes, I suppose so,' he looks quizzical. 'But who defines what is yours?'

'Well, we do.'

'And who is we?'

'Us?' the butterflies are beginning to stir inside me again.

'Us.' He examines the word, rolling it around his tongue. 'OK. Now define us.'

'Well, you and me to start with, and everyone else populating the world.'

'And we all have the same understanding of what the word "steal" means, do we?' His eyebrows have lifted – fractionally. The result is gently quizzical. Not combatant. Testing. Bandying words. Word games.

'I would say so. It's an accepted concept, isn't it?'

'Perhaps not. Not entirely. Circumstances might influence it, might they not? You cited some earlier – poverty, starvation. Maybe stealing isn't stealing then. It's something else. Survival.'

'Maybe. But that's more semantics, isn't it? Didn't you want to talk about morals?' *Get behind his words, dissect his understanding of them, then you'll know where this is leading.*

He ignores the question and leans back in his chair, taking up the relaxed position he'd first settled in at our initial meeting, ankle resting on opposite leg, insistently alpha male again.

'But are we entitled to own what we've acquired for ourselves through mere manipulation of society? What isn't ideologically ours?' I shake my head. I have no idea what is behind these words. My fists are balling up again and inside their tight buds, my nails cut into my palms.

'Consumerism and capitalism?' I venture. 'I'm afraid I can't get involved in political discussion. It's against Ethos' principles.'

He pauses, almost a double-take, then bursts out laughing.

'Oh Abigail, I'm not talking consumerism and capitalism. I'm talking about what we would have if we stripped away everything – all the trappings of society. What kind of people we would be, when all we had was our moral integrity – or lack of it. Not the position or standing that protects us from public criticism, but only ourselves. I want us to get real – address the really important things. How else am I going to sort out all these raging arguments with myself inside my head?' He sits forward urgently. 'For instance, do we even own our lives?'

Suddenly it's OK again. I'm excited by the notion of debating life ethics – the way I'd wanted to with Dada when he was in the mood. This isn't dangerous, it's stimulating – intriguing; the kind of challenge I hoped I'd find here. I study 'Xander' and his calm face and kind eyes. Alpha male maybe, but something more too. Like Dada in that sense too...

But remember the hard body under the soft clothes, the intoxicating sense of danger he exudes for me, his prey – like a gazelle might feel when a lion is close by. Remember why he's here. He's not debating word-meanings or values. He's a patient debating his view of the world versus yours. Yours has to be the carefully guarded view of the physician because of that. Whatever euphemistic names Ethos want to give him, he is still a patient. Remember what Director Anhelm said too – *Keep an open mind but your opinions to yourself... Bit late for that! You've given him Abigail. But that's just playing his game...* Oh, God, I need to stop arguing with myself! And he hasn't mentioned the death yet, either. He needs coaxing and I need stoppering. I uncurl my fists again and close my mind to his attractiveness. Role play. Choose your persona. Be Abigail, even; cool, calm, collected – smart.

'We have to own ourselves – accept responsibility for ourselves – so we must own our lives, mustn't we?'

'Unless someone has taken ourselves from us. Flicked the switch over.'

'No one can take yourself from you. You are as intrinsic to you as I am to me.' I almost laugh, but it would sound arrogant. My confidence is back though. I have heard so many of these kinds of philosophical debates raging between Dada and his students, ever since I was so small I didn't understand half the words used, but I can easily trade discussion on this score now, even if I couldn't then. I might even be forgiven for feeling a little cocky about it.

'And who are you? Don't you psychologists say that everything in the world has an impact on you and your understanding of yourself? Bad experiences give you baggage to carry around with you, and good experiences boost your self-esteem. If what happens to you in the world adds to your perception of yourself, why can't it also take from it? We are what we repeatedly do. Or we aren't what we repeatedly lose.'

'But you can't lose yourself. You can lose others you love or things you thought you had, but all the while you're alive, you have to have some sense of who you are, even if that's not who you want to be. You have to. You have to know who you are and accept it.'

'Are you who you want to be? And do you accept it, or do you want to be someone else?'

'Who else would I want to be? I'm fine. I'll be fine.' The mantra slips out automatically. I laugh to cover myself. 'It's what I tell my pa-clients with self-esteem issues to say to boost themselves ...' He tips his head to one side and his smile deepens. I wish I hadn't elaborated. He's got to me and he knows it. Time to wrap it up. I haven't wrung a confession from him – or a breakthrough – but he has progressed from patient to connected patient. 'But we're getting into the realms of philosophy and self-realisation here. That is a complex discussion and not really possible for us to resolve in the short time we have left today.'

'That's a shame.' Now I wish I hadn't moved to wind the meeting up – but I do need lunch and I do still have one more patient today. 'But I understand. I can't monopolise you.' He shrugs. His smile is twisted, yet still boyishly engaging. He can see I am wavering. That's why he's doing this. Dammit! He's turning the tables on me! He's psychoanalysing *me*, not the other way round. More mind games. Get a grip. You know how it's done.

'Not at all, but Rome wasn't built in a day. These things take time.' *Hypocrite! There you were hoping for a breakthrough today!* I ignore the dissenting voice in my head and continue with my psychologist-speak. 'We've yet to look at the issue – issues – you're having and trying to find ways of resolving them, haven't we?' I add quickly. 'We can carry on from here next time.'

'But that is one of my issues. You asked me what I wanted to start with. I want to start with stealing. If I'd stolen something, would that be right or wrong?'

I steady myself. Stealing. Was there something about possessing somebody else's possessions that I'd been missing all my life until now? First Jessica, and now Xander. Is this a game or a real issue? I wish the Director had told me what to expect instead of merely hinting at the difficulty of what might need addressing. This could far too easily get out of hand. A sudden, sneaking suspicion that maybe the Director had forbidden both Jessica Morgan and this man because he hadn't wanted to deal with them himself supplants the nerves that are beginning to overwhelm me. Maybe he'd deliberately done this to actually encourage me into involvement? Reverse psychology turned on the psychologist. Jenny had even said she'd been surprised he'd left a day before he needed to when normally he was a home bird. The possibility brings a spurt of anger with it. More manipulation! The Assistant Director title was more than just a sop for abandoning me. It was a façade to cover dumping on me too – all the clients he didn't want, private or tricky. The bright young thing with the qualifications and pedigree but no experience, and I'd foolishly snapped up the challenge. I should have realised. Dammit! But I *was* a chip off the old block. Aaron McCray's daughter could deal with this, even if she couldn't deal with other things. I'd better figure out fast why he so particularly wanted to sidestep these two now, though, and push them my way.

I press my spine against the back of the chair again, this time defying its plush ministrations. I push it ram-rod straight and assemble the right words to cut my patient's little games short or establish boundaries – whichever applied in this case. Sometimes you have to feel your way, and now was one of those times.

'In theory, wrong, but as we've already mentioned, there may be extenuating circumstances involved. Do you need to tell me something? Have you stolen something?'

'In theory, yes.'

We outstare each other, and I'm not backing down. I can't. I have to win this round. His gaze looks as if it's about to waver and that's when I press my point. My chance to turn the tables, I think – and I don't care that I'm pushing too hard now. The adrenalin is flowing again. I want the kill.

'A life?'

His lips part, then come back together. A soft self-kiss. 'Perhaps. Perhaps I'm thinking that a life *has* been stolen and I was responsible for that.' He looks regretful.

Well, fuck you Director Anhelm! You may have dumped on me, but I've crumbled the cookie.

'Ah.' I can't stop the sigh of satisfaction slipping out before the rest of his reply affirms it.

'But what if it was my cry for help?' he adds, the doe eyes now lava streams, overflowing.

I lean forward, the consummate professional, ready to show my compassion and empathy, replete with satisfaction at my first total win today – my first psychological kill, after all. He's broken. The barriers should veritably tumble down now.

'Do you want to talk about your cry for help?'

'No.' He smiles, slowly and deliberately. 'I want to talk about yours.'

Chapter 9

'*My* cry for help?' I laugh, but the stirring butterflies inside me make it too shrill. 'Why would I be sending out a cry for help?'

'Aren't you?' The corners of his eyes are crinkling – almost a smile but managing to be more surprise than humour. 'My mistake. Only your second day with no one around to explain procedures or background, following in the footsteps of so many men – I believe you are the first woman to be appointed an Assistant Director here too, and so young.' Now he is smiling, smoothly, calmly, charmingly. 'Anyone in your circumstances might appreciate a few pointers from an old lag, even someone with such an esteemed pedigree as yours.'

'I see.' But I don't. I'm horrified, breathless with dismay, petrified with alarm. I am a small jungle animal facing an alligator. 'Esteemed pedigree?' I murmur it before I realise I am repeating his words aloud.

'Your father,' he agrees. 'A force to be reckoned with.'

'How do you know who my father was?' That jolts me back to control. I sound sharp, suspicious. I reel myself in and try to soften the question with a smile.

'Abigail, surely you wouldn't expect Client X to not have done a little research on his new… ' he pauses, '… confidante.'

'Confidante? I am your psychologist, not your chat room companion,' I say, trying to sound equally light.

'Maybe, but I believe we are all confidantes for each other in different ways. We facilitate solutions. And that is the principle of Ethos, is it not? Facilitating solutions. And if you are going to facilitate understanding of my issues for me, I should reciprocate somehow for you.'

'Oh, no.' Now I am bewildered. Jenny's words are banging around in my head and I wonder if I should have taken her more seriously. Mere PA or not, she knows how this organisation works. I don't. 'No, not at all. It doesn't work like that.' Does he really believe that? His eyes are clear and his expression unassuming, expectant, even. I laugh but it rings false in my ears. Patronising. Don't be condescending or patronising with this man, whatever else you do. He is complex and clever, even if he is professing the wrong impression of what Ethos *does*. On the small amount of discussion we've had so far I know that he could run rings round me if he wanted to. Like Dada. 'I work for you, but presumably you are paying for that.'

'Oh no, Abigail,' he replies, shaking his head, and corners of his eyes – his very attractive eyes – really crinkling with amusement now. 'You don't understand at all, do you? And now you really are making a cry for help. I'm not paying for anything. No Chiaroscuro member pays for anything at Ethos, except in kind. So, whatever you do for me, morally, I must reciprocate. I must have a word with Robert when he gets back. Terrible oversight that he didn't explain that to you. Do you still have other clients to see today?'

Chiaroscuro? My ears are ringing and my head pounding. Wasn't that the organisation Jenny said Georges Thierone worked for? Hush-hush. And it was in the forwarded message from Director Anhelm too. So both my stalker and this enigmatic man are linked to something hush-hush, as Jenny had put it?

'Yes.' It's automatic, but my mind is still swarming all over his previous statement. 'What is Chiaroscuro?'

'Chiaroscuro?' His voice lingers on the word, caressing it. He smiles, as if he is rewarding me. 'We work with Ethos from time to time, and Ethos repays the debt by working with us when we need... solutions. Usually we do it by facilitating understanding on both sides. Enabling the flick of the switch. It's not always easy to fully understand the complexities of some of the issues that Ethos has to deal with, so we help by enabling a fuller appreciation of them. Your father was an advocate of that too, I believe.'

Before I can reply, he stands and saunters over to my bookcase – the one filled with so many tomes of professional expertise and wisdom by my predecessor, or maybe Director Robert Anhelm, who has seen fit to explain so little to me. He pulls a volume from it and crosses the room again, lays the book on my ice-white desk. He's gone straight to it like he was drawn there by a magnet, and he the opposing force. It's Dada's renowned first book. *We Are What We Do*. The assertion that we can only truly learn from what we experience, regardless of education and perceived wisdom. I recognise the book cover even at a distance – would recognise all of Dada's book covers even if I was blind. I'm sure I would sense them, sense the force of him through the very words.

'How did you know that was there?' I can't contain my curiosity.

'Natural affinity?' He grins, and he looks like that pleasant man in the street again – the one I would walk past, only noticing him for his gentle air of self-possession. He lingers by the desk, stroking the book gently where it lies. 'Look, I think we'll do just fine together if you'll just loosen up a bit and trust me like you want me to trust you.' His smile deepens, lingers on me, caressing my face and then my breasts, before returning to my eyes. 'I like you, Abigail. I already like you a lot. We are going to do a lot for each other, I think, and you really might be able to help me with my issues, but that comes later. For now, it's hardly fair of me to bombard you with moral complexities when you've only just walked through the door and haven't even figured out how things work here. I'm going to leave now, but I'd like to start addressing the real issues next time we talk.'

He comes closer, stands in front of me, is pulling me to my feet, warm hands encasing mine. I would like to resist but I can't. He is too inviting. Now he is the magnet and I the opposing force, being pulled close to him. We stand toe to toe. He is only a few inches taller than me. If I had been wearing heels instead of my working psychologist's flatties, we would be almost eye to eye. I have to tilt my head the smallest amount to look into his eyes and I am wrong. Those doe-brown eyes aren't merciless or dissecting me. They're earnestly examining me. The butterflies are frantic now, beating their wings against my breastbone and straying into my stomach and gut. One or two have even made it as far as my pelvis and are tickling me, tickling so I want to gasp and lean in and kiss him. I try to take a step back but his hands are holding mine locked tight by my sides. Instead I involuntarily thrust my breasts forward and they touch his chest. The sensation is electric. We both feel it.

'You need to let go of me. This isn't …'

'Sorry.' He drops my hands and steps nonchalantly away as if what has happened is the most natural thing in the world and not tingling in the nerve endings all the way down to the soles of my feet. 'I've left you something on the desk, Abigail. You need settling in time today, but I'll come back tomorrow, if that's OK? To be continued.'

I stutter. It comes out as some sort of 'yes'.

'Good, we're on the same page then. There's credit on it already, by the way.' And he's gone, leaving me standing in the middle of my new office, heart squeezed of blood, flooding the pit of my stomach and dribbling down my inner thighs like post-coital juice. Involuntarily I reach under my skirt to check – the sensation is so real – and am shocked to see my fingers are covered in blood. My period has started. Two days early. Well, at least I'm not pregnant. That really would have ruined my fresh start. The fumbled last night with Mark comes back to plague me – when I'd been deciding whether to take the job or not. It had decided me then. No going back, no standing still, no marking time, even with someone who'd give me the world for just a minute of my life. That was safe, but miserable. Dada would have told me that too, but the legacy that moment of decision-making could have left me with had worried me ever since. At least the fear is proved unfounded, to be replaced by – what?

I rummage in my bag and find a tampon. Rushing to the ladies' toilets, I strip off my pants in the cubicle and clean up as best I can. I toss the soiled pants in the rubbish bin alongside sodden paper towels and other female detritus. They're ruined anyway, and they'll only stain my skirt. Better off without them. Would Abigail do that? I try to picture Abigail's face. Pale gold curls coiling round delicate features? Baby-blue eyes? Or blue-green eyes that had a cat-like quality to them, ringed with long curling lashes. Coy but impish. Not a golden angel, a fallen one. Maybe Abigail *would* have tossed her spoiled underwear aside. Would have enjoyed the sense of sluttish abandon being knicker-less brought, whilst technically being unavailable to indulge sluttish behaviour. I feel oddly duplicitous as I wash my hands and stare at my face in the mirror. Unclean, yet uninhibited. I slather my palms with the expensive liquid soap that matches the hand lotion in the polished stainless-steel dispensers ranged along the washbasin area and scrub away the blood stains. My cheeks are still flushed from the encounter with Xander. Had he noticed or had the flood started after he'd gone? My cheeks flame a deeper red at the possibility he had known – had seen. Then I sigh. Too bad if he had. I can't change the past, not with him, nor with Dada.

Back in my office I push the door shut and check the time. I have ten minutes before my last patient – client – is scheduled for this afternoon. I sit at the desk and savour the few moments to gather myself, not wishing to review the encounter with Xander yet. There is a mobile phone on the desk next to Dada's book. I frown and then realise who it must belong to. In the rush to clean myself up I'd forgotten what he'd said as he left. Xander has left me a phone. That's what he'd meant by credit on it. Damn him – isn't it bad enough he's talking of reciprocation when I haven't the faintest idea what is going on? This is completely unprofessional, and he has no sense of propriety. I'm about to storm out into the corridor and go in search of Jenny to tell her to return it and reallocate Client X to someone else when I realise it is showing a text message has already been received.

I want to read it. And I don't want Jenny to reallocate Client X. That would be admitting failure before I'd even got started. My fresh start. Proving myself worth the pedigree – although God knows how! *And anyway*, that little voice prompts me, *you want him all to yourself*. I quieten it. It's not part of me, that voice. It's a tease – a lure. One I don't want to hear. The kind of voice Abigail would have – the fallen angel Abigail, that is. I resist the temptation to read the text for all of thirty seconds.

'Abigail,' it says. 'It's going to be so intriguing working with you. Finding solutions for each other. So much past. So much yet to come … Are you looking forward to it as much as I am? X.'

I toy with the phone. This is impossible! If I reply, I am buying into his agenda – whatever it is. But if I don't I will never know what it is – and nor will I be able to do my job. That is a lie. Of course, I can do my job. But not successfully with him. He doesn't play by the rules. He makes his own rules and plays his own games. Mind games. I already know that and how horribly dangerous this could be. I won't reply. I will put the phone in the desk drawer and lock it shut. Then I think about Jenny, and whether the fount of all knowledge might not also know precisely what is in everyone's desk drawers too. No. I'll take it home with me but return it to him myself tomorrow. I drop it into my bag and try to ignore the ping of another incoming text. It is two o'clock. Georges Thierone will be here any minute. My stalker – and my next challenge. I'm surprised he too wasn't included on the list of forbiddens Director Anhelm gave me. Whatever, he's self-selected me anyway – like I have selected Director Anhelm's forbiddens. It is then I first wonder whether it is not only Director Anhelm who has steered me towards the forbiddens, merely by making them forbidden, but also the forbiddens themselves. Suicide and muddying the past; anyone who knows anything at all about me would know that those two things alone would have me itching to delve further. Add to that Jessica's taunt about a predecessor I knew well and who was an ogre, and Xander's uncanny reading of my internal confliction and now his mention of the past … I am potentially a rat on a dissection table. Who else could my predecessor be but Dada, and what else could be the source of my confliction, but his suicide? But what else do they know about me and my past?

Deep inside me the kraken stirs.

Or what is it that I don't know about me and my past, and they do? Just as Dada's suicide needs explaining for me, now increasingly, so do the gaps in my memory that are become more and more obvious as some small but nevertheless significant detail makes itself apparent, like an air bubble popping inside my ear. Like Abigail. And like my father's mouth opening and closing in my repeating dream, not so much telling me why, as reminding me of a truth I may already know.

Chapter 10

'Cancelled, again.' Jenny's expression is comic. 'Tomorrow ...'

'How often does he do this?'

'Oh, all the time. It's not you, don't worry. Enjoy the breather. I expect you have quite a lot to write up about Client X anyway.' The curiosity is evident in her voice, but she knows I won't satisfy it. I'm glad of the time and space too. Jenny's face disappears from the screen and I lean back in my chair and reassess myself and my world. It is not so bad – if I can stop all the strands of it from unravelling all at once. I am still the professional, even if I am feeling my way some of the time. Everyone starts somewhere and learns from their mistakes. Letting Xander get too close was a mistake but I can rectify that. Yes, I take a deep breath in. I will start by making a full record of our conversations, then I am covered for the future.

The rest of the afternoon is taken up with recording what we said and as I review it, I rue my naivety. But I will be more prepared now. I took on a forbidden. I have to expect the forbidden to test me. As I'm preparing to leave the office, the gorgon in my bag awakes, the unexpected unfamiliar ping of the text making me jump. My own phone plays a gentle serenade to alert me to incoming messages. Xander's phone startles with a metallic crescendo of unmelodic chords.

'Good night, Abigail. We are what we do. Your father would be proud of you.'

I'm tempted to reply, except that it would be to tell him to piss off. That wouldn't be wise. Instead, I turn alerts to 'silent' and ignore it. Something tells me that he doesn't really expect a reply right now. He just wants to remind me of his existence and possibly niggle me a little. *We are what we do.* He's certainly done that. I put the phone back in my bag, and on impulse, instead of replacing the book he'd left there in the bookcase, hover over its title. *We Are What We Do: The Origins of Morality.* The image of Dada, at his desk, writing assiduously, is too much. I have to open it, to feel his words on the page. The fly leaf contains a personal inscription to its owner.

My darling Romaine, who has inspired me from the moment I first saw her and will continue to do so until the breath leaves my body. A. 14th Feb '91

I fling the book down. It remains open at the fly leaf. Romaine? Mum's name. OK, more accurately Romaine is my stepmother, but for me she has been Mum most of my life – only latterly becoming Romaine because now I am grown it feels more appropriate to acknowledge her individuality, rather than her role. How could a book my father has inscribed to her find its way into my predecessor's library? Unless my predecessor was my father – but that isn't possible. He's been dead for over a decade now. I remain fixated on the book until gradually the cover flips up and closes over again. My father's favourite portrait shot of himself smiles back at me from the cover, ringed by the title. We are what we do. We are what we do. We are what we do. I put my hands over my face and try to choke back the need to weep. I feel very alone. I'm not alright, Romaine. Mum. I'm not fine.

I wait until the worst of the storm is over before I gather my belongings to leave, but it's not so much the loneliness that has got to me, as a sense of the unanswered – as it always is. This time, the usual unanswered question *why?* is accompanied by the question hanging over the reason for my stepmother's signed copy of my father's book being in my predecessor's book collection.

We are what we do. Indeed.

What can I say about Dada? He was a man above men, a philosopher, an academic, an icon. He was my father and I trusted him above all people – even my stepmother. Why did he then just abandon us – me? I suppose it's as much that as the fact that he killed himself when I was fifteen that I struggle with. That a man so committed to helping people have the strength to cope with their problems and *live* should voluntarily choose to die. After the first wave of shock and grief Romaine said to simply accept it. It is what he would have told us to do, she claimed. We have a life to do what we want with. If his choice was to leave it, then who are we to dispute that choice? The philosopher's argument, but not so easy to accept when it is someone you love. Didn't you love him, Romaine?

Of course, I never asked her that. And in time, accept is what I did, outwardly. Inwardly I dwelt on it and Romaine knew that just as surely as I knew that she did the same – inwardly. We chose to accept a game of pretending that we'd both got over it. I forged on academically, scraping through my first degree, but being accepted for the Masters by calling in a favour from one of Dada's ex-students – now a head of faculty himself. My PhD was awarded with no corrections in a monumentally short two years, hence why I earned the accolade 'a chip off the old block', but sometimes I think that must have been luck rather than brilliance too. I chose the right research area at the right time and rode the wave of some ground-breaking results without having to do the ground work myself. Dada had achieved the same but in even less time, gaining his professorship at Cambridge only a year later. Unheard of. Incredible. Exceptional. But Dada was like that. Compared to him, I am a fraud. Compared to many, I am a fraud. But I am Assistant Director here, and this is my fresh start – on my own, no called-in favours, no dodgy moral supports, not relying on his name to open the doors for me – or so I thought. This was supposed to be on my achievements alone, and I damn well will achieve – even if it's in the face of Director Anhelm's manipulation!

I drop the book into my bag next to Xander's phone, grab my coat and exit the building like gas being released from a pressurised cannister. I haven't realised until now quite how oppressed I feel all time I'm here – even as I grab the reins of power with both hands. Power? I snort. Have I grabbed power, or has it grabbed me? Tomorrow I shall make a point of getting out again, even if only to grab something to eat from the little deli I found yesterday. For now, at least I've survived another day intact and in control. Then all the way home I think about the book in my bag, jolting against my neighbour on the tube, trying not to breathe in the stale air or allow the weariness that has suddenly overwhelmed me to drag me into sleep before I arrive back at my over-new flat with its still coffee-stained kitchen.

There, I do finally eat – a plastic-tasting pizza and wilted salad. It fills a gap, but not with pleasure. The wine does that. Well, why the hell not? It's been a hard day. I eat at the breakfast bar, trying to ignore the mess around me, and Facetime Romaine. Her face fills the screen, bright, fresh and happy. I push the wine glass out of view.

'Gab! How's it going?'

'How long have you got?'

She bursts out laughing, then looks concerned. 'Like that, huh? Good or bad?'

'How long have you got?' but I make a mock-rueful face to defuse the ticking bomb. This time I laugh, and she joins in uncertainly. I rush on, just in case I sound like I feel, despite the laughter. 'Three awkward customers, a know-it-all PA and no Director.'

'No Director? Why?'

'He and all the rest of the team are at a conference where they've just hit the big time. So that leaves just me and Know-it-all to hold the fort.'

'Oh darling! Are you alright on your own? Do you need me to ...'

'No. I'm fine. And I'm going be very busy this week, so I won't have time to worry.' I smile. I guess it must be over-bright because she looks anxious. 'And I'm a big girl now, remember?'

'I know, I know, but still... It's been tough and...'

'I'm fine. This is my fresh start. More to the point, are you alright without me?'

'Oh, don't worry about me. Just as long as you're not dwe–'

'Mum, I'm not dwelling on it. I've got too much else to dwell on.' I take a deep breath and am just about to ask her about the book and the inscription when she pre-empts me.

'You haven't called me that in years: Mum.' She sounds suspicious. 'Are you sure you ...'

'It's a Freudian slip,' I laugh, but now of course, I can't ask. The moment is wrong. 'And I'd better finish my pizza before it coagulates completely.'

'OK. Talk to me again soon, though? And Gaby ...'

'Yes?'

'You are remembering your meds aren't you?'

'Of course.' I mutter the lie.

'Only ...'

'I know. It's fine. I'm fine, really.'

'OK, well – tomorrow maybe ...'

'Tomorrow, maybe ...'

I ring off first. I feel guilty. I have lied. I don't lie to Romaine – Mum. But I am fine – really. And I don't need the unopened bottle in the bathroom cabinet. I don't.

Chapter 11

He is lounging in my office in much the same way as yesterday. It still feels like a glass cage and I have a hangover.

'How did you get in?' I ask. I can feel the butterflies starting to flutter in my chest cavity – also much the same way as yesterday. God, but he's good-looking, in a way I'd overlooked before. Those doe eyes are sensuous and appealing and his dark, dark hair has the merest hint of a wave to it, curling at the back where it meets his collar.

'The usual way,' he grins. Teasing me. He gestures to the doorway I'm standing in. 'Like you.'

I can smell him without there being any odour present. Pheromones, mine reacting to his. He's sitting with his back to a shaft of sunlight streaming in through the wall of glass overlooking the car park at the front of Ethos. He may even have been watching me arrive, park and enter the building from it. I'd taken his Ethos file home with me to read and absorb, but even the bumper bonus version Jenny latterly provided after I queried the original's emptiness had been virtually empty too; as enigmatic as the man himself. Apart from which, the amount of wine I'd drunk had been hardly conducive to concentration on the cryptic possibilities of the little there was in it.

'But I just unlocked it, and no one should have allowed you into my office in my absence without my permission.' He's watching me with curiosity now, like he might have been as he watched me arrive. The idea makes me even more nervous, trying to remember what I did as I walked in. Smooth my hair? Straighten my skirt? Pick my teeth? Muesli isn't always such a good choice to start the day with.

'Did you? Then I am a disciple of Houdini, keen to spend more time with his muse.' Me, his muse? Does he mean that or is it more teasing? It makes my pulse race – just a little bit more. Underneath that calm, urbane exterior does he feel the same – even the smallest amount? 'Is that alright with you? That I'm here this early? I couldn't wait, you see?' he pauses.

'Abigail.' It's said so softly, caressing and lingering on the 'ail'. My stomach lurches and the butterflies surge. Stop it, stop it, stop it! You know what you're dealing with. You decided that last night after re-reading the notes from yesterday, and the fact that Director Robert Anhelm sent him your way by device, not destiny. He's a killer, with something on Ethos. And he knows more than he's saying about Dada too. So maybe he is temporarily questioning his moral integrity; but he's still using Ethos to do so – and that means he's using you to square his conscience. This could even be a test by the Director, to see how well you cope – just like Jessica Morgan could be. You have to play the game to keep your job, but that means you have to adopt the sociopath's stance. So much for ethics!

'If you had an appointment booked in, its fine.'

'You didn't reply,' he says.

'No.' I say. 'You need to take it back.' I take the phone from my bag and put it on the desk.

'It's yours.'

'I don't want it. It's inappropriate between patient and doctor.'

He shrugs. 'That's fine,' but makes no attempt to move.

'What would you like to discuss today?' I add. My voice is scratchy.

'I thought we'd already agreed that?' He looks mildly surprised. 'Not so much discuss as share, though. We touched on the morality of stealing yesterday. Have you ever stolen anything?'

I put my bag in the bottom drawer of the desk, collect a pad and pen from the top drawer and slide into position in the chair opposite him. Its mink-coloured luxury moulds itself to my body. I cross my legs and his eyes follow the line of my right leg from thigh to toe before returning to my face via the left leg. They are long legs. I am proud of my legs, slim and shapely. An asset, together with my blonde hair and wide slate-blue eyes. Today, my legs sport *barely there* stockings whose sheen is caught in the same shaft of sunlight that spills over Xander. Normally I would wear tights to work. Stockings are for leisure, for seduction – for Abigails – but today I needed the confidence boost. I feel sexy. It makes me feel more in control, although God knows, I'm not.

'Of course not. Stealing is wrong – and there has never been any need for me to do it for any other, more complex, issues – such as we touched on yesterday.'

'Ah, yes. And then you suggested that you accepted stealing isn't, therefore, always wrong.'

'No, I said there may be exceptional circumstances that suggest redeeming features, not that it was ever right.'

'You are a pedant?'

'No, but if we are to understand each other we must ensure our communication is clearly understood between us.'

'I see,' he smiles, tapping the fingers of his right hand on the chair arm. 'Well that poses me with a lovely little challenge: to prove to you that sometimes stealing isn't only not wrong, but it's positively ethically acceptable. Will you take up a challenge?'

'Why would I need to?'

'Because you can't understand my dilemma unless you understand what I mean when I make that claim. And of course, that then means you can't help me find an ethical solution to my problem, and Ethos will have failed me.'

'Well, that's not pulling any punches,' I reply, trying to hide the tremor in my voice at what feels like a direct threat. How can this man so easily see what will rattle me? It's like he can read my mind.

'I'm a plain speaker. And I am here for help.'

'I am here to help you,' I remind him gently, forcing the butterflies to settle momentarily.

'Then you will take up my challenge?'

'What is your challenge?'

'I want you to steal something because doing so is the only ethical thing to do in the circumstances.'

The sun has started to move round the office, peering in the right-hand wall of windows now. The temperature is rising in the room and I'm glad I only put on a thin silk blouse today, anticipating heat of one sort or another. I'm still sweating though.

'What do you want me to steal?' My breath feels caught, trapped painfully in my chest.

'That will depend on you. You will decide on that, based on the ethics of the situation. You might need a bit of practice beforehand though – if you don't want to get caught. Training and preparation guarantee survival, not arrogance. That's what I tell my operatives.'

'Do you send your operatives out to practise stealing too?'

'If it will help them survive ultimately.'

'How can stealing help them survive?'

'If they're in the middle of India, and starving, I think that's obvious, isn't it?'

'Why would they be there?' I can't help it, even though I know I shouldn't ask about his work.

'Why wouldn't they?'

'On assignment?'

His expression is relaxed, giving nothing away. 'Assignment?' His smile is lopsided. 'Holiday, work, training... What do you think they or I do, then, Abigail?'

My skin crawls at the use of the name. 'Undercover work. You're Special Forces, or something similar.'

'Really? That's very romantic. Secret agent stuff you mean?' He shrugs and laughs, his amusement rolling around the room, making the glass reverberate – or maybe that's my head, pounding like it always does on the second day of my period. Hormones. 'My job role – for what it's worth – is Asset Assimilator. I recruit useful people. Secret Agent is someone else's job, I'm afraid.'

'Oh.' Now I feel stupid. The Director had me assuming that his work was something far more toxic. 'But Chiaroscuro?' The very name suggested something covert.

'Just a fancy name, like Ethos. Which sounds better, do you think? They both do similar kinds of things – find solutions to problems, they're just different kinds of problems and different kinds of solutions.' He's smiling at me like I'm a child. I suppose I am – naïve, anyway, despite my years.

'The Director said you had an unusual profile. I thought... '

'What did you think?' He laughs at my embarrassment. 'That I was something more than I am? Robert would imply that. Bigging me up to test you.'

'Then why are you Client X? Why not use your real name?'

'Who else do you have on your client list?'

'I can't disclose that to you. Confidentiality...'

'Not under any circumstances?'

'Only under oath or on a witness summons in the event of a crime.'

'Then your confidentiality rules aren't absolute. If I remain Client X, they are because you can't tell anyone I'm anything other than that.'

'If you need that level of security, then I still wonder about what you really do.'

'So do Chiaroscuro at times, but I get them what they want when they want it, so they play along. However, what I do to get them what they want has plagued me recently – the rights and wrongs of it: the ethics. So,

I'm here – seeking ethical solutions for what I do and how I feel about it, and in order for you to understand why, I'm asking you to experience some of the situations I have found myself in so you can rationalise them with me. And yes, what I do is classified, but not as secret agent crap. This is big business. Relentless, merciless and at times, destructive. I don't want it to destroy me in the process too.' He leans back in his chair and watches me. He no longer looks relaxed or easy. He looks taut and anxious. The sunlight is falling across the left-hand side of his face now, casting the right side in shadow. It sketches hollows under his eyes and I am moved with compassion at what appears to be the genuine desperation that is carving them out. His eyes plead with me. We seem to have gone round in a circle and are no further forward to where we were yesterday, except now I am confused. Maybe he isn't what I first thought him to be? Maybe he isn't a game player, and I have been overly cynical? I have agreed to play along to 'help' him, but now I think both he and I might mean it too.

'Whatever your secrets are, they're safe with me, and whatever your ethical problems are there are always solutions. We will find them. If your rationale for stealing is what you need me to understand, then I'll do my best to understand it.' *It may help you with Jessica Morgan too.* The thought coils round my brain and is absorbed into the sudden rush to prove myself, but not before it drags another one with it. It's not Xander who's playing games with me. It's the Director, testing my perspicacity. Why else land me with two tricky characters, both with the same issue, approached in different ways. Could I address the same problem with two perfectly tailored solutions for two totally different individuals? Understanding for Xander and absolution for Jessica?

'And then deceit and death.' His voice is thin and quiet.

'I thought you said there was nothing covert about you? Oh, I get it. You mean, once I understand how it feels to commit a criminal act, we can talk about the death that you...'

'Precisely. One sin leads to another, unchecked.' He seems smaller, filling less of the room all of a sudden. His body is still firm and toned under his clothes – a check blue shirt and faded jeans – but it no longer seems deadly.

'Is that what you're afraid of? That small things will escalate into bigger ones? Or that they already have?'

'You understand in part already then.' The thin quality has left his voice and he's smiling – an appreciative smile.

'Let's take one day at a time.'

'Sweet Jesus,' he winks. His voice lilts and I realise he is mimicking an evangelistic song and want to laugh. He knows too. I try to balance the thin, quiet voice with the brazen tease. He is both. The troubled soul and the ruthless killer. That is why he is here, I remind myself. And I want him far too badly to be his therapist, counsellor, facilitator, solution-finder – or whatever I am.

I stifle the laugh and nod gravely. 'I did want to ask you something actually – yesterday, after you'd left.'

'About your father's book?'

'Yes?' I hadn't expected him to get it so quickly. This man is a kaleidoscope of character patterns.

'You should talk to your predecessor about how it came to be here. I can't answer that for you.'

'Who was my predecessor?'

'Don't you know?' His surprise seems genuine.

'No.' I shake my head. He chews on a finger nail. 'Then it's not up to me to tell you. You'll figure it out. Much of what we do – as I'm sure you will remind me as our association progresses – is about figuring things out for ourselves, not expecting someone to do it for us. But there's our reciprocation. You research and I'll tell you if you're on the right track. In the meantime, are you ready to steal something and find out what it feels like?'

'Oh,' I laugh dismissively – the best way to deal with patient's inappropriate requests, I've decided. Especially this one's. 'I thought you were leaving that for me to decide on?'

'But you still need to practise or you'll get caught when it matters. Then how will you be able to help me from jail? Try something that's unimportant to its owner – you can square your conscience that way too.'

'And how on earth would I know what's unimportant to someone? Just theoretically.'

'Oh, you'll know. It's obvious, usually, but I'll prompt you if you need help. Otherwise, tell me when you've done it and then we'll talk again – from a different perspective.'

'I could tell you anything. Or lie.'

If it didn't matter to its owner was there no sin, no immorality involved, in taking a worthless possession?

'You could. But I would know if you're lying. Deceit and death, remember? That would be deceit, and we have a way to go before we progress to that.'

He is rising to leave and suddenly I don't want him to. I want him to stay and bandy words with me. That quality to him reminds me so of Dada. It's probably a good thing that my gut is aching and I need to change my tampon or I might have tried to prolong his visit. After he's gone, I realise he hasn't taken the phone with him. It is still lying, bold and brass-faced in the middle of my desk. I feel a sense of desperation that he hasn't taken it with him. Or maybe temptation. Only my second day here and already I am feeling trapped – in a snare of my own making. Dammit! I wasn't going to play patsy – already had plans to tell Jessica Morgan that and yet here I am doing exactly that with Xander. Xander needs help, but ethically the way he's electing to obtain it from me is wrong on so many levels, and the way I am allowing it is wrong too – and yet I need to.

What on earth could I steal that doesn't matter to its owner?

Chapter 12

With Xander gone, I go back to the files Jenny provided me with on Monday. The bottle of wine last night had negated all possibility of me looking at them in any sensible way, but to be honest, I'd probably needed the wine more than I'd needed information right then. Candy Myers is exactly what I'd figured her to be. I remember her platinum blonde pale similarity to me and squirm uncomfortably. I am not the proverbial escort in consultant's terms. I am far more than that. I set the file aside, resolving to let the Director carry on with her. I have bigger fish to fry – and to prove him wrong about my ability to cook with them.

My review of them originally had been cursory, looking for big answers to big questions, but there weren't any. Looking at things from a more enquiring perspective now, I see that the devil may be in the little details – the ones I hadn't bothered with at first glance. I'm not surprised by what is in Jessica Morgan's file, which is the one I tackle first. I am sorely tempted to dive back into Xander's instead, but I need to focus. Be professional. I acknowledge my interest in him has a personal element too. Rich – and powerful in her own right within the business world, spoilt, high-profile, Jessica Morgan is also charming, glamorous, quirky and the darling of the press. She has a philanthropic side too. It's recorded in some clippings I find tucked into the rear of the file. Third world poverty has been alleviated a small degree through her charitable donations – and it makes good copy. Could that be her self-imposed penance too? Debatable. It had started only fairly recently. Perhaps some self-awareness there? Now I waver over whether to refuse to treat her.

And now I also realise why her name rang a bell with me. Whilst her company is a big brand name, she is better known personally as The Shoe Queen. I should have recognised her as soon as she came into my office, not that a therapist would fawn over her patients. *Clients,* I remind myself. No, dammit – privately they are going to remain patients because that is what they really are. Maybe who she is influences how I lay down the law to her though. For Ethos, she is probably quite a coup. Rich, high-profile and needy. Everything Ethos could desire, based on what I've seen so far. There has never been any suggestion of anything other than generally law-abiding behaviour from her, so her petty pilfering is somewhat of a surprise. Kleptomania? I don't like gut-diagnoses but this one is screaming at me. She doesn't remember the act of theft, nor even where it occurs, just having the unknown and suspect objects on her. Then the guilt. Yes, genuine guilt because she has rationalised what she has done and wants to make recompense somehow for it, no matter how blasé she appears to be. I change my opinion of her. To be fair she does have a real problem, if only she can be persuaded to address it. Its roots will lie somewhere deep in her past. Her muddy water. The immediate answer isn't obvious from mine or the scanty notes made by Director Anhelm, only an oblique reference to a manipulative liaison when she was in her early twenties, and a period of rebellious behaviour that lasted some six months and then disappeared, along with any police records resulting from it, which, too, I paid little or no attention to in my original quest for a big truth and an obvious treatment path. Thereafter she was what she was – and what I'd judged her to be: brittle, bright and business-like. But underneath – that is what I need to get to.

I put Jessica Morgan's file aside and pick up an almost identical one for Georges Thierone. Political lobbyist and self-confessed serial liar. Really, that's what the file says! He wants to figure out how to separate the two parts of his life so that whilst he might lie professionally, he doesn't do so personally too. What? I lean back in my chair and allow its buoyancy to bounce me gently on the waves of laughter, like I'm a brightly painted boat full of happy tourists. He's actually asked to be coached in setting aside morals in his professional life – and he's in politics? The irony is almost too much for me. I wish I could share it with someone.

His appointment sheet records repeated failures to attend, last minute cancellations and unexpected insertions. A number of appointments are noted as 'off-site'. I ring Jenny. A brief conversation on arrival this morning has put us on even better terms this morning and I have now also found out that she is a single mother with two teenage children. Her life revolves around them and work. Kids and clients.

'It won't always,' she said to my expression that must have expressed dismay at the monotony of it. 'But for the moment, I'm doing what everyone needs me to do. One day I'll do what I want to do.'

Her greeting now is welcoming – none of the know-it-all of Monday morning. I'm relieved by the change. Or maybe my attitude has changed too? I pitch straight in after I've adjusted to talking both into the phone and to her image on the PC screen. 'Jenny, what does off-site mean in relation to appointments in Georges Thierone's file?'

'Ah, that. Synchronistic because that's exactly what your appointment is going to be with him today. He rang in barely three minutes ago. I've literally just put the phone down on him. He can't make it over to us in between meetings today so he's asked if you'd mind meeting him in Hyde Park. That's what off-site means. Between you and me, it makes it difficult to monitor the meeting. I think that's more his concern than having the time to get here.'

'Monitor the meeting?'

'Record it.'

'But we wouldn't, would we?'

'Only if it related to national security.'

'That's work for spooks, not us!' I want to laugh aloud at the incongruity of Jenny's statement – at the incongruity of everything here so far – but if I think about it seriously, it's not funny.

'We work with people who know a lot of things – sometimes things that they shouldn't have the power to act on, given they're here seeking help. We don't spy, we monitor.'

'Is that why Xan- Client X insists on anonymity?'

'Does he? I could tell you his real name if you want it. Or, the name he's given, at least. It is on record – everything has to be on record in case there's a need for witness statements, evidence – that sort of thing.'

I hesitate. I could know Xander's real name. Just like that, Jenny would give it to me. 'It isn't in the notes you gave me on him.'

'No, but it's in Robert's safe. It can be released on his say-so if you think it's necessary.' The expression on her face on-screen makes it feel like it wouldn't be a good idea for it to be necessary. And do I want the Director looking over my shoulder with Xander? Or knowing at all, for the moment, what I've done in countermanding his instructions?

'No, it's not necessary,' I say. 'Where in Hyde Park am I meant to meet Georges Thierone, and at what time?'

'Four o'clock by the Animals in War memorial. Apparently, it's only a few minutes away from the US Embassy and he's there all afternoon.'

'OK, tell him I'll be there at four and what I'll be wearing, so he can recognise me.'

'Oh, don't worry about him recognising you. Robert circulated a photo and information about you to our clients way before you arrived. They probably all know you better than you know yourself by now, I expect, given what they are.'

'Oh, my God, why didn't he tell me that?'

That would explain him knowing who to stalk...

Jenny laughs. 'Don't worry, it's perfectly normal and you haven't been singled out. Client care, he calls it. He did the same to me when I first joined, so it's nothing new.'

So, the Director is a control freak too. I wish I'd known that before I'd accepted the job too, but it's too late now. I'm here.

'Did he do it with my predecessor too?' I ask, suddenly inspired.

'Your predecessor? I don't think you had one.' Down the phone her voice sounds muffled, like she's moved away from the receiver, but the screen shows she's still there.

'Who occupied my office before me then?'

'No one. It's been empty for a while.' She hesitates as if about to say more but doesn't. 'It's an unusual one,' she concludes eventually.

'You can say that again,' I say with feeling. 'But it's full of books and it's one of the most luxurious rooms in the building? And I thought everyone was after it, from what you implied.' I admit to myself now that this has bothered me. My office is more well-appointed than the Director's – as I remember it – if also a goldfish bowl.

'Yes, well, after it in the sense of the kudos it implies. I guess it's become a bit of a library over time – any books that were of interest accumulated there, especially when there was limited space in the other offices.'

I don't ask about limited space. I simply make a note to inspect the other offices whilst their occupants are away at the conference. The Director's might be difficult, with Jenny fronting it, but I can check when she goes home and examine it then.

'When was it last used properly as an office then?'

'Oh, before my time – sorry I'm going to have to go, there's a call coming through.' Her voice clicks off and I put the receiver down. Xander's file is teasing me even though there are two more pages of the supplementary notes to wade through in Georges Thierone's file and Jessica Morgan is due here any minute. Resolutely I put all three folders away in preparation for Jessica's arrival, swivel the chair and angle it so I can survey the extensive book case behind me. Jenny's description of it is pretty good, actually. It *is* a library, with well-known texts on every psychological condition most therapists deal with from stress through to schizophrenia. Of course, it contains all of Dada's books. What good psychologist's library wouldn't? I pull them all off the shelf and check the fly leaves. None of the others are inscribed. I get the inscribed copy out of my bag, to reunite it with its companions. I'm prevented by the phone on my desk. It is Jenny again. The PC screen blossoms again with her cheerful face.

'Sorry I had to go like that, but good job I intercepted that call or you'd be twiddling your thumbs the rest of the morning waiting for Miss Morgan. That was her, calling to cancel, but asking for her own form of off-site visit. She's at a showcase for her latest autumn and winter designs tomorrow. Would you like to join her? She said she thought it might help you understand her world and what goes on in it. You'd be able to make a better-informed choice then. I assume you understand that?'

'Oh. Where is the showcase?'

'Paris.'

'Paris?' I can hear my voice rising half an octave but can't stop it.

'She'll send a car to take you to her private jet.'

'I don't know. I have other pa– clients ...'

'Who can all reschedule to the day after. Go and enjoy the experience.'

'Is this normal too, Jenny?'

'What's normal? It's different depending on the people and the situation. Where Miss Morgan is concerned, this is probably normal – wouldn't you say? Just like Mr Thierone's off-sites are normal for him.'

'And Client X?'

'Ah, now with him, I wouldn't venture to guess. That's your territory. I'll confirm the car pick-up for nine am, shall I? From your apartment or from here?'

'Oh, here! Most definitely here!'

The idea of Jessica Morgan – or any of my patients – having access to my private address makes me shiver.

'Will do. It'll take you about thirty minutes walking or on the tube from here to Hyde Park, by the way.'

'Thank you.'

My voice has dropped back to its normal cadence but it sounds stilted. Cold. It's not Jenny, it's everyone else, divvying up my life between them – even Dada to some extent. If he hadn't done what he'd done, maybe I wouldn't even be here? Maybe I would have followed one of the crazier and more exciting vocations I'd considered at fifteen. Vulcanologist, explorer, lion tamer.

'Thought you might like to know without having to look it up. You're getting all the curve balls there are to catch at the moment, it seems.'

The catch in my throat is unexpected and intense. Jenny is being as much mother to me as Romaine and yet she barely knows me. This time the thank you is warm and genuine. I think she gets the difference.

I go back to Georges Thierone's file. No mention of anything called Chiaroscuro in it, though – although Xander is involved in it too. I make a mental note to challenge Georges Thierone about it and close his file. Unlike Jessica's, but like Xander's it really does contain virtually nothing – even on detailed inspection. Need to know. Both of them, clearly … I close it up and sit at my desk, unsure what to do with myself. It feels too rarified for reality – in my glass cage with my three errant patients – four if you counted Candy Myers. What commercial psychologist had such a small case-load in an ordinary practice? But this isn't an ordinary practice and you aren't a commercial psychologist. You are an elitist psychologist, I remind myself, just as Ethos is clearly not one of the rabble. I wonder how many patients Ethos has in total. I shall ask Jenny, but in the meantime, I am here twiddling my thumbs with nothing to do until late afternoon.

I go back to Dada's book, but without real enthusiasm for the subject matter. What interests me more is the sudden spurt of resentment that produced the catalogue of ridiculous vocations I might have followed if I hadn't become a psychologist. Had Dada's suicide really changed the course of my life that much? What would I have been like if he'd still been around, throwing his own curve balls at me to field or fumble? And how would Romaine have behaved? Would they have still been together? Or would she have allowed the divide that is age to create a gulf between them that neither of them could bridge?

Romaine. Mum. The distinction has grown as I have. It is hard to define how, but she is both to me now. It is easier overall to just think of her as simply ever-present, a guiding influence when I'm not sure where I'm headed. She always seems to know where she's headed.

Such a typically Dada romantic gesture – to inscribe his book with his love for her. I go back to the flyleaf again.

MIND GAMES: MEMENTO MORI

My darling Romaine, who has inspired me from the moment I first saw her and will continue to do so until the breath leaves my body. A. 14th Feb '91.

I can feel the indulgent smile stretching across my face as I read it. Romaine is small, dark and perfect. Her hands are like falling leaves in autumn, graceful and incredibly delicate. Her eyes are smouldering blue – the blue of the deepest parts of the ocean. Her skin is softer and smoother than silk, and her voice lilts melodically in a way only Irish voices can. Romaine asked me to call her Mum from the outset – when I was four and she was nineteen. Now I'm twenty-six and she's forty-one, we're more like sisters than step-parent and step-daughter, but the cement has solidified in our foundations. She brought me up as her own – and *on* her own – for most of my young life. Dada died when I was just fifteen and she could have simply handed me over to other blood relations then, but she didn't. She dried my tears, listened to my rantings, calmed my wilder notions and encouraged me into academia. I am a bright young psychologist with a sparkling career ahead of me now as much because of her determined nurturing as my father's abrasive talent. *'My darling Romaine...'* Those words bring me almost to tears as I read them again. How he must have loved her, and she him, despite the age gap. That's why I never challenged her every time she coaxed me into acceptance of how things were – because she with her love, as great as mine, had to accept it too. She was coaxing both of us.

I close the book and put it with all of Dada's other books back on the shelf. *We Are What We Do* stands proud, despite all efforts on my part, so I remove the offending volume to see why it won't settle in place. There is another, slimmer volume behind it, running lengthways across the back of the shelf. The other books are smaller than this one, so are still able to sit in their correct position. *We Are What We Do* is bigger proportionately. If I had returned it to the exact spot I'd removed it from, it would have settled into place without a murmur, but here, the hidden book battles for position with it. I pull the secreted book out – because surely that is what it is? Why would it have been so carefully arranged behind the other smaller books if the intention hadn't been to hide it? It's not a print book but a notebook. It contains a name per page – at least a hundred of them, the pages after them blank and hungry to be filled. Most of the names I don't know, but three stand out like beacons: Jessica Morgan and Georges Thierone are two of them. The third is more ambiguous, but nevertheless, it can't just be coincidence. X. My patients.

What is written on their pages makes no sense. It could be dates or it could be code. It's not that which concerns me most. It's the handwriting that stuns me. It is mine.

Dropping back into my office chair, I sit for what seems like hours with the notebook in my lap. The sun moves round the building and takes up position in what feels like a spotlight only on me. The fish swims in the fishbowl – round and around in circles. It cannot be my writing. I hadn't even been in this office until two days ago, and I have never met – or even heard of – two of my clients until then either. Jessica Morgan, maybe if I dredged my deepest subliminal memories, I might track down lurking in some corner. The Shoe Woman. Far more than that. The Shoe Queen; but I've never really been one for shoes. They're functional mostly, comfortable necessarily, and fashionable as required – but I will have come across her name somewhere and at some time in the past. Even so, why would I record all three of them in a notebook that is hidden behind my father's books? I study the neatly scribed names again. The others I've never heard of at all. I swear! My stomach growls at me and I realise with surprise that it doesn't just feel like hours I've been sitting like this, racking my brain about the source of the notebook, it *is* hours. I swivel the chair back round to face the desk again and put the notebook in the middle of its empty space – the same empty space Xander had put the phone into yesterday. The glass expanse of my office is a yawning chasm and I the poor fool about to fall through it. I need to get out.

It is almost mid-day so I decide to take an early lunch. I'm entitled – and I'm Assistant Director. I slip the notebook into my bag and collect my coat from the minimalist coat rack by the door. As an afterthought, I slip Xander's phone and Dada's inscribed book in there too. Leaving the room feels like recovering my sanity, even if I have created and hidden a notebook of data I don't remember. I stop off at Jenny's office before leaving the building altogether.

She is assiduously filing – a stack of buff folders like the supplementary notes for my patients. Her room is just as polite and neat as yesterday and I envy her the three walls of solid construction and one of glass, softened by floor to ceiling vertical blinds, half closed so the cloud design etched on them shows in slitted strands of blue and white. It feels compact and organised. Like Jenny. I wish it was my office and wonder if I could swap. The thought is as ridiculous as it is unlikely, nevertheless... The filing range is to the left of Jenny's desk, a tall range of beech drawers proclaiming themselves to be A to F, G to O, and P to Z. Jenny is kneeling in front of G to O with a stack of folders on her lap. She looks up as I enter, dark hair swinging gently around her neck as she turns her head to greet me. She smiles and it's as comforting as the room.

'I really need to get out and clear my head so I'm going to set off early for my appointment with Georges Thierone and grab some lunch on the way. Is that alright?'

'You're the boss.' The corners of her eyes crinkle as she grins and I can't help noticing how few wrinkles she has for a middle-aged woman. I hope I'll be as well-groomed and youthful-looking when I'm her age.

'Well, perhaps not the boss,' I reply, shrugging my shoulders in what I hope is a rueful fashion.

'While the cat's away,' she responds, and we laugh together.

'Is there anyone else at all here at the moment?' I ask, thinking of the silent rooms I passed as I walked the length of the corridor to get to here.

'No. Silent as the grave, isn't it? Bit spooky at times but it won't last. When everyone's back next week there won't be a moment's peace – especially not for you. They'll all be wanting to meet the famous Aaron McCray's daughter.'

I laugh shakily. 'Is that how they were referring to me before they went?'

'Not at all. I don't think any of them, apart from Robert, even know you've arrived yet.' I can't quite stop my frown. *Apart from my clients*, I think. She smiles up at me. 'It's going to be quite a surprise for them to find you already here.' She retrieves a stray folder as it slips from her knees and onto the floor. Naomi Williams. Its companion is James Openshaw. 'Look, I think we got off to a shaky start originally. Let me just put these last two away and I'll walk down the road with you if you like – show you the best sushi bar in London.'

'OK,' I laugh a little again. I do like Jenny after all, and I'm glad she is here to be my moral support – better by far than having the Director here, peering over my shoulder. I don't like sushi much, but the way I feel at the moment, I don't care. The company is more important. She stuffs the two folders into the back of the open drawer and struggles to her knees. I watch her, trying to identify why the two names strike a chord with me, but have to admit defeat. There are times when my brain simply defies me. Luckily not when faced with exam papers or job interviewers.

'Oof! Getting old!' her lips twist in a moue of distaste. She straightens and smooths the wrinkles from her skirt, offhandedly kicking the drawer shut with her foot as she does so. It's a practised kind of move I can imagine her doing many times a day and the sort that only the diligent and co-ordinated could manage, like rubbing your tummy and patting your head simultaneously. She notices my admiration and laughs throatily. 'Jill of all trades, mistress of none. You get used to multi-tasking when you have kids.'

'How old?' She has already told me I think, but I have been immersed in myself.

'Thirteen and fifteen. The dreaded GCSEs loom next summer for the first time. There's a first time for everything, isn't there? Exams, success, disappointment.'

'Hopefully not the latter for them,' I say, since I don't know what it's like for boys. I remember well what it had been like for me, nightmarishly worse because of Dada's suicide beforehand.

'No,' she agrees. She pulls her coat on and cinches the belt tight. It draws attention to her hourglass figure. Really – it's better than mine. 'Ready? Let's go sushi!'

We fall into step along the rest of the corridor and I call the lift. We are surrounded by indulgence, private collection paintings on the walls, carpet that heels sink into – lucky I don't wear stilettos – and the aura of wealth at every turn. Ethos is solutions with a price-tag. Jessica Morgan must pay it, so must Georges Thierone and the Naomi Williams and James Openshaws of this world, but Xander claimed not to. What reciprocal service did he provide Ethos with then?

'So, are all our pa-clients high profile?'

We're standing either side of the lift now, facing each other. Its small box intensity is like a cocoon. I feel I can ask her more now we're companionably on our way to eat sushi and enclosed in this space that no one else is looking in on – ah! That's why I don't like my office. I feel like I'm being watched, crazy though that is as it's on the first floor so any spy would have to be airborne too.

'No, by no means,' she says, shoving her hands deep into her pockets and hunching her shoulders. 'Nor rich.' She grins at my surprised expression. 'Well that was obviously going to be the next question, given the ambiance of this place. But that's what the Director wants everyone to think. It creates a sense of exclusivity. That we're special, because you have to *pay* for *special*. But they all have an element of power attached to them.'

We've reached ground floor and the doors slide open to reveal the main reception for the building. Ethos has the suite of rooms that encompass the first floor, sandwiched between a specialist insurance firm below us and a private investigator above us. The building is based on a pyramid so the lower down the building, the larger it is. The ground floor encompasses reception, waiting area, and the management offices. Above the private investigator is a literary agent and above that a business without a name and a logo that is a black box on a black background. Don't think you'd be able to see that? You'd be surprised. The logo is very clever. Once seen, you'd never forget it. I'm about to ask Jenny what the business's name is but a shabby little man in an overly long grey mac and wire-rimmed glasses is stepping into the lift between us as we are trying to step out of it. We wedge in the doorway for the merest of seconds and panic fills me. I've never liked lifts. Fear of mechanical breakdown and consequent suffocation are at the bottom of it – not that I've ever experienced either. Somewhere, in my subconscious, though, there is some memory, some apparently insignificant experience of being enclosed and unable to get out has been whipped up by my imagination and shaped me this way. That is the problem with being a psychologist. You are always looking for the reason. Sometimes there isn't a factual one. Only a perceived one.

'Do you know all of them?'

'Not personally, but on paper, yes. Intimately. Jessica Morgan is probably our wealthiest client. Client X our most secretive. The others are all sorts of things in between. It's the fact that we offer solutions, not counselling, that attracts such a wide range of people and issues.'

'You sound like the Director.'

Her peal of laughter rings out as we cross the car park and turn left onto Wellington Road to start threading our way towards Marylebone.

'Maybe I am the Director and the last three years have all just been a dream?' She's giggling now and it makes me feel like we're two naughty schoolgirls joking about the head teacher. I giggle too.

'You obviously passed the test with flying colours though. I have still to survive it.' I say it without thinking it through first. Like a bubble has risen from my stomach and burst in my mouth, spilling out the fears that have been gathering in the pit of me.

'Test? What test?'

She stops by the pedestrian crossing and we have time to study each other. Her bewilderment seems genuine.

'I suppose I'm more acutely aware of it than you would have been.

Psychologist's mind games. This going off to a conference and taking virtually the whole office with him, leaving me to deal with three particularly tricky clients – that's a test.'

'I suppose it is, of a sort,' she says slowly. 'But I thought you chose to work with them, so isn't the test maybe self-imposed?'

God, what a fool I'm being! I know exactly what I've done – in psychologist's terms. Based on her comment about everyone wanting to meet Aaron McCray's daughter I've turned my latent egotism into a blasé assumption that she – along with everyone else – will hero-worship me for who I am, not what I am. In layman's terms, I've taken courtesy for camaraderie. I've been arrogant – and naïve. And too open.

'Well,' I laugh. 'Physician heal thyself! It would be a perfectly reasonable one, of course,' I add hastily. 'If it was. I'm untested as yet, in the professional world.' I smile warmly at her. She hesitates, then smiles uncertainly back. I steel myself for the kiss-off, the ignominy of having made a faux pas with a subordinate.

'I guess, although if I was being tested when I first joined, I'm glad I didn't realise at the time.' She gestures to the shop door we've stopped next to. 'But never mind all that for the moment. We're here.' My nerves settle with her deliberate dismissal of my exposed paranoia, and because of the shop sign. *Swish Fish*. And underneath, *Sushi, sashimi or just plain ol' fish n' chips on the go...* 'I usually just get the fish and chips. Gets tiring being contemporary and fashionable all the time, doesn't it? I only do it for show when I have to. I figured you for a fish and chips girl too, secretly – but the choice is yours.'

I follow her, trying not to let my smile show as she orders cod and chips twice. I want to giggle again. She is not at all what I thought she would be when I first met her. There is a kind of fuck you to her, without being confrontational. The fish and chips are delivered – in paper – to the eat-in area, four small square tables towards the rear of the shop, covered in red and white check tablecloths and sporting salt, pepper, vinegar, a bundle of white paper napkins, plastic cutlery. And chopsticks.

We eat in companionable silence, ignoring the comings and goings of the fish bar, secure and sedate in the murky rear of the shop.

'So, why did you figure me for a fish and chip girl?' I ask eventually.

'You remind me of me at – what? Twenty-eight, twenty-nine?'

'Twenty-six.'

'Wow, so you really are the prodigal daughter Professor McCray always boasted you'd be.'

'You knew him?'

'Yes. I knew him. He was my tutor.'

'Your tutor?' My voice has hit the high notes again.

Jenny clearly finds that funny, but somehow I don't find her laughing at me offensive now. To be honest, the way I'm unravelling currently, I would find myself funny if I could be an observer.

'I studied under him years ago, when you would have been tiny – four or five maybe? At most. I was all set to become the next best thing since Vygotsky – sociocultural shit gone crazy. My thesis was to have been on experience versus education – which mattered most. A little like nature versus nurture with added transactionalism.'

'Was to have been?'

'I got pregnant with Jack part way through my PhD. He's my oldest. I had a choice then. Abortion or motherhood. I couldn't bring myself to abort him so in the end there was no choice.'

'But couldn't your husband have –'

'There was no husband. Nor grandparents to help out. Jack was the result of a one-night stand just before Christmas when I drank too much Jack Daniels – hence the name. My parents died when I was in my early twenties.'

'Oh, I'm sorry.'

'So was I. My mother had high grade non-Hodgkins Lymphoma. They staved it off for years, but eventually it caught up with her. It went into her bones too. She gave up and my father gave up with her. I wasn't sorry for my mother – she was in pain and without hope. That must have been terrible. I was for my father though. His pain was the thought of being alive without her. He simply couldn't face it, even though it meant leaving me behind.'

'Oh Jenny, that's terrible. How awful for you, then and later.'

'We survive, Gaby. We survive because there is nothing else to do. Simply because someone gives up on you, it doesn't mean you have to as well. Jack was the model baby, so when I met up with his father accidentally a year or so later, I thought what the hell. I never believed in being an only child. I was one and it stank so Jack got a brother – not named after alcohol this time. I was stone cold sober.'

'What's his name?'

'Adam, for symbolic reasons.'

'Figures,' I laugh. 'How did your father die, though, if he wasn't ill?'

'Double suicide pact.'

'Oh my God! You make me feel weak and pathetic, you know. I've been trying not to dwell on my father's death, but I do still have Mum – well, my stepmother really. Romaine. I should be glad about that, not bemoaning my miseries.'

'You should. There are so many reasons to be glad when you look for them – including the fact that Robert wants to test you out. It suggests he's grooming you for greater things, perhaps?'

'I hadn't thought about that.' The idea settles in, grows roots. It would make sense of my three tricky clients too. 'Why didn't you continue with your studies when the boys were older?'

'Because we still needed to eat, so I needed to work. And Robert wanted someone who understood how things worked so he could keep his distance from them if need be.' I look askance at her. 'Oh, nothing terrible. Just Robert being Robert – he's extremely cautious underneath that blustery exterior, you know.'

'It must be galling working as a PA at Ethos though?'

'I had a problem. They had a solution. And it means I can afford to live in a respectable part of Fulham. I can fill all sorts of gaps when necessary too – albeit unofficially. Suits me. Practice without responsibility. Lets me flex my muscles without breaking sweat too.'

'You see clients?'

'Oh no. That would be unethical. I'm not employed as a psychologist. But I do sometimes facilitate when a specific outcome is needed and the client isn't quite responding the right way. Say the right thing, prompt the right idea. I'm only the secretary so everyone chats to me. Transactionalism is an absolute bonus in that situation and I am rather good at it.'

'Oh my God, this just gets better and better. How much more do I not know?'

'I think that'll keep you going for a few days,' she laughs. 'But Gaby, we're two of a kind in many ways. I do know what happened with your father and it must have been tough for you – losing him the way you did. I was an adult, but I still question it every day, even though I know why my father and my mother did it. That question, well, it raises even more about yourself in time, and those answers are sometimes harder to answer than the one you think you're asking. I'm there for you if ever you need me. Remember that.'

My eyes prickle but I hold her gaze. Her sincerity deserves nothing less back.

'Thanks. I will.'

She nods and wraps the remains of her cod and chips up in the paper. It is grease-stained underneath. She produces a plastic bag and bundles the oil-stained parcel into it.

'Often do this too,' she grins. 'Take it home for the dog. She loves anything that's not good for her. A bit like her owner.' She winks and before I can do the same with my own fish and chip bonanza Jenny is swinging one arm into her coat as she grabs the handles of her bag and flips them over the other arm with the same alacrity she'd displayed with the filing cabinet. 'And now I'd better get back before all hell breaks loose because I've taken lunch outside of my lunch hour.'

She's gone before I've got out of my chair. For a moment I consider staying, finishing the chips languishing in the nest of greasy paper, ignoring the world for a while longer. The stream of customers at the front of the shop has tailed off and I can see past the last lingerers to the shop window beyond them. It is pristine, despite the fatty atmosphere and the fishy odour. Clear, when it should be clouded. My thoughts are quite the reverse. I drop back onto the chair, ignoring its hard seat and the spiny discomfort of its wheel back design. The notebook behind Dada's books, the inscription in Dada's book, Xander and his almost animal attraction for me, Jessica Morgan and her equally instinctive fascination – and yet I am morally repelled by both. Why should it be this hard? It should be simple; clear-cut. They are the patients, I am the therapist and we have no past history that could have produced the little notebook – God knows how it was ever produced at all. I shake my head. It spins sickeningly, and momentarily I regret that I haven't taken any of the pills in the bottle in the bathroom cabinet for days. Maybe that's why I'm so uncertain about myself, currently. They did at least always dispel doubts and those nagging little fears my teenage peers used to have but I've never seemed to worry about – until now. Then it as if Dada is there with me right now, guiding me.

Forget that. Let it all go. Be in the moment.

Be in the moment. Yeah, right. But the moment is full of obscurities.

Give your mind permission to find its own solutions by letting go of your preconceptions for a while.

How can you let go of your mind without becoming mindless?

The banter was almost as good as the theory I learnt from him at those times: Dada's method of finding clarity when there was none.

We're never mindless, but sometimes we're too mind-full. Get it? Too much on our minds. And the more we turn all those things over and over, the more tangled they become – like tights in a washing machine. Let them drift for a while and unravel. Focus away from them.

How do I do that?

Be in the now.

That's hippy-speak.

He'd laughed like his gut would split at that.

Come on – are you forgetting theory because of prejudice? What about Broadbent? Treisman? Bottleneck theory? You know we can overload and then we can stop paying attention to the things that are important in preference to the things that are distracting us. Use your understanding of how our minds work to streamline the working of your own. Take yourself out of your head and into what is going on around you – the sights, the smells, the sensations. While your sensory receptors are concentrating on that overload, your higher cognitive function can tease out a solution to the mind muddle you've been creating. Overflow the right things to release the pressure on the things that matter. Be like a fully functioning psychopath and focus on just one thing – what you really want to achieve.

He was right. It did work if you could focus well enough. It had even negated the need for the little bottle in the medicine cabinet when I'd done it consistently. I wrinkle my nose. I don't want to concentrate on sensory overload in here though. Vinegar and over-ripe fish are hardly the nicest of overloads. I grab up the remains of my fish feast and thrust it into the swing bin by the entrance to the eat-in area. It swallows the treat whole and I attempt – unsuccessfully – to mimic Jenny's adept juggling of coat, bag, chair and graceful exit. The exercise propels me swiftly through the cloud of frying fish and into the fresh air again. I breathe in deeply and the cold bites the back of my throat, but it's a good pain. I let the breath out and take another in. I set off on that one, lungs clear but head still clogged with Xander, Jessica Morgan and Paris, Georges Thierone and off-site appointments, Dada and his personally dedicated book and the little notebook that quietly threatens me with madness from my bag. The road is a relatively quiet one for the approach to Marylebone and the heart of the city. The fact that the job was to be in London had been both a lure and a loathing. London buzzes, even when it's barely awake. That is exciting. It is also large and lonely. That is terrifying. What is also terrifying for me is living alone.

At university, I spent most of my time in halls of residence or sharing impoverished, untidy flats with impoverished, untidy students. In between was always Romaine and the stream of artists, authors and progressive thinkers she'd encouraged to use our family home as their place of retreat since Dada had gone. At times, I'd even had to wait whilst my bedroom was vacated if I made an unplanned visit home during term-time. But I hadn't minded. Busy was good. Progressing to grad studies had been worse – or better, depending on how important having a constant barrage of people and chatter around you was. Regard it as my sensory overload, but not to be in the moment – to be out of it: out of the moment when Mum – Romaine – had first told me about Dada's suicide, even though apparently I was there... I pause and consider that for a moment – or rather still calling Romaine Mum in my mind. It seems somewhat incongruous now I am twenty-six and an independent grown woman. If she'd been my real mother, maybe? And now I realise that Jenny is the first person in years who I've told that Romaine isn't my real mother. The last one was my own therapist, just after Dada died. That is significant, but I can't decide whether in relation to Jenny or my state of mind. Disassociation perhaps? Or rapprochement? That brings another train of thought that I banish because it could take me to a far-away destination where my real mother may or may not reside, with my latent guilt for never wanting to get in touch with her. I had Romaine...

Stop it. That's dwelling on things too. The now. Fill yourself with the now, like Dada said. That's what he would do if he'd been you right now. The now takes me from the deceptively quiet side road onto the main road and past a health and fitness club that looks more like a mosque than a get-fit sweat-shop. Its walls are white and smooth but the dome of the central section is lichen-stained and grey. The contrast between it and its leafy backdrop, now turning spiny red and gold as winter nips at autumn's heels, is extreme. There are still some green leaves clinging to the branches but the rich deep red of death is rapidly engulfing them. Another deep breath brings undertones of moss and mulching undergrowth. The sunshine of yesterday has long since fled and today is a dank, wet dog of a day. I kick a stone from the pavement and it rolls forlornly into the gutter, alongside discarded sweet wrappers and a fag end. *'Keep it clean, clear the scene',* the keep London tidy campaign posters scream at me from the waste bin tucked into a discreet alcove in the wall fronting the mosque-fitness place. A gust of wind tugs at my mac and hurries me along. It's going to be damn cold in Hyde Park at this rate, especially at four o'clock. It's going to be starting to get dark by then too.

Whatever is my unavailable patient thinking of? I shiver as the wind hits my neck and freezes my spine.

Park it. Park the doubts and the anxieties and the fears. Concentrate on the now. The hooting traffic, the open top bus swinging its way around the London tourist spots, the cat squeezing through the railings and disappearing into the carefully positioned shrubbery of the building next to the mosque-fit. The chatter of a group of Chinese tourists, sporting selfie sticks and iPads. The blare of a car radio as it passes, belting out heavy metal. The smell of autumn, and too much rain. England on the verge of winter. I cross the road, dodging the traffic but only making it to the island in the middle. London is a far cry from Oxford where I acquired my precious qualifications; the subject of much taunting and put-down from Dada, originally a Cambridge man, when precociously at thirteen, I'd first mentioned that was where I wanted to study. It was probably the only choice I'd made without Dada's guiding hand pushing me on towards the making of it. He teased, but I'd loved the place from the moment we'd stepped out of the car on a routine visit to Dada's publishers there. It had the grace and favour that London should have had, but didn't, and Cambridge aspired to, but hadn't. The glorious colleges and their rolling grounds; Magdalen had its own deer park, no less! The blend of old and new that mimicked the opposition of town and gown, but with a right now, right here feel. And when I received my qualifications – all of them – in the Sheldonian, I was sure he would have conceded my point. If he'd been there to do so. Skirting Regent's Park reminds me of the bowling green lawns of Trinity College, seen through the ornamental gates on Parks Road. Ironic I'm now on Park Road, heading towards Madame Tussauds and the Sherlock Museum. The buildings here are a mix of graceful neo-Georgian and block-modern. Baker Street looms ahead of me, and incongruously, a shop announcing, 'It's Only Rock and Roll'. I linger in front of its window. It's filled with cardboard cut-outs of rock icons, and Marilyn Monroe, draped in a Union Jack flag. When did Marilyn become British? Row upon row of fan T-shirts and memorabilia – none of it of any value – provide a backdrop for the phony rock stars. Something clicks in my head. Phony. But not why.

We're two of a kind.

I do sometimes facilitate when a specific outcome is needed and the client isn't quite responding the right way. Say the right thing, prompt the right idea. I'm only the secretary so everyone chats to me. Transactionalism is an absolute bonus in that situation and I am rather good at it.

That is hardly ethical and Ethos is all about ethical, isn't it?

I'm there for you if ever you need me.

Am I being played by everyone, including kindly Jenny with her trip to the chippy and her knowledge of transactionalism? But then why would that be?

Chapter 13

I cross the road, leaving the rock and roll years behind me, and head towards the far end of Baker Street. I will be in the heart of Marylebone shortly and Hyde Park will be mere minutes away. I am far too early for the appointment. It is only two-thirty. I decide to stop for a coffee and waste time. I opt for a small coffee shop cum bistro, next to the door for a private weight loss clinic. The coffee shop is advertising traditional English afternoon tea and the stickiest Danish pastries on earth. All of the ironies hit me at pretty much the same time and I give in to helpless laughter. Passers-by must think I'm mad. The irony of that causes a fresh wave of semi-hysteria. *But I'm a psychologist. How could I be mad?* I pull myself together enough to be straight-faced by the time the waiter arrives. He is clearly disappointed I only want coffee and not to increase my waistline with a Danish pastry. I smile sweetly and then have to feign a mild coughing fit as a fresh wave of amusement threatens more giggles. He leaves me to it with disgust, but when he's gone, it's my turn to recoil at the smell of stale vinegar and grease on my fingers. I must use the ladies before I leave – not just to wash my hands but to change my tampon as well. The second day of my period is always the heaviest and I haven't changed my tampon since just before I left the office. All the usual female anxieties about blood stained clothing and embarrassing personal hygiene smells beset me then and I want to go to find the loo straight away, but the other two free tables have now filled up on the covered frontage to the street and I don't want to have to go inside. It reminds me too much of the fish and chip shop eat-in. If I leave the table to go in search of the loo I either have to leave some possessions behind to stake my claim, and risk losing them, or leave nothing behind and risk losing the table. The kind of conundrum Dada would have enjoyed. *So, which is more important? Your belongings or your comfort? Your table or your well-being?* I'd learned – eventually – to make the right response. *All of them.* But it had taken years and much soul-searching before I'd realised that I could answer however I pleased and still be right, if the answer pleased me. I didn't have to please him too. The power of Dada. You always wanted to be right for him, even if it was impossible.

My coffee arrives and I stir the froth into the black underbelly of murky poison. Romaine would describe it as such, at least. She's a passionate health-freak these days. It was she who introduced me to decaf coffee, which I have to admit I'm beginning to take to. Full roast coffee tastes very bitter and a little strange by comparison. I only drink it when I need to snap to it – usually first thing in the morning. Romaine. That still has a strange taste to it too. Romaine, not Mum. I know she dislikes the change and I still need to explain why to her – but for that I will need to explain it to myself too. I'm halfway through my coffee when the unfamiliar – but growing less so – ping on the Xander phone makes me jump. Another text.

'Page 93,' it says.

I watch the text fade from the screen and the screen saver replace it. Even that is a tease. It is a photo of me – dressed in exactly the same clothes as yesterday. In fact, it was almost certainly taken yesterday because in the background are the row upon row of books in the bookcase in my office. I pull *We Are What We Do* from my bag and turn to page 93. I let the book slip into my lap and nestle there. I still need to ask Romaine how her copy of Dada's book got in my office. I still need to know – too many things. I'm tempted to ring her right now, but our conversation wouldn't be private.

The phone pings again. 'We need to understand each other, don't you agree? To help each other, we need to understand. X.'

I swig my coffee. It is full roast, not decaf. My head is spinning and my stomach churning. Coffee buzz and greasy fish and chips. I will not reply. I will not! I sigh, click the phone off and it lays silent in my hands. No more texts. I tuck it away in my bag and it sleeps like a gorgon in there whilst my misgivings growl awake. Looking back, that's when it really all went wrong.

I have too much time to wait before I meet with Georges Thierone, and the coffee tastes foul. The couple on the next table order a bottle of red wine and it glints, ruby-gold as they pour it into their glasses and clink.

'Cheers!'

Cheer – I could do with some cheer. I could do with some Dutch courage too. The forthcoming off-site meeting with Georges Thierone is making me nervous. Judging by my patients so far, at least my fishbowl office has one thing going for it – it is policed by Jenny. Out here, in the middle of a city I don't know, I am truly on my own. I give in to self-pity and am about to ring Romaine regardless of who is listening, then I think of our conversation the night before. She will wonder. She may even come to London to investigate. Then she will know I have lied to her about my meds.

The couple at the next table are obviously on a business meeting, not an assignation. Business and red wine? Maybe that is the norm in London. The butterflies Xander awakened are stirring again. I need to settle them and there's only one way I can think of doing that aside from taking my meds. I park the self-pity and signal the waiter instead. I am Assistant Director, after all. I ask for a glass of Merlot but he misunderstands and brings a bottle, pouring me a full glass and hurrying away before I can correct him. It loiters in front of me – a taunting, burlesque beauty. I hesitate, salivate and the taunt is too much. I can just drink one glass. I can correct the bill later. I drink – cheers – and the world seems less lonely. I half-listen to the business couple as I savour my glass of wine. They are negotiating some kind of deal – bartering and joking along the way. It is a nice way of making a deal and it makes me feel happier regardless of what I have to do later. See, I tell myself. The doctor was right when she told Candy that doing something she liked would make her feel better all round. I am about to giggle, when I realise it would be out loud. My head is humming. How many glasses have I had? I check the bottle. It is half empty. I push it clumsily away from me and it almost tips over. I steady it, and myself – but not enough.

Dada's book is still in my lap. How did Xander know it was there? How did Xander know my father? It is suddenly too much. I want some answers. I've lived my life too long without them.

'How did you know my father?' I text. Then curse under my breath. I have done it. It is too late. I am hot and cold, pinpricks of fire stabbing under my arms and into my fingers. I have committed the cardinal sin and engaged in private communication with a patient. Oh yes, taking the phone had been stupid, but this is lethal.

The answer is immediate as if he'd simply been waiting all this time.

'Why should I have known your father to admire his writing? I admire his daughter too. I would like her to help, to understand, and I will do the same for her. Will she do that, Abigail? Will Abigail really help Xander?'

94

I hesitate. Yes, I need to understand. I need to understand a lot of things. And I need help too, but not from my own patient. I wish I could ask Director Anhelm for help, even though I'm angry with him for leaving me with this tricky bastard to contend with. *Tricky bastard you're fascinated by*, the Abigail voice whispers. *That's why you're considering it even though you shouldn't.*

'Shut up,' I say aloud. The business couple glance over at me and then huddle closer. I duck my head down. Better than the Director, I wish Dada was here. He would tell me what to do without it being help. He would coach me until I found my own answer. Coach me. And this *is* a game. But maybe it is a game I'm going to have to play. 'Is it Dada?' I ask the book, silently. I imagine him smiling back at me. With nothing else to help me I take that as a yes. He's my client. This is my fresh start. Away from Mark and his pipe dreams of happy families, Mum telling me to just accept everything, and Dada's little oak plaque with his name and dates of birth and death but no answers to anything. This is my fresh start, and I won't ruin it before I even get past first base. Think out of the box, like the Director said. I have opened the bidding. Now I have to play the game. I'm a professional. I need to find my role and play it – even if it is unconventional. Even Director Anhelm said the rules were different in Ethos. I know how minds work. I can play Xander's mind games and win.

'Abigail will help Xander,' I text back. 'But she has to know what it is that Xander wants her to understand.'

'Thank you, Abigail.' I wait for more, but it doesn't come. I fidget, then just when I think he has gone, 'Are you sitting comfortably?'

I read and then in a fit of pique, ignore it. He made me wait… but he won't go away.

'Ready for a trial run?'

He knows that will pique me, and I've gone too far already. I need to keep this on my terms.

'No trial runs of anything,' I reply. 'I will do my best to assist you in finding your solutions, but you do not need to find any for me. I am here to help you, remember?'

'So formal, so cold? Abigail, I thought we were in this together? My solutions and your solutions, together? X.'

'I'm the therapist and you are the client. We are seeking your solutions not mine.'

'Maybe they are the same? X.' And then, 'Abigail? Why don't you sign off like I do? You are A and I am X.'

My fingers seem to have a will of their own, but I manage to stop them before they move faster than my thoughts. I breathe in deeply and hope the cold air will sober me. I delete the answer I am about to give and replace it with, 'I am Dr McCray, that's why.'

'You are Abigail and I am Xander. We agreed... How can we move forward if you keep going back on things? Reneging on a deal? Not good form. Your father would have agreed with me. *We are what we do*. X.'

I put the phone in my lap and try to stop my head spinning.

'Here's your chance,' the next one says. 'Fat man to your left. He's just tossed his credit card on the table as if it's a toy. Will he miss it? He's got a wallet full of others.'

I can feel my head shaking in disbelief. How? But the question of how he knows is lost in the bigger issue of what his message implies he wants me to do.

'That's stealing!' I text back.

'Of course it is,' he replies. 'That's the whole point!'

Chapter 14

I put the phone back in my bag without replying, but I eye the credit card lying boldly in the middle of the table the fat man is sitting at. He is puffy-faced and sweating even though it is cold. In fact, I wonder why any of us are sitting outside, regardless of how dark and cavernous the inside of the café looks from here. We're all mad, actually. It's early September, a miserable overcast day with more rain to follow and we're all sitting outside sipping coffee like its mid-summer. The bottle of white wine, chilled, the couple on the next table have doesn't even have any condensation on the outside. That shows how cold it is. And the credit card is still flaunting itself on the table. Displaying itself with lewd intend, waiting for me to despoil it. Involuntarily I rub my forefinger and thumb together as if they're preparing to pin it in a pincer grip. A hot flush spreads through me like my blood has started to seep out of all my pores. I can't take my eyes off if it. The phone pings again. I jump again, then try to make it look like I'm just repositioning my chair, which is difficult because it's canvas and sags in the middle. I and the chair rock awkwardly as I bend to retrieve the phone from my bag.

'You're scared.'

'No, I'm not, but I'm not going to voluntarily go about stealing.'

'You said you would.'

There's a pause and then another text follows the first.

'Abigail.'

I fidget with the phone. I don't want to take the card, and yet I do too. Abigail. But I am not Abigail, I am Gaby, and Gaby doesn't steal.

'But you undertook to be Abigail for Xander. You promised. You don't break promises. That's almost as bad as stealing. In fact, it might even be worse.'

That provocative little voice is back, teasing me. It makes me jittery. My heart beats a little faster and my stomach knots. The possibility of actually doing what Xander wants me to do makes the grey day bright. It makes my blood pump faster, my ears sing with the rush of it over my head, energises my sense of adventure. And I have no doubt I could. I can already see how. But I'm Gaby and I don't steal. Or I'm Abigail, and stealing to understand my patient – *patients, plural.* Isn't that acceptable? Perhaps. And I know I am bargaining with myself – trading one set of ethics for another. I watch myself doing it, amused and rueful in equal measures. Bargaining, like we all do all the time when deciding what is socially acceptable or not, what defensible or not, what desirable or not. We are human robots with computer brains, assessing and processing all the time: may the best logic win.

It isn't logic that wins this time. It is Abigail, but logic dictates that I plan it carefully in my head before I do it. I leave the money for my coffee and wine, plus a tip, in the middle of my own table, carefully reposition the chair so I can easily rise, drape my bag over my arm and stand. My legs feel weak and I want to pee but that is only a nervous reaction. Physical response to the fight or flight stimulus. I am afraid and the adrenalin is flowing. That's why my head is pounding in time with my heart now. Rationalising it doesn't alleviate the symptoms, but it does strengthen my resolve. I walk towards the fat man, unintentionally jostling the table next to him with my bag. Damn! My exit was to have been clean and unobtrusive, palming the card as I went. He doesn't even look up. His head is stuffed into his laptop, scrolling though list upon list of figures. The Stock Exchange. Dada use to dabble in it, so I recognise what it looks like on-screen. So, he's a stockbroker. A fat man indeed. His coat is thick charcoal grey wool. His briefcase, tan hide. His fountain pen, lying across the notes he's been making, is a Marte Omas. My God, how did I remember that from all those years ago?

If I ever win big on the Stock Exchange, Gab, I'll get myself one of these. The fat cat's pen.

He'd passed me the catalogue and the whole page had been taken up by the image of the pen. Conceived by three world-class designers, it is made of gold fashioned as a map of Mars, including mountains, deserts and lakes. It is decorated with rubies and the cap is encrusted with diamonds. It oozes wealth and writes in blood – the kind Mephistopheles might have extracted from the owner in order to scribe. Only thirty are made a year and it has a price tag to match, for the seriously wealthy alone. This man is. This fat man with a credit card he doesn't care about and a fabulously expensive fountain pen he scribbles rough notes with. I'd rather take the pen than the card, but the pen would be noticed, the card wouldn't. I nudge the fat man's table as I pass and it wobbles. This time he does look up but I've already looked away. I don't want to see his face and I don't want him to see mine either. All he sees is a tall woman in a blue mac with a grey and white scarf covering her head against the damp atmosphere, leaving the outdoor space of the café. He doesn't see what is in the hand tightly curled in on itself. He probably won't even notice the card is gone until the waiter makes his rounds again, and that won't be for a while because we have all only just been served. I have done it. I have stolen something that is unimportant to someone. I am mad! I want to laugh and cry all at the same time. My heads spins more than from the effect of the wine. Does it count as not mattering because he doesn't need it? Does it count that I won't attempt to use it, even though it is probably contactless and I could go on a spending spree all the way to Hyde Park if I wanted to? Does it count that I'm nearly peeing myself, or dear God, is that my tampon leaking and I am going to leave a trail of blood behind me, heading away from the café and to wherever I end up, cold, terrified of being caught and loathing myself? I walk, tight-limbed, as fast as I can down the road, teeth gritted and praying, praying I am not leaking. And what do I do with it now?

Get rid of it! Throw it in a waste bin.

No. It will have my prints on it.

Burn it then.

Do credit cards burn? But I haven't any matches or a lighter anyway.

Throw it in the Thames, then – or better still – the lake at Hyde Park.

I shove it in my mac pocket and stride to the end of Baker Street, senses now dumb to everything going on around me except whether there is a shout, a scurrying of feet, a fat man puffing after me. The phone in my bag pings but I ignore it. I need to put as much distance between me and the café as possible. Only when I reach Portman Square do I slow. The Hyatt Regency Hotel is on the other side of the gardens. I know that because Dada used to stay there when he was on a lecture tour in London. He used to bring me home the peppermint bonbons that were always left in the rooms as courtesy treats to the guests and they were wrapped in silver with the hotel name curving around them on a blue paper band. I could use the facilities there. There must be some in the reception area. Apart from the leaking tampon, I must look terrible – windswept, flushed, agitated. I need to tidy up and calm down before my meeting with Georges Thierone.

I enter the gardens that create the square and push the ornamental wrought iron gate shut behind me. It is a good spot to check whether I have been followed from too. I lurk just inside the gate and peer through the leafy screen of close-coiffed privet and berberis – not too close though in case I snag my tights or scratch my face. I pretend to be checking my phone to allay suspicion by any other passers-by and then I remember that I really do need to check my phone – not this one but the one Xander gave me. I drop my one phone back into my bag and fish around for Xander's. There is not one but several texts received on it. They read,

'Well done, now just keep walking.'

'There's a good place to check on whether you've been followed by Portman Square. The gardens front Baker Street on one side so you can look back along the length of it from there.'

'The Hyatt Regency has toilets to the rear and off to the right of reception. But you look great anyway.'

'In case it helps, you haven't (been followed), by the way. X'

I am speechless, and uneasy now. He has been watching me. That is the only explanation. He has been watching me, and yes, I have been followed, otherwise how could he know where I'm heading? Or that I haven't been followed by anyone else? I feel sick and double over as the nausea overwhelms me. Retching brings up the coffee I'd drunk at the café in an acidic brown spume, searing the back of my throat and leaving the metallic taste of blood in my mouth. I'm still clutching the phone when I'm finally able to straighten up without another wave of biliousness making my head swim and my stomach cramp. My thumb has involuntarily pressed the keyboard and the text waiting to be sent reads 'Gnbgmfhfhf.' Not that different to what I must have sounded like as I vomited out my fear and remorse. I delete it and replace it with, 'where are you?'

I wait for the reply. There's nothing, even after waiting for several minutes. I add, 'where are you watching me from?'

'Why would I be watching you? You're a big girl, Abigail. I am not your keeper. You do what you need to and go where you want to.'

The tone worries me. It has changed yet again and I know I am out of my depth now – should never have thought I could manipulate such a man, regardless of the list of qualifications I have in psychology and Dada's gene legacy. I need to take charge.

'This has got to stop. I won't play silly games with you any more. You are my patient and I am your therapist. I've gone along with this so far because I thought you really needed help, but I don't think that's what this is all about now. This seems to be more about some kind of perverted entertainment on your part. Tomorrow I will hand this phone back to you, and this nonsense will stop. Then I will make a full report to the Director when he returns.'

'Gaby bating? That would be boring – and pointless. This is about Abigail and Abigail helping Gaby understand Xander's perspective. Xander's problem needs a solution. Doesn't feel so good, does it? Actually stealing? But now you know. That was step one. The others can follow now. It will get easier from here.'

'No! No more. Tomorrow, 10am, my office and this ends there.'

His response is to invite me to join WhatsApp. What follows is a video. Me, stealing the credit card.

'OK. Till tomorrow then. X'

'You bastard!'

I take a step back further into the gardens, staring at the phone screen, anxious that a passer-by might have heard me. I should have seen this coming. How stupid was I?

There is a park bench just off the path leading staring across the gardens to the far side that borders Portman Square and the Hyatt Regency. I manage to get to it without my legs caving in and slump down. The phone nestles in my lap and the video replays. He seems to have made it into a loop somehow so I am endlessly stealing the credit card. The fat man looks up then back down, dismissing the intrusion. The Marte Omas gently gleams from the table. The woman slides the credit card from the table top like a master and walks briskly away, looking back over her shoulder just once before disappearing from view. Xander has freeze-framed that moment and woman is clearly me, tight-lipped and hawk-eyed, before the loop repeats. I want to weep but that will make my mascara run and then I will look even more of a mess for my meeting with Georges Thierone. I settle for allowing the sense of failure and self-loathing to fill me to overflowing, as I click the phone off and cover my face with my hands.

I sit like that for a while, unable to do anything until it dawns on me. This isn't just manipulation or some kind of sick game. This is also quite possibly blackmail. Then I am paralysed by the possibility of ruin. The faces of my judge and jury besiege me. All the people I've ever imagined saying I'd never be as good as my father, no matter how well I did. All the rivals for the position of darling of the academics, all the lovers who'd cursed me for being too devoted to study to give them a chance, all the people I'd surpassed and left behind, all the people who hadn't got what I had. I had just proved them all right. I didn't deserve this job – had messed up on only the second day. I didn't deserve my qualifications – had just reneged on my promise to behave with ethical propriety. And I didn't deserve Dada's pride in me or Romaine's support of me. I let my hands drop into my lap. Xander's phone shows it is now three twenty-five. I can't stay here much longer. I will be late for Georges Thierone if I do.

But how can I face him as I am? I can't. All I want to do is stay here and fuse to the park bench. Wither away like the autumn leaves. The sinking feeling in my soul seems to be perfect to do just that. It makes me too heavy to stand, move – even breathe. I am so still a sparrow risks fluttering down near my feet. It pecks optimistically in the grit, orbital eye keeping a close check on what I am doing. I am doing nothing. Statuesque. Turned to stone by the realisation of how badly I've messed up.

So? The little prompt that I am beginning to think of as Abigail prods me. *So, you've messed up. Haven't you messed up before? We all mess up, but you don't just lay down and die. Are you going to let that bastard walk all over you or are you going to pay him back in his own coin? Find out why he's doing this?*

Yes, why is he doing this? What has he got against me? And why did the Director lumber me with him like this too? I need to force myself across the road and into the Hyatt. Rearrange my wrecked face, hair and scruples and be the professional Georges Thierone is expecting to meet. What will happen with Xander tomorrow, I don't know, but tomorrow is another day. And now I have Abigail to spur me on. Then I remember I've agreed to go to Paris with Jessica tomorrow. Whatever I do, Xander holds all the cards for the next forty-eight hours or more.

'Fuck you, Xander!' I say aloud, this time not caring who hears me.

Chapter 15

Hyde Park may be a lovely place in spring and summer but in the autumn on a cold, damp day with the light failing, it's a place of shadows. Depression's hunting ground. By the time I reach the Memorial to Animals in War it is five minutes to four and the cold is getting to my bones. I feel the freeze, like hoarfrost, pervading my whole body and settling inside like rods of ice instead of a skeleton. I shiver and it makes me want to shake all over as if I am a dog. In sympathy, I stand in front of the dog statue and feel its pain.

There is no sign of Georges Thierone so I wander the memorial in an attempt to keep warm. It is spread over two levels, with a large wall, carved with images of the various animals who went to war during the twentieth century. Their silhouettes are ghostly renderings of the animals lost to battle. It makes me want to shiver again. Did the spirits of those animals wander here, as some thought the spirits of the men lost did across the plains of Ypres and the like? Romaine is a believer in life after death, and life after death even within life. We have discussed it many times over the years but she has never quite managed to convince me. If it were so, then Dada would still be with us somehow, somewhere. But he isn't. That brings an unexpected bolt of raw grief so intense it almost knocks my legs from under me. I gasp and blink furiously to keep the tears from welling up and spilling over. I have only just fixed my face in order to meet my enigmatic patient and I can't have it ruined by a moment of uncontrolled emotion. To distract myself I apply myself to examining again how Dada and Romaine could have fallen for each other – he, the pragmatist, the success-driven high achiever, and she, the idealistic young dreamer. It had been presented to me as a child as mere fact. I, became we, and eventually, once she'd been accepted as we, Romaine became Mum. It probably helped that my real mother had left when I was so tiny – less than a year old – I couldn't even hope to remember her. She is more a sensation, and even that probably imagined.

Someone who was there – comforting and warm – and then not. A sweetly perfumed shadow that was as much a will o' the wisp as the cavorting fairies in *A Midsummer Night's Dream*. Dada became both father and mother to me – with an assortment of nannies to deal with the practical requirements – until Romaine stepped into the breach. And Romaine is sweet and comforting too. And single-minded. I have needed single-minded over the years since Dada died.

It is now gone four and there is no sign of Georges Thierone. No sign of anyone here, in fact. On an impulse, I pull my own phone out of my bag and ring Romaine. Regardless of what she may think, I need to hear her voice to convince me I'm not completely mad. I ring the landline, not her mobile, because of an unexplained need to also know she is home, not roaming God knows where. She answers almost immediately, as if she's been hanging over the phone, waiting, ever since I last called her.

'Gab!' She exclaims at my greeting. 'How's it going? I expected you to ring later.' She sounds echoey, like she's in a cave, or underwater, the background rush of something taking her voice and distorting it. 'Sorry about that strange noise in the background. The boiler's on the blink and the plumber's here trying to get it to fire up. You'd think the system was in pain, the racket its making!'

'Oh dear!' The boiler has been a source of consternation for several months now. 'Why don't you just get it replaced?'

'Well, you know what they say? If it ain't broke don't fix it.'

'But it is broke.'

She laughs and her good humour reaches out to me down the phone. 'Yeah, but so am I, so it's just gonna have to soldier on for the time being.'

'If you've got money worries, I can help, now I've –'

'No, no, no! You need all your hard-earned cash for that exciting life you're going to start living now. It'll be fine. I'll be fine. Now tell me, what gives? Are you enjoying it more now? And what about the flat? Are you OK on your own?'

'Whoa! Slow down! It's going OK. The flat is lovely, the work interesting and the people... will be charming eventually, I'm sure.'

'And I'm a Chinaman!' I swing round at the interruption. The man who has interjected his own comment into my conversation with Romaine is tall and fair with blue-grey eyes. He looks a little like me, but he is clearly older than me – mid-thirties, perhaps? He is undeniably handsome. Almost too handsome. He smiles and holds out his hand.

'Er… Mum, I've got to go.' I inwardly curse the slip back to childhood. So much for moving on. I am continually regressing, at the moment, whatever my confusion over how to address Romaine. 'My client is here. I'll call you again later.'

'OK,' her voice disappears pathetically into the ether and I am facing the man I believe must be Georges Thierone. But he is not my stalker. I know that for certain. The physique is all wrong.

'Dr Livingstone, I presume?' he asks, his smile making the corners of his eye crinkle.

'Dr McCray, actually,' but I appreciate the joke and he knows it. We shake hands and his grip is warm and decisive – a therapist's grip. His expression drops into one more serious, but his eyes make him seem like he's still smiling. They are teasing eyes.

'Sorry about the unconventional meeting place but I am stuck in meetings almost all day, every day, for the next week, and I really wanted to talk to you as soon as I could, in case.'

'You're having problems?'

'I'll let you be the judge of that, perhaps. Shall we go for a stroll? It's getting a bit cold now so we'd be better off moving. Less opportunity to be overheard too.'

Instinctively I look over my shoulder. Does he know about Xander? Then I relax. What rubbish! Of course not. Patient confidentiality would see to that. I need to be calm, calm. Breathe…

'So why are you a Chinaman?' I begin, conversationally, to cover my nerves.

'Because whoever you were talking to just then – and sorry I interrupted – you were being very politely untruthful, probably to stop them from worrying.'

'Oh,' I don't know what else to say. Once again, one of my patients is turning the tables on me. Was it something to do with the kind of clients Ethos took on?

'I'm sorry, I really don't mean to be impertinent or pry, but you were, weren't you?'

'Well, I am here to help you, not the other way round.'

'On the contrary, we're all here to help each other, I would venture to suggest. The Christian way,' he adds.

'You are a Christian? That must make your issue – as I understand it – very difficult to deal with?'

'I see you've read up on me. Yes, indeed. It does. It's one thing being tricky professionally – sometimes it's the only way to get the job done – but I don't want that to spill over into my real life. I want to be a good person, not a liar or a cheat.'

'Do you feel that is happening? Is that why you needed to talk as soon as possible?'

'To be fair, it's probably always happening all the time with all of us. You've just been doing it with your mother. That was your mother, wasn't it?'

'My stepmother, and yes, in a way I have, but it was done – as you say – to stop her from worrying. The outcome possibly forgives me the method, even though it was, technically, lying.'

'Hmm, the end justifies the means?'

'Well, not really, but life requires a certain level of pragmatism. What is worrying you particularly, at the moment?'

'I suppose that I'm leading a double life. I am cheating on my wife.'

'You're having an affair?'

'No, maybe I'd better explain. I work in government – or rather in political lobbying. That means at times I'm working *for* the government, rallying support for initiatives it wants to be taken on and maybe even be pushed through parliament. At other times, I may actually be working against the government, impeding rash decisions and sowing seeds of disagreement when a better strategy needs to be adopted. For the moment, the government is my wife, and currently I'm cheating on her.'

'Oh, I see. That's presumably why you don't want to be overheard, then?' My nerves start to settle. I am back in the saddle, and this is a professional discussion, not another crazily off-piste conversation with patients I cannot control.

'Exactly.'

'That is difficult, morally, but I'm not sure I can help you with it. It's not as if it's a psychological condition.'

'But if it's spilling over into my private life?'

'It sounds like that might be a consequence of the job, and similarly it's not a psychological condition.'

'When I say spilling over into my private life, I mean I find I can't stop myself from lying – even when I don't need to. I'll lie about anything sometimes – about my friends, my job, my relationships: even what I had for breakfast. It's out of control. Now tell me *that's* not a psychological condition.' Having completed a circuit of the memorial, we stop in front of the wall depicting the ghostly war heroes. It is also carved with information about all the theatres of war in which animals lost their lives, and the names of all the animals who died. On the longer section of the wall, the names of all the major donors who enabled the memorial to be built are etched in another list. 'Me,' Georges adds, pointing to his name within the list.

'You donated towards this?'

'No. I lied. My name did. But I'm not Georges Thierone.'

'You're not Georges... I don't understand.'

'I'm his stand-in. My work, you see. It requires me to be a non-person so the rumours and manipulation cannot ever be attributed to me.'

'So, are you, or are you not Georges Thierone?'

'For your purposes, yes. For mine, no.' he grins suddenly. The light is failing now and we are standing in front of the wall in half-light. 'But then again, I might be lying.'

'I'm not sure I can help you,' I hear myself saying. This is too much like a game again. I am already in too deep with one trickster, I'm not being caught out by a second. Time to go – and all that wine is working its way through me again now, not to mention the credit card burning a hole in my pocket.

'Maybe not. Maybe I'm beyond help,' he agrees ruefully. He turns so the streetlight from Park Lane is falling on half of his face whilst the other half is in shadow. An open top bus turns the corner and parks up just along from the left-hand edge of the memorial wall. Its thin stream of passengers disembark from the bus, some via the front of the memorial. He takes me by the elbow and guides me to the other side so we are looking at the departing bronze horse and dog who face north into the gardens, representing hope. 'But you're not.'

'Me?' I wheel around to face him.

'Yes, you. What do you know about Ethos?'

'Well, I work for it.' I shrug, and gesture – it occurs to me afterwards, too vaguely. 'It's a socio-psychological counselling service based on strict moral and ethical solution-finding.' I'm trying not to show my confusion – or disbelief.

'OK, and what about Chiaroscuro?'

The name sends a shock through me, ending at my bladder. I squeeze my pelvic floor muscles together frantically. He has beaten me to it.

'Nothing, other than it's some kind of think-tank problem-solver. I only heard the name for the first time yesterday. And you – you work for it ...'

'Hmm. Alright, I'm going to trust you because my gut tells me you're OK. You wouldn't lie to your stepmother to stop her worrying about you if you weren't intent on doing the best for everyone. Do not repeat anything I tell you though. Do you understand? If not yours, my life could certainly depend on it.'

I pull away from his grasp but he doesn't let go.

'I'm not sure I want to know, if that's the case,' I protest. My heart is jumping from one rib to another in my chest and the knot in my stomach has looped itself round some inner hook and is tightening.

'It's not a case of wanting but needing. Chiaroscuro is a secretly funded covert organisation. I come into contact with it from time to time when I can't avoid it. Three months ago, I found out that Ethos not only counsels its staff, it may also contract with it too. That's why I won't come near Ethos' offices now. It's not MI5 or that kind of stuff. Its work is vaguer than that, but if there's a problem that needs fixing at the top and people like me can't fix it, Chiaroscuro takes over. On the face of it, it *is* a kind of think tank, solving problems with heavy-duty analysis of political, social and behavioural aspects. Beyond that – well, let's just say I wouldn't want to get on the wrong side of it. Power at its most raw.'

'Why are you telling me all this? It's nothing to do with me.'

'On the contrary, Dr McCray, it's very much to do with you if you're working for Ethos. You're right in the line of its war machine. Now tell me what you didn't tell your stepmother. Is everything as good as you claimed it to be?'

I hesitate. This man is a self-confessed serial liar, so how do I know he's not simply lying to me for his own perverse pleasure? I don't. He's also supposedly my patient. On the other hand, he seems to be far more knowledgeable about both me, my situation and what is going on at Ethos than he should be, and I need to know what he knows.

'It's somewhat more complicated than I anticipated it being,' I admit grudgingly.

He shouts with laughter. 'A master of understatement, unlike your father.'

'You knew my father?'

'I know his work and he does rather ram the point home. Psychology and Sociology joint first from Cambridge – your father's old hunting ground, I believe? After my time, though. Must have been tough growing up in his shadow.'

'No one was ever in Dada's shadow. He shone on everyone.'

'Is that why you followed in his footsteps as he groomed you to do, even though he wasn't there to make sure you did? That's true hero-worship.'

'It wasn't hero-worship.' I can feel my cheeks flushing despite the cold. 'He was a great man – a genius.' We face each other, each trying to outstare the other. 'And that was quite offensive, given you didn't know him and you don't know me.'

'I'm sorry. It wasn't meant to be, but there are many ways of lying, and one of them is to yourself. We are all potentially blessed with clear sight, but not if we create a belief and stick to it, come what may. I'd like to help you, but I can't if you don't park your perceptions and assess the facts.'

'And what do you think the facts are?' My voice is crisp with ice.

'Maybe more – and less – than you think. Don't be too hidebound by how things appear. Every image we portray of ourselves is a form of lie, fashioned to meet the needs of the person we are presenting it to. In there,' he waves his hand in the vicinity of the buildings behind us, 'in the US Embassy, I am a charming nonentity in a smart suit, who everyone talks in front of because they think I have the ear of no one. In reality, I have the ear of many and the voice of the highest bidder. In Downing Street, I have the status of useful mole, with the voice of the government and the integrity of a Services operative. In actuality, I am my own man, so I lie to Peter to persuade Paul, and vice versa as the situation demands. I don't have allegiances to either side, but nor do I have a quarrel with either too. I base my decisions solely on facts and a judgement of what will serve me best.'

'You are a sociopath.' I can't help the spontaneous diagnosis or the announcing of it. His expression darkens infinitesimally before assuming a clown's grin, so wide it almost splits his face.

'Ha! I like that. A sociopath and a serial liar. Better than being a psychopath, of course... Go with what will serve you best, even if that means going against what the renowned Professor McCray would have expected you to do. Be yourself, Gabriella McCray. Be a sociopath too, if that's necessary. Or even a psychopath. Copy me.'

'And that's how you're going to help me? What do you want in return?'

'Ah, *now* you're thinking clearly! I simply want you to keep me informed. Information is power, and if you can't cure my serial lying, then I'd best be sure I lie at the right time and in the right way to avoid finding myself on the wrong end of a gun.'

'You're not suggesting it's that dangerous, surely?'

'If you're in the thick of it, possibly. I don't particularly want to find out – and nor do I want to disappear if I get it wrong with the wrong person.'

'Is that why you don't want to come into the office?'

'Now you really are catching on!'

'I'm not sure I am.'

'Who mentioned Chiaroscuro to you?'

'One of my pa-clients. And our receptionist. She said you work for it.'

'Indeed? Clever. Testing you. And what do you make of them? Your other clients, I mean.'

'I can't tell you that. Anyway, it's confidential.'

'Have they something on you?'

'Of course not. Whatever gives you that idea?'

'That tells me all I need to know. Look, I've got to get back now, but let's say my next appointment will be same time, same place, next week. If you need to get in touch with me before then you can leave a message for me at the British Embassy. I'm there off and on from tomorrow. In the meantime, think about out why you're where you are right now. The facts only.'

He lets go of my elbow and walks swiftly round the end of the memorial wall and has disappeared into the traffic by the time I've gathered my wits enough to follow him. It's four-thirty now but it might as well be evening, night has fallen so quickly as we were talking. The cars and buses all have their headlights on and the streetlamps have lit up the sky like beacons. It is a bustling London scene just as you would expect it to be: smelly, noisy and vibrant, but for me it is cloaking something far more sinister – the knowledge that in the corridors of power, monsters tread softly and their footsteps might even echo in the corridors of my life. One monster, certainly. Xander. He works for Chiaroscuro. What did he want with me – or what did the Director want him to want with me? I had naively accepted my prestigious position with Ethos, assuming it to be based purely on my academic worth and – perhaps more than a little – Dada's reputation. OK, so that had been trading off my father, but why not? Hollywood starlets traded off their parental connections all the time and for far less good that they would do in the world. Am I so bad? I stand, watching the traffic stream past me, flashes of red and blue and silver. Across the road, the Georgian façade of

Mr Fogg's pub stares back at me, windows unblinking.

Think about out why you're where you are right now.

I'm here for many reasons. To meet a patient who turns out to be self-diagnosed as untreatable, and amused by it, but who has told me the organisation I've joined has depths I don't want to plumb. I'm here because the kudos this position earns me will stand me in good stead for a professorship in due course – like Dada – if I can survive it. I'm here because I trained to understand what was incomprehensible about Dada's suicide, yet still can't.

I'm here because of Dada.

That's the crux of it. I'm here because of Dada. His reputation got me the job. I see now that the Director's email virtually said so, and Jenny has said so too, in not so many words. Not for my achievements or my personality, but because I'm a chip off the old block. That's fact one. Fact two is I'm here, in this mess, because I've let myself be dragged into a game by one of my patients who has something to do with another organisation that I don't want to be involved with. Fact three is that apparently the respectable organisation I'm employed by, does. What does that make Ethos? Fact four, the notebook hidden in the bookcase says... Damn, damn, damn! No matter how hard I try to work that one out, I can't – unless I've been taking the pills from the empty pillbox in the bathroom cabinet and driving myself mad again.

Fact five, I'm totally out of my depth.

I feel intensely uneasy standing there in the start of the rush hour buzz, the passing buses full of unsympathetic onlookers and the cars full of impatient drivers. I want to be home, shut away from their intrusive stares. I feel physically wrong too. Damn again – I never did change my tampon. I hope the shivers and exhaustion aren't the first signs of toxic shock. I turn on my heel and trudge back towards Baker Street tube. The evening's prey is making its way down into the bowels of the tube snake in regular waves of peristalsis. I join the most recent wave, to eventually be regurgitated at Putney Bridge. Since the rush hour is in full swing, I have to stand, crammed up against a businessman in full navy pinstripe and overpowering aftershave and a European student, juggling folders and text books in a rucksack two sizes too small for even half of the books he is carrying. I hold my breath and count to twenty, taking a breath on each twenty mark to minimise aftershave overload. As we change at Paddington, the student drops one of his files on my foot but doesn't apologise. He scowls at me as if it's my fault, then scrutinises me as if there is something suspicious about me as he straightens. I feel like scowling back but that would be childish. Instead I exit the train quicker than him and head for the District line.

My bag pings at me as I'm balanced on the escalator going up but I ignore it. I don't want to know what Xander has to say – and how can he get through to me here anyway? There's usually no signal underground. It pings again and I feel self-conscious – like everyone is looking at me, unique because I can receive text messages whilst in the depths of the earth. We pass a series of posters advertising a ghost story coming to the West End shortly. 'When he calls'. The image on the poster is of a tall, fair-haired woman, wild-eyed and holding a mobile phone out in front of her as if it's an alien object. She could be me. I can see the likeness so my fellow travellers must be able to as well. I look surreptitiously over my shoulder. Blue pinstripe is directly behind me, his aftershave cloud billowing around him as the dirty air of the underground blows our hair and scarves away from our faces in long streams of brown and tawny and gold. Autumn leaves, falling into the earth. I still feel wrong, my body misshapen and bloated, my head muzzy and my limbs weak, crumpling.

'Steady!' Pinstripe nudges me upright. 'Are you alright?' I nod. 'Suffocating down here at times,' he suggests. I agree and we trundle on up towards the light.

I step shakily from the escalator at the top and head for the green District line sign. Eight stops and then a short walk to the apartment block overlooking the river. I can do it. I will do it. I feel so ill now. I imagine the bacteria invading my body from the saturated tampon, well past its 'best before' by now. I don't want to think about the mess my clothes may be in from the leakage. I'd like a seat on the train if I can get one but maybe it would be better not to get one after all, considering. The phone pings again. It turns my shivers to excessive heat. I'm hot and cold in turns the rest of the way home, the phone intermittently pinging to signify when the change should occur. By the time I get home there are twenty-four texts received, all from Xander, all saying the same thing.

'Tomorrow.'

Chapter 16

The walk home is the longest I've ever experienced, even though it is barely fifteen minutes from Putney station to my apartment. I am simultaneously shivering and burning up like a furnace. It's almost six now and completely dark. I plod past the closed shops with their sad window displays. So much to buy and no one to buy it. Under other circumstances I might have been tempted to linger in front of the window of the indie book store I spotted last night, seeing if I can find something new and refreshing – different from the titles that pack the high street book stores. Tonight, I trudge past it, head down against the wind, which is beginning to tug at my collar and nip my neck. The dreary, dank day is turning into a chillier night, with fog rising from the river. As I cross Putney Bridge the streetlights halo in the mist, turning themselves into great alien globes, filtering off into the night. They remind me of the Whistler's *Nocturne* painting of Battersea Bridge, the structure of the bridge and buildings shrouded in shifting, crepuscular light that might seep away into nothingness at any time. I almost wonder if my apartment block will still be there when I turn down the road alongside the river itself, or whether the evening mist – like acid – has eaten it away. Even the smell has changed from when I made the journey in the other direction this morning. Then it was moist but insipid. Now it is pungent with wet loam and mouldering leaves.

Halfway across the bridge I have to stop. My legs have lost the ability to carry me and my head is swimming. I think I'm going to be sick. I lean against the wall, expecting it to be smooth and cold, but it's encrusted with lichen, crumbling against my fingers. To distract myself from the nausea I explore its brittle, serrated edges, picking a piece off and examining it in my cupped hand. It is like me, clinging to a stronger structure but disintegrating on touch. I was not ready for this after all, Romaine. I was not ready at all and I am not fine. An overpowering need to cry drags me away from the wall and forces me onwards towards the three-headed Cerberus monster ahead of me that is one of the decorative three-lamp Victorian street lamp placed at equi-distances along the length of the bridge, determined not to make a fool of myself in public. My bridge-crossing companions overtake and disappear into the gloom as I struggle on, one foot in front of the other until I reach the shortcut down to Willow Bank. I follow the road round to Swanbank Court and I am safe.

I slam the door of my apartment behind me and rest against it for a moment whilst I wait for my head to stop whirling. It doesn't. The nausea is back, full strength this time, and I have to rush to the bathroom and throw up down the loo. Eyes smarting and nose running, everything else is forgotten for the moment. My stomach expels the greasy fish and chips, the coffee and a quantity of bile – and then miraculously I feel better. Cautiously I pull myself upright, flush the loo, put the lid down and sit on it, taking small, tentative breaths whilst I test whether I am going to pass out or stay in the land of the living. I am OK. No – really, I *am* OK. The biliousness has gone with the fish and chips. And goddammit! Now I remember! I need to clean myself up – except when I do so, I didn't need to at all. The tampon is almost unmarked – just a small, brown smear down one side – and my period appears to have dried up completely. I sigh. It has to be stress. There's certainly been enough of it over the last two days. I freshen up anyway, thankful for the pristine clean of the new bathroom and the fact that there's only me to foul it in any way. Examining myself in the mirror, I wonder what Georges Thierone made of me. I look the part – even windswept and tired – but I am not behaving the way a professional should. In fact, reviewing our conversation, right from the start of it he'd completely reversed roles on me, commenting on my little white lies to Romaine – and I'd let him! To be fair, had I been in control with any of my patients?

I sink in on myself. There is only one answer. No. It may not have mattered with Candy Myers – maybe even not with Jessica Morgan. But with Xander, I had metaphorically slit my own throat.

'I am no good at this,' I say to the pale face in the mirror. 'I am no good as a therapist or a solution-creator. These people are too convoluted, too devious for me. I need to go home.'

But you are home, Abigail's voice contradicts me. *You can't hang on to Romaine forever. You're an adult now, and she wants her own life.*

I admit to myself then, why I rang her landline, not her mobile number earlier. I want her to be home, where I know I can find her if I need her. My anchor.

And you really are all at sea! I can almost hear Abigail's laughter at my expense. Yes, I am. Even if there weren't nefarious undertones to what Ethos did, what Xander now had on me was enough to ruin me, and I had taken the credit card almost wilfully, knowing it was wrong – knowing all of what we'd discussed boiled down only to right and wrong and I had chosen to do wrong, based on the vicarious claim that I was *understanding* him by doing it. I had committed a criminal act, and I was trying to put myself on the moral high ground by comparison to him, or to Jessica Morgan or to Georges Thierone? I would be sickened with myself if I wasn't already so disgusted I could barely look at myself in the mirror, and yet I am still the same person as then. The same straight, wheaten hair; the hair of a child, soft and with a tendency to be fly away unless I braid it or pull it into a neat bun. Today I have done the latter, trying to be business-like. It occurs to me that no matter how business-like I make my outer exterior, it hasn't fooled either Xander or Georges Thierone. The same blue-grey eyes that question everything, the same set to my slightly too thin-lipped mouth, so I can look sullen when I am merely serious. Over the years I have learnt how to soften that too, by taking my lipstick past the edge of my lips so they look fuller and more inviting, but again, it's only a ploy, just as the confident and high-achieving young woman is, trading off her father's reputation. I am full of falsehoods. I don't belong here in this luxurious river-front apartment that goes with the job, or in this prestigious position that goes with a high achiever.

'I am not fine, Mum. I am not,' but how can I now go back on what I told her earlier? *And she isn't your mother, she's Romaine, who stood in for your mother, remember?* Abigail's mocking trill is caustic in my head. Yes, she is Romaine, who stood in for my mother and it is not fair to place the burden of either my issues or my behaviour on her.

I leave the bathroom and hang my coat on the stand in the hall. In the bedroom, I change out of my professional persona and lay the clothes on my bed – a therapist's body suit to be donned again tomorrow in the hope it will hide the quivering failure inside it. I slip into leggings and a baggy jumper instead, letting my hair down and shaking it free. Standing in front of the long mirror in my bedroom, I am a different person now. I am me, dishevelled, uncertain and irresolute. The opposite of my esteemed father. Where have his genes gone? They should be rooted in me, giving me backbone and conviction. What would he have done in this situation – not that he would ever have got into it? How would he have dealt with the moral dilemma I had got myself into? I wish I could ask him and for the thousandth or millionth time since he died I wish he was here again and I could ask his advice, take the worry out of making the decision for myself because Dada always knew best anyway. Then it occurs to me I do have a way of talking to him.

I cross the room to the photo of the three of us, Dada, Romaine and me, still lying flat on the chest of drawers, and prop it up against the bottle of perfume Romaine gave me for my birthday two weeks before I came here. He is smiling that smile I remember so well – almost smug, but Dada was never smug, only pleased when things turned out the way he said they would. I can't remember the occasion of the photo, or what had occasioned the pleased smile then – nor even who had taken the photo. It had been in pride of place on his desk for as long as I could remember. I was a gawky eleven-year-old in it, just approaching adolescence and without the benefit of understanding how to put on the requisite role model body suit or run my lipstick past the edge of my lips. I was as I was – and as I look right now. Vulnerable.

I can use Dada's manuscript notes to guide me, even if he can't guide me face to face. I had intended taking a look at the notes at the weekend anyway, to fill the days until I was back at work and occupied again. Maybe reading what he'd had to say would help me sort out the mess I'd got myself into now. Yes! I wedge the picture firmly against the perfume bottle and drop to my knees to pull the bottom drawer out. The manuscript is nestling at the back of the drawer in an opaque blue plastic folder where I'd put it for safekeeping. Apart from the top page – the title page – I haven't transferred it from the manila envelope it arrived in at university just before I submitted my PhD thesis, so it is doubly wrapped for protection. I had already applied for the job at Ethos by then, and spent the next month anxiously awaiting the results of both. The little note attached to it said, 'needs editing but a great tribute to a great man, if it could be published, posthumously.' I figured Romaine must have found it whilst she was clearing some of his old papers as she kept saying she was going to, and decided it was a good project for me to keep me on the straight and narrow – along with the little empty pill bottle that sits in the bathroom cabinet to remind me.

It's not a good idea given my recent sickness, and the excesses of this afternoon, but I pour myself another glass of red wine anyway, and curl into the check-patterned TV chair that is part of the interior designer's assumptions about my preferences. He or she is both right and wrong, because I hardly ever watch TV, but I do like the chair – big enough to curl your whole body into without feeling cramped as you would in an ordinary armchair. This one could accommodate one and a half people, just sitting, or one person, curled into a foetal position, like I am. It is nearest the mock-flame wood burner too, and I have already turned that on so the room is rapidly warming up.

'Morality has been a thorn in man's side ever since Eve fed Adam the apple,' the notes say. 'Was Eve wrong? Or was Adam? Were neither wrong? Why shouldn't they eat of all the fruit of the garden if it was there? Surely you don't grow something edible and then deliberately forbid it to the would-be consumers? That's immoral too isn't it, if it is immoral to tease and then condemn? So maybe God was the immoral one? That's the problem with morality. There are so many ways to approach it, and so many ways of it being actioned. It is a thorn in man's side, indeed!

So, what is morality? The dictionary describes the word's meaning as, "principles concerning the distinction between right and wrong or good and bad behaviour – a system of values and principles of conduct; the extent to which an action is right or wrong." A man of God would say that our morals are dependent on our beliefs, but religion does not dictate our morality. An anthropologist might say our morals are dependent on the culture we have created for ourselves, but what is morally wrong for one culture is completely acceptable for another, and there are many examples to validate this if needed – genital mutilation, stoning to death, and so on. The definition of what is moral or immoral for an individual will therefore depend on what he or she perceives it to be in terms of their beliefs, experiences and their understanding of the world they live in and of themselves. This poses a specific problem, of course, for the practising psychologist when assessing their patient's emotional and conceptual response to the world – particularly where anti-social problems, like violence and lack of respect for others' property are being treated. How do we decide what is morally acceptable? We cannot apply the same rules to every patient we treat because their perception of those rules may be different.

Perhaps the closest we can get to moral correctness and

to treating our patients effectively is to truly understand what they understand about themselves within their world. I have long advocated knowing who you are, accepting who you are and acting on who you are. Unless one does so, one cannot help anyone else to do the same. And acting on who you are may give you quite a different perception of your moral code when you eventually look back and review it. To illustrate, this examination of morality is going to follow several case studies, but one in particular: myself. I am going to start with petty theft. Thou shalt not steal... '

I put the notes down in my lap, and let that sink in. I turn to the acknowledgements page, to check if there have been any other contributors. There are several but one acknowledgement outweighs all of the others. Dada acknowledging his thanks to his colleagues at Ethos *'without whom this idea wouldn't ever have made it onto paper.'* Had my father already trodden the road before me?

Out in the hall, my bag pings, far too loud, but then the apartment is far too silent, apart from the artificial crackle of the wood burner, and the unsteady rasp of my own breathing. I don't want to know what Xander has said in his latest text, but paradoxically, I do too. I slide the manuscript back into its blue folder and lay it carefully on the coffee table beside me, next to the – as yet – untouched red wine. I take a swig before going to retrieve my bag. I may need it.

I sit with the phone on my lap for a long time before I can summon the courage to see what the text says, my mind drifting back to what I've just read. Outside the moon has come up and is sitting in the branches of the tree just outside my window – or that's what it looks like. Of course, it isn't. It's just the way I'm perceiving it, but it looks both impressive and bizarre; a huge white globe perched on a spindly branch. It occurs to me that it is exactly what Dada is trying to say. We all see things so differently, the only way to understand and therefore assist with treatment is to understand how a patient is seeing things. A startling notion starts its life as a tingling electric shock at the nape of my neck and travels its way down my spine until the circuit is complete and the idea is illuminated in my brain. That is exactly what Xander is asking me to do.

His colleagues at Ethos *'without whom this idea wouldn't ever have made it onto paper.'* But Xander couldn't have been a colleague. He is a patient – and not even around at the time Dada was writing his notes, surely? I try to guestimate Xander's age in a way I've not done until now. Assessed him and his physical state in terms of desirability, yes, but that had been entirely subjective. The firmness of his body under the casual clothes, the strength of his grip, the way his proximity sent my blood racing, the taste of his breath on my lips as we stood, almost touching, that first day, before he abruptly left. Oh yes, I have assessed him in that sense and found him desirable. He has aroused in me a craving that I shouldn't have – after all, he is my patient... But of what he really is; facts – as Georges Thierone had urged me to consider – I have little. I should have paid more attention when we were standing so close – observed the lines around his eyes, whether the whites of his eyes were clear or rheumy, his neck smooth or bagging. It's those little things that really tell age. Instead, he's age indeterminate – anything from late twenties to early forties, possibly – and I want him. Admit it. That's why I've done what he's asked me to so far. I want him. I want him, sorted, treated, off the books and then I want him. Are you going to cover that in the manuscript too, I wonder, Dada? The immorality of wanton desire for an object one shouldn't want – the apple Eve gave Adam?

Assuming Xander's in his thirties, it's just possible Dada could have come across him or vice versa. He would have been young – early twenties or maybe even less. A student? The similarity of what Dada was doing and what Xander wants me to do can't be coincidence, can it? If it is, why? Unless it's to help me finish Dada's book for him. He said he would help me find solutions too, had been most insistent about that. I go back to the string of texts from Xander.

My solutions and your solutions, together? X.

I'm the therapist and you are the client. We are seeking your solutions not mine.

Maybe they are the same?

I read his latest text.

'Tomorrow, we will really get started.'

I'm about to compose a suitably polite, but cool reply, bearing in mind what he's put me through today and the fact that he's openly threatened to blackmail me if I don't comply with his wishes when I remember again I'm going with Jessica Morgan to her show in Paris tomorrow. I amend the text to say so.

'I know,' he replies.

I stare at the reply. Then how can we get started on anything else tomorrow? I want to ask him but that would be engaging and I have promised myself I won't engage with him again unless I have to. He reads my mind.

'Now you're curious, aren't you? Listen and learn. We'll act on it later. Like your hair down, by the way. Don't drink too much red wine tonight, though. You won't enjoy the champagne tomorrow. Oh, and get rid of that credit card, won't you? X'

How the hell? My stomach lurches in a repeat of the bout of nausea earlier. I jump up, dropping the phone on the floor, and rush to the window. Outside the mist is still rising from the river, drifting gracefully across the land like swathes of white chiffon. In the distance, a fog siren hoots a mournful warning to the world, and the moon bathes me in its silvery light so I become phosphorescent, still floating all at sea. I press my face to the glass, steaming the window up as I breathe out, creating my own fog hazard. I wipe it away with the sleeve of my jumper, crane my neck and press my cheek to the glass to see as far to the left and to the right as I can. I could open the window and hang out of it to get a better orbit of view, but the idea makes me feel even more exposed – like my hidden observer might drag me out into the murky world outside. Common sense prevails. My spy cannot be outside – at least not that I can see. How could Xander be spying on me through the window, two floors up? No, the spy must be in the room.

I spread the curtains wide, examine the skirtings and architraves, the light fittings, sockets, lamps, slide my hands, palm downwards, across the smooth texture of the newly re-plastered walls. Nothing. I lift the rug and move the furniture. Still nothing. I go back to the chair and sit in it, trying to figure out where I could be being spied on from, heart thumping and breath short. There is only one obvious angle and that must be from the window, and yet there's nothing there. I get up and pull the curtains, frustrated and shaken, but there's nothing else I can think to do. Shutting the moon and my onlooker out makes me feel less anxious, but the feeling of being watched doesn't completely dissipate until I go to bed and turn out the light. Try watching me now!

Chapter 17

The car arrives at Ethos at nine am, dead-on. I am hovering downstairs in reception, world-weary and peering out of the glass frontage, and dodging the lettering *number thirty*, in flowing script, etched into it. Number Thirty, Wellington Road, NW8 is the full address. St John's Wood. Elite, but then it would have to be to attract the likes of Jessica Morgan. It is a limo with tinted windows and driver with a peaked cap – a chauffeur. The receptionist on the front desk gives me a curious look as I walk past her towards the sliding doors and the waiting car. I am wearing my most chic outfit, and not psychologist's flatties, this time – God help me. I will be crippled by this evening, but style has its price like everything else in life. Even so, I am not of the same standard as this car and the receptionist can see that. I'm tempted to catch her eye as I pass her but what kind of look would I give her? A companionable acknowledgement that I'm batting way above my league today, or snooty disdain that I am the one the car has been sent for, not her? To be honest I don't know. Both would require me to know how I am feeling right now and I don't. I am simply being; confused, unsettled, at sea.

The chauffeur opens the door and tips his cap to me simultaneously. It's the same kind of sinuous control of movement that Jenny displays and I can't manage at all. I can't even manage my thoughts, currently – let alone my body. I make do with levering myself onto the back seat with as much dignity as I can, conscious that the receptionist will still be watching. The look would have been snooty disdain, I decide. For the moment, I need to feel superior to someone, uncharitable though that may be. Jessica isn't in the car. I am riding in glorious isolation, sunk in soft leather upholstery trimmed with deeply burnished wood trim – walnut maybe? The car reeks of money and I smell as bad, sitting in it. It's a good kind of bad for once.

For a while I watch London speed past through the tinted window, the limo smoothly navigating jams and backlogs, the streets and buildings and foot passengers a blur of other lives and other dramas. My eyes lose focus and I shut them, laying my head against the backrest. I didn't sleep well last night. Despite the black out, I couldn't get out of my mind who or what was watching me – and from where. The chauffeur disturbs a fitful semi-dream in which I am running away from three-headed monsters with halos around their heads, trying to carry a huge sack of spoils with me. I keep tripping and dropping the sack and each time a credit card spills from it. No prizes for guessing what my sub-conscious has constructed that from. And damn! I still have the credit card in my pocket. I retrieve it and slip it into my bag – better hidden there. Better disposed of somewhere far away from home too – like Paris.

'About fifteen minutes to Heathrow, Dr McCray.'

'Thank you. Am I being met there?'

'Yes, ma'am. Miss Morgan's PA will be meeting us and accompanying you to the jet. Your departure time is scheduled for ten-thirty, so we are in good time.'

I relax in that knowledge. Despite being twenty-six, I am not a seasoned traveller. Whereas others have backpacked around Europe, taken a gap year to Thailand or volunteered in the Amazon, as a student I devoted myself to study. Study, study, study –determined to be the best, achieve the most, be good enough to be called Dada's daughter. I have missed out on other areas of education as a result. Mark took me on a holiday to Italy and Sardinia – to soften me up no doubt – before my PhD results came through, but I'd simply followed his lead then, happy temporarily to be cosseted and babied whilst I decided what to do next. Had I used him? Shamefully, I have to admit to myself I did. Small wonder he was so upset when I told him I was leaving and had never had any intention of settling down in the way he'd envisaged. He'd been Dada's Romaine for me. Unquestioning, undemanding, unwanted. That sits me upright.

Occasionally, deeply unwelcome truths surface when your mind is busy elsewhere – like the door to their prison just pops open. Maybe the lock has rusted and finally given way to the prisoner's persistent attacks on it. Or maybe you simply put the key in it yourself and turn it, rebelliously treacherous to yourself? I am not sure which type of revelation this is but revelation it certainly is – but also, it is not. Of course, Romaine hadn't been unwanted. She was his constant companion – and yet, she was also his shadow. Nothing was ever done because Romaine wanted to do it. Always, it had been something Dada wanted to do and Romaine had subsequently enthused about so I thought of it as something *they* had wanted to do. But the inscription in the book – it had said she was his inspiration, so why should this seditious and subversive idea about their relationship pop up right now? I have no reason to believe it and yet I know there must be a reason for it having been concealed and now revealed by my errant mind. I store it away again, but more accessibly this time, so I can concentrate on what the day may bring.

The turn off to Heathrow is being signposted now and the limo joins the logjam rolling tediously off the motorway and then to a full stop. The time is now eight minutes past ten. We have only twenty minutes to complete the journey, clear passport control and find the plane. My stomach growls at me like it does when I'm nervous. The sickness and red wine last night, added to the lack of sleep, have done nothing to soothe it and it is liable to become an angry wolf if it's aggravated too much by more stress. I notice the set of controls on the arm rest I am leaning on, fingers dangling over its buttons. I hadn't paid any attention to them before. One is marked intercom. I press it and the chauffeur immediately responds.

'Dr McCray?'

'Yes, er, are we going to make it – given all this traffic?'

'No problem at all.' I can hear the grin in his voice and I seek his eyes in the rear-view mirror. They are intent, but pleasant. 'We have flexible clearance from air traffic control. Miss Morgan always has it organised that way in case there are problems en route.'

'I see, thank you.' I press the intercom button and I'm back in my own silence again. So, Jessica Morgan is an organised thief, as well as a compulsive one. And with a great deal of clout if she can arrange for her take-off time to be flexible from as busy an airport as Heathrow. I reassess my patient and wonder if client might not be a better name for her after all. Why in particular does she want me to join her on this trip? It is not necessary for my understanding of her or her problem and her next appointment with me could easily have been re-scheduled to tomorrow. I had accepted the invitation almost without thinking, partly because of Jenny's presentation of it – matter of fact. Where do you want picking up from, not do you want to accept. Transactionalism. I laugh. Oh, my God – she'd used it on me too. I'd been so busy pigeon-holing her somewhere between subordinate, friend, and then latterly, almost peer, I hadn't paid attention to what she'd been ushering me towards.

Jessica Morgan wants to give or receive something from me on this trip, and Jenny wants me to be able to do so. Now was that as subordinate, friend or peer? My senses are on full alert now. No sleepy semi-dreams for me now. I am watching, observing – like a good therapist should be, and it comes to me too, that the half-observance about Romaine and Dada was the prompt to be so. I need my wits about me in relation to everything. I have walked into a prestigious job that is both more complex and baser than what it purports to be, with patients who are both more complex and baser than they are presented as being, and my own background contains seeds of the same.

The chauffeur is on his phone. I can tell from the way his neck is moving, belying the workings of his jaw as he speaks. The limo breaks free from the logjam of traffic, waved on by the traffic cop who has just slid into position ahead of us. We edge past the frustrated equivalents to the receptionist I left behind at number thirty, Wellington Road, NW8 and the engine purrs as we clear the worst of the traffic and ease off onto a slip road that arcs round the waiting traffic. I press the intercom button again.

'Was that just for us?' I ask. 'The traffic cop, I mean?'

'Routine assistance, Dr McCray. You have a plane to catch.'

He turns the intercom off himself this time and I feel like I have been kidnapped. We're moving fast again now and I can see Heathrow's sprawling buildings coming up in the distance. He sweeps past the multi-storey car parking and pulls in smoothly directly outside Departures, opening the door for me before I even have time to release the seat belt. A young woman with an iPad and an earphone dangling from one ear is already waiting for me as I swing my legs out. She steps forward enthusiastically, dark bob swinging in time with my legs, holding out her hand to me.

'Dr McCray, so pleased to meet you. I'm Mariah, Miss Morgan's PA.'

Her hand is perfectly manicured, and her coat is sleek – the kind of sleek that costs serious money. Shining hair, shining teeth, shining smile – she is exactly the PA I would have expected of Jessica – stolen from the likes of Virgin or Apple, no doubt – regardless of their contract with her.

'Hello,' I respond ineffectually. She shepherds me away from the car and into Departures, talking fast – the plane's schedule, the day's schedule, Miss Morgan's schedule. 'Is that alright with you? You'll have a little time to talk on the flight there and back, of course.'

My head is spinning again, like it had last night. I have the strangest feeling I may even have taken one of the pills from the little empty pill box in the bathroom cabinet. This is what they do to me on an empty stomach. We are heading for passport control now. I reach into my bag for my passport, but Mariah waves it away.

'Already sorted,' she assures me brightly. Her energy is exhausting me – and making me too aware of my inadequacies.

'But don't they need to see it?'

'Maybe later. Let's just get to the VIP lounge so we can give air traffic control the green light. We have a priority take-off slot of ten thirty-five if we can make it.' I follow her across the departure hall, dodging winding lines of heavy-eyed passenger and luggage trolleys. They snake, python style, across the expanse of polished floor, temporary barriers and meandering souls, immersed in their search for the right gate. An announcement echoes in the void above us, reminding us that abandoned luggage will be destroyed – maybe like abandoned people? But I am not abandoned or lost. I am being towed along by Mariah, still talking nineteen to the dozen without checking I have heard or understood any of it apart from the occasional, 'Is that alright with you?' which I nod and agree to, suddenly uncaring of what or how I am going to do anything today, other than get through it. My stomach is snarling like a whipped dog and my nerves are as flayed. Lucky, then, that we exit the departure hall and start along a corridor as straight as a Roman road. Mariah is walking a fraction too fast for me and I have long legs, but then I am wearing the killer heels that have me tottering at the slightest threat of a treacherous surface. Mariah, I notice, is wearing psychologist's flatties. I wonder what Jessica will be wearing, but don't have long to wait to find out as we turn off the Roman road and into a small, intimate lounge area, equipped with air stewardesses, magazines, filter coffee, croissants and Danish pastries. My stomach lurches with revulsion at the idea of greasy pastry and over-ripe currants sandwiched together with sugar. It's also equipped with Jessica and the rest of her entourage. She swoops on me as I enter and brushes Mariah aside.

'Dr McCray, we thought you wouldn't get here on time. I'm so glad Fred put his foot down. Such a busy departure time but it was all we could get.' I am overwhelmed by the greeting, teetering uncomfortably on my too-high heels. I have got it wrong, it seems. Jessica is in flatties too, stylish moccasins to match a nautical outfit that seems out of place but perfect when she tells me what the theme of the Paris show is. 'We're looking to catch the St Tropez luvvies of next season,' she explains. 'Boats are in – yachts, speedboats, even canoes, would you believe? Anything that floats, actually. It's Luisa Lomas's fault. She takes to sailing and so does everyone else. Aren't people inexplicable – and gullible?'

I'm not up on the Hollywood set but even I have heard of Luisa Lomas, current darling of the screen following a summertime blockbuster about paradigm shifts and bending reality to suit our needs. God, we do that all the time – why do we need Hollywood to tell us about it?

'Ready?' she adds. Her excitement shines from her like a child relishing an ice-cream or a new toy. What else is there to do but what I've been doing all morning so far? Agree. 'I love these show days. They're just so much fun – and I get to show off.' She links arms with me and we walk, lopsidedly, down the walk way towards the plane.

'No one has checked my passport yet. Won't that be a problem?' I ask, struggling both to stay in step with her and with my discomfort at having my role turned on its head. I was meant to be the psychologist, the therapist – not the hanger-on.

'Oh, really? Mariah should have sorted that. Don't want you refused entry the other end, do we?' She stopped and the whole entourage backs up behind us. 'Mariah, Dr McCray tells me you haven't checked her in yet?' There is ice in the air.

'I have, Miss Morgan. I did it online. I told her that when we were in Departures.' Mariah is frowning, not so much at Jessica's question as at me. I have made an enemy before we have even had a chance to be colleagues. 'You said you understood the procedure, did it all the time yourself,' she reminds me.

I have said nothing of the sort because I've never done it – don't even know what the procedure is, but everyone is looking at me, and maybe I implied it when I wasn't listening properly to Mariah. My head feels even more vague and detached from my body. I need something to eat. I covet the croissants and Danish pastries in the departure lounge now it is too late to eat any of them.

'I'm sorry. I must have misunderstood. I'm a little under the weather today,' I admit, hating myself for seeking the sympathy vote, but hating more the hostility on Mariah's face and the impatience on Jessica's. Jessica pounces on the explanation and the atmosphere changes again.

'Oh no! Poor thing – if I'd known I would have sent you back home again,' Jessica's expression is now all concern, and it seems genuine, even if it's not. Some psychologist I am. I seem to have lost the ability to read anything in anyone currently. Mariah is looking sympathetic now too – not hostile. Maybe she wasn't hostile before, just perplexed?

'I'll be alright, just off colour. Could do with sitting down and maybe a cup of coffee and something to eat.'

'Oh, of course. We can do that on-board. And are you OK in those shoes?' she asks before I can thank her. 'No, you're not. It's going to be a very long day and you are going to be absolutely pooped if you try to survive it in them. Andre, find Dr McCray something more suitable for when we've boarded, which we need to do right now.'

I have very little experience of flying. I have no experience of flying in a private jet. Is it like entering another world? Yes – to my limited knowledge. Is it better or worse than a scheduled flight? I'd have expected to have answered that question for myself as better, but then our experiences are coloured by our emotions. My answer, therefore, is maybe.

Jessica allows me long enough only to strap in, before I'm plied with breakfast and coffee, and for a while I do feel better. I even begin to relax, enjoy the experience – the room to stretch out, the reclining seat, wrapping itself around me like a hug, the unrestricted view of the sky – vast and uncompromising, our little plane balanced on the shelf of cloud like an ornament on a mantelpiece. I savour the smell of the breakfast which I hadn't realised I needed quite so badly until I start eating it – crisp bacon, perfectly round poached eggs, their yellow sun yolks suspended under a voile sheet of opaque white, golden-brown toast, cut into equilateral triangles and juicy oval plum tomatoes, skins gently roasted and crisp in contrast to the splitting flesh and pips inside. I am enjoying the tastes and the sense of fullness until I realise both Jessica and Mariah are avidly observing me, savouring the mouthfuls with me, one directly opposite me and the other watchful from a distance. I am conscious of their interest but the starving dog in my gut dictates I ignore them until it is satiated. Then I am uncomfortable.

'Good,' Jessica times her comment with the precise moment I scoop up the penultimate forkful. I chew and swallow with her eyes on me, watching my lips gently rotate as my jaw works. Mariah is tense and watchful too. Her eyes are as much on the back of Jessica's head – what she can see of it from where she is sitting – as on me, alternating between the two of us. Our seats are built into little bays, two by two, facing each other so that four could sit in a bay – a compartment – but only Jessica and I are in this one, opposite each other. Mariah is in the bay diagonally behind us with Andre. The bay next to us is empty but the one behind, I know, is occupied, although not by whom. 'Now you're ready for what we have on our plate for today – sorry about the pun!' She laughs and it trickles over me, a raindrop shower of amusement. 'Andre, where are those shoes?' she calls.

The lackey despatched to find me suitable shoes scurries from his seat and up the central aisle, bearing gifts – moccasins like Jessica's but brown and more brogue-like than her nautical extravaganzas. He kneels in front of me, Prince Charming making the shoe fit, gently slipping my own stylish heels from my feet and teasing me into the brogues.

'Are they comfortable?' he asks, looking up at me, eyes round and beseeching. Is Jessica really such a harpy? I hadn't expected her entourage to be this afraid of her. The shoes pinch my toes but the heels don't seem to rub. I spare Andre the guillotine. It is a far, far better thing I do…

'Yes, very,' I lie. His eyes thank me. He rises to his feet, fluid, lithe. Everyone seems to control their body so much better than me. Is it to do with the mind or the soul that I am so clumsy and inept with mine?

'Good,' Jessica smiles at him. 'Ask the stewardess to remove Dr McCray's plate, will you? And close the doors. We want to talk.' He gives a little bow and snaps his fingers at an unseen handmaid waiting further down the plane. She appears, like a nurse in crisp blue uniform, removing the dirty crockery and leaving a glass of what looks like sparkling water behind. Andre follows her, taking my shoes away with him. I lean forward to protest but Jessica intervenes. 'He won't steal them. That's my province,' and her laughter splashes over me again. The doors slide across the end of our bay and we are hermetically sealed from the rest of the plane. I accept the inevitable. We are to be closeted in our little world above the clouds, and far from the therapist being in control, the patient is pulling all the strings now.

'I think I ought to warn you that I can only continue to work with you if you are prepared to try to understand what your underlying issues are that cause your overt problems.'

'In layman's speak, you want to chop my head open and have a look inside it? Or wire me up to some machine and electric shock me into behaving better?'

'No, not at all!'

She laughs at my horror. 'Oh, I don't really mean it, but you want to work out what's going on in my head, don't you?'

'Only in relation to your issues. How can I help you overcome them if the root cause is deep seated and unaddressed? I have to be true to my profession. Ethos – it's all about ethics and these are mine.' I feel better for having said that. Strong, upright. Someone Dada would approve of. *Principles,* he used to say – *never give in on them, whatever the duress. Give in on one and it will impact on everything else.* Well, I've already given way dramatically with Xander, so with Jessica I must stand firm.

She purses her lips. 'We have to talk about things?'

'That is normally a good way to start – the things that bother you, interest you, need further consideration.'

'OK, I agree your terms if you then promise to continue working with me and my little problem.'

'I will.'

'In that case, let's start talking.' Her smile widens and I have a feeling I've just walked into a trap. Come into my parlour, says the spider to the fly…

'What would you like to talk about first?' I ask carefully.

'You,' she replies, bold-faced.

I had anticipated this so I am not surprised. Patients often have an unhealthy interest in or knowledge of their therapist. It's all to do with identification. They need to identify with you in order to bind and allow trust to grow. I accept the challenge but follow the accepted way of rebuffing the interest and redirecting it.

'What about me? I'm hardly relevant to your issues.'

'No, you're not, but that's not why I'm interested in you. When Robert told me who the new therapist was going to be – yes,' she laughs full-throated at my expression, 'for all his fancy talk about solutions and clients, you are a therapist, whether you can cure me or not – and no one else has so it will be interesting to see what you manage. Anyway, when Robert –'

'Director Anhelm?'

'Director Anhelm – Robert – told me who you were, I knew it had to be you I saw. He gave me a choice, of course, but really there was none, in my view.'

'Oh,' I don't know what else to say. I'm a no one – despite my plethora of qualifications and glowing academic references. Where could this be going – other than some connection to Dada again.

'I knew your mother… '

'Mum? I mean, *Romaine*?'

'Not Romaine. Anita. Your real mother. We studied together.'

'You studied together? What?'

She smiles quizzically at me. 'Fine Art for her, fashion design for me, but we were both at CSM at the same time.' My expression must be displaying my ignorance. 'Central Saint Martin's School of Art and Design. Katherine Hamnett is an alumnus – amazing designer. And Bruce Oldfield. Anita was more into Gormley. *Angel of the North* and all that?'

'Oh.' I am still confused. She absorbs my confusion like a bee sucking up pollen.

'Oh my God, you don't know anything about her, do you? She said he cut her off completely – even from her daughter. I didn't fully believe her at the time – didn't think anyone could be so cruel, but I should have known, since it was him.'

'I don't understand anything you're saying. My mother left – left my father when I was a baby.'

Jessica is watching me like I would watch her if she were talking to me. Her eyes are gimlets behind the false lashes. She brushes a strand of hair away from them. It has caught in the heavily mascaraed fringing around the blue bore holes. Her hand remains, caught in a curl and her lips have parted. The expression is almost sensual.

'Oh no,' she says softly. 'Oh no. It wasn't like that at all. Now I know I was right to ask for you. He said I should leave it all well alone; that it wouldn't do anything for me, but he was wrong. This really is stealing – candy from a baby.' She leans forward and beckons me to her. 'Do you want to know the whole story?'

I am looking into her eyes and I am reflected in them, a golden-haired prodigy, failing at every turn. I don't even know anything about my real mother – have accepted all these years that I shouldn't ask because it would upset Dada. I would never upset Dada. Then, later, because it would upset Romaine. I would never upset Romaine – for different reasons. But I want to know and I don't care who this woman is or that she is my patient or that she may be manipulating me for her own – God knows what – reasons. I want to know.

'Yes,' I reply.

'Hmm, but maybe not. If you haven't been told it yet, then perhaps you're not meant to know it,' she replies. 'You shouldn't have something you're not entitled to. Isn't that stealing?'

'How is it stealing to tell me what you know about my own mother?'

'It's stealing my memories. They're mine, not yours.'

'That isn't stealing. That's sharing.'

'Is it? So, you want to share my memories? What will you share with me in exchange, then?'

'I don't know. My time? As your therapist? Free of charge?'

'Money? Oh, I don't care what it costs. Dr McCray, what do you think this jet costs, just for today?'

'OK, what do you want me to share then?'

I can feel my fists clenching and despite the full stomach, the angry wolf inside my stomach is growling again. It is gnawing at my guts until they are raw, aching agonisingly.

'I'll think about that.' She pauses, then takes my hands, pulling me forward so our faces are barely a foot apart. 'He forced her out. You were six months old, a veritable cherub. She would have immortalised you in stone if he'd let her have enough time with you. He made her go. You didn't argue with him – he had that way about him. You know what I mean. I can see it in your face. So, she left. She told me the day before, sobbing her heart out, clutching you to her. She had no choice, you see. Her or the baby. One of you would suffer.' She snorts. 'The Judgement of Solomon, and he thought it was his right to apply it to her – and you.'

'I don't believe you. My father wouldn't lie to me about this. My real mother left because she was a drifter – a wanderer. She wouldn't settle and one day she just left and he never heard from her again. He always said the North Wind took her.'

She drops my hands and leans back into her seat, settling herself into it. Her eyes are half-open, still watching me along the long lashes trimming their edges. Her mouth is set, a scarlet gash. She looks older than I first took her to be. Late forties, definitely, whereas my first impression of her yesterday had been of someone nearer her late thirties. It is the make-up, ironically – and the grim expression. Less is more, they say. I lean back too, assessing what she has told me. She could be my mother's age. Late forties would make her early twenties when I was born.

'Believe what you want,' she says, and turns her head to one side to stare out of the cabin window.

'How old were you both then?'

'Twenty-two. Just finished art school. I'd got myself an apprenticeship with a designer. Took them over eventually. She got herself your father. I think I was the luckier of the two.'

She's looking at me again now, eyes narrowed. I am about to ask where my mother is now when the air hostess opens the sliding doors a fraction and says apologetically, 'Landing in five minutes. Can I ask you to buckle up again, please?'

Jessica directs her smile like a spotlight at the air hostess. 'Of course,' she says smoothly. 'What's your name, honey?'

'Francine.'

'OK, thank you, Francine. Could you help me with this?' I can see the charm working on Francine even as Jessica waves the buckle at her. 'Just done my nails and I don't want to smudge them.' I could feel my jaw dropping at the outright lie – and it was obviously so. There wasn't a bottle of nail varnish in sight, nor the tell-tale whiff of acetone that always accompanied it, but Francine's expression didn't even twitch. Maybe she was used to it? Or maybe she didn't even care? Service was her role and that was all that mattered. It mattered to me though. Could I now believe what Jessica had just told me? 'And open those up too, would you, honey? I need to talk to my PA now.'

Francine pushed the sliding doors fully open and Mariah was immediately alert, leaning forward to catch what Jessica was saying to her. It was rapid-fire instructions, ending in, 'and see that Dr McCray gets a front row seat, won't you?' Turning back to me, she says, 'sorry I won't be with you much of the day, but I have buyers to schmooze. Mariah will make sure you find your way round, though. Fill you in on anything you need to know.'

'I'd like to ask you more about my mo–'

'We can talk on the way home,' she interrupts. 'Other priorities right now.' She turns her face to the window again, shutting me out. 'And, oh, look, we're in the clouds now,' she trills, making me wince as my ears pop. The sensation of falling takes my stomach with it. I accept defeat for the moment. Jessica has me right where she wants me and I am a fool both for having agreed to come on this trip and for letting her know I knew so little about the situation between Dada and my real mother. What is wrong with me? I am a trained professional and yet my three patients have already pushed all my buttons and got me right under their thumbs. The acknowledgement of how badly I am failing makes me want to cry, but I can't. I am Dr McCray, Ethos Consultant. I am an adult. I need to look invulnerable, even if I'm not. I watch the plane's descent through banks of drifting white – not unlike the mist from the river last night – until we exit into an iron-grey sky, reminiscent of yesterday. The impression of déjà vu is intense and unsettling. Jessica is as complex and calculating as Xander in her own way. I see that now it is too late. The question is, how do I extract myself from the situation I have got myself into with her – and with information I can trust? I am going to have to learn to play her games back at her, and before the flight home.

I clasp the arms of the chair and lay my head against the head rest, swallowing and concentrating on the call hostess button in the panel above my head. I remember this now as the part of flying I'd hated most when Mark had taken me to Italy. Why do I put myself through these hateful experiences? Mark had been kind, holding my hand and telling me how to swallow to equalise the air pressure in my ears to minimise the discomfort. And I'd been as trusting as a child, but with him that had been alright to be because he'd been as caring as a parent. I close my eyes tightly but the tears still squeeze through the lids and I have to pretend I have something in one of them to hide the wetness. Is Jessica watching me out if the corner of her eye, or is she really so intent on the landing she hasn't noticed my badly disguised distress?

'We're down,' she says, head swivelling in my direction as I hastily blow my nose. The plane bumps along the tarmac, making my head bang against the headrest with the first impact. We can't be crashing. We're landing. But I haven't experienced it this bumpy before – not in any of my vast experience of three flights. My stomach turns itself inside out and back again, leaving me swallowing frantically again, but this time to keep my breakfast down. Jessica smiles at me, a knowing but innocent smile that doesn't reach her eyes. 'That's better. We can pull ourselves together now.' Her eyes haven't left me since they re-connected with mine just as the wheels hit the runway. 'Mariah?' She doesn't wait for a response, but I can see she already has it, with Mariah unfastening her seat belt and leaning forward. 'You are in charge of Dr McCray now. We will meet back here at five. The show will be over by then. Only the reprise to watch on our way home.' Her smile twists her lips into a one-sided grimace. 'And then you can tell me what you make of my world.' I realise belatedly that she is now talking to me. I nod, head and mouth too full to risk speaking. 'Good,' she nods back. And she is swinging out of her seat, showering the air hostess with more honeys and sweeties as she makes her way to the exit whilst the plane is still taxiing, interspersing them with barked orders to Andre and a so obviously gay man called Jed, who I'd missed in the mêlée of hangers-on at Heathrow. Jessica's team numbers six, each adding their piece to the jigsaw puzzle that is her. By the time I see her making her way down the steps from the plane, she has been re-clad in a different version of herself – fur coat, glasses, high heels, Gucci bag. She is every inch the starlet, with her obsequious cohort trailing behind her in an unravelling multi-coloured thread that matches her outfit. My team numbers two. Mariah and me, and without Jessica there, Mariah now seems openly hostile.

'Why did you say I hadn't checked you in?' she greets me with as I rise from my seat. She crowds me back into the compartment. I sit back down abruptly. 'Are you trying to undermine me? She won't find a better PA than me – or one that puts up with her moods as well.'

'No, no – I'm sorry. I'm not feeling great today – like I said. Wrong time of the month, and I just misunderstood.'

'Oh,' she sits down in Jessica's seat and studies me. 'You do look pretty rough, actually,' she concludes. 'You need some blusher to put colour into your cheeks. You look sallow otherwise. That probably doesn't help.'

Sallow. I hadn't heard that word used in a long time. It was the type of word Dada would have used. Subconsciously that warms me to Mariah, but I'm aware of that little psychological aberration so I'm cautious with my response.

'No, probably not. I don't really wear a lot of make-up.'

'I can see that,' she replies dryly, but her eyes are sympathetic. 'Let's get off and we'll brighten you up a bit in the airport loos.'

She leads the way down the steps and across the tarmac to the airport building. On the flights to and from Italy, there was an airport bus to transport us from the plane to the terminal building. I have never walked across the runway before. I pause and look back at the jet. It is tiny by comparison to the jumbos I can see lining up and taxiing in and out in the distance. If I had known how small it was when I'd been about to board, I might not have. It is sleek though. The kind of sleek that says wealth and influence. There is a rush overhead and a plane seems to skim us with its landing gear as it takes off. The engine noise is deafening. I duck instinctively and Mariah laughs. She takes my arm and hurries me inside where it is quieter but clinically sparse. Her comment is a nod to my reaction.

'Charles de Gaulle – not one of my favourite airports. The French trying to be efficient. Only the Germans do that effectively. The French should stick to what they know. In fact,' she adds pointedly, 'we should all stick to what we know. If you're not trying to undermine me, what on earth *are* you doing on this trip?'

'Miss Morgan asked me.' We are nearing passport control now and Mariah motions for me to find my passport. It is almost as pristine as the terminal building, although the building has seen far more traffic than me or my passport.

'And you always do what your patients ask?'

For a number of reasons, I don't know what to say back. Firstly, answering the question will confirm that Jessica is a patient and I don't know whether this is an educated guess by Mariah or an indication of trust in her by Jessica. Secondly, how am I to ask the question truthfully and retain professional credibility? The honest answer would be – *yes, it seems I do, at the moment.* The professionally correct answer would be, *only when it is expedient for their treatment.* Neither are the right answer though; not for this sharp-eyed woman, potentially in cahoots with her unscrupulous employer. I settle for 'no,' and we filter through passport control and into baggage collection and customs. 'I would have thought there would be an equivalent VIP area on arrival as at departure,' I add to change the subject.

'There is,' Mariah agrees, 'but I thought it might be better to detach ourselves from Jessica for a while. After all, she's consigned you to me for the rest of today so let's enjoy the freedom.'

'Freedom? That sounds like you don't enjoy what you do – and no, whatever you say won't find its way back to Miss Morgan – Jessica.'

'Oh, I enjoy what I do, but its grip is somewhat vice-like. Unexpected freedom from 24/7 supervision is like a good fuck and a good work-out all in one – liberating!' She laughs and it is husky and intoxicating. Her dark bob swings coquettishly about her face and her eyes sparkle. I am struck by how attractive she is – and how refreshingly obvious she is compared to Jessica's obliqueness. I have never been attracted to women, but with Mariah, I could be. The thought makes me recoil in alarm. It must show in my eyes because she stops laughing and pinches her lips together in mock horror. 'Sorry, didn't mean to shock. I thought you psychologists had heard everything?'

I laugh ruefully. 'Almost everything – and I'm not shocked, just… ' The rest of my explanation gets lost in an announcement – in French so I don't understand it, but as it contains the words *baggage* and *explosé* I'm guessing it's another baggage warning. Mariah is nodding her head in time with the rhythm of the announcement, as if she's nodding along to a tune.

'Same old,' she comments when the announcement is finished. 'Have you visited Paris before?'

'No.'

'Then you have a lot to see in a short space of time. Shall we?' her head is nodding towards *Douane* and *Sortie* now. 'Let's start with the Champs-Élysées and the Arc de Triomphe. Everyone has to see them, then maybe we'll go via the Place de la Concorde – where they chopped off all the French revolutionaries' heads. It never fails to get me, that. Why chop off someone's head simply because you disagree with them?'

'To create fear and therefore control. All control is based on the fear of something.' It leeches out of me automatically – psycho talk.

'I thought control was based on a counterbalance of wants and needs?'

I look at Mariah with renewed interest. 'Did you study psychology, by any chance?'

'Anthropology, actually – and a little sociology. Surely everything we do, every culture we devise, every community we grow, is based on a counterbalance of needs and wants. What one individual has, another individual covets and so they trade off each other. It can be information, wealth, social standing, necessities for living, people – we all trade. That's not fear, that's commerce. We live a commercial life and commerce creates power – and control.'

'In a materialistic way, but not in a psychological way. What has the greatest power over you? Life or death?' I am enthusiastic for her answer, breathing quickly and shallowly. I already know what it will be though.

'Death, I suppose,' she hesitates. 'Because it's inevitable. I don't really like to think about it, actually.'

'Exactly. And how does the idea of death make you to feel when you *do* have to think about it?'

She laughs. 'Afraid.'

'So, what is the power rooted in now?'

'OK, but that doesn't hold good for everything. Death is an extreme example.'

We are climbing into a taxi now, heading away from the airport with me barely even having noticed what the arrivals exit looked like other than it was guarded by gendarmes with barely hidden holstered firearms.

'Où est-ce que vous allez?'

The taxi driver is peering over the back seat at us, politely impatient.

'Oh, pardon. Nous voulons aller…' she delivers our preferred route in

French as rapid-fire as Jessica's instructions.

'OK.' He shrugs and the sheer Gallic-ness makes me want to laugh. The car pulls smoothly onto the Allée du Verger and picks up speed. Behind Mariah's head the line of trees and small hillocks bordering the autoroute flash by in a blur of green. I focus on Mariah instead, eyes aching. Mariah nestles next to me on the back seat, and we begin our discussion in earnest.

'Maybe,' I resume, 'but finding the thing that produces the most extreme reaction often gives us our most definitive answers.'

'But sometimes we cannot define the most extreme reaction for ourselves because it is a number of things that co-relate and co-react. For example, today you don't feel great. Add to that your fear of flying – yes, it is obvious to me, because I hate it too – and then round it all off with Jessica and her high-handed treatment of everyone and you get the way you feel today, which is… ?' she waits. I know better than to answer. I know better than to do a lot of what I've been doing over the last couple of days, but I need someone to talk to. Mariah's comments in the airport about freedom make me want to risk talking to her.

'Like I'm being psycho-analysed,' I say dryly in the end. She laughs aloud with delight. 'And uneasy,' I add because of her amusement despite the rejection.

'And my fear of losing my standing with Jessica and the number of times she's mentioned you over the last few days, together with being excluded from the show preparations in order to babysit you have made me suspicious. Maybe we ought to join forces, Dr McCray. Trust each other a little. Wants and needs.'

'Gaby.'

'Gaby.'

We smile at each other and a voice inside me tells me she finds me attractive too. The voice belongs to Abigail. Mariah leans across and kisses me. It is soft at first, then more insistent. I am unresponsive even though I want to be. Her mouth tastes of sugared almonds and her lips feel firm but soft, all at the same time. Inside me a little spark fires against the tinder, nurtures a flame, then voluntarily stifles itself. She leans away from me, head cocked to one side. I wish she would lean back in and kiss me again, but it's not me who wants that. It's Abigail.

'I'm not sure I… '

'It's OK. I was just testing. Let's enjoy the day, shall we? There's a lot more of it yet, and we will have to make an appearance at the show or both of us will be out of a job.' She settles back against the seat and starts a running commentary of the places we are passing as we enter Paris. Her voice soothes and kneads me so I am smooth and rounded, like rising bread. I swell, expanding to consume the moment, all of the 'now', so it is overflowing, whilst I try to tease a flame out of the little spark. But it will only glow, a tiny ember in a cave of darkness and I am an empty vessel. Miserably, I know what would fan the ember to a flame and then a burning furnace and that is what I fear most – more than death. Xander.

The Champs-Élysées and the Arc de Triomphe are iconic. We circle the Arc several times so I can photograph it. The taxi driver offers to park in one of the side streets so we can stand underneath it and admire its grandeur. Mariah regretfully declines or we won't have time for me to see some of the other sights. We do linger just off the Place de la Concorde though.

'Awash with blood then,' she says when I marvel at its sepulchre whiteness. 'It's been scrubbed clean since.'

'On hands and knees?' I joke.

'Not so unlikely actually. But more probably jet blasting,' she replies with a half-laugh. 'Still, to think that so many people lost their lives here because of social manipulation.'

'Social manipulation? Well, it was the aristocracy of the time who were beheaded so maybe it was just rewards – not that it should have warranted such barbaric treatment, but their luxury was many others' poverty.'

'True, although actually the revolution was fuelled initially as much by the aristocrats as the desire for reform. Desire and power, an explosive mix. The Marquis de Lafayette, and the Duke of Orleans – Louis XVI's cousin, and one of the richest men in France – were in the thick of it, not just Robespierre and the masses. And even after Robespierre and the Republic were in situ, some aristocrats still found ways of staying in power – the Marquis de Sade, for instance. When you have power, it's addictive – and self-perpetuating if you're cool-headed, or psychopathic, enough.'

'Oh,' I study her, surprised she is so knowledgeable. 'I didn't realise that. I thought it was an archetypal socialist revolution.'

'By no means,' she smiles. 'Although unfair taxes, bad harvests and clever inflaming of prejudice against the privileged, including the clergy, probably kicked it all off. Facts can get so easily buried or transformed with a bit of spin, can't they?' Her eyes are on me, clear and expressive.

Facts. What Georges Thierone had urged me to establish. Am I so obviously lacking in facts to both of them? I study Mariah. I suspect she is telling me something more than about the French Revolution, but I don't know what.

'So, you're saying that what I think of as the French Revolution is actually only my own version of it?'

'Or a version of it,' she shrugs. 'There's no such thing as just one angle, is there?'

'No,' I agree. 'There are usually many.'

'And the trick is seeing all the angles and all the facts and being able to marry them together.'

'Or discount those that don't,' I agree. She is still watching me and something in me is shifting; a stone rolling away from a cave.

'Power, politics, control, and the world's intervention. Those are the facts of the Revolution.'

'Not greed at all then? The aristocrat's greed?'

'Oh yes, that too. There's always greed, isn't there? Everyone suffers from greed – the kind that feeds off others. People greed.' I stare at her. I hadn't suspected such a depth of anger or disenchantment in her until now. She catches my eye and laughs disparagingly at herself. 'It's not a real anthropological term and I'm not preaching, but it's something I've noticed as a possible reason to describe why cultures have risen and fallen over the centuries. You must have come across it in psychological terms too. Some people simply have to feed off others. They gorge themselves on them – their weaknesses, their willingness to be manipulated, their failings, what use they can be turned to. I suppose you would call them psychopaths?'

'More likely sociopathic, if you're talking about feeding off others. A psychopath doesn't need anyone. They make and need no emotional attachment. A sociopath can, although they often manipulate it. All psychopaths are sociopaths in that they manipulate, but not all sociopaths are psychopaths.'

'You know many?' she asks dryly.

'I hope not,' I laugh. 'But they do fall within my remit.'

'And mine,' she replies ruefully. 'I suppose it's when we lose control of our need to feed off other people that we destroy ourselves. Politics is greed. People are greed. Power is greed. All the great civilisations did it – became too powerful for their own good. Or too weak.'

'It's an interesting idea,' I reply, doubtfully. The politics of power have never been my bag. Dada's maybe… Mariah's cheeks are flushed and her eyes sparkling.

'Some people can become almost like a leech, feeding off others – or being fed off. Emotions, needs, desires. If you can't find enough stimulus to satiate your own, you draw on others to supplement the need. Use or be used.' She stops abruptly.

'Are you talking about a specific person?'

'Am I?' She grins suddenly. 'I think we need to get to that show now or we'll both be for the chop, Revolution or no! Even the Judgement of Solomon wouldn't save either of us then.'

We're still looking out across the wide expanse of the Place de la Concorde, with me now imagining the teeming crowds, the wooden platform streaked with reddish-brown stains from previous displays, the stench of fear from the prisoners who have just been brought to its steps on the rickety cart. In the middle of it all is Madame Guillotine, a paper-cutter gone mad, slicing through the pages of over forty thousand books of life two hundred or more years ago. The place must indeed have been awash with blood. The spatters on the ground and up the walls of the buildings mock me with other blood spatters I can imagine, but not place. Mariah's portrayal of the Revolution has left a sour taste in my mouth too – sour because I recognise some of what she is talking about, hovering in the depths of memories I instinctively know are as intrinsic a part of me as my dream of Dada and the forever-withheld explanation for his suicide. There's something of that I should be seeing, some fact, that marries the others together, but whilst knowing it, I cannot see it from the right angle. Confused I turn away towards the greenery of the Jardin des Tuileries and the more spiritual history of the Louvre. The definition of psychopaths and sociopaths I have just given doesn't help. We both know we know someone with at least some of those traits.

'Sorry, we won't manage there today, nor the Seine.' Mariah is gesturing towards the Tuileries. I am disappointed. I recall Romaine's description of the Jardin des Tuileries when she and Dada had visited here for their honeymoon. And the banks of the Seine. *We picnicked there – just like in Seurat's day.* It would have been interesting to have walked in their footsteps – not that today would have measured up to Seurat's rendering of the bathers and their grassy bank today. No golds and greens or blues to revel in today, only dun coloured embankments and steely grey waters flowing on to the River Styx, alongside the blood of the many – innocent or otherwise – from the Place de la Concorde.

'Nor the Louvre?'

She doesn't answer that but steers our conversation away from power games and fears, real or otherwise, and back to the fashion empire of Jessica Morgan as if she is merely continuing the same conversation.

'She's best known for her shoes, but she has other strings to her bow too. Bags and accessories mainly, but believe it or not, interior design too.'

'Strange for a shoe queen?' I probe.

'Not really. She farms it out. In fact, there are many areas she farms out to people she's collected across the years. They all pitch their ideas and she takes credit for the most successful.'

'But that's – ' I'm about to say dishonest, but stop myself just in time. Mariah supplies a different spin on it, but I know she has registered what I was about to say.

'Entrepreneurial. That's what she calls it.'

'So, they get paid, or get more commissions from it?'

'I guess so, or presumably they wouldn't keep doing it. We're back to trade, aren't we? We all have something someone else wants, don't we? She has reach, they have talent.'

'But her shoe designs?'

Mariah smiles enigmatically. I'm about to follow up on the lack of reply, then I understand what she's not saying and drop the subject. She is deliberately feeding me information about Jessica, specific information that discredits her without having been openly critical. Mariah hates Jessica, and yet she is aggressively defensive of her position with her. I study her, trying to decipher the enigma. 'So how did you come to work for her? This doesn't quite seem the role for a social anthropologist?'

'Why not? It's all about manipulating people and their culture.'

'But I didn't think you liked manipulating people. And is that really what anthropology is all about? I thought it was about understanding people and their culture.'

'Touché! Well, maybe that's why we're talking about Revolutions and how bloodshed comes to happen. If we understand history, the worst of outcomes can be avoided in the future – according to historians. Do you understand history?'

'Oh.' Again, I feel there's something more to the question but my head is still stuffed full of cotton wool and the cries of the dying, as well as Mariah's implicit censure of Jessica. Maybe because of that I'm starting to feel nauseous again too. 'Can we move on from here,' I ask. 'I think history is making my imagination work a bit too hard.'

'Ah, it's got to you then. I told you it was like that, but it's good to have an imagination. It helps you put flesh on the bones of other people's problems. Makes you able to apply the Judgement of Solomon in an empathetic way. That has to be a bonus in your line of work.'

'Sometimes, but let's not put too much flesh on the bones or I'll end up imagining flesh-eating zombies here.'

I pretend a melodramatic shiver and a rueful smile but it becomes too real to be convincing. She waves her hand and our taxi, which has been idling illegally in one the pull-ins off the square, meanders towards us through the rest of the traffic. What Mariah has said is jiving with what Jessica said earlier. The Judgement of Solomon. It's the third time I've heard it said. I can't remember the first time, but it has to be more than coincidence that both Jessica and Mariah have referred to a biblical passage that has very little to do with what is going on today – and Mariah has quoted it totally out of context. On the other hand, she has mentioned learning from history, and corrected my faulty knowledge of it. I'm prevented from asking her anything else by the taxi driver's torrent of nasal French. Mariah leans into his window and replies. I don't understand a word of it except *le Louvre* and I'm touched that she is deliberately tailoring the tour to meet my demands even though we have to fit in Jessica's show too.

Mariah slides in next to me and raps on the window between us and the driver in the front.

'Do we really have time for the Louvre?' I ask, in return for the kindness in responding to my request. 'I can always see it another time – in fact maybe I should. There'll be far too much to see in just a short visit?

'No, we don't, I'm afraid,' her bottom lip protrudes in an adult version of childish disappointment. 'But we're going there anyway. Or rather, to the Carrousel du Louvre and La Pyramide Inversée – the shops leading into the Louvre proper and the central atrium. They're the location of the show. Commerce, you see. Jessica has something they want and they have something Jessica wants. Trade, and power – but it's nothing to do with fear this time, it's good old money. She's making a major donation in return for the use of the venue. Quite a coup, but what Jessica wants, Jessica gets.'

'I think you're warning me off?'

'Do you? Then take heed!' She winks and the moment is forcibly lightened. I have to laugh back but the warning is heeded. The Judgement of Solomon – the choice between a lie and a truth. The taxi draws up near one of the lines of temporary barricades fronting the Louvre itself on the Place du Carrousel.

'Ici?' The driver asks Mariah.

'Ah oui, bien.' She rummages in her bag and thrusts a card at him. He's about to refuse it, then studies it more closely.

'Naturellement, mademoiselle.' Now he's all smiles and Gallic charm, jumping out to open the door for her and waiting politely for her to slide out, before rushing round to repeat the performance for me.

'The power of Jessica,' Mariah says in response to my bemusement.

'I'm beginning to see,' I reply. We are talking more in code than in plain speak now. I'm not sure I want to stop it, but nor do I like it. The thing that was so refreshing about Mariah initially was her outspoken honesty. She nudges me towards an empty section between the barricades and we stand in silence for a while, admiring the gravitas of the largest dedicated space to art and history in the world. Behind us the Paris traffic hoots as the taxi slides into the slip stream and disappears in the melee of blue and grey. For those few moments we are in a cocoon, fortified from the world, the wandering crowds, randomly overheard words.

'I plan on leaving at the end of the month, by the way. I'm working in China next.'

I reel with surprise. So, what does that make of her private agenda now?

'That's quite a change.'

'Yes and no. It's still all about commerce and manoeuvring people, but in a different way. I'm working *for* 'the people' out there, not against them. A government change initiative.'

'Does Jessica know?'

'Not yet.' A tourist weaves through the barriers near us. Mariah leans towards me on the pretext of brushing something from my shoulder, but she isn't grooming me, she is whispering to me. 'I'm trying to help you. Be careful.' She steps away and surveys me. 'There. That's better. Must have brushed against something and for this show, you need to be immaculate.' She laughs ruefully. 'It's not just Jessica and her designs on show but all of us too. Her whole team.'

'I didn't know I was – her team, I mean.'

'Oh, my goodness, yes! You've been co-opted just as surely as her interior designers and other talents have been. Why else would you be on this trip?' I can feel my mouth working but no words are coming out. The couple who have been photographing the Pyramid pass by us and Mariah guides us into another open space. 'Do you want to take a photograph? Here's good.' She smiles politely at me and at least the psychologist in me is working well enough to take the hint. I rummage in my bag for my phone. Mariah looks hastily around her and then reaches round me to adjust the angle I am holding my phone at. She says under her breath. 'Gaby, you're trained to observe. What do you see around Jessica?' Her lips are so close to my ear I can feel the warmth of her breath on it.

'A lot of frightened people,' I murmur back.

'Exactly. Now make your deductions.' Her speech is hushed and breathless. My brain is still full of mist from last night. I'm sure now I must have taken one of those pills from the little empty pill bottle in the bathroom cabinet, but not how. I frown at her, disturbed at the turn this taking.' Aloud she says, 'Here, how about a selfie?' She pivots us around the camera and reaches towards it to press the button. Her whisper echoes the click of the camera. 'She's seeing you for a reason – for therapy. What is it?'

'I can't tell you that. It's confidential.'

'I know you can't. It was a rhetorical question. I know what she's seeing you about. I know everything about her. That's why I'm frightened too. She's come to you because she steals – a pair of shoes here, a scarf there. Maybe even a purse, but she'll discard it before she even knows what's inside. She does it involuntarily. Has she told you that? She can't stop herself, but she doesn't care. She doesn't want to stop it – or need to. We take care of it for her. But it's not just personal possessions she steals. It's much worse than that. It's emotional possessions too – memories, friendships, status. It's what else she wants from you that's more important.'

'You can't steal memories,' I protest. I reposition the phone and pretend to take another selfie of the two of us. She deliberately nudges the phone as I press the button. The image is blurred beyond all recognition.

'Oh dear! Try again,' she says loudly. Then quietly, 'Can't you? I heard her on the plane. You tell me she didn't steal something from you then.'

'How? We were closeted away in that compartment.'

Mariah moves away from me and I realise for the moment, the crowds have all passed us by. She shakes her head, and opens the top of her bag so I can see inside. Lying on the top of the other contents – purse, opaque make-up bag, hairbrush – is a small white box with earphones, attached to a thin snaking wire, plugged into it.

'Let me take one now.' She delves past the little white box and pulls out a phone identical to mine. 'Come on, smile.' She pulls me to her and we hunch together in front of her phone. 'I hear everything she does – when she wants me to. It's her way of controlling. Whatever you've discussed with her, I've either heard or it's been recorded for me to hear. Then I have to comment on it and you. Culture placement. How can you be nurtured for her personal use? If you don't fit in one way, she'll try another. Professional can overflow into personal, personal can overflow into intimate, intimate can overflow into manipulated – with careful handling.'

'She only told me something I didn't know – even if it was a surprise. That's hardly stealing.' I am so confused now, battered on all sides by conflicting opinions, conflicting people. *The Judgement of Solomon.* It rolls round and round in my head. 'But I can see what you mean about the professional and personal divide being compromised. Thank you. I'll be more vigilant in the future.'

She takes a final photograph and is putting her phone away. A rag-tag group of people are heading towards our private spot, presumably with the same apparent intention as us – to take photographs. It is a good spot – for photographs and private conversations.

'More than that, Gaby. She took a belief from you and replaced it with another that you don't know yet, whether is accurate, but now you have lost confidence in yourself and your sense of what your world encompasses as a result. She has already stolen that from you. She has already manipulated you.'

'And you said you didn't study psychology?' I ask, the sarcasm making even me wince. My opinion of Mariah's private agenda is back to where it was originally. All the friendliness has clearly been only to erect a barrier between me and Jessica after all, except now I don't understand why.

'I didn't need to. I study what I see and the conclusions are obvious. She wants something from you and she's going to twist you into a little rag to get it. Remember that, Dr Gaby McCray. When I have escaped and she is looking for a replacement for me... '

Her sarcasm matches mine but it isn't said with venom. It's said with a twist of sorrow on the side, but my attention is diverted before I can factor that in with everything else she's told me today. My eyes blur as I stare at the graceful structure of the Louvre itself as it spreads either side of the glass pyramid in front of it, and at something that shouldn't be there at all.

'How… '

'How?' Despite my caustic reply she is frowning, a humorous, bemused kind of frown. 'Haven't I – '

I point, my arm wavering in front of me. Mariah turns as an approaching tourist jostles against her, and then me, before passing on by. I barely notice the tourist in my daze. Mariah stands firm but I lose my balance. I cannon into her and now she stumbles. We fall, like a pack of cards, tumbling the other jostling tourists nearby. I reach wildly for a handhold in the thin air and find, instead, a hand. It steadies and rights me. I turn to express my thanks to the generous stranger who has saved my dignity whilst the others sprawl in a heap across the chequered paving. It is the briefest of impressions of my saviour, but it is enough. Then he is gone, swallowed whole by the crowds now surging around us, helping the fallen to their feet and expressing concern about their welfare whilst eying me, the perpetrator of the accident, with disdain. I don't care about their contempt. I care only about what I've just seen, mind fighting to make sense of it. I drop heavily amidst the writhing bodies of the people I've knocked over, careless of the cold stone, the tangle of limbs, the protests of the ones still struggling to their feet that I crush. My head hits the stone as my mind forms the connection. He is the figure that should not be here. He is Dada.

Chapter 18

'Gaby, Gaby!'

I am asleep. I know I am. Dreaming. He's going to tell me why he's done it. Really, he is. He's calling my name to get my attention and then his mouth is opening and the words are hovering on his lips, ready to fall – a great gush of explanation... I open my eyes and my head is cushioned on something soft, yet lumpy. My head is pounding. Maybe it is my head that is soft, yet lumpy. Mariah's face floats above me, pale and tense. Her mouth is opening and shutting, forming a word, over and over. I squint to focus on her fish-like lips, opening and closing.

'Gaa-aah-bee.'

It is Mariah who is calling me, not Dada. Calling me back. And behind her float other concerned faces, now watching me with pity not contempt. My limbs feel heavy and my attachment to reality shaky, the milling crowd of onlookers all so far away, and drifting further. Maybe I am dying, leaving them all behind? Skull disintegrated like Dada's? Like father, like daughter.

'Ga-ah-bee. Ga-by!'

I reach up to touch my hair, my head, my face with trembling fingers. Nose, lips, forehead. They are all intact, not blown apart like Dada's would have been. My head has no holes or jagged edges to it, no cratered skull. So, I am not dead, and I am not asleep. The leaden sky above me takes on a more foreign twist to the leaden skies above Putney Bridge. I am alive, and lying on the cold hard stone leading up to the buildings of the Louvre, but I feel so very *removed*. I try to get up but, Mariah stops me, gently, but firmly.

'You fell. We all fell, but you cracked your head too. We've called SAMU – the paramedics out here. They'll be here shortly. Just lie still.'

'But I'm alright.' I push against her restraining hand. It falls away enough for me to I sit semi-upright, propped on my elbows. My head spins and throbs, but settles.

'But you may have concussion,' she insists, hand now on my shoulder, pressing me gently but firmly down so I cannot sit fully upright.

'No, really. I'm fine. I'll be fine. Just need to get my bearings.'

'Can you see straight?'

She holds two fingers in front of me, and then adds a third. I hold my own up in mimicry, copying the sequence.

'See? I'm fine. Only my dignity's damaged, not me.' The crowd is drawing back a little around us now, losing interest. I'm relieved. I hate being the centre of attention; would far rather be the observer. My eyes are already gazing past Mariah, towards the triangular form in front of the main buildings, the glassy alien structure that I know is the Louvre Pyramid. It also the direction the figure I think is Dada was heading in. As the crowd dwindles I'm able to see beyond them, scanning the straggling figures winding away from us. Could that be him? Mariah lessens her pressure on my shoulder and I manage to achieve a right-angled stance, legs spread out in front of me and looking particularly child-like with the Morgan brogues still firmly in place. The distant figure is lingering, not moving – as if watching us. 'And we need to get to Jessica's show, don't we? You said yourself there'd be trouble if we didn't get there on time.' The sense of urgency that is gripping me is also making me feel irritated with her. If it is him, I might be able to catch him up, talk to him, but she is stopping me.

'Well,' she is debating. I see the conflict in her face – the need to maintain her position and the need to do the right thing. *Do both,* I want to scream at her, *but quickly, before he moves on!* but the voice in my head tells me I have to look calm and logical – not concussed. 'Alright, but only if the SAMU team say you're OK.' A smartly dressed man in a grey wool coat behind her asks something in French and she replies. He nods his head sagely, and crouches alongside her, heedless of the potential damage to his trousers.

'Je suis docteur.' He pauses. 'You must be err, check,' he advises me in heavily accented English. 'La commotion cérébrale… ' He shakes his head. It is no good. With two opponents, I am defeated. I mentally mark the distantly departing figure and try to estimate where he is heading, but he is too far away. If he wants you to find him, he will, reason advises me. I am surprised. Rationality isn't something I would have expected of myself at this particular point in time. It harps back to an earlier – almost forgotten me. *Yes,* the voice in my head says. *Oh, yes. And who do you think you saw?* Reluctantly I acknowledge the impossibility of it all. My mind is playing tricks on me. Even so, I want to be able to get up and leave here.

Luckily the wait isn't long, and I manage to convince the French paramedics that I am indeed OK. I am allowed to go on the basis that I will seek immediate medical attention if I display any of the symptoms of concussion later. The symptoms are translated by Mariah and relayed to me. I nod enthusiastically even though it makes my head pound. I do not want to get stuck here, any more than I want to be caught stealing. Halfway through that thought, I remember with panic that I never did get rid of the stolen credit card yesterday. It is still nestling at the bottom of the bag my head was resting on when I came round after the fall. Now, more than anything, I want to get away from everyone and simply get rid of the card, but of course I can't. For the rest of the day I am under close supervision by Mariah, but with nothing else to say on the subject of Jessica – perhaps unsurprisingly since from the drama outside the Louvre, we move rapidly to the drama inside the Louvre, and Jessica's show. It is a lavish affair and under other circumstances I might have enjoyed it, but the lights are too bright, the noise too loud, the area around the catwalk in the centre of the Pyramid too crowded, even though Mariah and I have front row seats almost opposite Jessica. I can just see the top of her head, from eyes upwards, peeping above the catwalk, deliberately built higher than the norm to focus the audience's attention on the shoes rather than the outfits. Mariah explains this to me. More manipulation because the show is more than just Jessica's shoes, but Jessica is the major financial contributor so of course, everything is ultimately done to suit her. All roads lead to Rome.

I watch the parade of stilettos, brogues not unlike mine, courts, sandals, peep-toes, boots, until they become a blur and me, round-eyed with exhaustion and the pain from the headache which has now developed from a throb to all-encompassing agony. The only relief from it is to shut my eyes, but I can't do that, or – just as I can see Jessica, so she can see me. Instead I go inwards to Abigail, shutting out the camera flashes that leave blue and pink after-shocks in my eyes if I'm mistakenly looking directly at them as the press records the day, and deafening myself to the buzz of the fashionistas around us and the steady thump of the music accompanying the models down the catwalk. *The Judgement of Solomon* stays with me through all of it, and the journey home. So does that brief impression of the man I'd worshipped since I was old enough to remember conscious thought.

149

Logic overcomes hope eventually, as I turn over the possibilities in my head, still rueing my inability to have jumped up and run after him earlier. It couldn't have been him, though. He is dead. Of course, I haven't seen him dead. I'd been kept from the house as the police filtered in and out, followed by the forensics team in white scrubs and ballooning plastic covers over their shoes, and lastly the morose, green-gowned officials from the mortuary. But I'd seen him leave the house with them, wheeled sedately on a trolley covered by a green sheet the same shade as the green gowns, and into the back of the waiting ambulance. The sighting earlier had produced the same spurt of insane hope I'd experienced then. The small grassy peak that was his nose under the green cover seemed so incongruous with death. If I'd been able to have pulled the cover back, wouldn't he have announced 'surprise!' like you did when you played silly games with kids? And if he was going to hospital, surely he wasn't dead, I'd reasoned then – although I knew they wouldn't have covered his face unless he was.

They thought I couldn't see, but I saw everything from across the street, from the frothy pink bedroom of Mrs Redmund – designated appropriate adult in Romaine's absence – together with the young WPC who didn't know what to say to me. Romaine was late home, delayed by an accident on the motorway after visiting her aunt in London. She would have been home hours before if it hadn't been for that. Instead it had been the cleaner, doing her 'lick and spit' as she called it, last thing on a Friday afternoon, so the flotsam and jetsam of the week was cleared away before the weekend debris accumulated. A Dada-ism. He liked everything – and everyone – in its place. I sometimes wonder now if he'd known that it was to be Mrs Noakes who found him, whether he would have changed the timing of his suicide so that it occurred after she'd completed her rounds so her cleaning routine wasn't affected. She never came back after that day and Romaine had to do all the cleaning – in a haphazard fashion – with my occasional help. Too isolated, she said, but really she meant she didn't want to go in the room he'd died in so horribly. He would have much preferred Romaine to have found him, I surmised. Even though the emotional impact would have been greater, the impact on the practicalities of our daily lives would have been far less. Not that he was without feeling, or the ability to surprise. And he wasn't a creature of habit – more of controlled planning.

Strangely there didn't seem to be any blood anywhere when I peered in the study as the forensics team were leaving. That was two days later, when they'd finished their sweep of the room.

'You can come in here when we leave – if you want to.'

The woman from the forensics team was youngish – in her late twenties – and serious faced. Her wire-rimmed glasses were all the rage then, but they didn't suit her at all. She had long fair hair and grey eyes – not unlike me now. I remained at the door, restrained by the yellow and black ribbons that said *Police – do not cross* as she clasped her briefcase shut, balancing it on the chair I'd last sat on in the room Dada had last been alive in. There should have been blood – great spatters of it everywhere. I wanted to ask her why there wasn't but instead I asked why they had to be so thorough. If it was suicide, then why all the swabs and evidence bags? She looked confused, the way I imagine myself looking now when I think back to it. The pieces of the puzzle didn't fit for her, as much as they didn't fit for me.

'He's – he *was* – a prominent figure. We always have to make sure with prominent figures.'

'Make sure of what?'

'That he wasn't murdered.' She tried to make it gentle, but it wasn't.

'And was he?' She probably looked more upset than me at the question. I could hold it all in then – had done for weeks, until realisation dawned.

'I don't know.' She looked apologetic and I wondered which she thought was worse – that someone had deliberately taken Dada from us, or that Dada had deliberately taken himself from us. 'There was the gun too. Where did it come from?'

I followed her out and roamed the house, taking possession of it again now it had been returned to us. I left the study to last, when Romaine thought I'd gone to bed, exhausted from weeping, but my tears were dry ones, hot and heavy inside me. I lingered in the hall, listening first. I didn't want her company in there. She was on the phone to her aunt, telling her in hushed tones what had happened, periodically lapsing into sniffles. She was repeating herself a lot. I noticed that particularly, so clearly I must be like Dada – able to detach myself from the situation, even when the emotion is the most extreme. And yet, I'm also completely unlike him in that respect because whilst I can detach myself, I cannot reconcile myself with the detached being. I stand aside and watch, but with my conscience pricking all the time. How can I be so unaffected? How can I be so calm? How can I be so logical? Or at least, I used to be able to. That was the Abigail in me, even then. I seemed to lose that ability over the years that followed – and certainly most recently – but that night I must have still had it.

I take myself back to that evening, seeking out the emotions I felt then – the curiosity, the dread, the ghoulish excitement. I crept into the study, twisting my body under the yellow and black ribbons the last man out had forgotten to remove, despite their thoroughness. Or maybe by leaving them there they thought we would remain discouraged long enough for what had happened in the room to lose its significance. Obviously, Romaine hadn't faced it yet or the ribbons would have been already removed. I put the lights on but left the door open, so I wasn't doing it covertly. I had a right, hadn't I? Standing in the middle of room, in the hush of death, with only Romaine's intermittent murmuring on the phone penetrating the void, I asked him why. Why? WHY? The only thing that popped up in my head then – as now – was *the Judgement of Solomon.* A harsh regimen but an effective one. Sacrifice the child to wring the truth from the warring claims. Something of it spoke to me now as it had then, but I'm not sure what. Had he said it? When? Or had he applied it? What I do know is that now I am caught between three warring claims on me – Xander and his mind games, Jessica and her power games, and Georges and his information games and I need help. The Judgement of Solomon would sort the true amongst them from the divisive, but am I the sacrifice? If I'm not to be sacrificed to any of them, I need to toughen up and think straight. My head hurts less when I admit that to myself. It's clearer too. Dada is dead. I cannot have seen him, but perhaps the vision was my mind's prompt to look beyond ghosts to the facts Georges Thierone urged me to seek. Maybe Dada's ghost was trying to lead me to a solution – or it was a presentiment of what I had to face to survive now; the Judgement of Solomon, and what I had to be prepared to sacrifice to arrive at the truth.

By the time we are on the plane home I have little energy, and no desire to press Jessica more about my mother. I cannot make her relevant when she has had so little relevance to me over nearly all of my life. What is maybe more relevant, is why Jessica so wants to raise my curiosity about my roots and my childhood, but the fact that Mariah would be listening in kills it dead, although something has settled in me that was upset and anxious this morning. Strangely, Jessica shows no inclination to talk either. Her conversation is limited to, 'did you and Mariah have fun on your little trip round Paris?' Had Mariah been recording what we had talked about even as she'd been running Jessica down? Has Jessica garnered information from her that now revises her plans for me? Mariah is playing a dangerous double game if so. Part of me admires her spunk whilst another abhors the deviousness, but both are curious about her and the symbiotic relationship she and Jessica seem to have. The two parts of me fuse over that. I smile at Jessica and effuse about the Champs-Élysées and the Arc de Triomphe because that is what she seems to be expecting.

'And the show?' she asks dryly.

'Oh, that too. So impressive! Were you pleased with it?'

'Oh, you know. These things are exhausting, but necessary. I presume Mariah filled you in on how things work?' It was said without facial expression or vocal inflection, but my senses are on full alert to the dual possibilities. I decide to take the middle road, allying myself with neither of them. I may need Mariah one day and Jessica clearly has plans for me if Mariah is to be believed.

'I'm intrigued. I didn't know so much went on in the fashion industry.'

'So much goes on in any industry, sweetie,' Jessica laughs. 'I hope this little insight goes some way to giving you an idea of how to help me. Now you know the pressures and the prizes. My team could do with someone like you too.'

'I'm thinking about it even as we speak,' I reply, smiling over gritted teeth to hold it together – the fatigue, the fear, the fury.

'Good, then perhaps we can talk again in a couple of days' time and you can make some suggestions.' She pulls an eye mask from her bag and slips it over her head. 'Oh, by the way, how's your head? I hear there was a little accident?'

'Fine. I'll be fine.' I can hear Abigail saying it in my head as I say it aloud.

'Good, then I hope you'll excuse me but *mine's* splitting. We'll talk on Friday. I have some things you may want to follow up on.'

Or you can do some detective work yourself, Abigail informs me.

I now knew where my mother had studied, and when. I could start there with a last known address. Or the hospital where I'd been born. I could piece my own story together without anyone stage-managing it for me. But do I want to? Mariah's claim that Jessica would use it to manipulate me has me thinking. Have I already become one of the frightened entourage, without even a threat being voiced towards me? Or maybe Mariah does all of Jessica's dirty work for her and today has merely been one, long threat? Friday would probably reveal the answer to that. In the meantime, I need to hold my nerve, do nothing and wait.

One thing I do, nevertheless, on my way home from Putney – having unbent enough to allow the chauffeur who picked me up to drop me off there, instead of the Ethos offices – is to stop by the supermarket in the middle of the high street and buy a roll of food storage bags. I would like to claim it as my idea, but it is Abigail's really. I scuff my way along the high street until I've collected sufficient stones to fill one of them, then stuff the credit card inside it and tie the top in a double knot, having polished the card with the corner of my coat to remove any finger prints. In the middle of Putney Bridge, Abigail and I wave goodbye to the Hon Mr Jeremy Orland-Roper and the first bit of evidence that could damn me. Tomorrow we will find a way of doing the same with the other, whatever that might turn out to be.

Chapter 19

'So.'

He is here before me again, lounging in the chair I usually sit in this time.

'So?' I try not to let him see I am unsettled by his easy access to my locked office.

'So, how was the day in Paris?'

Something tells me he already knows exactly how the day in Paris went. Quite possibly he was even there himself, watching me – somehow.

'Interesting,' I say, laying my bag on the desk and collecting a note pad and pen from the top drawer. Someone has put a large jug of water with an open neck on the table. Next to it are two glasses. It must have been Jenny. 'It's always fascinating to peer into other people's worlds, and the fashion industry is certainly another world!' I take the pen and notepad over to the seat Xander had occupied yesterday and settle into it. Ironically, I find I prefer it to the one I should be sitting in. It faces away from the window so I feel less exposed and it is harder, more supportive than the plush consultant's chair.

'Isn't it just?' he replies, watching me with amusement. His mouth is tilting upwards, on one side only though, so it gives the amusement a flavour of mockery too. We sit watching each other for a minute or two, each waiting for the other to broach the subject we know has to be broached at some point today. Damn you, it's not going to be me who asks first. You can go to hell... But that twisted smile is still getting to me, rousing the butterflies in my chest again. I lick my lips and find them taut, but not pursed. More, pouting in defiance. Abigail lips. His smile widens and straightens. 'Would you like me to make a suggestion?' he adds.

'A suggestion?'

'That we stop sparring and start working together.'

'I thought we were working together? I'm helping you with your issue. What are your thoughts on that right now, by the way?'

His smile is a grin now. 'Ambiguous,' he says through the grin. 'What are your thoughts on stealing?'

'That it's wrong and reprehensible.'

'No softening at all then?'

'None.' My lips are pursing now. Something like anger is replacing the butterflies. Anger and anticipation.

He takes his phone from his pocket and rests it on his knee. 'You are a feisty lady, Abigail.' We both eye the phone. I could grab, throw it to the floor, stamp on it – or maybe submerge it in the jug of water. Drown it. I don't. He toys with it. 'Good. I'm glad you stick to your principles, but I still maintain there are times when stealing is forgivable – or at least explainable. On the other hand, there are times when it isn't.'

'Are you going to hold that over me, and if so why?' There. The subject is broached. Now he must twist the knife and I must be prepared to play him at his own game or pay the piper. It's not such a good job after all – divisive, difficult, devious. I could do better – after I've done my time. Or maybe I could go back into academia? Pretend I'd been depressed or fazed by the move. Delayed grief, possibly? The possibilities go round and around in my head.

'Do I need to?'

'You have a recording of me. On there, I presume.'

'Indeed. For your further analysis one day.'

'Not blackmail?'

'Blackmail? My dear Abigail, why would I want to blackmail you? We agreed you'd experience some of what I've experienced in order to understand me – like you peeped into one of your other client's worlds yesterday. I hope the experience taught you something useful about both of us – and yourself. My suggestion now is to expand that understanding further. Would that be OK?'

'How?' This has to be a trap.

'You asked if I'd had any more thoughts about my issue. I could ask you the same thing?'

'Oh, no,' I was half-standing, the notepad and pen bouncing at my feet, before I could stop myself. 'Stealing a credit card is one thing – and I wish to God I hadn't now – but killing someone in cold blood is quite another!'

'Killing someone in cold blood?' he is still grinning; grinning like his face will split – a Hallowe'en pumpkin ready-carved. 'What on earth do you think my issue is? Serial killing?'

'You have killed someone,' I hesitate because of the expression on his face. 'By accident, maybe... '

'Who told you that, because I haven't?'

'I-I,' I don't know whether I should tell him the Director has told me – but then, why shouldn't I? He must have told the Director and it is relevant to my treatment of him. 'It's in your file, Director Anhelm... '

'Ah, more bigging me up!' He laughs, clearly enjoying my discomfort. 'Is that why you're so antagonistic towards me? You're passing judgement?'

'I am not passing judgement!' I can feel the butterflies and the anger battling against each other inside me now. 'And I'm not antagonistic!'

He's on his feet too now, moving towards me, careless that his phone has joined my notepad on the floor.

'Aren't you? I think you've been antagonistic from day one. Wouldn't tell me your name, holding your position against me like it was a bomb threat, spouting your moralistic claptrap about stealing and owning yourself at me when at the smallest encouragement, you voluntarily steal yourself. Why do you think yourself so much better than me, Abigail?' His eyes are coals, glowing fire at me. No softness in them today. He is angry. I am angry.

'You've manipulated and coerced me,' I spit back. The theories clump in my head. Simon and Braiker. Oh my God, why haven't I put this together before now?

'Have I now?' We are barely inches apart. 'Or have you let yourself be? Wanted it in fact?' I can feel his breath on my face, smell the faintly sour tang of coffee on it. My eyes are drawn to his lips, hypnotised by their movement as he denounces me. 'You've been doing it deliberately ever since we first met. Testing me, taunting me. Judging me. Condemning me.' Have I? His jaw is taut, his lips thin and brutal. 'You want me to turn on you, don't you? You don't want to help me. You want me to take you down.' Briefly I register danger, before a perverse kind pleasure kicks in and I acknowledge what he is saying is true. What kind of psychologist does that make me? What kind of therapist? What kind of woman?

I know the answers to the first two questions but to the last? I am all fire and ice like Shakespeare's Cleopatra – frozen in Gaby's world of right and wrong, raging in Abigail's of jeopardy and excitement. The coffee smell turns my stomach but it also makes the hairs rise on the nape of my neck.

I try to step backwards but my legs won't work.

'No, I… ' The contrary thrill trickles down my spine and into the pit of my stomach. He is so close now, we are touching, sparking off each other, both enraged. 'I… ' I'm gazing into his eyes and they are flickering fire – not rage, though. Desire. We fuse. One minute we are toe to toe, about to tear each other to shreds. The next we are spread-eagled across my expansive desk, my skirt up round my waist and his hands sliding into my pants. Feebly, I protest but he pushes my fluttering hands away and drags my tights and pants to my knees. I kick one leg free. It is wrong, wrong, wrong, but I want him. He unzips his fly and pulls me bodily towards him, my legs dangling either side of his hips. The contents of my bag scatter around me and I am rolling on something small and cylindrical but I don't care. His body is strong and hard under his clothes, just as I'd thought it would be. It excites me even more. It excites Abigail even more. He pushes my legs wide and I welcome him in, thrusting my pelvis against his crotch. He leans over me, forcing the backs of my hands flat against the desk top and I am pinioned by both his arms and his penis. He thrusts and I writhe, panting. Oh God, I'm panting like a dog, grinding myself against him. He draws away from me, just far enough to be able to see my half-closed eyes, my arching back, my gasping mouth. The pain on my arms and hands as he uses them to counterbalance himself is extreme, but I ignore it. Every sensation in my body is focused on my vagina and the wonderful agony of him forcing harder and higher inside me. Sweat trickles from his forehead and drips onto my face, running in a salty rivulet into my mouth. I swallow and let the waves of pleasure-pain wash over me as we settle into a tortuous rhythm that has me mewling like a kitten. He looms over me, grinning devilishly until his grin becomes a rictus and my waves are a tidal wave carrying me away to a watery grave.

He pulls out of me as abruptly as he'd entered me, tucking himself away and zipping himself up before pulling me to a seated position.

'So,' he's watching me with that twisted smile again. 'Now we know, then? Are we still arguing, or can we get on with the job in hand?'

'You bastard!' Abigail is gone. Gaby remains, disgusted with herself.

'You wanted that as much as I did.' He's retrieving his phone as I'm climbing shakily off the desk, rubbing my aching limbs and balling my fists to get the blood flowing back in them. Pins and needles puncture the skin of my hands and arms and I wrap my arms around me to alleviate the discomfort. He looks up from where he's kneeling, picking up the contents of my bag and piling them on the desk. The cylindrical thing I'd been rolling on is my lipstick, minus the cover. I hope it hasn't left lipstick marks on my back. He laughs. 'And people in glass houses shouldn't throw stones.' He jerks his head towards the glass wall ahead of me, and the vista of grey car park, random parked car pattern of blue and red and black, and the steadily flowing London traffic outside.

'Oh my God!' I back away towards the only solid wall of the room and collide with the bookcase. Its inhabitants poke stiffly into my back and I jump forward, grab my pants and tights and try to pull them on, hopping to stay upright. He watches, laughing. 'Shut the fuck up!' I hiss at him.

He holds up his hands, still laughing. 'OK, OK, but you stop the can-can act.'

'Shut up and I will.'

If I could have ripped him apart with my bare hands then, I would. Instead I manage to pull my tights up past my knees and straighten them. He resumes the collection of my bag contents, ending with an, 'interesting?' He is holding up the little notebook I found behind Dada's books in the bookcase. 'Client notes? Maybe I ought to see what you've written about me?'

'Give it!' I swoop on him and snatch it out his hand before he can stop me. 'It's none of your business.'

'Oh Abigail, everything that is your business is my business too.' He pulls the phone from his pocket and scrolls to the image folder. He taps it and we watch a replay of us getting it on spread across my desk. 'Would Robert think that was suitable client-facilitator behaviour, do you think?'

'Oh my God – what have you got against me? Why are you doing this to me?'

I want to cry but I won't let this animal see me break down. My throat burns with swallowed misery.

'I'm helping you, like you're helping me.' He seems quite genuinely surprised. 'I thought we'd already agreed that, Abigail, so it's strange I keep having to remind you. You're going to come across some tricky people working here. I'm preparing you so you know what to do.' I am paralysed, literally stopped in my tracks by his latest trap. He reaches across and plucks the notebook out of my hand and opens it up, placing the phone gently on the edge of the desk near my open bag. 'My, my. You say this is nothing? I think this is *something*, and so do you.

D. B. MARTIN

Something to do with your father? It looks like his writing.'

'It's not,' I say flatly, trying to take the book back from him. He eludes me, dancing round to the other side of the desk and then back again as I follow him. We end up both in front of the bookcase again and he pulls out the same book of Dada's as the first time we met. He holds it up in front of me and the inscription to Romaine cavorts in front of my eyes. His other hand waves the note book at me. I freeze, mid-attempt to grab at the notebook.

'That's not the same handwriting?' he asks, brows lifting questioningly.

'I- er.' I stare at the two pages. '*My darling Romaine, who has inspired me from the moment I first saw her and will continue to do so until the breath leaves my body. A. 14th Feb '91'* and on the other, '*Some would call me amoral, but morality is a lethal game. It just depends who you play it with whether it's you or they who get destroyed. I'm just keeping myself alive here.*'

The handwriting looks similar, but it can't be. The writing in the book is mine. I know – without the shadow of a doubt, but why, I can't say.

'It's in the tails of the g and y. The capital R and M, too. Also, the way the letters are attached. But you think it's someone else's writing, don't you? Whose?'

'It doesn't matter, and it's nothing to do with you either. Why are you playing this cat and mouse game with me? I haven't done anything to you, and I don't think you're the type to fixate on anyone either.'

'You mean I'm not a psychopath?'

'I wouldn't go quite so far as that.'

'Neither would I,' he laughs. 'Not all the time, at any rate.'

'You're a sociopath, though, manipulating me for some private agenda I don't yet understand.'

'Really?' he tosses the book on the desk but continues to hold onto the notebook. 'So, being a clever psychologist, you've decided to play along to find out – you just didn't realise the stakes would be so high. Does that make you ethical? Or any better than me? We're alike, you and I, whatever you think of yourself.'

I make a wild swing at the notebook and manage to wrestle it from him. It pulls on my already weakened arm but at least I have the notebook back. Now if only I can get to the phone before he does this time I will drown it or stamp on it. Amazingly, the jug of water is still on the far end of the desk, near the phone system, and unspilt. He follows my gaze and

160

shakes his head sadly.

'Oh no, poor Abigail, you're far too obvious. You did much better with the credit card. Good job I sent you a copy of that little episode so you can watch and learn from it. It's all automatically backed up to cloud storage. If you wipe that version, there's still a master version somewhere up there in the ether. I think it is really time for you to learn a bit more, since you're such a bad liar and so unobservant too. I'll be in touch – the usual way.'

He starts to move past me. Unobservant? The irony of that gets me. He's casually leaving without realising that excitement has obviously continued after the moment of ejaculation for him. I spit at him as he brushes past me. The dark stain on his jeans near his crotch is now matched by one on his shirt. He pauses and looks at me with surprise. I look at him and his dark stain with loathing, then can't resist a small satisfied smile at the way he is about to expose himself to the rest of the world if he leaves like that. He looks down at himself and laughs softly.

'Oh, right. Not the done thing at all, is it? To walk around displaying the aftermath of sex with your therapist!' and before I even register the fact that he has raised his arm, the back of his hand is swinging across my face and my cheek is stinging like it has been attacked by a swarm of bees. 'Never think you'll get the better of me.' I drop the notebook and clasp my hands to my face, eyes smarting as badly as my cheek as I try to force the tears back. 'Gaby.' I turn, more in response to the fact that he's called me by my real name than in wanting to know what else he has to say. 'Maybe I am a psychopath, but don't forget what that could make you. Let's stick to Xander and Abigail and not get into who we really are, for now. Better the devil you know, huh? I'm going to go and clean up now. I think you might want to as well. Appearances are everything in our game, aren't they?'

Chapter 20

The door closes softly behind him and I am left, clutching the notebook. I hate him. Yet this is all of my own doing. I cannot believe I have allowed myself to get into this situation. Correction, Abigail has got me into this situation. *But Abigail is your own creation, so don't blame her.* He has tapped into a part of me I would rather deny. Blasted wide open the protective shell she is hiding behind – that Abigail part of me. The memory of how I forced myself onto him and writhed in pleasure in turn makes me want to writhe with revulsion. He is right. I am no better than him. I have already stolen, lied and betrayed my professional ethics. There is only murder left to totally condemn me. I give in to the tears that I wouldn't let Xander see, and collapse in a small, squalid heap on the floor behind the desk. At least there I can't be seen, hidden from view in the glass display cabinet that is my office. Only Jenny would see me if she came in unannounced and somehow, that no longer seems to matter. I sob until there are no more tears to come out. I am dried out. Dessicated. A desert with no shelter from the remorseless heat of my own shame. I am exhausted too. I shuffle on my bottom until my back is resting against the bookcase and stare down at the notebook in my lap. It is cheap, spiral-bound. The kind of thing you'd buy for a few pence in the stationery section of a supermarket. It even has a price on the back cover. A few pence. It should cost more so it isn't current – several years old, in fact. And it *is* my handwriting, I'm sure, although the little tremor of doubt Xander has seeded in me makes me uneasy. I pull myself unsteadily to my feet and retrieve the book with the inscription on the flyleaf from the desk where he tossed it, sitting back down in my semi-supported position against the bookcase. With the two of them open in my lap, I acknowledge why Xander could have thought the writing in the notebook was my father's – on a cursory glance. But I know it's not. I know for certain because a deep, private part of me can imagine writing the words – forming the loops and joining the letters. Both the inscription and the notebook make me feel anxious. The psychologist in me acknowledges too that I need to find out why I wrote the words but why I don't actually remember writing them.

Am I sick? I had a spell of anxiety attacks and depression just after Dada committed suicide but the little bottle of pills cured that – so completely that I'd decided to stop them when I moved here for my fresh start. They cleared my mind of the worst of the memories. I can't even remember precisely when or how I arrived home that terrible day, in fact – a good thing, I've always thought. I thought my memories were so clear I could have stopped taking them long before, really, but I'd been lazy – making it easy on myself. And it had been understandable. Everyone said so. How many teenagers lose their parent that way? I lean my head against the bookcase and the spines of the books crenellate my scalp. I imagine them imparting their wisdom directly into my head through the contact. Osmotic learning. I laugh, an explosion of air and ridicule. Much good that would do if it were possible, anyway. I've spent the last eight years of my life learning the classic symptoms of all the classic psychological conditionings and just succumbed to the most obvious myself. That's what Xander has used on me. Classic manipulation theory. Simon and Braiker, and he'd used almost every manipulation technique Simon had recorded in his summation of the way manipulation is achieved. Oh, I'd been such a fool! But it was true I had played along with his games to achieve my own ends. So maybe that does make me a sociopath, in the narrowest sense of the word?

The phone on my desk buzzes. I'd like to ignore it, thick-headed and sore-limbed that I am, but if I do that, maybe Jenny *will* come in unannounced to see why I'm not answering. I lever myself to my feet again and answer the phone, placing the two books side by side out of view on the desk but pinning a smile onto my public face which is in-shot.

'Ah,' she says, 'I wasn't sure if your client had gone or not but I thought I'd better just check your diary for today with you as everything is a bit fluid here at the moment.'

'My diary?' A heaviness settles in my stomach at the thought of facing anyone else today.

'Yes, you added the appointment on-line on Tuesday, so I guess it was set up as a repeat? Same time, same place, kind of thing? Georges Thierone.'

'Did I?' I don't remember. I shake my head to clear it but it merely

163

sets off a buzzing behind my eyes and makes me feel nauseous. The repeat meeting arrangement with Georges hovers there too. Yes, I had agreed to meet again even though we'd agreed I couldn't do much for him.

'Yes, today at four o'clock again,' Jenny's voice has a question in it. 'That is right, isn't it?'

'Uh, no – no, next week. Are you sure?'

'It says confirmed here. Maybe I should have explained the system to you better when you first arrived but I really thought the Director had given you the basics. I wrote them up for him, so there's no excuse if he hasn't.' There's an indulgence to Jenny's voice now – a cadence suggesting camaraderie beyond that of a PA for her employer. 'When an appointment is definite, it's marked as confirmed. When it's tentative, it's marked as provisional and other clients can fill that slot if the appointment isn't confirmed first. That's what I mean by fluid – first come, first served.'

'It should be down for next week – next Tuesday, if anything.'

'But it does say confirmed. Shall I ring him and check for you because Jessica Morgan is also looking for a late afternoon consultation too?'

'Oh. I guess you'd better.' The heaviness in my stomach has dropped all the way down to my groin. All three of them, all in one day?

'OK, I'll ring him and let you know the outcome.'

'Wait,' but she has rung off already. I was about to tell her to ring the British Embassy to get hold of Georges, but maybe she already knows. She seems to know everything else about my patients. I pull my laptop out of my bag and log in to my emails. The one from the Director is still in my inbox, but marked as read. I click on the attachments and apart from my client list, the Ethos personnel list and the door codes to get in, there is nothing else. No 'how it works' attachment. The phone buzzes again and I grab it before it manages a second chirrup.

'He didn't send me anything,' I say defensively.

'Pardon?' I recognise the voice as Georges'.

'Oh, sorry. This is Dr McCray. I thought you were someone else – the receptionist here.'

'It was Jenny who put me through,' he says. I think I can detect a note of irony in his voice. 'She wanted me to confirm our appointment this afternoon.'

'We didn't make one. It was for next week.'

'I know, but you sound as if we need one.'

'Really – me? I need one?'

'Yes. You sound hassled.'

'No, no – just… surprised.'

'Surprised? I'm confirming then. I like surprised – especially when it's someone else and not me.'

'Oh, but… ' But he's gone too, and now I'm saddled with an appointment I don't need at all. I put the phone down and lean forward, laying my head on the desk. It feels cool and soothing against my forehead. It's the only part of me that does feel cool and soothed. The rest of me feels sticky and used. Sore too. The sex was brutal – pure animal need, nothing human about it at all. I need to go and clean up, like Xander suggested. Maybe cleaning up will help me sort my thoughts out too.

I come back from the ladies loo feeling marginally better. My tights and underwear I've straightened and dabbed dry, and cold water on my face has cleared the flush from my cheeks and the smudged mascara from my eyes. I look scrubbed and fresh – more schoolgirl than tramp. Inside still feels raw though. The light on the phone system is blinking at me. I think it means there's a message waiting for me. There is. It's Jenny.

'All confirmed now, then. Four o'clock, as before with Georges Thierone and five-thirty back here with Jessica Morgan.'

Four o'clock, and it is now eleven. I have five hours to waste since I have no one else to see and nothing else to do until the Director returns and allocates me more clients. I'm starting to master that at least – clients, not patients. God knows how I'll cope when I have more of either. I start by googling chiaroscuro. It's a mode of representation of light and shade in painting. Well, what did I expect to find? A secret organisation? I abandon the search and buzz Jenny.

'Would it be OK if I went out for a while? I've got some work I could do at home, and at the moment I'm just kicking my heels here.'

'You're the boss,' Jenny replies. 'I'm just the filing clerk.' Her expression is semi-ironic.

'OK, well, you can get me on my mobile until 4pm,' I reply. I put the phone down, the remembered image of her on her knees, stuffing buff folders into the filing cabinet, supplanting all else. It is a strange image and I wonder why it has stuck in my head. Like it's skewed – Picasso-like – looking at one object from too many angles. I fold the lid down on my laptop, and tuck it and the notebook into my bag. Dada's book I'm about to replace in the bookcase when on impulse I stuff that in my bag too. It's

165

all skewed – my whole world. Patients who are clients who are manipulators. Directors who leave the newest recruit in charge with no instructions, PAs who know as much as the therapists and a father who killed himself for no apparent reason. I need to make sense of something – anything.

I pull my coat on and leave the office, thankful to be away from its goldfish bowl quality when I am far from suitable to be on display. Jenny's office door is open but she isn't in there as I pass it. I pause there nevertheless, replacing the empty room with the remembered image of Jenny on her hands and knees, trying to work out why it bugs me. I still can't.

I leave the office, deliberately ignoring the ping I hear coming from my bag. I want to know what Xander has sent me, but I know, in my current state of fragility, it isn't something to find out in public. As I walk sluggishly to the tube station at St John's Wood the muggy cold freezes the ache in my crotch – the drag that usually accompanies the fullness of my period, but any sign of that has long since disappeared. It slowly invades my bones, freezing them to icicles so by the time I enter the station I am brittle and ready to break. Luckily the Jubilee line is quiet and I get a seat at the far end of an almost empty carriage all the way to Green Park. The Piccadilly line is similarly quiet and I make it to Earl's Court in record time, jolting and rattling with the rumbling of the train as it stops and starts, teeth chattering despite the stale warmth of being underground. It is ridiculous to go all the way back to the flat in Putney when I have to go back into the centre again for four o'clock, but it's the only place I can think of to secrete myself away and think. It is only when I get there and close the front door behind me that I remember how Xander had been watching me the night before. I drop my coat and bag in the hall and hide in the bedroom, burrowing under the bedclothes for warmth. It is there, in a foetal position, that the reason for the image of Jenny filing bothers me. Why did she file the folder for Naomi Williams with the one for James Openshaw in the G to O cabinet? It is not a mistake she would make. She is too able, too literate, too clever. It occurs to me that I would like to see what is in the files in that filing cabinet – in all of the files, actually. I dwell on that thought as the softness of sleep shrouds me.

And I dream. I realise that when I wake but of course when I'm dreaming that is real too. I dream I am walking up to my front door, opening it and being surprised. *I like surprised – especially when it's someone else and not me.* But it is me. I'm the one who is surprised and I'm fifteen, not twenty-six. And there is Dada, mouth open and the words tumbling out – *why* – as I wake. And this time I am glad – relieved – I have woken before I could make sense of what he was saying.

It takes me several minutes to get my bearings. I've pulled the covers so far over me they are covering my head and everything is dark. I thrust them away from me, gasping for air, and clawing the sticky plastic from my face, but there is no plastic over my face; no bag. It is simply part of my dream, I rationalise – a dream of being trapped, and not understanding. I lie there, waiting for my heart to stop pounding and my breathing to normalise. I fix on the photo of me and Romaine and Dada and slowly I relax, placing the events of the day into an order they hadn't had before. I haven't slept long. It is still only just after one. I should get up and eat, but I don't feel hungry. Everything tastes like cardboard recently – even the red wine last night. Still, I need something because the day is probably only going to get more difficult; I have still to read what Xander has sent me.

Reluctantly I climb out of the cocoon of bed covers and go out the kitchen. I make coffee and take it back to the bedroom, collecting my bag from the hall on the way. Back in the bedroom I close the door and nestle under the covers again, careless that I am still wearing my shoes and they are probably leaving dirt stains on the pristine white of the new bedding. It is like me now – soiled. An apt description, as it happens, because Xander has sent me a copy of the recording of us having sex on my desk. Watching it once would normally have been enough – more than enough – but there is a wildness to me I don't recognise in it. In fact, it fascinates me to see myself as he has. Is that really me, that hard-faced aggressive woman? It troubles me too, until the explanation comes to me as suddenly as the realisation that Xander has used classic manipulation techniques on me did. It isn't me – not really. It is Abigail. It is the me that is also Abigail. Wanton, maleficent, risk-taking Abigail. I sit up straight and examine the whole concept of Abigail as if I am now a patient. Not classic schizophrenia. I am not mad, nor even ill. Not schizophrenia at all, but an extension of role-playing. When I'm scared, she's bold. When I'm confused, she's objective. When I'm enraged, she's icy calm. When I'm frigidity, she's desire. It had happened before – that last night with Mark. I wouldn't have slept with him at all if it hadn't been for that little voice inside me that had said just do it. You're leaving anyway. No messy emotions, no lasting commitments. Just do it.

There's a mark on the paperweight next to the photo. I hate it when anything mars its glassy surface. It drags me out of bed again to polish it against my skirt but it won't shift. I replace it reverently next to the photo anyway. They're my only remnants of Dada – that and the manuscript. I gave him the paperweight when I was ten. It's corny. It says 'love' inside its crystal dome, but at ten, I couldn't think of anything else I would substitute for the word where Dada was concerned. Whether he loved me or loathed me in return, I was his acolyte, his worshipper, his avid follower. He would understand this splitting of myself between me and Abigail. He could do it too, cold and impersonal when he was busy, charming and gregarious when he was in the mood for fun. I loved him none the less for the times he ignored me or sent me away, or even plain lied to get some peace and quiet. It was simply Dada, working on something as monumental and astounding as he. I had Romaine, anyway. The mother who'd been there when my own hadn't – had become my best friend as well as my stepmother. She never sent me away, never ignored me, never lied so it was fine. It was all fine. It would all be fine.

But it won't unless I do something about Xander.

It is now two-fifteen. It will take me three quarters of an hour to get to the Animals in War memorial to meet Georges. I have an hour and a half. I touch the paperweight gently with my fingertips – skeleton fingers. They've always been too long and bony. The mark on the paperweight is still there, like a mark on my soul. It's the mark that never seems to go no matter how hard I polish it; an abrasion that scars its smooth perfection. I use it to replace the perfume bottle propping up the photograph until I can get the broken frame fixed. That hides the mark too. I need a shower and a change of clothes. At least that will wash Xander from my body, if not my mind. The phone Xander gave me pings again. It's a text this time.

'For the record,' it says. And then, 'Tomorrow I'll have your final challenge for you. Then the reciprocation will be complete.'

I can't even bear to think what my final challenge might be. For the first time since I got it, I turn the phone off completely. It doesn't get rid of Xander, but like washing, it at least allows me to bring an objective approach to the problem – free of the taint his whispering, calculating texts bring with them; not that I can manipulate him back. He – and I – have called me a sociopath but I am not truly that; I am a poor excuse for one, thinking that as she knows the sociopath's rules, she can play them and win. There's only one sociopath living that I know of currently who could do that, and it occurs to me now, I'm going to see him this afternoon.

The journey back into London is easy too – going the opposite way to most of the commuters. I reach the Animals in War memorial ten minutes early and spend some time reading the lists of battles and the numbers of animals lost that it commemorates. Underneath 'Animals in War' there are two inscriptions:

This monument is dedicated to all the animals that served and died alongside British and allied forces in wars and campaigns throughout time.

The second, larger inscription reads:

They had no choice.

I study the depictions of the heavily burdened beasts, labouring to their death and I am close to tears again. How can we treat any living creature so heinously? How can we treat each other so heinously? Can't love make us kind? The love written into the paperweight I gave Dada was given unconditionally. I want to turn away at this, but force myself to remain staring at the inscription until my eyes blur and then refocus. The same butterflies that Xander disturbs in me are flying free inside my chest, but I don't know why.

'Indeed, they didn't, which is all the more reason for us to make the most of our ability to choose.' Georges is standing quietly beside me, immaculate in a dark wool coat and light blue tie. It has a sheen to it that suggest silk. He suggests silk; smooth, slippery, expensive.

'I didn't think we really needed to meet this afternoon,' I begin.

'Didn't you? I thought there was more need than ever. What surprised you? I could tell by the tone of your voice it wasn't a good surprise.'

'This is very odd. I'm meant to be your therapist and you my patient but here you are suggesting you help me.'

'Reciprocation,' he smiles and his teeth are white in the failing light. Shark white.

'I've heard that before but that's when the surprises first started.'

'I've heard that before too.' Now he's grinning. I hesitate. It's tempting. This man could easily play Xander back at his own game but then what would Georges want me to do *in reciprocation*? 'Look, you came out of your nice warm office to meet me on Tuesday, knowing nothing about me or what I might want from you. You were upfront with me when you said there was little you could do to help me because basically, what I want is impossible. I'm living a lie and have to continue with that. But still you came out to see me again today. I don't get much honesty in my game so that, in itself, is refreshing. However, it's clear to me that you are like a little goldfish swimming in a sea of piranhas. Do you need my help? I am reciprocating, not asking you to.'

His smile seems genuine – and anyway, what can I do for him? What can I do for myself? I do need help.

'You're right,' I say. 'I'm an innocent abroad. I may know all the theory but dealing with examples of it in practice... Well, I have some way to go with some things. I'm being blackmailed.'

'Whew,' his eyes are bright like his teeth now. 'A biggie! I didn't realise your problem was that big. Who by, may I ask?'

'One of my pa- clients.'

'From where you were before?'

'No. An Ethos client.'

'But you've only just joined Ethos.'

'Yes, but this is no ordinary client.'

'Ah. What have they got on you?'

'Two recordings that could ruin my reputation, maybe get me into trouble with the law too.'

'My God, you don't do things by halves, do you – and in only a few days. I'm impressed.' He starts to laugh and the streetlights come on, irradiating both of us with a dirty yellow glow. Today the memorial is deserted apart from us. Maybe it's the cold and threat of fog.

'Look, if you – '

He takes me by the arm and leads me round to the far side of the memorial – to the two bronze donkeys toiling up the steps.

'I *am* impressed, Dr McCray. I wouldn't be offering to help you if I wasn't. Your father had an imposing reputation and I've no reason to think his daughter isn't equally as brilliant – given a chance. It struck me from day one that you are out of your depth though. In time, you can probably bat with the best of them, but for the moment, you need a break. One day I may need a break too and you can help me then if it's within your power to do so. How I'm going to help you is really very minor. It's this. Do whatever you can to get the recordings back.'

'I will but I would have to do something pretty major to do so. I don't know what it is yet, but I've a really bad feeling about it and the danger is that they still won't play ball and they'll have even more on me by then.'

'OK. So, you want a permanent solution?'

'Is there one?'

170

'Maybe, but it's a big step to take. And there really would be reciprocation with it.' He's watching me closely. He exhales in a cloud of mist. It blends with the already murky atmosphere, engulfing him in vapour. The cold is getting to my feet, turning them to ice blocks and bonding them to the stone floor. I stamp gently to keep the circulation in them but the vibrations jar all the way up my body and make me shiver.

'What?' My breath joins his.

'You mentioned you'd heard of Chiaroscuro and I told you a little of what they do.'

'Yes.' The condensation seems to have been sucked back into my lungs and is drowning me. I struggle with my breath. Just the word alone makes me apprehensive. Xander is connected to it too.

'They could probably find a permanent solution for you.'

'For one of their own?'

'For anyone. An agreement's an agreement. If they accept the proposition, they honour it, whoever it involves. You'd have to accept that they might one day want the favour returned, though.'

'I don't know.' I stop stamping and allow the cold to creep up my legs. He is right. It would be a big step – into a very uncertain unknown. 'What if they wanted something back in return that was against my principles?'

'I don't think they ever ask for something someone isn't able to give. What is the point of asking for something they won't get? They're pragmatists – like all businessmen.' He's still watching me. 'Look, think about it. If you want me to get you a number to make contact, let me know. In the meantime, watch your back – and the camera!' He's turning to go and my whole body suddenly comes alive.

'No, wait. Get me the number anyway. I'll think about whether to use it when I've got it.'

He looks at me uncertainly. The yellow light from the street lamp skims the top of the monument so he's half in shadow, half golden Adonis.

'Alright, I'll see what I can do for you, but it'll only work once so be sure you're going to go through with it if you ring it. I doubt I'd get a replacement for you. Too risky.'

'Too risky? Against the law, you mean?'

'I don't know. It depends what you agree with them to do. You need a solution, they can provide it. It's up to you what you agree with them, but if someone asks then backs off, they're a risk, whatever it is they're asking for. You might do or say something out of turn if you get cold feet. Collateral damage. Do it or don't do it, it's up to you but you'll only get one chance.'

I nod. 'I understand. Get me the number please.'

'OK. Then we'd better not meet here again. I'll only be in touch if I need to once I get you your number.'

This time he does leave, walking swiftly and respectably into the distance. A businessman en route to a meeting. A city financier on his way home. An ex-soldier paying his respects to the fallen – animal or human. The yellow street lamp is creating a foggy holocaust directly beneath itself and it looks positively inviting compared to the dank grey stone of the monument and the shadows falling long around it. *They had no choice.* But I have and I don't know what it will be. I am frozen to the core but I cannot move from here until I have decided. It seems only right since they had no choice whilst I do. I go to stand under the misty yellow beam. It falls round me like I'm in a spotlight. I am under a spotlight. This is a spotlight of right versus wrong. No! I cannot contract with some shady organisation to do something intrinsically wrong. I have to make the right choice, and the right choice is to face whatever may come as a result of my foolhardiness. Tomorrow I will face Xander and tell him to publish and be damned. My father raised me to be a proud and decent person, a respecter of human life and morally upright. I stamp my feet and this time it is a tattoo to march to. I set off, back towards Marble Arch and the tube. Damn Xander! If he wants to spy on me in my own home, let him. And if he wants to report me to the police, let him do that too. I have the phone and what is on it to prove that he is blackmailing me and he'll ruin his own reputation too if he tries to compromise me. This is bully-manipulation but I know that bullies also back down when challenged.

The shops along Park Lane are all starting to expel their customers in preparation for closing time. Now I've decided to be bold and reputable I linger outside a jeweller's shop window, complacent with my moral superiority and aghast at the prices. The shop window bling dazzles me. I wonder what it would be like to be able to afford any of this. I can't even conceive of being wealthy enough to afford ten-thousand-pound earrings. And therefore, what is the point of Xander blackmailing me? I'm worth nothing. I have no money, no property, no claim to fame. Now Jessica Morgan, she'd be a different proposition altogether. I shove my hands deeper in my pockets and hunch my shoulders against the evening air.

And yet there must be a reason for it. Whether he's a sociopath or a psychopath, there is always a reason for the targeting – baffling and inexplicable as it may seem to anyone on the outside. Maybe I should try to figure out Xander's reason for targeting me before I act against him? I review our conversations – what he's had to say to me – and draw a blank, other than the fact that he knows I'm Dada's daughter, but then everyone seems to know I'm Dada's daughter so that can't be the underlying reason. And why did he say we are two of a kind? I am nothing like him, nothing! He is a cold-blooded manipulator, a man who works for whoever pays him most and for an organisation that – according to Georges – has no morals. The irony, the sheer irony that he has come to Ethos for help with morality issues! The question then remains, did he ask for me – as Jessica did – or did Director Anhelm simply decide to foist him on me because he didn't want to deal with him? I need to see the file in the Director's safe. I wonder how I'm going to gain access to that. Maybe Jenny? My phone is shrilling at me, breaking me from my wide-eyed bedazzlement. I rummage hastily in my bag and catch the call just before it dies. Of all people, it is Jenny.

'Hello, all OK?'

'It's five fifteen,' there is heavy emphasis in her tone. 'Jessica Morgan?' she adds, and the rest of the arrangements for today come tumbling back to me.

'Oh, gosh! I'd forgotten her. I'm on my way back right now.' I hitch my bag back over my shoulder and stumble off in the direction of the tube station, the over-bright brilliance of the window display leaving blind spots in my eyes, and pink and orange floaters drifting across my vision until I adjust again to the dull half-light of the rest of the street.

'The door downstairs will be locked by the time you get here, then. The receptionist goes dead-on five-thirty, as do I usually. The code is three, four, zed, two, zero, nine. You'll need to use the same to get out when you're done, and set the alarm system.' She sounds inhospitable. I suppose I would too if I was waiting to go home to my kids.

'I'm so sorry, Jenny. Will you be gone by the time I get there?'

'Hardly, I can't leave Ms Morgan alone to make her way through all our other client's files in my absence, can I?'

'She wouldn't do that, would she?'

Her laughter as it exits the phone at me is loud and rich. 'Probably not, but I wouldn't put anything past any of our clients, would you?''

I laugh nervously back. 'No, I guess not.'

173

'I will go once you're here, though, if you're OK on your own? Adam has football practice tonight and I need to feed the ravening beastie before he terrorises the football pitch. Jessica only pretends to be a lion, anyway. She toys with you. Take her playthings away and she's a pussy cat.'

'Her playthings? What are they?' Jenny the transactionalist would clearly know about Jessica's props. I rather thought that Jenny probably knew everything – including the code to the safe.

'Oh, purely a manner of speech. I mean whatever she uses as her props. You'll know what they are, not me. See you shortly.'

The phone screen blanks out and I am left with silence ringing in my ear. I struggle with my bag whilst trying to maintain a brisk pace, puffing out clouds of cold vapour – a horse on a frosty gallop, cantering towards the tube station – brain also galloping nineteen to the dozen over how I can extract the safe code from Jenny and Xander's file from the safe.

Chapter 21

I don't need the door code on the way in, as it happens. Jenny is downstairs both seeing off the office cleaner and greeting me and Jessica, who arrives just as I'm thanking Jenny for waiting. It is five-fifty so both Jessica and I are late.

'You know the door codes so I just need to show you how to set the alarm as you leave,' Jenny greets me.

'Do you need to go right now?'

'Ten minutes, max. I've told Jack to put pizza in the oven but I won't be back in time to get Adam to training unless I leave pretty soon.'

'I'm so sorry. I got distracted.'

'Don't be,' she hisses as Jessica sweeps through the main door. 'But do keep your eye on the ball with her, pussycat or no pussycat. She knows a lot of people. Her reach is further than you'd expect. Just remove the toys, OK?'

She steps forward to greet Jessica and I turn to face her too, grin fixed to my face. It feels like a rictus at the moment.

'Sorry it's such a late-night affair,' she drapes herself over Jenny. 'How are your lovely boys? Not keeping you from them, are we? Dr McCray can cope without you, can't you?' She turns suddenly on me, accusatory glare desiccating me so even my rictus crumbles.

'They're fine Miss Morgan, and Dr McCray is in charge anyway regardless of whether I'm here or not. I was just doing the handover. The alarm settings and that sort of thing.'

I barely even notice our joint movement towards the lift until we've entered it, crab-like and I notice – belatedly – that Jenny has her coat on. She really must be in a rush. She catches my eye and smiles minutely at me. She has saved me again. A rush of gratefulness makes me want to hug her. I am not normally demonstrative but right now, I would give almost anything for the kind of generous, maternal hug she probably gives her boys.

'Don't let me stop you then,' Jessica says as the lift stops and she precedes us into the corridor. 'I'll wait.' She leans against the corridor wall and watches us, slit-eyed.

'Would you like to wait in the reception room? I have to do this in confidence, I'm afraid.'

'Not really. I'll just make myself comfortable in your office, Dr McCray. That is alright, isn't it? Robert never has a problem with it when I come to see him.'

'Well,' Jenny looks doubtful.

'Unless you don't trust me on my own in there? Think I might steal a couple of books?' She is looking at Jenny more than me, laughing, but challenging too.

'I'm sure they'd be very edifying if you did,' Jenny laughs back. 'I'll open up for you.'

I mentally review the state I might have left the place in this morning 'Oh, I can do that,' I interrupt, fumbling in my bag for my keys, but she is already striding off, and Jenny is shaking her head at me. Jessica is wearing her ugly shoes again. She must be doing some kind of penance. Jenny guides me into her cosy cocoon of an office. I follow her, protesting. 'But the door is locked.' She hands me a bunch of keys. 'The spares,' she explains. 'Just in case. If all else fails, you can simply unlock all the doors with them and override the system.' She pushes the print hanging neatly above part of the filing range aside to reveal a square plastic cover behind it. She presses it and it springs open. 'Pressure release,' she explains. 'It controls everything, so don't tell anyone it's there, will you?' My eyes are saucer-wide. The plastic door is covering a box with a number panel and a series of key holes. The key holes are numbered. How many security systems are there to turn off, then? Jenny turns the key in number three. 'That'll keep her happy for the moment. If you want to we could lock her in too.' I shake my head, horrified. 'OK,' she giggles. 'Then let's get you sorted.' I realise then that the numbers correspond to the consulting room numbers. Mine is five. The Director's is one and Jenny's – strangely enough – is two, despite being right by the entrance. There are five more. Five other colleagues I have yet to meet – if I manage to avoid professional suicide in the meantime. We are seven – seven deadly sins, maybe, not seven ethical consultants; although maybe that is unfair on my colleagues. Maybe it is only the Director and I whose morals are compromised.

'I thought only I had a key to my room. I didn't know anyone could just walk in even if I'd locked it.'

'They can't. These are the master keys. Nobody normally has access to them other than the Director, or acting Director. I've only got it because he's away. Once you lock your room, it's secure. This is for emergencies only,'

'But you've just unlocked my room for Jessica.'

'How we understand the word "emergency" is fluid,' she replies. 'Stopping her from looking over our shoulders right now qualifies, I think, or she would know how the whole system works. If you'd arrived earlier, it wouldn't have been an emergency.'

I am suitably chastened. I listen intently, trying to take it all in and feeling like a naughty child as she explains the security system and the routine for setting the alarms when leaving. She is speaking fast and I am conscious she is keen to get away to her boys – to a personal life that actually has someone and something in it, unlike mine. It is only when she reiterates that the master key for the system will override *all* the doors that a different kind of alarm clangs in my head. All the doors must include the safe door since it is wired into the same system from what Jenny has said.

'Will you be alright with all that?' she asks, glancing at her watch as she swings her bag onto her shoulder and pushes the security system door shut with an elbow that manages to simultaneously flick the edge of the picture frame. It slips back into position as if part of a finely tuned precision system. Jenny is a master of the simultaneous, it seems. Maybe that is why she has been designated acting Director in charge of the master keys this week when really, it suddenly occurs to me, it should have been me – naivety and newness aside.

'I'll be fine.' The mantra slips out automatically. I have managed much more complex security systems than this. The one we had set up at home before Dada died was far trickier, and I had no problem with that. I knew precisely how to turn it on and off without anyone knowing I'd been in and out when I shouldn't have been. It was how I slipped in and out as an errant teenager when I wanted to go out with my friends but Dada had banned it. Come to think of it, it was how he kept Romaine home when he went out. In theory, neither of us could go anywhere if he'd turned on the security system to keep us safe. I push the mean little thought aside. Dada wouldn't have done it to keep us in. It was to keep thugs like rapists and murderers out. *But it didn't,* Abigail taunts me. *Did it? Not all of them.*

Jenny is on her way out the door and I need to be attending to Jessica.

'Remember, remove her playthings,' she whispers before she steps into the lift. I nod, uncomprehendingly and set off down the corridor to my room, thoughts still on the incredible opportunity that might have presented itself to me to make Xander *my* plaything.

'All primed and dangerous?' Jessica asks as I enter the room. She is standing by the front wall of glass, looking down over the car park in front of the building. I join her and together we see Jenny exit, march across the car park to a small blue mini, slither into it and drive away. Her tail lights flicker as she pauses before entering the flow of traffic along Wellington Road.

'Primed, at least,' I reply, trying to sound light and relaxed. She is here to continue the conversation from the plane, but I don't know quite how. It occurs to me as I watch Jenny's tail lights merge with the rest of the boogie woogie beat lights of the home-going traffic that cat and mouse is probably how – and I am the mouse. It does nothing for my already squeamish stomach which is threatening to rebel again. I've never suffered so much from nerves and queasiness as now. Even if I can manage to survive the stress until next week and the Director's return, I'm beginning to think I will be grateful to be fired.

'Good, then let's get on with this. It's been a long day and I'm tired.' She leaves the window and settles herself in my chair – just like Xander did. These people! I'm beginning to positively loathe them – even Georges, the least loathsome of the three, but still vague and ambiguous in everything he does. I like clarity, certainty, solidity. I also like to be in control. That smacks me in the gut too because whenever I think I have control it abandons me – dramatically. One occasion particularly is needling me, at the corner of my mind, just out of reach. An occasion that means something but is playing cat and mouse like Jessica – or spoof spy, like Georges. 'You wanted to know the whole story behind your real mother. Turn that thing off and I'll tell you.'

She's looking at the phone system on the desk. The jug of water and two upended glasses from this morning are still next to it, the meniscus on the water now dusty and the water full of bubbles condensing against the glass. There are red streaks on the white desk too, speared like streaks of old blood. My lipstick. I can feel my face flushing as I look, and look away.

'The phone? I'm not sure I can. It's plugged in at the exchange downstairs, I would imagine.'

'No, the remote record function.' She gets up and fiddles with the buttons on it. Look, here.' I join her at the desk. 'Here, she repeats irritably. 'I don't play games. Uh!' she slaps the panel of buttons in exasperation but I am completely lost.

'But there is no record function. It's just a phone.'

Jessica ignores me and moves around the room, examining the walls. Of course, there isn't much to examine. They're nearly all glass, but she runs her hands across them anyway. Her damp palms make a squeaking noise as they stick and bind on the smooth surface. She stops when she reaches the book case wall and stands back. She looks across at me, the desk and the bookcase, then she drags a whole shelf of books out and throws them onto the floor.

'No, no, stop it!' I exclaim but still she ignores me until mid-shelf she encounters a book that will not move. In fact, it isn't a book at all. It is a small structure with a pin prick hole in one the 'o's of *Psychology of Mankind*. It looks like a book on a bookshelf, but actually it's a hidden camera. 'Oh!' my breath seems to leave my body completely empty. She picks up one of Dada's books from the floor where it has been heaved from the shelf and starts beating at the structure. I skirt round the desk and stumble over the dejected books languishing on the floor. 'No, don't! You'll ruin it. That's one of Dada's.'

She stops, briefly, and examines the book she is using to bludgeon the camera structure. 'Huh! A blunt instrument to batter it with – perfect. She tosses the book onto the rest of the pile and starts to wrestle with the camera box. The bookcase wobbles and I am afraid she will topple it altogether.

'Jessica, this is ridiculous. You're going to pull the whole thing over.'

'Then help me with it,' she rasps. Her cheeks are flushed and her eyes glittering. I hover helplessly as the box comes away in her hand and she grunts with satisfaction. 'Hah! Knew I'd get it.' A wire snakes from the camera to behind the bookcase. She tugs on it and the whole thing unravels. She tosses it on the floor and it lies in the wreckage of books like an all-seeing eye, closed.

'I don't understand.' And I really don't.

'I've got one just like it. As soon as I saw it on your desk I knew what was going on. I'm hardly so gullible as to believe Robert Anhelm doesn't keep enough stuff on all of us to shaft us whenever he feels like it. I've been in business a long time. I know the value of information.' She goes back to my chair and settles back into it as if she hasn't done anything but sit sedately there ever since she arrived. Only the flush in her cheeks confirms I haven't been hallucinating.

'You mean he records patients?'

'And staff.' My cheeks are flaming at the possibility that Xander recorded me using the device but he is not the only viewer of the resulting porn film. She's watching me and now she laughs out loud. 'Oh, poor you – didn't you realise that?' I do hope you haven't been doing anything in here that you wouldn't want caught on camera.' I am a mouse in a running ball now, and she is not the only cat after me. A whole gang of alley cats are out for my blood. 'The most sophisticated versions of them can use satellite to track targets if they've been tagged – a phone or something like that. They can record through the ether. Very useful for keeping an eye on rivals, but I've never gone quite that far with my system. Only record conversations when I've been out of the room. Great ploy that is. Wind them up sufficiently and then give them a bit of breathing space when you're not in earshot. Amazing what comes out when they don't think you can hear them. Robert and his cronies though, they're a bit more extreme. Oh, the pursuit of power!'

'This is totally heinous if it's true.'

'Oh really, come on. Don't be naïve. You knew what the deal was when you took the job. The dirtiest problems, the cleanest solutions. Your father would have been brilliant at it if he'd been allowed to live.'

'What do you mean, allowed to live?'

'Well, really... Oh, I suppose this is where I should explain. Your father and suicide? Never. Utter rubbish. You know why?'

I blunder across the abandoned books, and sit heavily in my patient's chair.

'Why?' It is more croak than question.

'Because he was a selfish bastard and he would never give up anything that was his – and certainly not life.' I'm shaking my head, stunned and angry but the words I want to spit at her description of Dada stick in my throat and become little more than a crow's caw. 'Oh yes, he was selfish alright. Got your mother pregnant, then completely lost interest, but he had to marry her or what would the King of Morality have looked like then? But as soon as she was Mrs McCray, he was back to his old ways. There was this girl, you see? In fact, there was always a girl in tow – a student or a wide-eyed innocent involved in one of his projects. That sort of thing. She got fed up eventually. Told him she'd report him to the university if he didn't clean up his act and then his projects would all be curtailed – especially one particular project and one particular girl at the time. So he got rid of her.'

'What do you mean, got rid of her?'

'He had his ways. She went, but she got her own back. She left you behind.'

Her words are like acid burning into my soul. 'You're lying. I don't think you knew my mother or my father at all.'

'Oh, don't you?' She leans back in the chair and smiles. Then she lists every detail of my birth certificate, right down to the time of birth. 'I registered you,' she says to my shocked and haggard expression. 'He was on a jolly. A convention. Did a lot of those, didn't he? You ask your stepmother. How she put up with it, I don't know – or why, but she did. She was in the wrong place at the right time for him. Maybe it was because of her nature that he picked her next. She took the sting out of the punishment by all accounts.'

'I was not a punishment!'

'Of course, you were. A man like that – do you think he wanted a kid hanging round his neck like a millstone? He didn't want you. Didn't want kids at all.'

'That's not true either. He loved me.'

She shrugs, foot swinging. 'As you wish, but I'm telling you the truth. We all need to acknowledge the truth about ourselves, don't we? The underlying issues? You said that to me the first time we met so you must believe it or you're as much of a hypocrite as him.'

The ugly shoes aren't worn for penance today. They are a foil for the role she is playing. She is enjoying this; baiting me, tossing me around in her jaws until she's ready to snap my neck. She isn't here to deal with her kleptomania. Maybe it doesn't even exist. She is here to deal with me. Well, I'm not playing. I don't have to play. I decide there and then that I'm going to tell Director Anhelm exactly what he can do with his job and then Xander and Jessica Morgan can both go fuck themselves.

'This is not what you or I are here for. We are here to work on your problem with stealing, not my personal tragedy.' I force as much calm into my voice as I can.

'Your personal tragedy – yeah! Having a liar and cheat for a father.'

I stand up and walk to the door, ready to usher her out. 'This is rubbish, I'm not listening to any more of it. It's all totally inappropriate to the situation between us.'

'No, it's not. If I'm to be treated by you, I want to be treated by someone who can acknowledge the truth about themselves, not spout platitudes at me whilst believing complete crap about herself.'

'Then don't be treated by me. I'm not sure how I could treat a compulsive kleptomaniac bitch who doesn't want to be cured, anyway!'

Her mouth drops open like a fish gulping in water. 'You really have no idea, do you?' she says quietly when she's recovered enough to speak. 'I'll email Robert when I get home, then.' Jessica brushes past me, cold air like ice flow freezing me in her wake. The door slams behind her.

I know I have gone too far – way too far. I won't be telling Director Anhelm what to do with his job, he will be telling me and I am not quite ready for that yet. I stand in doleful silence for all of thirty seconds then run after her. Not only have I been rude and unprofessional, I have potentially made an enemy. I also don't know what to believe about what she has told me. What is the point of making up lies like that? She is already halfway down the corridor as I enter it. It stretches ahead of me, replete with its limited edition print walls and plush carpet hush. It is such a short road to degradation and self-reproach but unless I walk it, for all my high and mighty ideas of telling everyone where to go, I cannot afford professional suicide. I am not Dada. I am not renowned, sought-after, or eminent. I am a lowly, recently qualified psych with a famous father who has opened a door for me, albeit where that door leads to I've begun to fear. Nevertheless, having the door – all doors shut in my face – would be worse. I cannot claim anything I've done is from the moral high ground because I am also a criminal. I have been a fool to think I can challenge Jessica or Xander and win.

'Jessica, I'm sorry.' I am breathless, trying to catch up with her. 'I shouldn't have said that. Please wait.'

She stops and turns slowly. She is abreast of a print of Klimt's *The Kiss* and I feel like the desperate lover in it, wildly flying to suck a snatched breath from his love. 'No, you shouldn't.' The shadow cast by the arc of the globular overhead lights in the corridor turns her mouth down at the corners and her eyes into hollows in her skull of a face.

'Can we start again?'

'I'm the compulsive kleptomaniac bitch who doesn't want to be cured. Why would you want to?'

'Because I was wrong. We can all be cured, we just need to know the illness. Mine is not being able to accept he's gone, or why.' Her mouth softens, but she says nothing. 'Please?' We stand, barely a foot apart and really look at each other for the first time. There is pain in her mouth as well as displeasure.

'I'll think about, but only if you accept what I've told you. You need to stop lying to yourself and face some home truths.'

'Why is that so important to you?'

Jessica just shakes her head. 'I know what happened. With your father. You should too. Ask Romaine,' she says.

Chapter 22

She departs on a mutual part-agreement. She will think about things, and so will I. But what am I to think of anything? She won't explain what she means by, 'ask Romaine,' nor add to what she'd said leading up to it. I stand by the Klimt painting and watch her enter the lift, the doors sliding across and cutting her slowly into an ever-smaller segment, angry and confused with myself. From the moment I arrived here, I have been messing up. My fresh start has become my nightmare, but it isn't just me causing the problems. These people – these patients – they all have private agendas that seem to involve me.

The Kiss is almost directly opposite the Director's office door. It stares bold-faced back at me. Robert Anhelm. Director. *Director.* Yes, I do feel as if I'm in some strange, divisive play where I am being directed in a role that has no script. Well, I may not have a script to follow but I do know where some of the playwright's background notes might be, and I have the keys to their safe place. I have the keys to THE safe.

I go back to my bedraggled office and the strewn books. First, I should tidy up or someone will be asking other awkward questions tomorrow when they see my littered floor and the mangled camera-book. If its destruction can be concealed for a while, it also gives me an advantage over Xander if he thinks he can film me – maybe even using this, for all I know – and blackmail me again. I work swiftly and methodically, my back to the three window-walls, trying to ensure the order of the books makes sense so any previous disturbance is undetectable. The camera-book too, I wedge carefully back into the same place Jessica ripped it from. With surprise, I find I am enjoying the tranquil deliberation of assessing where each book should go, alphabetically. It is logical, reassuring; strategic. I file my thoughts about Jessica in the same way. Manipulative, narcissistic, power-hungry and a kleptomaniac. But on some kind of crusade too? What is it she wants from me? What is it Xander wants from me? What point is there in ruining me when I have no standing or power in the first place? My professional life is hanging in the balance and yet I am serenely filing books as I contemplate it. The butterflies are unfolding their wings and shivering inside me, and yet I am calm too – the kind of calm that accompanies the aftermath of the worst thing that could happen to you, and its acceptance. Have I felt like this before? It is a familiar feeling. Cool logic in the face of utter disaster. Maybe I have tapped into some secret strength I'd forgotten I had? The counsellor Romaine made me see before I was prescribed the pills had said there was an inner place of calm to be found within any storm. I hadn't been able to find it then – until the pills – but I had understood what he meant. It was the part of me that could step aside from the tumult of emotion and rationalise. Plan. It was Abigail.

When the bookcase is intact again I collect my own bag and coat, and give the room one last visual sweep. It feels even more like a goldfish bowl tonight, with the dark of the evening outside, punctuated only by the flash of passing headlights. It is a lightbox and I am standing in the centre of it, spotlighted to the world – with all my inadequacies and uncertainties. Why Ethos had approached me and invited me to apply for this job suggested a spotlight had been on me even before I got here. Well, time to find out why right now. The keys are jangly in my coat pocket where I'd put them after Jenny gave them to me. I drape the coat over my arm and pull them from my pocket. Seven consulting room keys, Jenny's office, the main doors both upstairs and down, a set of small keys on a separate ring and one other. The Director's safe?

Back in the corridor, I feel less exposed but the butterflies have started to fly, banging against my ribs and grazing my internal organs. Some have even reached my throat, making me want to gag and swallow hard as I insert the key numbered 'one' into the Director's consulting room door. It turns smoothly, a slick slide, and I am inside, breathing in the essence of the man who'd catapulted me into this nightmare. I flick on the lights and the room is illuminated with a soft pink glow. It takes a moment or two to adjust. No brash, commercial spotlights in here – like my room. It is all gentle lines, curves, rounded edges. I cast my mind back to my interview. Had it been like this then? I hadn't noticed particularly, but then I had been focused on the man and his questions.

'Would you call yourself dedicated?' He'd pushed his glasses up his nose and peered at me through them, eyes magnified by the strength of the lenses so they looked huge and owl-like.

'I think so. I think my academic record demonstrates how fully committed I have been to my studies.'

'Commitment and dedication. Two powerful motivators. So, if you had to do something that impinged on your personal preferences but you knew was important, would you prioritise your personal life or your professional life?'

'If it was that important to my professional reputation and standing, of course I would put professional demands first.'

He'd smiled at that. A pleased smile and I knew then I'd passed his test. 'Professional demands are sometimes hard to shoulder. Are you ready to be challenged?'

'Absolutely. Keen to be, in fact! My father always relished a challenge and so do I.'

'Keen? Well,' he'd smiled again, this time amused rather than pleased. How many emotions a smile can communicate! 'We need to feed that keenness. And we need to continue the good work your father started with you, and nurture you and your talents.' He took his glasses off and rubbed his eyes. He looked different without them – naked, younger. He reminded me of someone I'd confided in once, years ago. Who'd encouraged me and my talents then, too, even though I hadn't been able to appreciate it at the time. I must have stared because he tipped his head to one side. Quizzical.

'I'm sorry. You reminded me of someone.'

'My son?'

I shook my head. I didn't know anyone with the surname Anhelm. 'I don't think so.'

'You would probably know him as Stephen Anders. Anders-Anhelm is his full surname but he dropped the Anhelm when he dropped out and opted to become a counsellor, rather than a psychologist.'

'Oh.' Stephen's smiling face came back to me, shambling, but also intense and kind. If this was his father, then... 'You know about all that?'

'I know about all that – and sympathise. All professionals should avail themselves of some counselling during their professional life. We are human, after all.'

'But it should have been confidential.' I bit my lip. I'd just impressed this man – head of one of the most prestigious private counselling and psychology practices in the UK – and now I was criticising him.

'Indeed. It should. Romaine asked me for a recommendation. I know about it on a personal level and endorse it on a professional one.'

'Oh.' I didn't know what else to say. He would probably also know why I'd seen his son then. Romaine would have had to have explained. But it was reasonable, wasn't it? I'd been fifteen. My father had committed suicide, without leaving a note. What fifteen-year- old wouldn't have been traumatised? And if this was Stephen's father then how could he not understand? 'It was a long time ago. It was... helpful. I haven't needed counselling since.'

'Gaby, please. There's no need to defend yourself. I understand completely. It was essential and very helpful for you at the time. And here you are, an astonishingly talented and able young woman. I think you would be an excellent fit here, if you would like to join us? Take on a challenge? You come recommended by Stephen too.'

The rest had flowed so easily from there – the job, the company flat no one was using currently. *Perfect for you to get you started here, Gaby. Start as soon as you can. We're delighted to have you. Whatever makes starting here easier for you...*

Well that was crap, wasn't it? He'd deliberately got me to start when there was no one else here to help. A challenge – yeah, it was that alright!

I cross the room and sit at his desk, looking outwards. What does it feel like to be Director Anhelm? Is it the same sense of power Jessica Morgan feels when she orders her team around? Or Xander, when he orders me around? I place my hands, palm downwards on the desk. It isn't pristine white like mine. It is a delicate, burnished walnut, with elegant brass handles on the drawers and a tooled leather centre for writing. His chair, too, is different to mine. It is harder, more supportive. Decisive, not soft and insidious. It makes me feel decisive too and the butterflies settle, folding their wings in on themselves. The sharp, logical edge that dominated when I was restocking the bookcase takes over again. The walls are filled with more of the type of popular prints that hang in the corridor, but they are mainly by artists like Klee and Kandinsky, turning reality on its head. I scour them for a suitable cover for a wall safe. If Jenny's is anything to go by, it needs to be a decent size, and about shoulder height. The rose soft light gives the whole room an air of fantasy – of drifting, dream-like. One of those lucid dreams in which I could reach out and turn on a light, except my arm won't move. But it isn't the same in here as that interview day. The furniture, I remember, but not this sense of unreality. Maybe it is the lighting that does it?

I swing the chair full circle, swivelling on its ball feet and identify a contender for the safe cover right behind me. It is by the father of cubism itself, Picasso, and the ironist in me appreciates the joke. A cubist painting, defying rational shape and form, fronting a cubist hiding place – a small white box safe – defying entry. And it does. The unnumbered key on the ring doesn't even fit the lock because there is none. Entry is by a numbered keypad, and I don't know the combination. Dammit!

I sit for a long time, wondering what to do next. Of course, it would have been too simple, and it had been stupid of me to think I could find out about Xander and what he wants from me so easily. Klee's *Twittering Machine* mocks me from across the room. I appreciate the irony of that too. I am also a *Twittering Machine*, chattering and twirling pointlessly, and veering between full volume and disorientated silence as the handle is turned. I need to regain control, rationalise what I'm doing and why. Plan. I need to go home, although where home is is now too diffuse for me to decide on tonight. Jessica and her malicious defamation of Dada has soured my childhood home, and yet that is where my roots most are – with what there is left of him, and Romaine. I need to think, and above all, I need to reconnect with *my* memory of Dada, not the squalid one Jessica has tried to supplant it with. I will go home and read some more of his manuscript. That is where I will find him again.

My journey home is full of Dada and Romaine and all the things I can remember about our lives together. Dada in his study, barricaded from us by piles of books whilst he wrote his next book or lecture notes, and Romaine leading me gently away to cookies and warm milk in the kitchen so we didn't disturb him. Dada, playing host at one of the drinks parties he occasionally insisted was held, buried inside a tight knot of students, all anxious to hear his wisdom, whilst I hung over the banisters – too young to be allowed to join in, but watching and listening with envy. His interest in them was intense and absolute. In me it was occasional and patchy. I wasn't good enough, you see.

Romaine would sometimes come and sit on the stairs with me.

'You don't have to sit up here. You're old enough to join in.'

She would laugh. 'I am, but maybe I'm not smart enough.'

'You are. I'm the one that's dumb.'

'We're both smart enough, then. Smart is what you make it.'

Or Dada, propounding some theory to me when I'm older and he's using me as a test subject, only half understanding but not wanting to say so or he'll sigh and wave me away. Romaine often intervened then too, with a well-timed coffee break or a reminder that I had this activity, or that piece of homework to complete – before his patience wore thin.

'You'll understand it all too, one day,' she told me on numerous occasions.

'Will I? He is just so clever. He is awesome.'

'Where on earth did you get that word from?'

'It was in an article about Dada in *The New Statesman*. Awesome. He is.'

'It's never good to be totally in awe of anything,' and she touched my cheek with her finger. 'We're all awesome – in our own ways. You especially.'

'Not like Dada's awesome. A newspaper has even said it about him.'

I arrive back at the door to Willow Bank and have to kick a child's ball away from the door when I go into the lobby. It is bright red and has a yellow smiley on it. It is the kind of ball I would have had as a child. In fact, I probably did, but the memories of Dada and Romaine and I don't dredge up any with red balls and smiley faces. Only more of the same as the ones I'd been lost in on the way home, a sense of foreboding accompanying them – and Abigail, of course.

I was given Abigail when I was six. She was my sixth birthday present in fact. I think I really only got her because Romaine noticed how deeply I fell in love with her on a visit to Harrods. We'd gone to get Dada a specific kind of tie – which I later found out was a white bow tie – because he was speaking at a convention and the formal dinner was what he kept calling *a white tie event*. Romaine wasn't going, even though some attendees were taking their families. She had to stay home with me. I thought she'd be cross, but she wasn't. She almost seemed relieved. I wasn't. I was disappointed.

'It'll be nice, just you and me. We'll make some fairy cakes and go to the park. Maybe even go swimming.'

'There's a swimming pool at the hotel.' I couldn't keep the wistfulness from my voice.

'How do you know that?' she sounded amused but surprised.

'It's in the leaflet thingy on Dada's desk.'

'You didn't move anything, did you, Gab? You know how he hates anyone touching the things on his desk.'

'No. I didn't. He will be back for my birthday, won't he?'

'I'm sure he will, but if he isn't it'll be for a reason.'

I never did find out the reason, but I did get Abigail to make up for it, and he even wrote the label himself.

A perfect doll for a perfect daughter.

That's what the label said. Romaine wrapped her up though. I know because she cut herself trying to curl the ribbon round the parcel and had to wear a plaster to stop the bleeding. I heard her tell him, so it must be true; it must be, mustn't it?

'Ouch!'

'What's that?'

'I cut myself.'

'Clumsy! Don't get blood on any of my papers, will you?' Then, *'How?'*

'Oh, er, the scissors – trying to make the ribbon curl on Gaby's birthday present. You have to run the sci–'

'Yes, alright. I don't need a blow by blow account. The bloody thing has wasted enough of my money without wasting my time hearing how you wrapped it up. What am I meant to write on this bloody label?'

'Something nice. You're going to miss her birthday altogether so say something she'll treasure.'

'Like what? I don't know what kids treasure. That's your job.'

'How about a perfect doll for a perfect daughter?'

'Huh, half true at least – a perfectly bloody expensive doll, maybe... Why doesn't she want one of these modernistic things wearing what they dress in today? That would be more appropriate. Not something out of the last century with ringlets and petticoats. It's a hard world out there. She needs to grow up learning how to live in it.'

'Not everyone wants to live in a hard world, Aaron.'

'They don't have a choice. There, I've written what you wanted me to, but she needs to toughen up. OK, look sweet and pretty, but underneath, know how to kick ass too. Not rely on ringlets and petticoats. You know that... '

I try to un-remember, but I can't. The little stab of pain under my ribs isn't real, like the memory – I don't think. It still hurts though. I dribble the ball over towards the lift and when it arrives, I kick it into the lift with me. I don't have Abigail any more. I kept her until I was fifteen, then I smashed her face and threw her in the river. I think. I hadn't remembered that until now either. I threw her in the river with the bags. The butterflies are stirring once more and I'm feeling sick again. I should have eaten better at lunchtime, not rely on coffee to keep me going.

I would have liked a red ball with a yellow smiley on it. I would have liked to remember kicking it around the park with Dada and Romaine, but

I can't. Only Romaine. I remember Romaine kicking a red ball when … I would like to forget what I've just remembered about Abigail, but I can't. Inside my flat, I drop my bag and run to the bathroom where I'm sick in the washbasin. The red ball rolls in behind me like some truant child is trying to tease me, and idles in the doorway. I sit on the side of the bath and cry until I can only sob, dry gasping sobs and there are no tears left. Why did my real mother leave? I must have asked Romaine that at some stage. And she must have known, even though she never told me. Too young to understand, too hurt to understand, too long ago to understand? Whatever the reason, I don't want to understand now but I need to know if Jessica Morgan was telling me the truth. Something deep and essential to my sanity needs it.

I swill the puke down the drain and rinse round the wash basin. It's not much more than greenish-brown bile anyway. It leaves a stain on the white of the porcelain that I can't be bothered to deal with now, and a rancid smell in the air. The smell makes me feel nauseous again and I hang over the wash basin just in case, but the sensation passes and I end up staring at myself in the mirrored door of the bathroom cabinet. I have dark red-brown rings under my eyes, like they are scalded, but my skin is otherwise pasty. An unhealthy tallow-white, surrounded by lank fair hair, hanging in shredded yellow ribbons round my face. My smart work blouse and skirt are wrinkled and puke stained. Not ringletted and petticoated. Worn and jaded. But Abigail hadn't been a just a doll from the last century. She had been something else – a symbol of everything that wasn't real in my life. No wonder I remember her as a coy coquette with the devil lurking behind her pouting mouth and rounded cheeks. She was innocence lost, belief destroyed, love rejected.

I stumble into the bedroom, abandoning my coat and the rest of my clothes on the floor. I stand naked in front of the full-length mirror and examine myself again. I have a good figure – full breasted and with a neat waist – but today it looks solid and lumpy. There is a bruise on my left thigh too, angrily red, turning to purple. It is striated on the outer side, and with a heavy circle on my inner thigh. I grunt with dismay. It is a hand mark – Xander's, probably, from when he first pulled me around him. I don't want to look at it any more. I disgust myself. I turn away and rummage in a drawer for some jogging bottoms and a top. Now at least I am decent to the sight, even if not to the soul.

I slouch into the kitchen to make myself something to eat – I ought to eat, really, I ought to eat – but I feel nauseous again so I settle for dry toast and builder's tea. I take it back to the bedroom with me, with Dada's manuscript, and slide into bed. As far as I can tell, Xander still can't see me in here – and with the camera now broken, maybe he can't see me at all. Plumping the pillows behind me, I manage to nibble my way through the toast whilst surfing the manuscript. Crumbs accumulate on the bed covers but I am so long past caring whether my bed, or anything else in my life, is pristine, I let them. The stench of my own decay is strong in my nostrils, and the foetid smell of puke still lingers from the bathroom. It takes all my will power to just chew and swallow, chew and swallow, as I turn the pages. Having read all of Dada's books many times over, I'm disappointed to find that much of what I'm skimming is a re-hash of what he'd already written. Or maybe my attitude is subtly different. My eyes begin to blur and I lean my head back against the pillows. I will read one more chapter and then sleep. The manuscript isn't doing what I'd hoped it would do. In fact, it's doing the opposite. Even my professional admiration for him is waning because of a sense of anti-climax at how insipid the manuscript is. I turn the page and chapter six defines itself as being about *Amoral Beings*. It begins fairly dryly, but halfway down the page, it starts to open up, like a can of wriggling, invasive worms.

'It's not that we're immoral. More often we're actually amoral – lacking in an understanding of the moral. Who is to say what is moral and what is immoral? It depends on culture, history, tradition, psychological processes and conditions, expediency. Is war morally acceptable? No, in general. Was war against Hitler morally expedient? Yes. And we are continually adapting and refining our terms of morality against events happening in our world and our lives. Abortion is believed to be morally wrong by some, but what if it is to save the mother's life when the child cannot survive anyway? Stealing is morally wrong, society says – but if taking a stale loaf from a supermarket shelf manages to keep a starving child alive, is that immoral?

Perhaps what we need to do – more importantly than defining what is moral and what isn't – is to put ourselves in the position of those facing moral dilemmas, and experience those dilemmas for ourselves. In doing so we become moral beings, making a judgement of what is acceptable that might not be possible with as much compassion and understanding if we hadn't experienced those difficult choices.

As a moral being you need to develop a range of apprehensions of the world, a range of experiences and a range of conclusions based on those beliefs – not the ones that have been drummed into you by society. These may potentially be quite different – and yet equally defensible – as the beliefs another moral being has, based on their specific experiences and apprehensions. By opening up your mind to temporary amorality you allow yourself to fracture outmoded conventions and find new and better ways to live successfully in a world that is grey-scale, not merely black and white. Become truly modern man, responding to the challenges of reality. Not a repressed, restricted version of what custom and religion say is right, but adaptable, tough, incisive and REAL. A psychopath, in fact.'

I lay the page I am reading on the rest of the pile on my lap whilst I inwardly digest what he is suggesting. He is saying that no one set of moral beliefs is right. In fact, moral beliefs that some would denounce as actually immoral could – under some circumstances – be perfectly acceptable. Well, yes – I would agree with him there. I have already had this argument in part with Xander. But to be able to make true moral judgements, you need to experience both ends of the spectrum, and everything else in between? Be amoral in order to determine what is moral? That is a contentious idea to put forward. Fracture morality so we can see its constituent parts before reassembling it? Extrapolating what he's proposing, we should all abandon our historical moral code and persona and live for a while as another. One person's morals aren't another's but that doesn't necessarily make either right or wrong, just right or wrong for that particular person. Shift the persona and the morality issues shift too. Even more contentious is to pose the claim that a psychopath's standpoint is a suitable moral standpoint to adopt.

But is that what Xander has been pushing me to do? By being Abigail I become a different moral being, with different apprehensions of the acceptable – and therefore a different way of coping with morals in others that I can't accept as Gaby? I'd wanted the sex – as Abigail – but abhorred myself for that as Gaby. Abigail had been excited by stealing the credit card. Gaby had been horrified with herself.

The idea is both exciting and disturbing and my professional curiosity is piqued. What an incredible experiment to conduct to see if actually doing that changed morals completely, or developed a kind of hybrid of

193

the two. Who else but Dada would have been capable of such original thought? When I'd called him awesome as a child, I'd been right, although the memory of the context I'd used it in now makes my lips twist. My memories and childish nostalgia are warring and I'm not sure which is going to be triumphant. Xander is invading them too. Could Dada and Xander have known each other even though Xander claims not? How could Xander come up with precisely the concept that Dada was writing about here if they didn't – and decide to apply it to me? Or is he hand-in-glove with Director Anhelm and this is one of the challenges referred to at the interview – one that, despite what she claimed then – Gaby can't cope with. There are only two people who could, it seems to me. The creator of the idea itself, and Abigail.

Regardless of what else Dada has written in his manuscript, I can no longer rely on him, or what I remember of him. I will have to rely on Abigail, God help me. Abigail, with her ringlet curls and wide blue eyes. Abigail with her cold deconstruction of a situation and wilful defiance of control. Abigail, who could have sex on her desk with one client and then coolly walk away to meet another in order to arrange a clinical removal of the first one. I set the manuscript to one side and close my eyes, picturing how I think Abigail would look if she were real. How she would walk and talk, react and counter-react? What she would accept and not accept? I do not know. That is the problem. There is some of me in her and some of her in me. I need to separate the two.

I fall asleep, with Abigail on my mind and filling my dreams. When I awake, it is nearly dawn and a thin, tentative light is filtering through the window despite the closed curtains. The open weave allows it though in glimmers of grey; patchy promises of the world that is mine today. I lay, blank-minded, breathing in the early morning cold, until I slowly start to remember yesterday. Leaden, my heart sinks at the thought of who and what I need to do today. And yet – do I? I watch the digits on the clock click over to six-fifty. At seven the alarm will insist I get up and face reality, but for now, I can think. Ten minutes of thinking would not usually solve a problem for Gaby, the moral resolute, but for Abigail, the solution is clear. Set morals aside in the same way my patients have. As the alarm buzzes, the sun breaks through the curtains and the grey pinpricks turn to brilliant white light.

I swing my legs out of bed. The carpet still feels too soft and too obvious, but the smells of fresh paint and too-new wool have diminished today. I focus on the sensation of clouds under my feet – buoying me up –

that the pile of the carpet mimics. I stretch and the stiffness in my back reminds me of yesterday but I ignore the discomfort. That too will ease.

Will you be alright? You're going to be entirely on your own there.

Of course, I will. I'll be fine. And I'm not on my own...

The photograph on the chest of drawers laughs at me, upright now from where I have propped it against the paperweight. Man, woman and child, smiling up at me as if there would never be any questions to answer. There are even more now than there had been then – questions I already sense the answers to. I brush the glass with my fingertips then lay it flat, exposing the paperweight, with its irritating blemish. On reflection, I prop the photograph against the paperweight again. The lesser of the two evils.

I breathe slowly in and out and do some stretches to loosen up. The ache in my back eases a little, but it still nags at me. I straighten up and pad to the bathroom. The smell of puke has gone but the washbasin still looks soiled. I run hot water into it and swill it round. It swirls and settles with an oily slick on the top. I pull out the plug and leave it to drain. I'm going to have to clean it properly but for the moment I haven't the time, inclination or the energy to pitch into housework. I peer at myself in the mirror on the bathroom cabinet as the water gurgles away, leaning heavily on the rim of the basin. The position pitches me forward so that I am leering at myself close-quarters, every pore of my skin reflecting back at me. My hair looks lank and greasy and my face pallid. Only my wide blue-grey eyes have anything of Abigail in them. Mutinous. My back twinges and I try to calm it by stepping back and hunching my shoulders so my spine is lengthened. That only makes it worse. Maybe I actually pulled something yesterday. The sex *was* rough – very rough – and the desk top unforgiving. There are painkillers in the cabinet, but today I don't want to open it and see the empty pill bottle in there too, although I may have no choice if this spasm doesn't ease of its own accord.

'Oh, just do it.' I sound irritable and abrupt – completely unlike myself. And I'm talking to myself too! Shit! I yank open the cabinet door and stare at the empty space where the empty pill bottle used to be. That can't be right. I saw it there only yesterday. I push the contents of the cabinet around, dislodging the bottle of painkillers in the process. It falls into the remains of the murky washbasin water that is still draining, and floats there; a message in a bottle, but the message in the missing bottle is more disturbing.

'I haven't moved them. I haven't.' Now I sound whiny and pathetic. I hate myself.

Are you sure? You've been doing some weird things lately. Can you be sure of anything?

'I'm sure?' The whininess is less, but pathos still hovers in the question that I am posing of myself.

If you're really sure, then someone else has.

'No. No way.' But Xander had recorded me, even in my own apartment...

I grab up the bottle of painkillers and gulp down two, then replace it in the cabinet and slam the door shut.

'This needs to stop,' I say to my reflection. 'Today, this needs to stop. Get a grip, Gaby.'

I step into the shower, turning it on full force. It hammers on my skull and shatters into droplets over my skin. I can see a shadowy reflection of myself in the shiny new shower screen until it mists over. Now I've disappeared. I run my hands over my body, skimming the curves, lightly touching the curling down around my vagina and remembering the urgency of the need as I'd pushed myself onto Xander yesterday. I slip my finger inside and clench round it. The urge is still there but I control it. I let my hand fall back to my side as the water purges me. It's good to have a sense of yourself. *Know who you are. Accept who you are. Act on who you are.*

I rub the condensation from the shower screen and I reappear, a rippling, transient form, blurred by water droplets. Blue-grey eyes observe a partial me emerging from the steam. My hair curls in Medusa tails and my lips pout.

'And I know who I am now,' I say to it. 'I am both of us. And today, Abigail will be just fine.'

Chapter 23

Jenny's office is shut and locked when I arrive, but of course Xander is already in mine. I expect no less. He lounges in my chair, smile a brilliant white against the new addition to my room – window to window voile drapes, obscuring the blazingly bright autumn day sunshine to a muted glow.

'I like them. Always felt like a goldfish bowl in here, not that it seemed to matter yesterday.' He winks and I am astonished by his gall, and yet – again – unsurprised.

I cross to my desk, trying to appear impassive. I abandon my bag on the corner when I see the post-it note stuck to the phone.

"Meant to tell you last night, but was in too much of a rush. Hope you like them. They've been kicking around for ages but as no one was using the room, rather got forgotten. Got the caretaker to put them up first thing. Thought you might appreciate some privacy."

It's unsigned but I assume it must be from Jenny. Who else? My office door has stopped, halfway to closing, and in the corridor the sound of a banging door makes me jump.

'Good,' I reply coolly, stuffing the note in my top drawer – not that it matters. Xander would no doubt have already seen it, but how had he got in if I had the spare keys? I'd like to ask, but it will expose my ingenuousness. I go back to my door and peer down the corridor. There is no one in sight and from where I'm standing, I can still see that Jenny's door is closed. There would be a square of light falling on the wall print opposite otherwise, and making a pattern on the glass. I step back into my office and Xander is watching me with alert interest. If he'd been a dog, his ears would have been pricked. 'So, I think we have business to attend to, don't we?' I push the door and it slides jerkily shut, displacing whatever had wedged it before.

'Do we?' he is settling more comfortably in his seat as I turn to face him, his eyes narrowing.

'You wanted me to do something in exchange for what I want returned to me.'

'I haven't taken anything from you,' he says, face an icon for innocent surprise.

'You have taken a great deal from me, actually, but now I want it back, starting with those recordings.'

'Why, Abigail, you really do mean business then!' he laughs, but I ignore the mockery.

'Yes, I do.' I feel strong and unafraid as Abigail. I should have done this years ago. Dada was right. Temporary amorality *is* liberating. And Georges is getting me a number, anyway…

'OK,' he is openly studying me now. 'Things *have* moved on from yesterday. Alright, let's not mess around. In return for the items you would like from me –'

'And all of them – no keeping another copy to come back on me with later.'

'I take it you mean the recordings?'

'The recordings. The films. Whatever.'

'OK. All the films – no copies and no double-cross – I have one last thing I would like you to do. A kind of final challenge.'

'Final, and then no more? You'll leave me alone? No more pretending to be a client, because I know you're not. This is all one big game for you and I will tell Director Anhlem that when he returns.'

'Really? Well, there's the Abigail I was hoping to meet. Shame we have to part company as soon as I do, but… No, I'll leave you alone then. You do what I ask you to and after that we'll wipe both phones and destroy them.'

'And the cloud.'

'And the cloud.'

'Alright. What is it you want me to do?'

'I'll be in touch. The walls here, well, I think you know what I mean.'

He is getting up to go and contrarily I don't want him to now – not until I know why, anyway. I stop him in his tracks with, 'I have one more question for you before you go.'

He is almost to the door and I think for a moment that he is going to ignore me, but he stops and turns.

'And what is that?'

'Why?'

'But you know why, Abigail.'

'No, I don't. I wouldn't be asking you if I did.'

'You have it all written down. Just like your father would have expected you to. I saw it yesterday.'

'The notebook?'

'Yes, the notebook.'

'What has that got to do with you and the way you've been persecuting me?'

'Persecuting you? Oh, I think that's a bit strong. I thought we were having quite a lot of fun yesterday actually. But, never mind. Maybe you should be asking yourself what has it got to do with you, Dr McCray? You're your father's daughter. Work it out.'

He turns on his heel, a clipped, military turn, and he's gone, leaving me staring after him, open-mouthed. Well, Abigail had achieved something at least – a deal, but what had he meant about the notebook? And why the sudden reversion to calling me Dr McCray? Was it because the game was over and his acknowledgement of me as me signified that, or was he suggesting the contents of the notebook related to me?

I rummage in my bag for the notebook, and there it is – alongside the empty bottle of pills I had expected to find in the bathroom cabinet this morning. Full. Abigail or no Abigail, I could cry, but she won't let me. *I wouldn't cave in so neither will you. I am not a wimp and I will not let you make me one. Get a grip, Gaby.*

The notebook has fallen open at the page after the one I last read.

"Choose what you do with it, right or wrong, but choose for yourself. If we are entitled to nothing else in life, we are entitled to make our own choices."

And on the next page,

"... others' views of morality are not valid unless we validate them ourselves. Only our own view of morality is right for us."

I hang over them, arching my back as I rest my elbows on the desk and my chin in my clasped hands. They read so like Dada's words – something I would expect to find in his notes now I have started reading them in earnest – and yet they're mine. Maybe I have copied them from his manuscript? But then why have I written them in the notebook without remembering having done so? Or hidden it behind the books in the bookcase here? I puzzle over the two pages. It is my handwriting, even though I think they are Dada's words, not mine. I sigh, and Abigail loses her grip on me. My back is aching again too. The painkiller's relief has been so temporary I might as well have not bothered. I pull the chair out from behind my desk and slump into it, shuffling the notebook and the pill bottle so they are centre stage on my desk, directly in front of me. Both are mysteries. Both rely on my memory being accurate and neither feature in anything I can remember over the last few days, let alone further back. At least I can succumb to despair and confusion in privacy, thanks to Jenny and the drapes – except Abigail won't let me do that either. Her irritable prod comes at exactly the same time as Jenny's phone call.

'Ah, you are in. I assumed you were but I wasn't sure of your movements this morning.'

'Yes, I'm in – and thanks for the new additions.'

'Oh,' she sounds bemused.

'Your note and the curtains?'

'Curtains?'

'In my office.'

'Oh, right. Should have organised it before you moved in. No one likes living in a glass house – unless they're not worried about being a target. I hope they make you feel more at ease there.' There's a pause and then, 'and I have a message to pass on to you. It's from Georges Thierone. He's at the Embassy if you need to contact him. He said you'd understand.'

'Oh, thanks. I do.'

'Good, and would you mind if I asked a favour? I'm not feeling wonderful today. It's why I was late in so it was a good job I gave you the spare keys last night. As there is only you in, but no clients due in today, would you mind if I went home again? Tomorrow is the weekend anyway and the Director and the rest of the team will be back on Monday. Could you hold the fort and lock up when you're ready to go?'

'Of course. You go. I'll manage.

'Thanks, I appreciate it.'

The phone clicks to a soft purring sound and I hang up. So, Georges has something for me. I pick up the receiver and the phone is still purring at me. I put it down again. Or maybe I should use my own mobile? No possibility of anyone listening in then, and I'd feel easier ringing if I know Jenny isn't even in the building too. This phone call feels far too significant to make with witnesses around. I slide out from behind the desk and open my office door. The corridor is as deserted as before and there is still no square of light reflecting on the glass of the print on the wall opposite Jenny's office door. I debate whether to check or wait a little longer. I decide to check.

Her door is locked when I try it, but I have the master key to it so what the hell. I slide it into the lock and turn, holding my breath. What will I say if Jenny is in there, waiting? *Stupid! Why would she?* Abigail's voice is scathing in my head. *She's already told you she's going home.* Resolutely I turn the handle and push the door open. The room is empty, the only sign of Jenny the slightest trace of her perfume, lingering on the air. Otherwise the room smells stuffy, shut in. The sunlight streaming through the window doesn't help, heating it up like a small greenhouse. I change my mind about preferring Jenny's office to mine. Now with the cocooning drapes, mine is by far the more desirable. Strange how such a small change can make such a major difference. I straighten my shoulders and walk inside the room. And actually, my back ache seems to have eased again now as well. Abigail feels good; in charge – and ironically, she is, until Monday.

The filing cabinets grin back at me from their home along the back wall, handles like clown mouths upturned and amused, hanging under the nose which is the range card A to F, G to O, P to Z, and the two eyes which are the double locks. I retrieve the bunch of keys from the office door and examine the separate ring attached to it. These must be the keys to the filing range. Naomi Williams next to James Openshaw. I really want to see why. I unlock the G to O cabinet and get onto my knees so I can rifle through the bottom drawer. And there they are; Naomi Williams and James Openshaw nestling together like lovers. I pull both of them out and spread their contents out across the floor. They don't take up much space. They contain one sheet each, which says *'refer R. Anhelm 3-1-2010'*. I replace the pages and put the files back into the filing cabinet. None the wiser. I am about to close the filing cabinet when I wonder what is in the other files. I pull out two at random. One is exactly the same, apart from the date, but the other says *'refer A McCray 24-6-2005. C/AG review'*. A McCray – not G McCray. The patient's surname is Jeffries, not that it matters. It's who the referral is to that matters. Not a typo, not an error, because I wasn't a part of Ethos then. For God's sake, I wasn't even fifteen then. That came four days later. Four days before Dada died. I pull out another and it says the same, but again with a different date. Six more produce more dates and the same instruction, M. Norrish, G Heland, L Morton, A Parsimon, J Orland-Roper. They also have the endorsement, *'candidate Chiaroscuro'*. The last of them has the same phrase but the date is only this year. I look at the name on the folder and nearly drop it. G A McCray.

Gabriella Adele McCray.

'That's me! It must be.' I scrabble to remove the other papers from the folder because this one actually contains more than one page.

'6th April 2004. Proposed as suitable candidate for C/AG review. Monitoring commenced.

24th June 2005. Access A McCray only. C/AG review to commence.

27th July 2005. Re-presented with extreme depression following death of father. C/AG review postponed. Regression and aversion therapy replaced by Sineptin. Discharged 22nd October 2005 to parental observation. Remote C/AG review in due course if still suitable.'

Sineptin? The pills in the little empty pill bottle that usually resided in my bathroom cabinet but now sat on my desk, full, were called Primaton. Sineptin is an expensive and rarely used drug. Dredging my memory, I think I may have come across it before, when I was studying drug use in psychology, particularly the psychology of depression, but it's not something I'd anticipated coming into contact with in relation to myself. I remember it as a combination of wipe-out medication and an attempt to manipulate neuropeptides. I can't have been on Sineptin. I wouldn't have a memory at all! This must be wrong, like the suggestion that I was once a patient of Ethos. It was the Director's son I'd seen – entirely independently and without even knowing Ethos existed at the time. And what is 'C/AG review'? That is first mentioned *before* Dada died. Could Dada have once worked for Ethos? In fact, given the dates of some of the referral notes, had he been working for Ethos *when* he died, and been the person originally referring me for 'C/AG review'? The whole thing is disturbing to say the least. I feel like a lab rat under observation. I can feel my heart connecting with my ribs and making me unsteady, like my whole body is pulsating. This is all wrong. Everything is all wrong.

I collect everything back up and re-file it. In the meantime, Georges is waiting for me to call, but I will definitely use my own phone now. I close the filing cabinet and go back to my room, having locked everything back up in Jenny's. The day has lost its brightness and the clouds are rolling over again. It mimics my mood. The corridor is still bright, like sunlight, because the overhead lights come on automatically –

movement sensors, I guess – but instead of my room being flooded with admittedly *muted* light, now the voile drapes are in place it's gloomy and full of foreboding. The bottle of pills and the notebook wait for me in the middle of my desk, reminding me that I am quite possibly out of control. I open the bottle, pressing down hard on its security cap, and it releases its treasure. I tip the pills onto the desk top and count them. Twenty-six. The label on the bottle says thirty. Four are missing. Two days' worth. Have I been taking the pills for the last two days without remembering? Would it account for my less than rational behaviour recently? The pills do have side effects, but it was so long ago that I was told what they were that I can't remember them now, although neither I, nor Romaine would have accepted me taking anything potentially risky. And I had taken them continuously without ill effect for years. Primaton is a minor mood-lifter and hardly indispensable. I could almost have been taking a placebo for all the effect it probably had on me really. It had only been the irony of how inappropriate it was for a therapist to be on medication herself that had made me decide to stop taking them. Ironic that we look after ourselves less than we look after others. I drag my laptop out of my bag and search the internet for Primaton. The side effects are minor – insomnia, sweats, diarrhoea. Well, I've suffered from none of that. Discontinuance? Fatigue and sometimes a feeling of being unsettled until the body adjusts. They are a very minor SSRI. No big deal. Sineptin, though… It takes a while but eventually I find a paper on it from about fifteen years ago. Also an SSRI, but not in common usage.

"SSRI form of anti-depressant, used mainly for depressives with aggressive and/or self-harming tendencies. Boosts neurotransmitter activity and serotonin levels on a counter-reactive basis by modification of neuropeptides. Side effects: neurotransmitter activity may be volatile, leading to mild to excessive confusion, depending on dosage and use, plus a higher level of susceptibility to suggestion than the norm. If stable after a monitored period of use, may be used long term. However, regular monitoring should be sustained and care taken to avoid exposure to situations that may cause abnormal stress. Inclination to paranoid delusion may be increased in these circumstances."

I remain reading the screen over, and over again. Inclination to paranoid delusion. Regular monitoring. Have I had regular monitoring?

Certainly not by a doctor. OK, so maybe I exhibited no signs of side effects but if the medication officially required regular monitoring, I should have received it. I hadn't so whoever had prescribed it for me would have been struck off for their lack of control of my care. But then why record I have been treated with it – and by whom? I grind my teeth and the butterflies are swarming in my chest again – no, not butterflies. Angry hornets. How could Romaine let this happen? But that's only if it has – if the record is true. It could be a complete fabrication – nonsensical though that would be – by the Director. It occurs to me that Jenny would know what is in my file as well since she is the queen of the records. Maybe she knows what a 'C/AG Review' is too. Or Romaine. She has to be party to everything that involved me back then – and until I came here. The hornets swarm, and my throat burns with rising bile, but the only people that I can ask about it are unavailable for the moment – the Director and Jenny until Monday morning, and Romaine... Actually, Romaine, I could visit over the weekend. I have more than one question for Romaine now. I close the laptop and put it in my bag, replacing it with my mobile phone. I toy with it. *Go on.* Abigail is impatient.

'There's so much I don't know – don't understand yet, though.'

Makes no difference to Xander. He's a thorn in your side whatever else is going on. Sort that problem out first then you can concentrate on the others properly.

'But Georges was clear. It's a big step.'

So was coming here, but you did it – moved away from Romaine and the easy life you could have had with Mark.

'That was different.'

How?

'This was to be a fresh start.'

Yeah, was... Until Xander interfered.

She's right. Whilst I wait for the questions about myself to be answered, there's one I answer for myself with just a phone call.

'Georges Thierone, please? I've been advised I can get him on this number?'

'US or UK contingent?' She sounds bored.

'UK, I imagine.'

'And who shall I say is calling?' Sing-song bored. She must ask the same question a hundred times a day.

'Dr McCray.'

'Thank you.'

There are beeps and clicks on the line and then Georges' voice comes through, muffled and distant.

'Dr McCray? Thanks for calling back. About that research you wanted. I'm afraid I can't help but I have the number of someone who might. Have you got a pen and paper?' He barely pauses before rattling it off. 'It's 07795 343267.'

'Is that Chiaroscuro's number? What do I say to them?'

'You simply tell them your problem and ask if they can do something about it for you.'

'And what will it cost me?

'That will be up to them.'

'But I'm not rich.' I think of Jessica Morgan and her private jets and team of sycophants.

'It won't cost in cash. But only ask if you're prepared to do whatever they ask in return. Only do this if there's no other way of dealing with the situation. If you can defuse it yourself, try to.'

'I don't know yet.'

'Then wait until you do, but the number is only current for one call, and I won't be able to get you another – OK? Remember what I said about them.'

'I remember.' At least my memory is clear there – Georges' stern expression and eagerness to leave after he'd agreed to provide me with a number. These people meant business and I need to give this some serious thought before I find out exactly what business that might be with me, regardless of Abigail's insistent urging. Yes, I want the problem solved, but the price has to be affordable.

He is gone without a goodbye and I suspect it's the last I will hear from him. I turn my phone off and put the slip of paper in my purse. Suddenly I am exhausted – and feeling queasy again too. All I want to do now is go home and sleep, and amusingly, as boss for the day, I can do just that. The notebook follows the phone into my bag and the pill bottle is just about to as well, when I hesitate. The chemist's label isn't the usual one from home – Romaine's home now, not mine. It is local to my new home. The address is 36 Putney High Street. I may be going home to sleep but there's one errand I need to run before I get there. Who prescribed the pills for me and who got the prescription filled? I stuff the bottle into my bag and zip the top shut. It bulges with my secrets, sacred and profane, and I carry them with me like the mark on the paperweight, some of them flaws I may never be able to cover up if I get this wrong.

On my way to the tube station, a familiar ping from my bag makes my heart sink lower into my gut.

'Quid pro quo,' it says. Then, 'media to follow.'

The media is a photograph of Jessica Morgan.

I stop and balance my bag on the low retaining wall of the building next door to Ethos' offices, careless that it is muddy and lichen-covered and it will stain my expensive cream leather bag that was a present to myself for landing the job. Not quite Jessica Morgan standard but it had taken a fair chunk out of my bank balance. I text back, 'I don't understand.'

'Remove her.'

'What does that mean?'

'Whatever you want it to mean. Just do it, conclusively. Media memory will be wiped when confirmed, or distributed to press in forty-eight hours if not.'

'Wait – you mean kill her?' I wait but the screen remains blank. 'Xander, please explain. Why?'

I wait longer. Still nothing. Then I try ringing. It rings out. I try again and again and again and it is on the sixth attempt that I accept he isn't going to reply or explain. It is what it is. Remove her. Or else. I ring Georges again and go through the same sing-song questioning routine with another bored female voice. After what seems an age, Georges answers. Overhead the threatening clouds drop their payload and the rain starts to teem down, soaking me through within seconds. I splutter through the rivulets that flow from my rat's tail hair, down my face and into my mouth, trying to explain what has just happened.

'What do I do now?' I blink as the rain makes it through the curtain of my lashes and makes my eyes smart.

'That's up to you.'

'Kill her?'

'If that's what you think he means? You have to decide that for yourself.'

'But why? Why would he want me to kill her?'

'He gave you no reason?'

'No.' The desperation in my voice makes it high and reedy.

'You must already know then.'

'I don't! Oh, my God, I don't!'

'Think, Dr McCray. What connection is there between them?'

'None. Apart from they're both my clients.'

'And what is it they are being treated for?'

'Jessica for...' I hesitate. The last vestige of client confidentiality – and my ethics – is about to be abandoned if I tell him. 'I shouldn't say.'

'Then I can't really help you, can I?'

'Client confidentiality,' I mumble.

There is a pause, and he asks gently, 'Jessica who?' I bite my lip. 'Look, I have no chance of helping you figure out what the connection might be if I know nothing at all.'

'Jessica Morgan,' I blurt out. There. It is done. I have completed my damnation. 'And Client X, but I don't know what his real name is. Jenny could find out for me, but I'd have to explain to her why I wanted to know, then the Director would get involved because the name is in his safe and... Georges, I have made such a mess of things, and now I've even contravened professional guidelines.'

His chuckle is rich and disconcerting. For a moment, I wonder if he is setting me up too.

'Dr McCray, I think you've done a lot worse than contravene professional guidelines, but let's not pick up on semantics. This Client X, he is the one with links to Chiaroscuro?'

'Yes.'

'Has he mentioned Jessica Morgan at any time?'

'No.'

'Has he mentioned what he does at any time?'

'No – well, yes. Asset Assimilator.'

'Ha!' This time the chuckle is preceded by an abrupt bout of laughter. 'What would you say is the defining characteristic of your Jessica Morgan?'

'Power. She's power-hungry.'

'And has she mentioned Chiaroscuro to you – ever?'

'No, I don't think so. She's been more on about... ' Self-preservation stoppers my mouth. Not that there is anything to damn me more than I already am, but there's a vibration lingering on a string somewhere that tunes me into danger. 'She's been more overtly interested in me, than anything else.'

'You.' His voice is quieter. I can imagine him turning the word over and examining it – and me. 'Then the link is you. There is something about you that links both of them, and requires your Client X to neutralise your Miss Morgan – maybe before she passes on to you what that link is. Is there anything at all that is common ground to both of them?'

'Dada,' I say eventually. 'My father. Jessica paints him quite differently to the way he was. Client X knows a lot about him too.'

'Then maybe they also know each other through him, or something he was involved in?'

And there I am, back to Dada, the reason I am where I am. The reason I'm always questioning and never sure. The reason I'm wondering now why there are things I don't understand but think I should. The reason there's a file on me labelling me as a candidate for Chiaroscuro?

'Jessica claims to know why Dada died.'

'Does she? Then maybe your Client X had something to do with that too.'

'And Chiaroscuro... Oh God, no!'

'Maybe.'

I can tell he is waiting for me to go on. I can hear the anticipation in the silence.

'Would Chiaroscuro, even though... '

'Like I said before. Chiaroscuro offers a solution, whatever and whoever is involved. If you think they have a solution for you, that's your decision. All I've done is give you a contact.'

'Do I ring it or text it?' I ask, then clamp my hand to my mouth. Do I seriously want to know? 'Oh my God, this is terrible. I don't know what to do. Oh my God!'

'Dr McCray, you have a problem. You have to fix it. That is all. Detach yourself from how it is fixed. That is Chiaroscuro's problem if you decide to use them. I must go now. I'm in meetings – and I should tell you I'm not on this number after this call. Moving on to my next project. I'll be in touch if I need your help in the future in return for the number. Thanks for your time and the information. It's been very helpful. Good luck.'

I sit heavily on the wall, with the phone in my lap and the rain, pouring, pouring as I drown. What should I do? There is not even an amoral answer to this question. A lorry thunders past and the puddle he disturbs splashes up onto the pavement and over my feet, but I no longer care. I feel sick, exhausted and miserable. There is only one thing I can do, whether I am Abigail or Gaby for now. Go home. To my childhood home, and the only person I can ask for help – and perhaps, answers, if she will give me them. Romaine.

Chapter 24

The house looks exactly the same as when I left it a week ago. Wisteria curling around the front door and gnarling its way across the front of the house. Skeletal, now that the foliage and blooms have all died off. Bone white fingers crawling the house. I always think it's such a shame – so beautiful in summer, so blasted in winter. Seasonally sad, like some people are. Me included, perhaps? Except this season seems to have lasted almost half my life so far. The melodramatist in me would say the sun went south permanently when Dada died. The psychologist would possibly agree – but with clever technical interpretations and methodology too. The realisation shocks me like a firecracker thrown at my feet would. There – I've admitted it to myself now. Why I haven't done so until now, I don't know. It is so obvious! I am permanently winter-laden. I'm not sure if it's that way for Romaine too. She has never shown any interest in meeting anyone else since, but she doesn't seem to labour under the weight of grief I still do.

I still have my front door key but it seems wrong to just let myself in having now officially left home, and it was about time at twenty-six! I ring the doorbell instead, counting to three as I always used to as a child before I was granted the honour of my own key, and waiting for the first chime of the bell to strike. Ding-dong, ding-dong, ding-dong, ding-dong... The Westminster Chimes. Probably the most common chime in the whole of the UK, but it seems peculiar to my home and my world with its three-second delay and prolonged last resonation. I take a step back from the door step and take a fresh look at what had been my home for pretty much the whole of my life, the firecracker still popping and hissing at my feet. It has taken leaving here and coming back to clarify something that should have been blindingly obvious to me all this time – particularly with my professional training. I have been revolving round *why* Dada had died, but really it was the fact that he *had* died that has unsettled me for the last eleven years. The why is probably irrelevant, in

209

the end... I can hear Abigail goading me about it, even now, whispering in my ear – taunting with suggestions that I already know why anyway. *It was you. He didn't want to be around you any more. You caused it. You know you did.*

'I didn't. Whatever caused it, it wasn't me!' I say it just before the door opens and Romaine greets me, surprised but with genuine pleasure.

'Gab!' She pulls me into an all-encompassing embrace. I have always wondered how such a tiny woman could give such capacious hugs. I tower over her and yet she manages to enfold every part of me in reassurance. As I revel in the luxury of love, up close, I notice she has grey hairs growing amongst the rich brown. She gently releases me and holds me at arm's length. 'I knew,' she says.

'What?'

'That you were... uneasy about something.' The Irish brogue is muted now but still redolent in the way she pronounces 'r' – a kind of 'urr' rather than 'r'. I used to try to mimic her when I was younger, thinking that if Dada loved her so, it must be because of the way she was different to other women. The accent, the tiny stature, the dark curling hair. I tried dying my hair once – with disastrous results – luckily whilst he was at one of his conferences so Romaine was able to whisk me off to the hairdresser before he returned and salvage something of my ruined locks. He didn't seem to notice the rather straw-thatch texture it had for ages afterwards, anyway. Of course, I could never do anything about my height – other than round my shoulders and slump. Probably why I get back ache from the soft consulting room chairs now. The damage of the curvature is so well set in, their ergonomics simply prod it into life.

'Can you read me that well, even over the phone?'

'I always know when you're unhappy, Gab.'

'Have I ever not been?'

She looks a little sad. 'To be honest, no.'

'Wow. That's pretty blunt.'

'I wonder if blunt might not be what you need now. I think you've come home for some truths.'

She is right. On both counts. The firecracker fizzes a last gasp at my feet. I have been unhappy for as long as I can remember. Even before Dada died. The childhood memories the red ball in the lobby to my apartment block resurrected jump around with the firecracker as it dies.

'You're right. I have,' I say and the tears start falling and won't stop. She pulls me gently inside and I let her take over. I am a child again and

Romaine will make it alright, whatever the problem. I no longer want to challenge her over what she knows about my real mother, or about why Ethos seems to have figured in my life for over a decade without me knowing. I just want to be comforted.

It takes some while and several mugs of tea to calm me. Maybe it is also the familiarity of everything here. No new wool carpet smells or fresh paint. Just the well-remembered smell of sunlight on beeswax, old tea garden roses and the occasional whiff of incense, musky and exotic, quixotically underlying the otherwise essentially English aromas. I suppose that sums Romaine up too. She is her own person. She might be other people's person too – Dada's and mine – but she always has that still core to her that defies definition. She is simply Romaine. Perhaps it is that which Dada loved about her and which no one could emulate, no matter how hard they tried by dying their hair, copying her accent, or hunching their shoulders? It also strikes me, now I am reviewing the me of the last twenty-six years – or rather, Abigail is prompting me to – odd how I have never felt any resentment towards her for the fact that Dada had loved her, but not... *Yes,* Abigail nudges me. *Say it. But not you.*

'If I ask you something, something awkward, will you tell me the truth, no matter how unpleasant?'

'If you want to know it, Gab, I'll tell you.'

She is sitting in the rocking chair opposite me, almost swallowed up by it, a blue patchwork cushion spilling out one side between the seat and the arm. By accident, or maybe by design, I am sitting in Dada's chair. The old dun brown leather wing-back chair that he always said was the only chair in the house with enough gravitas for an academic to sit in. It is as hard as iron and the leather is slippery. Why anyone would want to sit in it, I don't know. I would like to move but I don't want to interrupt the moment.

'Someone told me something about my real mother. I want to know if it's true.'

'What did they tell you?'

'That Dada left her for a younger model, and she abandoned me with him as a punishment. Because he didn't want me.'

'That's a very cruel thing to have said. Who was it?'

'It doesn't matter – just someone who says they knew her and Dada at the time. Is it true?'

'Which?'

'Both.'

'He was never good with children, that much is true. What went on between your mother and him? That I don't know.' She shakes her head gently at me. 'And nor should you let someone's malicious take on events of twenty-five years ago affect you. You are your own truth. Everyone else's version is purely that – a version.'

'But recently I've been remembering things that call my version into question – amongst other things.'

'In what way?'

'Well, what do you remember most about my childhood?'

'I remember you as a loving but somewhat vulnerable girl. Like most girls.'

'But what do you remember us doing – you, me and Dada. Do you remember us picnicking in the park, going to the seaside, playing catch? Because I don't. Not the three of us, anyway. The two of us – you and me, yes… '

'But Dada wasn't like that, Gab. He was an academic. You remember what he called himself. A dry old psychologist. He wasn't a ball games in the park kind of person. He wasn't good with children. He did other things with you – talk, explain, teach. That's why you've achieved so much at only twenty-six.'

'I wasn't just children. I was *his* child.'

We watch each other in silence. She takes a deep breath in, and then gets up and goes over to the Welsh dresser at the far end of the room. A stray frond of bony wisteria has escaped its bindings and is tapping against the French window. The room is warm. Romaine has lit a fire and it is crackling happily. The watery sunlight is even attempting a come-back against the puffball clouds filling the sky, but I feel cold nevertheless. Romaine returns with a pile of albums. She spreads them on the rug in front of the fire and invites me to join her.

'Your father was a complicated man, Gab. He didn't always show love and affection when he should, but it doesn't mean he didn't feel it. His life was his work – with distractions. I was a distraction once. Other things and people have been distractions too. That doesn't negate any of what he was, it just makes it more complex.'

She opens the first album. There is a photograph of Romaine, Dada and me at the seaside. He looks impassive. Romaine looks happy and I look very small and awkward, clutching a giant-sized ice-cream.

'Pretty much our first photo all together.' She smiles, clearly remembering it well – unlike me. There is an inscription underneath; a slip of paper, stuck on. 'June 1994, Torquay.'

'I don't remember that.'

'No, I don't suppose you do. You were very small. We'd been together properly for about a month then. A family.'

'How did you meet?'

'Oh, university stuff. I was helping with a project. That sort of thing.' She turns the page and there are more of the same – but in different places, different clothes, different times of the year. Variations on the theme, often without Romaine. They range from 1994 to 1997.

'There's not that many of you.'

'I was usually official photographer,' she replies, smiling ruefully. 'That was my role – the archivist. I didn't mind. It was nice doing it. It's always nice recording good things.'

'I don't see a red ball,' I can't stop Abigail's thoughts slipping out.

'A red ball?' Romaine looks bemused. 'I don't think you had one. You had a doll you adored, though.'

'Abigail.'

'Yes!' her face lights up. 'She was a special present – from Dada because you fell in love with her as soon as you saw her in Harrods. She cost a small fortune at the time. I don't know what happened to her, but there were specific ways he showed his love and those are what you need to remember about him.'

'I remember things that suggest what I was told was right though.' She turns another page and there is a clipping about an award Dada had won – one of many. 'Recently I remember him more interested in his work than me. Or you.'

She turns another page and a portrait shot of him stares back at us. It was taken at one of his book launches. In the background the crowds mill, awaiting the master's return.

'Perhaps he was, latterly. I tried to be there for you though, Gab.'

'And you were, but the gaps showed.'

She looks up at me, forehead creased with frown lines. 'You say recently you've been remembering things? How recently? And what do you think has prompted this? What has been said to you?'

'Part-memories seem to just be popping up – different to how I'd been thinking life was.'

'Are you still taking your medication regularly?'

'I stopped.'

'Oh, Gab!' her eyes are wide and her mouth open. 'Don't do that.

You need it.'

'Why? Why do I need it? I'm not mentally ill or depressed. I'm confused and disappointed.'

'When did you stop taking it?'

'A while ago. Before I left here. I decided that as it was fresh start, I would do without it.'

'Oh dear,' she shakes her head and she's very Irish now. 'No, Gab, you can't just stop taking it. At the very least you should have talked to me about it and then withdrawn slowly from it, under observation.'

'I've read up on it. It's a SSRI anti-depressant, that's all. And I did withdraw slowly – over a month or more, so I'd stopped by the time I left.'

'It's more than that. It activates neurotransmitter function. It stimulates activity too. It's not widely used because of that, and probably what you read was the bare bones about it.'

'And?'

'I was told when it was first prescribed for you that removing the stimulation without replacing it with something else could leave you fluctuating between depressive and excessive.'

'Meaning?'

'Susceptible to suggestion, and... '

'And?'

'Suppressed thoughts and the memories linked to them could re-emerge, but possibly distorted because they'd been stored in your long-term memory without having been rationalised first.'

'You mean I'm not remembering things right?'

'I don't know, but if you're finding your memories confusing, perhaps. This is how it was, Gab.' She turns the pages back to the first photo of us all on the beach. 'We were a family and maybe Dada wasn't the most child-friendly father around, but no one is perfect.'

'And his work? The work he was so involved in? What did that entail?'

'Well, probably much as you recall. He lectured, he mentored, he had to work away a lot... '

'Doing what?'

She shrugs and I know – whereas she has been telling her version of the truth before – she is hiding something now. Romaine might know me brain and soul, but I know her too. 'Conferences, assignments, projects he contributed to.'

'Ethos?'

She shuts the album, and reaches for another. I put my hand over hers to stop her opening it.

'Ethos,' she agrees, looking up at me apologetically.

'Why didn't you tell me when I applied to them?'

'Why would I? It didn't make any difference to you.'

'But it does. They have a file on me, Romaine. It says they were treating me even before Dada died!'

'Oh dear,' she says again. 'You weren't meant to know about that, but they weren't treating you. They were observing you. It was long-term project Dada was interested in. Recording the potential and the ultimate achievement of children with identifiably high-attaining parents to see if it was nature or nurture that would push them on most.'

'I was a lab rat? My own father made me into a lab rat?' I can barely contain the disgust in my voice and I don't know whether it is me or Abigail who is expressing it now.

'No, not at all. You were a kind of control because – obviously Dada was the one recording your progress and running the research. Of course, he would protect you in the process, so although I didn't like you being part of it, it was difficult to object. After all,' she adds sadly. 'You were his daughter, not mine. I'd never have allowed anything to have adversely affected you because of it, Gab. You must believe that.'

She places her other hand on top of mine and presses it hard, sandwiches it between hers so I can't remove it. There are tears in her eyes. I believe her again, but I am still angry. Abigail is still angry too. Muttering in the back of my mind, *you see, you see. That's why. You do know why.*

'It said that Ethos treated me after Dada died too. I thought it was Stephen Anders.'

'It was.' She's frowning again.

'Stephen Anders-Anhelm. Director Anhelm's son.'

'Oh. You found out?' Her mouth has dropped open once more.

'Director Anhelm told me when I went for the interview. He assured me it was fine – not important – so I left it. It seems it obvious why, now.'

'Oh no. I wish you'd told me. I would have... ' she pauses. 'I don't know what I would have done,' she concludes miserably. Her mouth turns down at the corners and now I want to comfort her. We have both been betrayed. 'I didn't know that, Gab, really I didn't. Stephen came highly recommended by one of Dada's colleagues – I can't remember who now – and you were so angry and mixed up at the time, I was at my wit's end. You wouldn't come out of your room, wouldn't eat, wouldn't talk. Just sat there on the floor cradling that paperweight you'd given him in your lap, or hitting yourself with it so you had bruises all up and down your arms and legs.'

'I don't remember that.'

'That would be the Sineptin. It helps suppress the memories that are destructive – that undermine you –'

'I know. And releases them when you stop taking it. So, it's true. That's what I'm taking? Why didn't you tell me? It's heavy-duty stuff. I should have been told the side effects of what I was taking. I am an adult!'

'You weren't then. You were under age and I was advised that telling you what the drug could do would be counter-productive because you would have fought it – actively tried to remember what the drug was attempting to suppress until you were in a more robust frame of mind. It was never intended as a long-term solution. The counselling was what should have taken over from it, but after a couple of months, Stephen suggested that counselling then wasn't the best way to approach things. He recommended we continue the drug and that he and I monitor you. If I noticed any return of the symptoms, to contact him again, but otherwise letting sleeping dogs lie was the best solution until you were older. Then counselling might have a positive use. I was going to talk to you about it all once you'd settled into this job, but... well, here we are now, talking about it anyway.'

'So, what is a C/AG review?'

'Where does that come from? Your file?'

'Yes. It says I was identified as suitable for Chiaroscuro, but after Dada's death the C/AG review was to be deferred until after I was treated. Or done remotely.'

'And who has this file on you?'

'Ethos.'

'Ethos? Oh.' Her face closes in momentarily.

'And what is Chiaroscuro?'

She shakes her head and then says slowly, 'I suppose it's something to do with Dada's project, but I don't know what it stands for. I didn't know anything about what he did for them. It was confidential.' She looks away, picking at a loose thread on her blouse.

'I'll bet. And what about the manuscript you sent me?'

'What manuscript?' She stops picking.

'You sent me the manuscript he was working on when he died. With the suggestion that I edit it so it could be published as a kind of epitaph.'

She shakes her head again, eyes deep drowning pools.

'No. I know nothing about a manuscript. I didn't even know he was writing anything else before he died, and anyway... ' she pauses, and shrugs her shoulders. 'He was away so much... '

'It was on his desk that day – ' I stop, the memory slipping away like sand filtering through my fingers – the sand from the beach pictures, the memories the drug has suppressed but that are now trickling back to trick me. Romaine is waiting for me to finish, a strange expression on her face, quickly replaced by a too-bright smile.

'You're probably remembering a manuscript from before.'

'No, I have it. I actually have it. Back at the flat. It's in a blue plastic wallet and it's all about amorality. He gave it the working title of *Fractured Morality.*'

'Are you *sure,* Gab?'

Now I'm not, even though Abigail is prodding me. *Of course you are. You've been reading it the last two nights. But don't tell her. She's been less than honest with you. Why should she know all your business?* I want to protest aloud 'because I need her,' but I know Abigail will throw scorn on that so I say nothing, swallowing it down like bile. Abigail is a double-edged sword. It's enough to stop me mentioning Xander though, and that is good. There is enough doubt being poured on my clarity of thought already without me telling Romaine that I'm being blackmailed for the two shameful acts on my part, and to cap it, I'm considering getting a contract taken out on him.

I mutter instead that I'm feeling tired and maybe we could have something to eat? My stomach growls, conveniently for me, and Romaine at last removes her hand from mine. I whip mine away before it can be trapped again. She struggles to her feet, taking the albums with her.

'Getting old,' she mock-grumbles. I think of Jenny and her transactionalism. There is something of that to the photo albums. A record of what should be, now what was.

'You're not old,' I say, unfolding my longer limbs and stretching them before clambering up.

'Forty-one,' she replies. 'Next stop fifty. That is getting old.' She leaves the albums in a pile on the edge of the Welsh dresser. 'In case you want to look at them again,' she adds lightly as she heads for the door.

217

'How about some home-made soup? I have a batch on the hob at the moment. Carrot and coriander.'

'Sounds good,' I say, equally casually, although the stomach growling feels more like stomach mutiny now. I follow her out the kitchen and lounge in the doorway as she collects up bowls and soup spoons.

'There's some fresh bread over there too. Will you cut and butter it for me?'

Romaine has her back to me and the grey streaks are even more evident from the rear. I'm suddenly engulfed with grief at the thought of her growing old and dying – leaving me. On impulse, I leave the uncut bread and go over to her, wrapping my arms round her as she stirs the soup. She half turns and smiles up at me.

'It's good to be home,' I say, to cover my emotion.

'It's good to have you home. Like old times.'

Romaine's hair tickles my arms. It reaches almost to her waist and it will always be her crowning glory, even with streaks of grey.

'Has your hair grown even longer?' I ask.

'Probably. I'm becoming quite unkempt these days,' but there is a lack of concern to her tone that is typically Romaine. And unkempt is so far from describing her, it's a joke.

'You could never be unkempt.' I release her and go back to the bread, warm and content inside – something I haven't felt in a while now. She continues stirring the soup but now facing sideways on to me so she can look from me to soup pot and back to me again without moving. 'You know I always wanted long hair, but it never grew past my shoulder blades.'

She laughs. 'I know. You wanted me to buy you a wig once – when you were about twelve. A long blonde curly one.'

'Did I?' Abigail hair. Another thing I don't remember. I want to both laugh and groan. My Abigail fixation has been a long time growing. The psychologist in me wants to sigh ironically – or maybe that's Abigail. 'When did you start growing yours?'

'Seriously? When I was about the same age. It took until I was about sixteen to see any real results though. At sixteen I was also going to become a scientist – save the world from disease. But things don't always turn out the way you intend them to. In the end, I flunked my exams because my mind was on other things and I eventually became your stepmother instead.'

'That doesn't mean not becoming the world-saving scientist was a failure. You saved *my* world.' And I mean it. The fervency with which I mean it shakes me to my core. Without Romaine I would have been a lonely and lost child. I can feel my eyes smarting as the tears threaten to well up again and I concentrate hard to force them back down. This time *she* comes across to hug *me*. When she eventually goes back to the soup I say, 'I found a book Dada gave you in my bookcase at Ethos too,' because I need to offer her something back. A love token.

'Which one?'

I tell her and repeat the inscription. I can feel myself blushing and falter before I reach the date of it.

'I wondered where that had gone,' she says, cocking her head to one side, smiling. 'I'm glad it's in your bookcase and not simply lost. Several things seem to be misplaced after... well, after he died. Like the window pole in his study, of all things – and that doll. I always wondered what happened to her. And there was one photo I particularly liked too. You, me and Dada, just before he died. I always remember it as one of the few he wasn't being terribly serious or terribly professional-looking in. As you've observed, he found it hard to relinquish his professional self in favour of his emotional self.' She looks reflective. 'The real Aaron McCray. He was so popular with all his students. You know, Gab, he may not have been great with young children, but with his students he was as much a father as a teacher. We all have our strengths and weaknesses, don't we? It's what makes us who we are. What made him a... ' she pauses to choose her words carefully, 'an impassioned man; even if he found it hard to show love at times.'

Deep inside me Abigail disagrees, but I choose to ignore what she's trying to prod me into remembering. What's more important and challenging now is eating Romaine's home-made carrot and coriander soup and not immediately throwing it back up. The urge to gag makes me swallow hard and I manage only half a bowlful before having to admit defeat. Romaine removes it but says nothing. I file away the ideas that are beginning to surface and make connections, and our conversation turns to more mundane things. What my new apartment is like, London, how she'd always hated the dirt and stale air of the tube.

'Like being buried alive.'

'It's not that bad, and there are compensations.'

'Such as?' she teases. 'Bad breath from your neighbour, sweaty armpits in rush hour, and there was always a flasher lurking somewhere. I remember once sitting opposite an old man in a mac, and as soon as I looked across at him and smiled, he pulled his mac aside and he had all his bits all hanging out through his flies. Disgusting!'

I laugh despite myself.

'Luckily no one's flashed me yet.' *Only had brutal sex with you on your desk.* Shut up Abigail!

I spend the rest of the afternoon browsing the house and soaking up its atmosphere. It is comforting. I feel like a child again – the kind of child who would have had a big red ball as well as a giant ice-cream. There's only one place I don't go. Dada's study. The door is shut, but I can still see the yellow and black *Police – do not cross* tape that was strung across its open mouth that day. Unfortunate because the bookcase is in there so I am without anything to read. I should have brought Dada's manuscript with me. Whoever sent it to me – since it was apparently not Romaine – was still right in that it would be a suitable epitaph if it were to be edited and published by me. More and more, I am thinking that Dada was his work and his work was Dada. Romaine and I were by-products – and I had been research material too, it seemed.

Romaine has to go out to a book group in the evening – she is leading it. One of the things she started doing even before Dada died because she was so often left to her own devices whilst he was working away. Inevitably I find myself drawn back to the photograph albums she's left on the dresser. This time I settle in the rocking chair, plumping the cushion behind me but the rocking motion brings the nausea I keep suffering from back so I resort to the rug and its tassled knots instead, spreading the three albums across the rug like before. I start with the earliest one – the one with the photograph Romaine remembers as being only a month after we became a family – studying us and our expressions. Looking for what I'd always wanted from Dada, but realise now I never had. I'm disappointed. By the time I've got to the end of the first album, there's no evidence of it whatsoever. I move on to the next one. I'm older, Dada's older, Romaine is older. There are more people intruding into our threesome now too. They look like they could be Dada's students. Of course – I remember now. His Friday night soirées. The ones where he held court for his brightest and most unique students. Co-admiration. The last date recorded in the album is 2001. There are lots of articles and photographs of Dada in award-receipt mode in this one too.

The last album is the one Romaine hadn't opened earlier. There's much of the same as the one before in it, with the students becoming predominantly female as the years wear on. It's the last two pages that really surprise me. They're of me. Or rather, they're of me and some of my friends. One must have been a birthday party because there's me, grinning back over the top of a birthday cake smothered in candles. Regardless of what Abigail has to say about the girls clustering around me, waiting for me to blow out the candles, this brings back fond memories. Janie, Tia, Sandra, Marie and a small dark girl whose name I don't recall. In fact, I don't really recall her at all but the others I do. We have long since lost touch, but that summer before Dada died had been a good one. 2005. 27th June 2005. My birthday when I was 15. Four days later and Dada was dead. I shut the album, the dates jumping around in my head. Abigail is putting them there. 27th June 1990. My birth date. June 1994 – the first photograph in the first album and Dada, Romaine and I had all only been together a month. 14th February 1991 – the date of the inscription in the book.

"To my darling Romaine, who has inspired me from the moment I first saw her and will continue to do so until the breath leaves my body. A. 14th Feb '91"

I wasn't even one when Dada wrote that inscription, yet he was already professing his love for Romaine – more than three years before the time when we were supposedly first all together. Jessica had said my mother left before I was one. Romaine would have been sixteen if she's forty-one now. I can't deny the connections this time, however much I would like to. Romaine was the student Dada had been having an affair with. No, not even a student – a schoolgirl who'd wanted to be a scientist and save the world, but flunked her exams instead because she was being distracted.

Chapter 25

I pile all the albums together and put them back where Romaine had left them on the dresser. I need to think but I am too cold to. The room has grown chilly because I have let the fire die down too far. The warmth the home-made soup and Romaine's welcome created inside me has gone too. Everything in my life seems to have been built on shifting sands. I put another log on the fire and shiver whilst I wait for it to catch, then I have a better idea. The radiator. I'll sit with my back against that and warm up the way I used to as a child. I push Dada's chair to one side and slide down against the radiator, only to pitch forward immediately again. It is cold – freezing. I check the radiator at the far end of the room and that is cold too, as is the one in the hall. Why on earth has Romaine got the heating off? The whole house is icy! Upstairs I rummage in the airing cupboard for a blanket and wrap it round myself, then decide I might as well go to bed. I don't want to talk to Romaine when she comes in anyway – not until I have got my head round how I feel about her being part of Jessica's 'truth'. I go back downstairs and turn off the lights in the lounge and kitchen, leaving only the hall light on. Across the hall the door I don't want to open looms large in the muted light of the big old Tiffany lamp that Romaine has hung there. Far from brightening the place up, its elaborate glass design throws coloured reflections on the hall floor, muting and diffusing the light. It is elegant, true, but not particularly practical.

Go on. Look inside. You know you want to.

'I don't.' I'd like to oust Abigail right now. She is insidious and disruptive as well as bold and self-assured.

Don't lie. You do. You want to see if it's the way you remember it. All of it.

'It will be the same as it was then. But even if it isn't, it's irrelevant. Facts are facts.' That sounds more like Abigail than me and it makes me want to grind my teeth. 'And get out of my head, anyway. You're a fiction created for Xander, that's all.'

I can imagine the toss of the golden curls and the mutinous pout, even find myself doing it until I pull myself up short.

I haven't been in the room since the day the police left. I wish I hadn't then, so why would I revisit it now? Now, I have enough to cope with without having to remember how it had been on that day. The whole landscape of my childhood has just changed with one small detail. The woman I'd trusted above all else is a liar, and the memories she says I have confused are far from that. They are merely suppressed and now finding their way up from the dark well of despair they've been drowning in for the last eleven years. It was alright for Romaine. She still had Dada in her head exactly how he'd been – even if that was less than perfect. She still had the romantic moments amidst the failures. She still had the fact that he'd dismissed my mother for her, and she had the reassurance of the fact that three years on he'd still wanted her. Had married her, made her my stepmother. And no, none of it meant I loved her any the less for all that she'd been to me since then, but still I felt betrayed that she hadn't told me the truth today. Or ever.

Betrayed.

That brings another disturbing emotion. Blind rage that has my heart pounding and my breathing heavy. But not with Romaine. On impulse I cross the hallway, fling the door to Dada's study open and flick on the light. I am back to the 1st July 2005, dithering in the hall, staring at the suitcases that are piled there. They are the suitcases that I last remember containing the whole family's belongings when we went to Ireland for Romaine's mother's funeral. We stayed there for two weeks, immersed in Irish burrs and Catholicism and spontaneous bursts of music and strong black beer whenever more than two of her family were gathered together. It had been a bewildering mix of the sacred and the profane, and the suitcases had been as full to bursting as they were now. Romaine had gone to visit her aunt in London, but I hadn't thought she'd taken a suitcase, let alone a stack of them. It was just a day trip.

'Romaine? Are you back early?' I'm silent, afraid of the reprisal for bunking off school. 'Oh,' Dada emerges from his study and stands awkwardly in the doorway. I linger behind the suitcases and we gaze at each other over the top of them. 'They're mine,' he says, smiling – that smile he has when he wants to win you over. Eyes as well as lips engaged. Not the bleak little apologies that I usually got. But when Dada went to one of his conferences he only took an overnight bag or a carry-on. Not a great pile of luggage that surely must contain the whole of his wardrobe of clothes. 'I'm going.'

'Going? To another conference?'

'No. Leaving.'

The words dance in my head. Their choreography belongs to another time, another person.

'Leaving?'

'Yes, sorry. I intended being gone before you got home. I didn't think you'd be back this early.'

'But what do you mean, you're leaving?'

I don't really need to ask. I understand instinctively what he means. I can feel my heart stuck in my throat whilst still pounding away in my chest. That little voice that so often questioned things even now was questioning how my body could do that without being heard – or seen – then.

'I'm leaving, Romaine, I'm afraid. You'll be better off without me anyway – dry old psychologist that I am.'

That usually raised a dutiful rebuttal of him as dry or old, like I'd been trained to do ever since I could understand that Dada said these kind of things to be contradicted – to have his ego stroked – but the affectation annoys me today. I say it anyway – Pavlovian to the last.

'You're not dry and you're not old.'

'Thanks, Gab.'

'But I still don't understand.'

He motions me to follow him into his study. Unheard of usually. I follow, my heart still filling my throat and closing over my larynx. The rest of the words choke behind it. He indicates to the chair in front of his desk but I can't make my legs work well enough to reach it. I loiter awkwardly in the doorway. He moves behind his desk, nevertheless. It is his trench and between us is no-man's land.

'I've met someone.'

'Met someone?'

'Louise. She's – she's different. Much younger, but that's not it. She makes me feel alive.' He sits. The action seems to free up my legs. Then I am walking without controlling them. Someone else is controlling them. 'I need to be free of all this.' He's swinging his arms out wide, encompassing the room. 'Free of this stolid respectability, this sterility. I'm going to write.'

'But you already write. You've written lots of books.'

'Oh, not that kind of thing. Real writing. My imagination running wild. Senses and passions engaged.' He indicates the pile of papers on his desk. We're going to live in the sun and I'm going to write. It's going to be just us.'

He's beaming at me and I'm dying inside.

'But you can't. We're your family. I'm your daughter.'

'I'm sorry, Gab. It's like the Judgement of Solomon,' he's saying. 'Sacrifice me for you or you for me. This time it has to be me. I have a choice now. I didn't when you were tiny. I've written you a letter but I guess you could read it now. There's one for Romaine too.'

He rummages under the pile of papers in the middle of his desk and finds an envelope. It is one of two. The other is addressed to Romaine. He tucks that one into the book lying next to the pile of papers. I take the one addressed to me from him, fingers numb, unbelieving.

'You can't just leave us.'

'I have to be me, not who you or Romaine want me to be. And anyway, I'm no good for you. Never have been. Didn't even want to be a father in the first place. Your mother foisted you on me. I wouldn't have told you normally, but well – you need to know now. Read it.' He nods to the letter, pinned between my fingers, a specimen butterfly stained with its own blood. 'I took such a long time writing it. The hardest thing I've ever done, but I have to be true to myself.' In the letter, he says that too.

"What you end up with isn't always what you thought you'd chosen originally. Situations change, people change, wishes change; we change. It's called accepting yourself, or being who you really are, even if you don't like what you see."

And who are you? I thought you were Dada, who I could rely on, even if you don't love me. But you aren't. You are a stranger coolly handing me an envelope before abandoning me. Intent only on himself.

Your mother foisted you on me and then left...

Chapter 26

Who is she, this Louise? I don't need to ask. Suddenly I know who Louise is. She's the girl who came to my fifteenth birthday party with my best friend Tia. Her cousin, inflicted on her for the summer – Tia's words – and traipsing faithfully behind Tia whenever she came over. A puppy, always at her heels. Dark-eyed, dark-haired and pale-faced. An Ophelia, lost in her own thoughts. A Lady of Shalott, bearing her tragedy with her, downstream. Her mother had died – that was why she was staying with Tia. Some unpronounceable illness and whilst we gabbled nineteen to the dozen and did all the things fifteen-year-olds did, she'd sat so quietly in the corner I'd almost forgotten she was there. But Dada hadn't. He'd talked to her. Self-belief and the power of the mind – the kind of things he talked about with his students but I was always excluded from. I'd thought him kind, taking the time to make her feel at home. My God! He hadn't been kind, he'd been pursuing her. The grandmother clock in the hall bing-bongs half-past twelve. Ten minutes ago, my life was completely different.

He's clearing the things out of his top drawer as I read – the drawer that's always locked. The gun is the last thing to come out of the drawer. He lays it on top of the manuscript he'd been working on; black, squat and ugly. I stare at it, shocked and uncomprehending. Since when did Dada have a gun? I know about the manuscript because I creep in here when he's not around sometimes and roam the room, absorbing his possessions, the things he treasures. Once he left the desk drawer unlocked. He'd gone off late to a meeting, and obviously forgot to lock it in his hurry to be on time. That was when I saw the manuscript, and read what it's about, but there was no gun in there then. All his treasures are in this room. I put my paperweight in here too, tucked behind the photograph of Romaine. The last time I looked, it was still there, unseen.

The letter doesn't make sense, or maybe I don't. I try to read and comprehend but the words just snake round and round in my head, a boa

MIND GAMES: MEMENTO MORI

constrictor squeezing the life out of me, and all I can think about is that gun and that Dada is leaving us. I try to concentrate.

"*...other's views of morality are not valid unless we validate them ourselves. Only our own view of morality is right for us."*

The manuscript is about morality too. How can he comment on that? Louise is my age. I look up from the letter but he's still absorbed in what he's doing, gathering up his treasures. Preparing to remove them with himself. The photograph of Romaine joins them. And the gun. My paperweight doesn't.

No! I want to shout. *You can't.* Instead I whine beseechingly, 'But you're my father. You can't just go like this. I need you.' I can hear the break in my voice quite clearly; the supplication, the desperation, but he can't.

He looks up now, still smiling, sadly. I hate that patronising smile.

'Oh, Gab. You've got Romaine. You'll be fine.'

No. I won't. You're my father. You can't leave us – not for a girl only the same age as me. That's sick. Disgusting! And you're mine, not hers...

The sound I make is like the yowling of a cat, and my face is crumpling like paper. I can't stop it folding in on itself. Self-destructing. *Your mother foisted you on me and then left ...*

'I'm sorry, Gab. Don't cry. It will all be alright. You'll see. You're growing up. Almost an adult. You don't need me, but Louise does. And I need her. I've been starved of life and love for too long.'

'But Romaine?'

'Romaine has you. You'll be fine. You'll both be fine. Remember, know who you are. Accept who you are. Act on who you are. That's what I'm doing, and you should too. Unless you do that, you cannot be who you are for anyone else.'

'But you're my father – that's who you are.'

He's shaking his head sadly. 'Oh dear, this is why I wanted to leave whilst you two were out. Gaby, we're not defined by what people want us to be – or think we are. We're defined by who *we* think we are. I may be your father biologically, but it doesn't follow that I am required to be here for you simply because you think I should be. Or Romaine thinks I should be, come to that. If I wanted to be here as your father and Romaine's partner, then I would be. But that would be because I had chosen to do so. Do you understand?'

'No.'

I've stopped crying now. The tears seem to have dammed up behind the hard lump in my throat. And I don't feel desperate any more. I feel hopeless. The kind of hopeless that can't see beyond the suitcases in the hall; can't see anything or any point to anything beyond the suitcases in the hall. I'm still holding the letter but my hand feels numb, hanging uselessly by my side.

'No,' he says heavily and sighs. 'I thought you wouldn't. Look, I've spent my life thinking these issues through. You must have picked up something of what I've taught my students over the years from the times you've hung around, listening in, but this is it in a nutshell. We are formed of a series of choices. The choices make our lives what they are. We are encumbered by what society calls morals, and more often than not coerced into choices governed by those beliefs, even if they aren't ours. I was never cut out to be a father, tied to home, restricted by responsibilities. I'm a free thinker – a lover, not a fighter,' he smirks, 'although you won't get that joke; but I was born to question custom and practice, not conform to it. Through Louise I can do that. She frees my spirit and understands my need for self-determination. And it's all in here.' He pats the manuscript. 'My best work yet – everything I've learnt about the advantages of amorality and the freedom of choice that finally gives you. The fount of all knowledge – or all mine anyway! I shall finish it with Louise's help and then move on to other things.' He pauses. 'Like you and Romaine will. Read the rest of the letter. You'll understand better now I've explained the theory.'

He sounds like he's talking to one of his students, not his daughter. I gaze at him, dumbfounded, no words on my lips but a thousand in my head.

'But… '

'No.' He's shaking his head again.

'But why today?' I insist, my voice small and thin. 'Now?'

'I thought I'd spare you and Romaine any upset. Thought I'd go before either of you got home. Just shows what thought does.'

'Killed the cat,' I said.

He laughs humourlessly. 'Yes, well, these sayings… ' Do you want to read the letter while I'm still here or after I'm gone?'

He's anxious to go. I'm anxious to delay him.

'I'll read it while you're still here.'

'Good. You read it and then we'll talk about it if we need to. I'll finish clearing out my desk in the meantime, and then get going. At least I can avoid Romaine.'

I go over to the window. He smiles brightly at me as I pass him and pulls the top drawer wider. There's a box in it. Bullets. Aren't guns meant to be locked away? It's illegal to keep firearms and ammunition in the same place. And no one is meant to keep a handgun. That's illegal too. We learnt that at school the other day when we were debating whether gun ownership for pleasure was socially acceptable. They showed us a video beforehand – all the terrible things owning guns caused. The Dunblane school massacre; *this could have been all of you if owning a handgun was still legal.* And what firing a handgun at point blank did to a melon; *imagine this is a human head.* Did you know that more men commit suicide by putting the gun in their mouth than women? And that just firing a gun will deposit gun powder residue on your hands, so you're immediately marked as a suspect? I hate the ugly black gun on his desk, crawling over the manuscript on morality like a bloated fly.

'Done yet?' he asks, not even turning round.

'Not yet,' I say, trying to focus on the words dancing around in the letter again.

"...others' views of morality are not valid unless we validate them ourselves. Only our own view of morality is right for us."

I give up. The words mean nothing. They are just an excuse. It takes me barely thirty seconds more to scan the rest of it – this letter he says has taken him so long to write. And he's still dismantling his desk, his life with us, humming softly under his breath. If I walked round the front of his desk to see his expression, I know it would be smug, self-satisfied. The gun sits on his desk, with the rest of his treasures. My paperweight sits all alone on the cupboard under the window. It says 'love'. I pick it up. It is heavy – what they would describe as a blunt instrument in a crime novel. The clever words ring round and round in my head, taunting me.

"Some would call me amoral, but morality is a lethal game. It just depends who you play it with whether it's you or they who get destroyed. I'm just keeping myself alive here."

He is bending over the drawer, hooking out the last of the contents. I haven't noticed until now that he has developed a bald spot at the back of his head. Maybe I've never been close enough, or maybe it is the careful way he has arranged the surrounding hair over it. He always looks so young, I've never thought of him as ageing – or middle-aged. It's the aquiline features and sharp blue-grey eyes. I have inherited those from him, even if I have inherited nothing else. I hate him so much right at this moment. The thousands of words in my head rearrange themselves into just one and someone speaks it so clearly to me it cannot be wrong; a girl with golden curls, defiant eyes and pouting lips.

No.

And it is all so clear then what I should do. He's even said so himself. I should make my own choice. That's what I'm supposed to do and I am my father's daughter, and always obedient to what he tells me to do. Maybe that is what has defined me most until now. My choice is for him not to leave with Louise.

The bald spot is the perfect target, simultaneously vulnerable and pathetic. I smash the paperweight down on the back of his head. The impact jars all the way up my arm and into my jaw. He falls forward onto the manuscript, a small explosion of air escaping him as he merges with it, and the choice is made.

I stand, paperweight in one hand, letter in the other, the summer's day sunshine streaming in around me and him and the bloodied spot on the back of his head, barely believing what I have just done. There is something white peeking through the red, like a shark's tooth. I'd wanted a shark's tooth pendant when we went to Torquay last year but he'd said it was a fake. I peer at the white, fascinated but sickened. This is a fake too. It is bone. I recoil in horror, sweaty and faint. Oh my God, what have I done? I have killed him. All I can do is stare at the bloodied patch, that protruding bone. I have killed him. I have killed him. I have killed him. I am a murderer.

We're frozen like that for what seems like forever, the sweat trickling down my back like the finger of death stroking my spine, but it can only have been a few minutes. In the hall, the grandmother clock chimes again. The quarter hour. Twelve-forty-five. I should be getting back at school. Class starts back at one-thirty. No one knows I slipped out for my gym kit. I need to get back or I will get detention for bunking off. But what about him? Oh my God! I start to shake and I can't stop. The earthquake is inside me, splitting me in two, opening a chasm I am falling into, down, down, down.

That's when I am first truly Abigail. She takes over so naturally, calm and efficient; computing the possibilities, assessing the risks, devising the plan. She takes the same length of time as it took for me to scan the letter to take control and I am amazed but relieved. I am me, but not me.

The letter goes on the cupboard. The paperweight on top of it. Bloodstains contained. Then she forces me to stand next to him and assess. I exclaim at the state of the book and manuscript, neither quite trapped there by his shattered head, but the dust cover of the book has blood stains on it. I gingerly remove them too. The book is one of his earliest ones. It is inscribed – one of the few that are. *To my darling Romaine...* The way his head is positioned I can only see one eye, and it is open, but dulled; the pupil a gaping black hole in its centre. He is definitely brain-dead, or close to it. The gun has been pushed to one side and is lying next to him. It still looks like a bloated insect and I shiver with distaste at both. Abigail makes me breathe in and out, shakily, and maintain control. But what now? He is dead and I have killed him. I will be caught, found guilty, sent to prison. Reviled and hated.

Why? What good will that do?

None, but I'm guilty. I did it.

He egged you on. He asked for it.

But I killed him.

You made a choice. "Other's views of morality are not valid unless we validate them ourselves. Only our own view of morality is right for us." That's what he said. He is morally wrong to do what he was going to do. You put a stop to that. Make what you did worthwhile.

Oh my God. I don't want to go to prison. I don't want Romaine to hate me.

Then don't let that happen. "Some would call me amoral, but morality is a lethal game. It just depends who you play it with whether it's you or they who get destroyed. I'm just keeping myself alive here." Play the game too.

How? Think, think, think!

The gun. And the bullets to go with it.

But how. I don't know what to do.

Yes, you do. The film, remember? Load it the way they did. Fire it the way a man would.

The gun. Yes. I see.

I try to push him upright by the shoulder nearest me but he doesn't budge. Frustration displaces squeamishness. I have only three quarters of an hour before my absence will be detected at school. My friends are all at lunchtime drama club so I'm free and clear for the moment, but not when classes start back. I'm sweating and my breathing is ragged but I am ice-cold inside. I stand behind Dada and reach over to drag him back against his chair. His head lolls and I have to jump away to avoid getting his blood on me. Strange how he has become an object now, not a person. A bloodied body. But I need him to stay upright! How?

Prop him up.

I swing round and round, searching for something to prop him up.

But they'll know!

Then remove it afterwards. Get rid of it.

The window pole. I could prop him up with the window pole and then pull it away afterwards. It's long enough not to get in the way.

And don't get blood on you.

Don't get blood on you, don't get blood on you...

I collect the pole and position it, hook end into the nape of his neck. I have to change the position several times until it works. Then I realise I won't have enough space to be able stand in front of him and hold the gun to his head so I start again, having first heaved him and the chair away from the desk. His legs sprawl awkwardly as I manoeuvre the chair and I have to prop them into a right-angled position too. They are thin and bony. There is nothing soft about him, I decide – quite objectively – from the skeletal legs, to the hard features. How have I adored him so unconditionally all this time when there is no softness in him? And none in me either?

Eventually I stand in front of his desk and study him critically. He's almost upright, both eyes staring at me and mouth open as if he's about to speak. It unnerves me and for a moment all I want to do is run away, knees knocking and heart rattling against my ribs at the enormity of what I am doing. I take two steps backwards and the clock chimes again. One o'clock. Shit! Thirty minutes now. I want to pee too.

That is fear. You don't have time for fear.

I go to the kitchen and find two waste bin bags, cut holes in one for my head and arms, and wrap the other one round my body like a black shroud. Am I doing this right? Fingerprints. There are rubber gloves there too. Little thin latex ones. Romaine uses them for what she calls 'dirty jobs'. I take a pair of them from the box and pull them on.

And your head. Cover your head. The melon went everywhere.

I find a smaller, see-through bag for recyclables too. I don't know what else to cover my head with and still be able to see. Back in the study, I fumble a bullet into the gun clip. One or a whole clip? What would a suicide do? One. No point in any more, and I'm not sure my cardboard fingers could load another one anyway. I lay the gun carefully back down on the desk. Dada is still watching me glassily, disapproving. I avoid his eyes and collect up the manuscript, and book from the cupboard behind him, surprised to find a photograph tucked into the book. It is of Dada, me and Romaine in Torquay last year. We are all smiling – even Dada; and he has his arm round me. It sends a shock wave through me. I remember the day well. But the smiles are a lie. It was the day he'd refused me the shark's tooth and told me I was too ingenuous. Dumb. I needed to grow up and learn when a fake was a fake. The chasm reopens but I refuse to fall into it. I have learned what is fake today. My whole life. But the photograph and the book and the manuscript will be mine. The book because it has Romaine's letter and the inscription inside it and she mustn't see it. I will remove the cover and keep the book. The photograph will serve as a reminder of everything I haven't admitted until today, and the manuscript? A tribute. One day I'll read it properly, maybe even get it published posthumously. Make it mine too. It's the least I can do since he said it's his greatest work yet. I laugh out loud at the craziness of it all. And my composure. I am a murderer planning the perfect crime. I am Gaby, ingenuous and dumb. I am Abigail, calculating and clever.

No, I don't know who I am now. I am in transition.

I put all three in a neat pile by the door, together with the letter and the paperweight. I will decide what to do with them later if I'm not in prison. The idea rises on a tide of panic inside me, and I start to tremble again but Abigail is impatient to get on.

You will be fine. It will be fine. Just do it.

I place the recyclables bag over my head and peer through it. It's frightening, but I can still see and breathe – just. The bag distorts my world, the circular arrow design obscuring the centre of my vision and 'cyc' dancing in front of my eyes. It balloons out as I exhale, an astronaut's dome, then a collapsing balloon, shrink-wrapping my head. Panicking, I claw it away from me.

'I can't! I can't do this. Oh my God, oh my God, oh my God.'

Shut up! Stop it. Control yourself. Don't gasp in air. Take it in slowly.

I count to five and take a small experimental breath sucking it through my compressed lips. It's OK. I try it again, slowly and shallowly so the condensation from my breath doesn't plaster the bag to my skin. The bag wafts gently in and out as I inhale and exhale, but doesn't attach itself to me again.

OK. Now get on with it. Do it now.

I have to straddle him. Like Louise might have. I gag. I sob. I can't do this. This is terrible. I can't do it.

But I must.

Knees shaking, I take his right arm and curl the hand round the gun. The forefinger I thread through the trigger space. But now how am I going to make him pull it? We are opposite sides of the equation. I support the gun and his hand round it with mine on the other side. My own forefinger slips into the trigger space like this, whilst the rest of my hand stretches away from the gun and its barrel. Actually, that's perfect. The powder burns will mainly be on him, not me. Not that they'd show with the gloves on, but he needs to have looked like he pulled the trigger or the police forensics people might wonder. Lucky we have such bony fingers that they can both fit in that tiny trigger space. I breathe out, slowly, slowly, softly… The bag swells and deflates around my face. And again. I guide the gun to his face and push the nozzle into his mouth. He looks surprised. I pull on the trigger, pinching his finger against it. It is awkward, fiddly. And there's only one bullet to get it right with. I'm sweating and dizzy, the summer heat amplified by the plastic bags and my nerves. His eyes are glazed, staring into the far distance, lips cupping the barrel of the gun like he's sucking a lollipop.

'I'm sorry,' I say, suddenly overcome by the indignity of this for him. He has always been so dignified, so exalted, but all he is now is a corpse that I am desecrating. I am crying inside the recycling bag, steaming it up with my shuddering sobs. It is all so unfair. None of it should have been like this. Abigail is shouting at me but I'm struggling to simply stay on my feet, let alone pull the trigger. And I wonder where you go when you die, too. It's something I would have asked him one day when maybe he had time to discuss things with me. He would certainly have had something to say about it. Now it is too late.

Wherever he is, he is already there.

Yes.

I stop sobbing. Wherever he is, he is already there. But still I can't do it.

Do it!

'I can't.' I can feel my face crumbling in on itself again. 'I can't! What if I do it wrong?'

Too late now. This is your only chance if you want to get away with it. You're not killing him. He's already dead. Just fire it, for God's sake!

I fire, despairing, as the world explodes with crimson.

Chapter 27

The place is still freezing in the morning. My nose is an icicle and my face, sheet ice. I curl into a ball and bury my face in the bed covers to thaw it, but it's not unlike being inside the recycling bag and I burst free almost as quickly. My head is throbbing and I know I have been crying in my sleep because my nose is thick and my eyes sore. Now I am properly awake, lying in bed unsettles me. I need to be up and doing something to take my mind off last night. It feels like a bad dream but I know it's not. I can imagine, almost without trying, the abrasion on the otherwise smooth surface of the paperweight. And I know where the letter is – where I hid it. I can't ignore any of it, as much as I might want to. It's like the atomic bomb. Once created, it can never be uncreated, just like, once detonated, the radiation particles will forever contaminate the air it exploded into. I am contaminated air. I am toxic. I am a murderer – and of my own father. I prop myself up in bed and allow that to really sink in. I do not need Xander's challenge or Chiaroscuro's reciprocal charge in return for getting rid of Xander for me to make me into one. I have already done it for myself. Far from my world being upended by being caught out for stealing a credit card or having brutish sex with a patient, it was already in reverse.

'I have killed someone. I have killed someone. I have killed someone.'

I say it softly under my breath, trying to accept it.

Know who you are. Accept who you are. Act on who you are.
Unless you do that, you will always be weak; at everyone's whim.
But how do you act on being a murderer?

I could have a fascinating conversation with Xander about that now. An expert's view, in fact. I laugh without humour. I am so many things I thought I wasn't. I examine it from another angle. Yet it wasn't just me. It was Abigail too. OK, she isn't real and I'm not so psychotic that I don't know that. I'm a psychologist, for God's sake! But she's is part of my psyche. I have been incorporating her into myself ever since I was six. She is everything Gaby is not. She is pert, proud, perfect. Careless if she is perceived as something from the last century. Careless if she is despised or reviled. Careless of other's opinions of her. Secure in herself. That means some part of me must be secure in myself too. I have to find that part of me and cling on to it for dear life. Like Abigail said, I had made a choice to stop Dada acting immorally. I had to make that choice worthwhile. There was no worth in also being destroyed. The destroyer destroying the destroyer, because he had just as surely destroyed the girl that was me as I had the man I'd called my father.

'Gab?' Romaine's voice floats up the stairs. 'Are you awake? Like a coffee to warm up. The boiler's packed in again.'

'In a minute.' I call back, my heart pounding and my ears singing. I am not ready to face Romaine yet. How can I? How can I ever? Then as an afterthought, 'Didn't you get it fixed after the last time?'

'I did, but it was a quick fix – on the cheap.'

'You need a new boiler.'

'Don't I just! A new boiler for an old boiler! Needs must though. Come down when you're ready, and I'll put the kettle on again.'

I slide back down under the covers and pull my knees up to my chin, dragging the covers round me into a cocoon. I nestle inside it, incubating. Butterfly or whoever or whatever I am, it's going to have to emerge soon or Romaine will as likely simply make a mug of coffee and appear with it. I worry about that as I try to gather the constituent elements of guilt, objectivity, self-loathing and self-preservation together. What else had that letter said? I try to picture it, the neat crease lines breaking up the sentences as I held it in my trembling hand.

"Choose what you do with it, right or wrong, but choose for yourself. If we are entitled to nothing else in life, we are entitled to make our own choices."

Including murder?

"Some would call me amoral, but morality is a lethal game. It just depends who you play it with whether it's you or they who get destroyed. I'm just keeping myself alive here."

Like me.

'Kettle's on again, Gab, and I've made up the fire in the lounge. Should feel warmer soon.'

'OK.'

'Don't be long.'

The idea of facing Romaine makes me despair and the idea of coffee makes me queasy. It is the latter that takes priority in the end and I stumble wildly to the darkened bathroom – the blind still drawn from Romaine's early morning shower, no doubt. I'm heedless of the cold floor and thin cotton top I'm wearing, which exposes more than it covers. My new wardrobe, including nightwear, purchased the week before I'd left, had anticipated not only a fresh start but a fresh romance at some stage. I manage to make it to the toilet just in time to empty the contents of my stomach into it. The remains of yesterday's carrot and coriander curdle in the bottom of the bowl and an incongruous thought has me both laughing and crying simultaneously. There's always carrots in puke so at least you can see in the dark if you're throwing up at night. Some comedian's line that has stuck with me, but in this case, is true. Especially when the light blinks on and I hear Romaine's, 'Oh dear. I thought you were looking peaky.'

I squat back on my heels, eyes still smarting and the burn of bile setting my throat ablaze.

'Something I ate, probably.'

'Hmm,' she says. I realise, too late, what I've just implied.

'I didn't mean there's anything wrong with your soup.' I look up at her imploringly and the moment I've been dreading is happening. I am facing her.

She kneels on the floor next to me and strokes the hair away from my face.

'I didn't think you did. But there is something you're not telling me isn't there?'

'Oh God. You know?'

The queasiness is replaced by the sense of falling. The chasm that I'd opened up in myself eleven years ago is claiming me. It doesn't matter what I may tell myself about choices and morality. Romaine will never forgive me.

'I wondered before you left. The way you so suddenly split with Mark and were so adamant about taking this job even though you were going to be on your own – and you've never been good on your own. It was like you were pushing us all away.'

'I'm so sorry, Romaine. How can you ever forgive me?'

'Forgive you? I'll always forgive you, Gab. I love you like my own daughter. You are my own daughter. What other child do I have?'

'But what I did... '

She puts her arm round my shoulders and I realise then I am shivering. Teeth chattering and hands blue with cold. The sickness has gone, replaced by a hollow ache.

'Come on. Whatever you've done isn't going to be made any better by catching pneumonia.'

She guides me downstairs, collecting a pair of thick socks and a blanket en route, and settling me in Dada's chair. I start to object but she shakes her head. 'The rocking chair won't do you much good. Nor will the floor if you're already cold.' She pushes me into it, wrapping the blanket round me and slips the socks onto my feet. I am Jesus and she is my handmaiden. No, I'm not. I'm Barabbas, forever damned unless she forgives me. I start to cry again. I do not know how to effect the metamorphosis that I need to survive.

'I'm sorry, I'm sorry. I'm sorry, I'm sorry... ' I just can't stop saying it.

'Gaby, stop it. Whatever is wrong, it's fixable.' She settles at my feet, a curled Madonna in floral pyjamas and a grey polo neck. 'Do you want to talk about it?'

'I don't know what to say. I'm ashamed of myself. So ashamed.'

'Is it not working out for you? You know you can simply come home if it isn't?'

'I know, but I can't. I need to deal with this. It's just... difficult.' It isn't me talking. It is Abigail, coming to my rescue. 'If I deal with it, I'll be fine. It will all be fine.' Not metamorphosing. Taking over. Lying. How can it ever be fine? Don't! I want to tell her, but I haven't the strength.

Romaine hesitates, then begins speaking with that tentative carelessness that usually masks specific intent.

'Mark is always asking after you, you know. I saw him only yesterday.' She pauses, and I pick my nails, avoiding her eyes. 'A bit of provinciality and a family wouldn't be such a bad thing maybe. I've always counted you as the biggest blessing in my life.'

I look up at that. 'And Dada?'

I am playing with fire and I know it, but I can't stop myself. The words are out and hanging in the air. I sound like a jealous schoolboy, seeking approbation. I shrink into the blanket, hating myself even more. She takes a while to answer, and then it is measured, treading carefully between the broken shards of our past.

'Dada too. But he was a race apart, Gaby. I know he was your father and you adored him, but you have to understand him to understand what he really was to either of us.' This time I wait. She continues, slowly, tiptoeing into the void. 'None of us are perfect. We wouldn't be human if we were. The trick is understanding our flaws and living with them. You know what he always said. Know who you are. Accept who you are. Act on who you are. Well, that includes knowing who others are too, and accepting what they are as well.'

'So, what was Dada?'

'Is this what you really came home for? The truth you needed to know? I didn't really think it was about your mother. You would have asked me about her years ago if you'd really needed to know about her. But I knew this would come one day. Who your father really was.'

I try to hide my surprise. It isn't what I came home for and yet it is what I have discovered – alongside myself. But what does Romaine believe the truth to be about Dada? I had thought that was obvious. Her belief in him had always seemed to be absolute. Maybe we are both reaching into the depths of ourselves and admitting something hitherto denied.

'Yes.' I am still picking my nails but blindly, eyes on Romaine's face and her sad eyes.

'He was human. He... ' Her lips compress. 'You really want the whole truth?'

'Yes,' although I can barely hear myself.

'Alright. He was exceptional... And fallible. He was kind and he was dismissive. He was brilliant and he was thoughtless. He was passionate and he was inconsiderate.' She pauses again, and takes a deep breath. 'He was flawed, like all the rest of us. He was my husband, but he was also profligate. He was two men, one faithful and one faithless.'

She looks me straight in the eye, defying me to disagree. I can't stop my jaw slackening and my voice rising a pitch.

'You knew?'

'All those conferences, Gab? Of course, I knew. But I accepted it. He needed his freedom, whereas I needed stability. You needed stability too. And you needed to believe in him. You'd already been abandoned as a baby. You didn't need the one real parent you had to disappoint you too. But if you're comparing your ability to his then maybe now it's time to see him for who he really was so you can be Gaby, out of the shade, not always in his shadow. Oh, I've watched you so many times over the years, hanging on his every word, adoring him, even idolising him. I could see he was a symbol to you of everything you wanted to be, but he wasn't that perfect person and that blind belief has held you back. I wouldn't ever have said any of this to you if you hadn't asked but now you need to be free too. Be yourself. Be proud of who you are. I am.'

'But you don't know what I've done. Who I really am.' One of my fingers feels sore and I realise I have picked the skin so far away from the nail that it is bleeding. I watch it blossom, gradually turning the nail as crimson as my morals. 'I'm so ashamed of some of the things I've done.'

'We all make mistakes, and none of us ever know fully who the people we love are. I am not in your head and you are not in mine. I'm sure you've told your patients that many times already. It's who we believe we are, that matters. I believe in who you are, even if you don't – yet.'

Who we believe we are? I know who I am, I am a murderer. Even Abigail wouldn't deny that, and yet here I am taking reassurance and comfort from Romaine, like I am an innocent. I disgust myself, but I am weak too. I need someone to grant me absolution even though I don't deserve it.

'But there are things… Oh God! There are things I'm remembering that… '

'It's because you've stopped taking the Sineptin. It confuses things. Ignore them.'

'I can't!' The blanket is swaddling me, suffocating me. I push it away. 'How can I ignore what I'm remembering? I tell my patients to face themselves. I'm a hypocrite if I don't do it myself too.' I picture Jessica Morgan's sneer, Xander's cruel amusement. Oh my God, if they only knew what their therapist needed to confront and accept, they'd be crying with laughter. 'And why should I ignore them? Shouldn't I face them? Face what I've done?'

'Some things are best left in the past.' Her jaw is tense and there is a tic making her right eyelid flicker as she says it.

'Are they? How much can you leave in the past? How much be forgiven?'

'More than you'd imagine,' she replies quietly. And then I know, I'm not the only one with memories that have been buried until now.

'You knew.' I can barely hear myself saying it, but I know I have from the expression on her face. 'And you knew he was leaving.'

'It's in the past, Gaby, and the past is a closed book. Open a new one.'

'How can you tell me to pretend it never happened?'

'If you hadn't stopped the Sineptin, I wouldn't need to.'

'But I did.'

'Yes, you did. Now you must set it aside without the drug's help. I did what I thought was right. If it wasn't, well, then... ' She shrugs and she looks small and sad. The house itself seems to be waiting for her to continue. The silence is total and all-encompassing. Even the clock in the hall has stopped ticking. She sighs. 'I've always counted you as the biggest blessing in my life. Nothing changes that. Not the past, present or future. And some things are best forgotten for the sake of the future. That's the way I see it.'

'Everything is fixable – even this? Mum, I'm a m – '

'Shh,' she puts her finger to her lips as if I was a naughty child trying to but in. 'This is fixed. It's in the past. You just need to leave it there. Don't try to make more of it than there needs to be.'

Do I accept what she says? Leave it behind me, regardless of what I've done? How can you leave murder behind you? How can she forgive me for destroying the man she loved? We sit watching each other for a long time, my limbs slowly stiffening from the cold.

'But you loved him and I – '

'Shh,' she says again. 'Past tense. This is the present. This is us as we are now. Time to accept who and what we are.'

Maybe she is right. Maybe now is all that matters. That afternoon is a long time dead. Irrelevant to what our lives are about now. She looks adamant, her eyes still determinedly on mine, lips still gently curved, defying me to revive the argument. The clock has started ticking again and reality is Romaine, and me and an icy house. The hornet's nest inside me has settled and, all of a sudden, I feel strangely calm. Like it never existed at all, that red-spattered room with its stench of death and betrayal. The blanket has fallen over the side of the chair arm and is lying on the floor next to me. Romaine must have put her boot socks on me because her small pointed feet are turning a mottled blue and my arms are pinpricked with goose-bumps. The here and now is all about a freezing house and freezing limbs. I drag the blanket back round me.

'Why don't you get the boiler replaced?'

'No money,' she pulls a wry face.

'But I thought Dada left... ' I can't bring myself to continue.

'Dada left me everything? He'd spent it all – that summer.'

'On what?'

The girl, Louise? Deep inside me the kraken stirs, but she shakes her head and I soothe it back to sleep for now.

'It's in the past, Gaby. Let it go. I have.'

'And why did he have a gun?'

She sighs. 'I don't know. They never fully explained that, except to say that it was definitely his finger on the trigger, whatever the other anomalies.'

'Other anomalies?' My stomach lurches. We have never discussed that day before, or the police investigation and Coroner's verdict. I have lived out the last eleven years blissfully unaware of what I'd done and how close to or safe from discovery my crime has been.

'Technical things. But since his finger was definitely the one on the trigger, they were deemed irrelevant. After all, even the experts have to allow for human fallibility, and he had problems he hadn't admitted to anyone too, so there was a reason.'

'Problems?' This had to be the girl.

'Gaby, I really don't want to talk about it any more. It does neither of us any good. It's in the past. It would only sully his reputation and ruin lives if it got out. Let's leave it as it is. A tragedy we've moved on from.'

'But I haven't. I'm still trying to make sense of it – all of it – and now I find I've been taking a drug that is mind-altering for years without knowing that; years when I have been an adult...?'

'I'm sorry.' She looks overcome with guilt and my self-righteousness is temporarily quashed. 'I should have told you. I know I should. It's just that everything seemed to have settled down and I didn't want to stir it all up again.'

'But – oh my God, what have I done?'

'You've only done what was to be expected. Look, there was a project Dada was working on, like I said. It involved young people with exceptional potential. He'd included you in it. I didn't like the idea because it went against the grain to use your own family as test subjects but he said it would be advantageous to you one day. That's no doubt what the C/AG review was all about. He was recording your psychological responses to phenomena and how you dealt with situations. He was developing a kind of super-elite psychological response. That's all you've done – responded to an excess of stimuli.'

'But that's so clinical, and why, why…?' I pause, not sure what why I want answered first. 'What stimuli, and why haven't you ever said anything to me about all that before now?'

'Why would I? It all stopped when he died. It was his project and only he knew who his research subjects were. I only knew about you by default. I challenged him about something and it came out then.'

'What?'

'It doesn't matter now.'

'It does to me.'

'It's irrelevant, Gaby. We can't change what happened and like I said, I've always counted you as the biggest blessing in my life. You are still here, so I am still blessed. He isn't and so that is all in the past, whatever it entailed. His stimulus was successful, shall we say? And he suffered the response to it. I should have told you about the drug, but it was doing its job and all seemed well. I was wrong, but if you've stopped taking it, then you've stopped taking it. Just remember that whatever you think you're remembering is muddled – like a confusing dream. Forget it in the same way as you'd forget that when you wake up.'

'But… '

'No buts. There's really no other way if we want to keep moving forward.' She looks fierce, like she might actually physically fight me if I continue to dispute it. 'Once you force something into the open, there's no way of ever covering it up again.'

More questions tumble through my head but they're supplanted by one – apparently trivial. So, do I also leave the fact that she and Dada were a couple before my mother was safely out the door? *To my darling Romaine, who has inspired me from the moment I first saw her and will continue to do so until the breath leaves my body. A. 14th Feb '91.'* Do I leave everything – my whole past – in the past and try to forget about it? Romaine clearly has – despite what I have always assumed about her feelings for Dada. Her eyes are knives, their shiny tips pointing straight at me. They are a warning. The cuts will be lethal if they become necessary.

I realise, again, I have no choice and the chill of the room reaches my soul then. Romaine wants me to say nothing, positively wants to cover this up, and weak that I am – afraid that I am – her want is greater than mine.

'I guess,' I say hesitantly.

'Good. Now, shall we get some clothes on before we both freeze to death? I thought I'd show you my vegetable patch. I'm growing my own now – my latest economy drive.'

There is nothing else to say. She has shut the door and locked it, but can something as momentous as the act of murder simply be buried with the corpse? It wasn't even defensible on grounds of self-defence. It had been a wilful act. A deliberate act of destruction. However, Romaine has made it quite clear that whatever the moral chasm my actions have caused, she has bridged it and cut the ropes adhering it to the rocks on the other side of the abyss. I am still digesting that when I leave later that day, certain she will never betray me, and yet frozen to my core that her love for me may have infected her with my immorality too. And still there's that question I wanted to ask – that feels integral to something – but now no longer can. *'To my darling Romaine... '*

I've damned her to forever bear the weight of my guilt with me, so I suppose it's a small thing to bear the weight of her lie for her.

The bottle of Primaton – or Sineptin – still nestles in the bottom of my bag. I haven't taken any more. What is the point? I have remembered. Most of it, anyway. I have remembered too how I snapped the window pole in two and bundled it up with the bin bags and gloves, leaving the gloves to last because of the blood. Oh God – the blood; there was so much of it... I shake the memory away and focus on the facts. I remember it all in fine detail now. I wrapped the bags round the pole and each other, tied the bag ends together and tossed it all in the lake on the way back to school. I rinsed the blood and bone splinters from the paperweight and initially hid it in my room with the photograph and the manuscript and the book and the letter, but the abrasion on the paperweight seemed to hold the stain of the blood no matter how hard I scrubbed. The suitcases stared at me from the hall but I hadn't time to empty them and store them back in the spare room, without being late back to school. I decided to come back to them, but they had gone by the time I got home, breathless from sprinting to arrive before the cleaner did her Friday afternoon visit at four o'clock. The alarm that had accompanied that discovery; I could still feel it now. Legs trembling and stomach alive with crawling maggots of fear. Yet no one was around and Dada still stared blankly at me from his boudoir of blood. How? Who?

Running upstairs, I found the suitcases were back in their normal home and Dada's clothes had repopulated his wardrobe. I stared. Not possible. And yet it was. There was no denying it. The papercut one of the manuscript pages had given me as I bundled it into an envelope –

stinging and bleeding like the cuticle skin I have picked raw now – proved that what had happened was true. So, did the paperweight and the bloodstained book and the letter, all hidden where I had put them earlier. I retrieved everything and ran back downstairs again, collecting another bin bag from the kitchen before slipping out the front door just as Mrs Noakes arrived. My relics lived in their new hiding place for years – the derelict coal bunker at the side of the house.

Yes, I remember it all now. There is no need for Sineptin. Only punishment.

I rev the car and pull away from my past, but it drags behind me, a clatter of old tin cans announcing the bride and groom's departure – me and the sin I wedded more than eleven years ago. I can hear it following me all the way back to London. The honeymoon has long since finished but the marriage is going to be a long and dismal one. Abigail finds it amusing. She would.

Oh, come on. What better outcome could you wish for? You've remembered what happened, even been forgiven for it by Romaine. Now you know why he died and that's been bugging you all these years. Now it won't any more. It must have been Romaine who removed the suitcases. She must have come home early, worked out what must have happened and removed any suggestion that it was anything other than suicide by unpacking them again.

But why?

Who cares? The subject is closed. Leave it in the past like she said.

But she loved him – even if he was unfaithful to her. She loved him enough to put up with it. Why cover up his murder?

Because she loves you more. Because the status quo is more important. Because she doesn't want anyone digging around too deeply. Who knows? Who cares? You've got other things to worry about at the moment.

Yes, other things. Xander and Jessica Morgan.

Sickness, sore breasts. When was that last fling with Mark?

I don't answer myself – or Abigail. The thought elbows all the other worries out of my head temporarily. But I've had a period. Of a sort. I pull over and drag my phone out of my bag. I google pregnancy, and read the tell-tale signs. Including false periods lasting a day or two and turning into nothing. Oh shit! I scroll through the calendar on my phone and try to pinpoint when I had sex with Mark. Have I miscounted? Was it later or before I thought it was. I'm now not sure of anything other than my memory plays tricks on me. I'm not even sure when my period should have been due. Like I hadn't remembered restarting the medication I'd stopped taking. Or killing my father.

The road is clear most of the way back to London and the chemist named on the pill bottle is still open when I arrive. I park down a side street and walk back to the main road. It is one of those leafy suburban roads that house the respectable and the righteous. My right to a place on it, other than in passing, has long since been forgone, but then given the way appearances are, perhaps its residents are less than perfect too. I'm still processing Romaine's cover-up for me. What does it say about her morality – not that I have any right to criticise that. Maybe Dada is right and morality in its truest sense doesn't exist at all – only what we decide it is. Abigail cheers that idea on.

So, the logical conclusion to that is?

'We're all damned.'

She laughs and I wonder if I am truly going mad. Me, and the whole world with me. Or to hell.

The chemist is halfway along Putney High Street, lights ablaze and a steady stream of customers around the cosmetic and vitamin supplement aisles. I head straight for the prescription counter and tackle the problem head-on.

'I'm so sorry, I've forgotten my prescription receipt but I left one to be filled here earlier. Gabriella McCray. I can give you my address, if you like, and my GP's name.' The girl stares blankly at me. I might be talking a foreign language for all the comprehension in her face. 'I want to collect a prescription,' I repeat.

'I know, but you already have,' she replies, still staring at me.

'I already have?'

'Yes. I served you on Monday, Miss May.'

'May.' My throat constricts at the name. 'But that was for Primaton. This is for Sineptin.'

'You collected both on Monday.' She is eying me, suspicious. 'Are you OK? The pharmacist could have a word with you, if you need to.'

'Oh, no! I'm so sorry!' I shake my head and grin sheepishly. 'It's been such a week this week. Of course, I did! My mistake. How could I forget that? No wonder I haven't got the receipt!'

The girl eyes me strangely, and looks as if she wants to delay me but I hurry away, hiding myself down the feminine hygiene aisle whilst I recover. Abigail May. God, I'd forgotten that too – buried almost as deep as that morning in July. Gabriella McCray may not, but Abigail May. Abigail may do anything; anything she wants. It was what I'd told the doll the day I got her, angry at what I'd overheard. A beautiful doll with the wide blue eyes and ringlet curls, why shouldn't she? Abigail was perfect. It was Gaby who was flawed. But Abigail had helped Gaby. Covered up her flaws. Stopped Dada going away with Louise. Abigail may have to help her again, now.

I told you that ages ago.

'OK, so it's taken me a long time to accept it.'

In front of me are the pregnancy testing kits. I select one at random and take it to the till nearest the door and furthest from the prescription counter. How I was going to sort this one out, I had no idea.

You have me. It will be simple. Everything will be simple if you leave it to me.

Chapter 28

I stare at the little blue line. I have used both tests in the pregnancy testing kit and they both say the same thing. Positive. The line accuses me of all the things I have been doing wrong. Red wine. Too much coffee. Not eating properly. Casual sex. Lies. Theft. Murder... Murder... How can I possibly bring a child into the world? I may not even be at liberty to raise it the way things were going. And yet, how can I *not*? I believe in the sacredness of life, despite being a murderer. I count back, ignoring what I'd thought a period starting. It must be Mark's. Thank God for that, at least. The alternative makes me shiver.

I place the condemnation of the little blue line on the washbasin. It raises a whole new set of moral questions that I'm not equipped to answer. And I am revolted. Yes, that is the right word to use. Revolted that a body as vile as mine should be able to reproduce – to make a copy of myself. Whether it is that revulsion or pregnancy itself, but I am overcome with nausea that won't be denied this time. I vomit into the washbasin because there is no time to make it to the toilet, and with it seems to come all the shame and self-reproach I have been storing up since I was fifteen. When I finally control the urge to turn myself inside out, I hang onto the edge of the basin as if to the edge of a precipice. I am drained. And yet I am full of a life that isn't my own, and so it continues; when have I ever been my own person? When have I ever been normal? Just a girl, growing up into just a woman. Ordinary. Not conflicted, or manipulated or psychologically damaged? Just ordinary, able to make ordinary rational decisions and do ordinary rational things. The answer is in the hollow pit of my stomach and the ache in my chest.

Never.

So how do I face this now, when I am already facing the murkiness that is myself and that I am not sure I can live with. I need help. Oh God, I need help. With that I descend into a kind of hysterical amusement. The one person who would have been able to have a handle on this kind of desperation was Dada. The contradictory was his forte. The hysterical amusement and curiosity prompts me to retrieve Dada's manuscript and see if he had anything to say on abortion. Given the fact that he hadn't wanted me, it would be interesting to see what he would have espoused if my mother had given him the choice. I abandon the bathroom without even swilling out the washbasin – it's a suitable comment on my life – and sit on the end of the bed, spreading the manuscript out across it, dividing it into chapters. Sure enough, there is one on abortion. Unsurprisingly he doesn't come down on either one side of the argument. It is the moral choice of the individual, dependent on circumstances. A cop-out. He loves the contradictions, but won't commit himself to supporting any of them.

"Remember that a child is not a child until it is capable of independent life. There is an argument that until a foetus is born it is only that – a leech, drawing of its mother's incubating body. Against that, some will argue that merely the spark of life is sufficient to render it murder to abort at any stage of a pregnancy."

Thanks Dada.

"I am neither a proponent of abortion nor of slavish insistence on the sanctity of life, whatever the circumstance. What if the foetus is irreparably faulty because of genetics? Or the mother unable to support the onerousness of pregnancy? Conventional morality would have us follow one course above the other at the risk of being labelled callous and selfish if we don't. Is that fair? Is it not a choice what a woman does with her body? She is as much a creature of self-determination as a man. Are we required to procreate? Our world is teeming with the unhoused, the unfed, the uncared for. Adding another to the heap would surely be ill-advised and irresponsible. But what if we don't? Or what if procreation became the activity solely of the unenlightened masses, uncaring of how else they may reach their potential, and the highly intelligent and educated reserve the right to live their lives unfettered by social and domestic demands?"

I guess it at least tells me which category Dada would have put himself in if he had been a woman. My gut reaction is to immediately remove myself from that category as definitively as possible, but he does have a point. I should be a creature of self-determination, and I have been far from that all of my life. Everyone has decided for me – from giving me life, to preserving me from the possibility of incarceration because I took a life away. It seems to me now that at no stage have I ever made a conscious decision about anything for myself.

I wonder how Jenny decided? I think back to what she'd told me about her unplanned pregnancy. '...in the end there was no choice ...' Yet another instance of life trapping you? But Jenny is the farthest cry from a prisoner of denied choices that I can imagine. She regulates the Director, manipulates the client base, provides access to information that shouldn't be accessed and generally does what she thinks she will. Over the last week, I've come to realise that far from being a victim of circumstance, Jenny is a master of what the Director aspires to – to be seen but not accountable. I wish I'd talked to her more now. What a turnaround! The PA I'd dismissed and tried to belittle had more control over what was going on in our little world than anyone.

Transactionalism, that was what she'd referred to; how she applied herself to the manipulation of her world. She made each interaction a commodity worth the barter and providing reciprocation that ultimately made the lack of choice an acceptable compromise. Ethos had needed a PA who was more than a PA. She'd needed a job. She'd moulded the job into one that allowed her to apply her knowledge without taking formal responsibility for it. She'd felt morally obliged to keep her child, so she'd turned an unplanned pregnancy into a planned single parent family. She knew herself and her limitations. She accepted them, but didn't allow them to limit her. And it wasn't that she'd had no choice. Her choice was merely governed by her morals.

This decision I will make wholly alone, with complete clarity about what and who I am – after I have decided what to do about what and who I am.

I look up and I am staring straight at the photograph of Dada, Romaine and me, just days before I killed him. His smile no longer seems wide and charming. It seems artificial and disingenuous. Romaine's seems too bright, and mine seems awkward. He is no longer the man I have remembered him as all these years, but neither am I the person I thought I was. I am both me and a refraction of me – an opposite. I have to be, or Abigail wouldn't exist in my head and nor would I have been able to calmly kill my own father, without remorse or regret. In conventional terms that would make me a psychopath, and yet I know I am not because I do suffer from remorse and regret at other times. I hate even swatting a fly. That makes me schizophrenic then? I search my mind for all the various aspects of schizophrenia I have drummed into myself as a student, with the sole purpose of one day being able to correctly diagnose the condition. Can I diagnose myself? The characteristics: an altered perception of reality, seeing or hearing things that don't exist, believing that others are trying to harm me, or that I'm being watched... With that, it hits me that I have experienced all of these things recently. So, I'm schizophrenic? I get up and go over to the mirror to look at myself. I look bemused – the kind of bemused I can imagine I have been looking all this week. Gaby and Abigail. And what if I hand over the reins to Abigail? Relinquish my thoughts to her – what she would think as she looked at herself. I can feel and see my jaw tightening and my eyes widening but it doesn't make me a different person, nor think I am a different person. I can merely sense how she would approach things. And how could I self-diagnose if I am so out of touch with reality or so paranoid I can't separate the real from the imagined? Objectivity would be an impossibility. No, I am not schizophrenic. The effect of the pills, on the other hand – after having stopped taking them for a while...

I collect my bag from the hall, acknowledging my paranoia about being watched with a wry smile as I shut the bedroom door firmly behind me. Theoretically, if I am being watched, I am being watched in every room – even the bathroom – so what the hell?

'You'll know I'm pregnant then, too,' I say sarcastically to the walls, as I slide the laptop from my bag, balance it on top of the manuscript sheets and switch on.

It's as hard to find information about Sineptin as it was last time I looked, but after a variety of searches I do. Sineptin – otherwise little-known as PTSD. PTSD? I dredge my PhD student memory. Post-trauma-symptom-disruptor. Yes, it's as heavy duty as I first thought it was. This time I don't just read the first page-ranked information sites. I drive down into the lesser read pharmaceutical reviews where the real name is used and the chemical composition revealed. A disturbing picture emerges of the medication I may have been taking for years. Sineptin is routinely used to enhance mood in psychotically disposed patients but generally only in private practice treatment facilities – mainly because of cost. It is most used as a precursor to longer-term therapy involving CBT, hypnotherapy and regression treatment for those suffering from trauma potentially leading to suicidal tendencies, or at risk of self-harming, although it can be used on its own. Then it acts as a blanket, covering up painful memories and burying upsetting experiences. Prolonged-use patients report side effects such as memory loss – partially rectified on discontinuing treatment – but also cite other symptoms on discontinuance. Memory cross-over is the most often-reported – a belief that something remembered from the long-term past has only recently occurred. Past-role confusion is another, where observed actions are believed to have been executed by the observer, not the observed. It literally changes personality traits in some. Only a relatively short period of time without the medic-ation caused confusion and psychosis in one group who had previously been treated with Sineptin for more than two years, hence why it's not usually a long-term treatment option. For periods of under one year, the patient returned to normal memory function/behavioural patterns relat-ively quickly – hence the need for other therapies in conjunction with it.

If what is written in my Ethos record is true, I must have been taking this drug for eleven years. And Primaton? The girl at the chemist had said I'd collected that too. The bottle in my bag claims to be Primaton, but in that case, where is the Sineptin? I'd consciously taken my last dose of anything the day before I'd taken up residence in London. Four pills gone means I've missed only about five or six days in total of whatever the medication in the bottle is. If it was Sineptin, my memory should still be more Swiss cheese than Cheddar, yet the memories are flooding back, vivid and horrific. I can understand why Romaine thought it better for me to forget, but what if my recall isn't accurate? Or it's confused? Given I now have no idea what medication I may have been taking, in the past or recently, could I be mixing memories like those other long-term Sineptin patients who went cold turkey? Could what I'm remembering be skewed, right from filling my own prescription on Monday to firing a gun at the father I have hitherto remembered as having been adored? There's one way I can test a part of that theory, at least. I set my laptop aside and collect the photograph from the chest of drawers. It's more of a hunch than a memory, sliding the backing from the photo frame and peeling away the layers to reveal the photograph itself and what it conceals. Folded – once crisply – into two, edges are now curling and dirty from constant handling. The flowing script blossoms into a blue flower – a forget-me-not – where a water droplet or damp has attacked it, but it still reads easily.

My dear,

By the time you read this I will have gone; left. Not morally acceptable behaviour in the eyes of many, but other's views of morality are not valid unless we validate them ourselves. Only our own view of morality is right for us. Call this a lesson in life. Choose what you do with it, right or wrong, but choose for yourself. If we are entitled to nothing else in life, we are entitled to make our own choices. This is mine.

Why am I leaving? It's a sad fact that things change. That's another life lesson. What you end up with isn't always what you thought you'd chosen originally. Situations change, people change, wishes change; we change. It's called accepting yourself, or being who you really are, even if you don't like what you see. I don't like myself much at the moment, but I have to do this if I am to be true to my choices for myself. I am not a doting father, or a faithful spouse, or a dedicated teacher. I admit I am basically selfish. I want what I want, and I intend getting it. Life is short. Dreams are fragile. People are weak. I've found a way to achieve what I want, albeit at others' expense. For that I'm sorry, but not for choosing what is right for me. I hope one day you too will find and choose what is right for you, regardless of what others think.

I am also, perhaps, running away – but that is another concept altogether in an altogether different game of morality. By running away, maybe I'll dodge a bullet for both of us, so I'm taking that to be my makeweight for leaving. Some would call me amoral, but morality is only a game, and a lethal one at that. It just depends who you play it with whether it's you or they who get destroyed. I'm just keeping myself alive here.

There's just one other thing I want to say to you – although whether I'm now entitled to do so, I don't know. Know who you are. Accept who you are. Act on who you are. Unless you do that, you will always be weak, at everyone's whim. Be strong. Be a shooting star, blazing your own trail.

Regrettably,
Aaron

I put the letter down on top of the dismembered photograph frame and scattered manuscript. There is no doubt now. Accept what you are. The truth of Dada's homily now rings out like a warning bell. How could I have this letter if what I remembered wasn't true? And how could I have transcribed the key elements of it into the notebook hidden behind the book in the bookcase in my office at Ethos, the once blood-spattered book I'd taken from Dada's desk because it contained a letter. It makes no difference whether I am schizophrenic or not, can self-diagnose or not, am rational or not. There remains one undeniable truth. I have killed. Deliberately.

The day wears on, but I don't go with it. I am stuck on one theme. Maybe I should stop this the way I'd thought Dada had stopped things all those years ago? Maybe suicide would be best. Then there would be no need for Romaine to cover up for me, no need to face my guilt every day for the rest of my life, no need to decide what to do about yet another life and how I might destroy it. Yet that would be murder again... I sit amongst the flotsam of my past, lost in my attempts to rationalise everything that has happened over the last week. Ironically, whilst they are completely separate, everything recently now seems inevitably and inextricably connected, the common theme being the question of my own immorality. How can I judge my father for his failings? At least he admitted to them – accepted them and chose to move on instead of perpetuate them. How can I damn Xander for whatever he has done? I am no better. How can I take the moral high ground where Jessica is concerned? I am far worse.

Maybe it is synchronicity, but on that thought my laptop whirs back into life from sleep mode. The icon in the bottom toolbar shows I have incoming mail. I don't want to look at it but the fact that it's an envelope won't allow me to ignore it. I click to expand it and there it is. A message from Jessica, 'sent from my iPhone', saying she will give me another chance, but I have to prove I have accepted the truth. God dammit! What business is it of hers what I accept or deny about myself? I really don't need this. Not now. I'm tempted to simply delete the email, pretend it never arrived, but Abigail interferes.

You still need to keep her sweet until you decide what to do.

I hesitate, finger hovering over the delete button, then decide to email back.

'All truth is relative. I know my truth and am always ready to assist with yours.'

The reply is immediate. My God, she must be hanging over it, waiting.

'Then admit your truth.'

My truth is far too near my self-destruction. I feel the sweat accumulating under my arm pits and the prickling in my fingertips, and with that I know that my thoughts of suicide are self-indulgent. If I'd been seriously considering it, I wouldn't be afraid of being found out now, and Jessica is precisely the kind of person who would make it her business to find me out. Her issue isn't her own identity, it's possessing everyone else's, but she can't know what mine entails.

Then do something about it, Abigail inserts into my ear like an ear worm. *This can't go on. Nor can it go down in writing.*

She is right, but I don't know how to deal with it – nor whether, right now, I have it in me to deal with it. I look at my hands and they are trembling, and my heart is pounding so hard it could break through my ribs any moment.

Shut her down, Abigail prompts. *You know how to do it. So, do it.*

'How?' I ask her aloud. 'I don't know how. How?'

But she's right. I do know how. I know it even as I'm protesting I don't. I even know what to do if I can't. I find Xander's phone in my bag and ring the number on the bottom of Jessica's email. At least Xander and his phone have some positive benefits, like being untraceable. I have to consciously steady my voice as I talk, but fear seems to simultaneously calm me and inspire me. I listen to my voice with a sense of distant unreality. It is me, and not me, speaking. Not Abigail though. She has deferred to me, it seems. Perhaps that means I am equal to this task, after all – even though I don't feel it?

'Jessica, it's Dr McCray. I don't really think it's appropriate to carry on a conversation via email. What is it you want to discuss?' I stifle the tremor that threatens towards the end of the question.

'It's encrypted my end but OK. You know what I'm referring to,' she replies, clipped and business-like.

'My family background?'

'Yes, if that's the way you want to put it.'

'But it's irrelevant to however I can help you. And it's personal to me.'

'It's personal to me too.'

'I'm not sure how.' I feel a little more confident now. The cheek of the woman – the downright cheek! 'I mean, OK, so you and my mother –

apparently – knew each other. But that has nothing to do with my treating you via Ethos.'

'Doesn't it? What about Louise?'

I sit bolt upright, the hairs on the back of my neck straining like a dog about to fight. 'Louise?'

'Yes, Louise. You know who I mean don't you?'

'I have no idea what you're talking about.' My heart is pounding again.

'Louise Morton, fifteen, recently bereaved, sweet pregnant. He told Anita about her and Anita told me. He had this ridiculous ability to be so crass when he was so clever. Fancy rubbing Anita's nose in the fact that he'd got bored with the woman who'd replaced her. He told her she might even have to be a mother to you again if Romaine couldn't cope. How dare he? How dare he use her like that?'

This time, Abigail does speak for me because the words seem to just pile up and strangle Gaby. Abigail, the bold. Abigail the controlled.

'Really, Jessica. I don't know what on earth this is all about. First you want to stir up things about my mother. Now you are asking me about some girl I don't even know. This is all highly inappropriate.'

'Highly inappropriate.' She laughs, a small sneering snicker. 'It is, isn't it? Especially for a therapist. So why suicide? Can you explain that? Why? Makes no sense when he was about to leave you both for Louise. I know, Dr McCray. I know.'

The silence between us crackles with tension. Abigail has abandoned me again. It must be me who replies this time, and there can only be one reply – not that the consequence can be changed by it.

'What do you want?' My voice sounds unnatural; wooden, splintering – a wooden window pole broken in half and covered in blood.

'I want you to work for me. Mariah is leaving, temporarily. You'd be ideal as her replacement.'

It takes me a moment to rein in my surprise. 'Your PA? But I'm not a PA, I'm a psychologist.'

'She's not a PA either. She's an anthropologist. Your receptionist at Ethos isn't just a PA either. Qualifications don't mean a thing. It's connections that make all the difference, and you have some excellent ones. Connections are power.'

'I have no connections at all, Jessica, and definitely not ones that would be useful to you.'

'Oh, you do, Dr McCray – Gaby. You have connections you don't even know about yet. I want them too, and you're going to make the introductions.'

'This is ridiculous. I really don't know anyone you could want to... ' My head is spinning, whirring with confusion. She knows, but all she wants me to do is to introduce her to useful people I don't even think I know.

'Let me share some other names then. Stephen Anders, The Hon Mr Jeremy Roper, Alexander Parsimon – Xander to you, I believe. Interesting relationship you two have, isn't it, by the way? Quite unconventional – and certainly unprofessional. But apart from that, do you know what the link is between all of them?' My throat has completely closed over and not even Abigail's slick patter would be able to slide its way through the barricade now. 'Chiaroscuro, Gaby.' In the silence as she waits for me to understand, the links enchain me too. Chiaroscuro. They are all Chiaroscuro. I am Chiaroscuro too, whether I like it or not. Xander set me up. That is what she must know. Jessica's voice cuts through the fugue in my brain. '*I know*, and I want in. There are answers I want from them. And changes – to the status quo.' That pause again, and I imagine her smiling at me on the other end of the phone. Smiling about all the things she thinks she already knows and now I do too.

Wait and listen, see? Abigail is back in my ear. *It's not so bad. You can shut this down, easily. You don't always need me. You're learning fast.*

'You want in?' I repeat, stupidly.

'Yes, and you're going to arrange it. That's how you're going to work for me. I can get a PA from anywhere, but I can't get to Chiaroscuro – except via you. I'll see you on Monday. Give you some thinking time, should you really need it... Oh, and Robert's back on Monday too, isn't he? I wonder what he'd make of you and Xander?'

She rings off but the threat is still ringing in my ears. Robert – the Director. Chiaroscuro. Xander. Maybe even Dada. Maybe... me. Maybe the whole can of worms, or at least enough of it to set me crawling. I want to be sick. Abigail wants to think. Jessica knows – enough, if not everything. Enough to open up the ground and for me to be swallowed by it. Even if she doesn't pass on what she knows about Dada's death, if she talks to Director Anhelm about anything I've been up to recently, whatever my intention to put a stop to it, or Romaine's staunch support of me, I am ruined. But more than that. She knows something about

Chiaroscuro too, and Jessica understands power. Momentarily, the revulsion with what I've done is replaced by an overwhelming terror of public humiliation, condemnation and then a life of imprisonment and degradation. I can't stand it. It is worse than my remorse, far worse, whether that makes me a monster or not.

I need to get out – get some fresh air. I feel stifled here – stifled by the past and guilt and remorse and confusion and fear. I don't know what to do about anything any more. Romaine wants me to just forget – forget what I did. Pretend Dada really did commit suicide. My body wants me to carry a child, one conceived in nothing but lust, or maybe self-loathing. My conscience wants me to confess, pay the price of sin – *the wages of sin are death* – and my basest instinct wants me to protect myself even if at the expense of others, but I, I don't know what I want to do. I grab my coat, and stuff my feet into shoes as old and ugly as Jessica's atonement shoes, leaving the house without anything but my front door key. It is early afternoon and the sun is shining after days of blustery wind and rain. The wind is still sharp, but the sun tempers it. The good weather has brought out young and old as I walk the length of Putney High Street – for want of anywhere better to go. It is almost as busy as on a Saturday. I shove my hands deep into my coat pockets and hunch myself into my coat, collar high around my neck. I want to be inconspicuous. A nameless face on a nameless street, walking off the after-effects of a glut of self-hate. The biggest irony currently is that – after days of feeling nauseous – I actually feel suffused with a sense of well-being right now, as if my body is trying to lull me into accepting its proposed biological task.

I pass a young woman with a buggy, the baby inside swaddled in a dark blue check quilt. Only its eyes and nose peep out above the muff. They are bright blue, squinting into the sun and beyond me into the wide blue sky, full of awe. I can't bear to look at them. My child's eyes could be as bright a blue yet I am still considering whether to allow it to be born. I look away but catch the eyes of the mother by accident. They are cornflower blue too, and her hair a deep auburn. Her cheeks are pink, whipped strawberry marshmallows, and her lips red – red liquorice snakes like the ones Romaine used to allow me to devour as a kid on what she called our treat days when Dada was at one of his conferences. Sweet and sour. You could dip them in the sherbet and wince as the powder burst on your tongue, or you could chew until the liquorice dissolved on your tongue, tangy and redolent of raspberries even though there were no raspberries in them at all. She smiles at me, one young woman to another, indulgent. She thinks I am looking at her child and wishing. If only she knew I am looking at her child and despairing.

I smile for form's sake and walk briskly past. She stops to tenderly tuck the quilt higher round the child and I hope she hasn't seen me look back. The small act of devotion makes me ache. I don't deserve smiles from young mothers or to see a baby's awe at the sheer enormity of the world. I shove my hands deeper and trudge on. The black cloud follows me despite the brightness of the day and my fellow walkers. I avoid their smiles and polite greetings by fixing my gaze on the shop windows as I traipse the length of the high street. The shops are all full of early Christmas displays – my God, and it's not even October! This one is of fancy confectionery. Swiss chocolates and sugared almonds. The next, gifts and trinkets, and the one after, toys. I stop in front of the toy display. Teddy bears. Soft brown mounds of fur with button noses and twinkling eyes, twist-curled traditional types that probably bleat 'mama' if they are tipped forward and back – like they used to when I was small – and funky mods, dressed in their own designer wear. Every kind of bear for every kind of child. I have never been particularly precious about teddy bears. I had one as a child, I hugged one as a child, I confided in one as a child – but never as I confided in Abigail. Yet today, the very idea of them makes me want to cry. Bears and babies. They go together. My baby would have a teddy. I would choose it – with the utmost care and love – and give it with the utmost joy and delight. But I am still considering whether to allow it to be born.

I turn away, tears stinging my eyes and the wind turns them to icicles that the sun wants to melt. Why had Romaine called me a blessing? I am a curse. She counted me her biggest blessing. She counted me her child, because she had no other – and here I am considering whether to allow mine to even be born. Maybe I need a blessing like Romaine had once thought me? Maybe a child would change me for the better – redeem me? Replace a lost life with a new one? I hunch my shoulders less as the sun intensifies its warmth away from the shadows cast by the shop buildings. I walk on from the end of the high street and along the main road towards Putney Heath. The drone of the traffic is countered by the drone of a plane overhead. I look up into the wide blue sky like the blue-eyed baby had, trying to see it as he or she had perceived it. For the briefest moment, I understand their awe – the awe of a child for a world unexplained. I could gift that awe to someone even if I no longer deserve it for myself. I could gift that awe to my child. I stand in the middle of the pavement and stare upwards until my eyes blur and the green of the trees merges with the blue of the sky, bright little sunspots of yellow peppering where they fuse. The world spins and renews, winter into spring, spring into summer, summer into autumn. I am winter, becoming spring, and my child would be the flowering of the summer. A car hoots me as it passes and I drag my eyes away from the intensity of the sky and its cycle of the old renewing, to the absurdity of some of the creatures that crawl under it. A youth is hanging out of the car and making rude gestures at me as it cruises past. I watch him with distaste as he disappears into the distance, followed by a sudden spurt of anger. Who the hell does he think he is? How dare he encroach on my appreciation of something so remarkable with his coarse ignorance? The flame flickers and grows. He's the disgusting one, not me. I am part of this remarkable renewal cycle – if I want to be; and now I want to be. I may have taken from the world, but I can give back too. I can give a child, to grow up, not tainted like me, but fresh and luminous as the bright bold blue above me. But to do so, I need to do things very differently. Abigail says so too, and for now, because this will be our child, I know I must trust her. Together, we will protect our child. Together, we will make this the fresh start it should have been a week ago.

And then I am marching at top speed back towards Putney High Street, back over Putney Bridge, back into my apartment block, back into my flat and slamming the door shut. The renewing life of the bold blue pulses through me. I feel good. Not disgusted with myself any more. Not afraid. Not uncertain. Sure. And I will atone – in some small way – like I showed Jessica how to. I can give life not only to something fresh and new – unsullied by the mistakes of the past – my child – but to something directly from the past that would have been born if I hadn't taken its creator's life away first. I will see Dada's unpublished manuscript into the world, like my innermost self had determined to do even as she pulled the trigger all those years ago. I will publish it and I will make it a tribute to him; a celebration of all that was exceptional about him. Abigail even has some ideas how I can achieve that, but first there is a stumbling block to remove.

The phone shows thirty minutes of credit remaining. Xander's use of it and me must be almost done, but if Xander follows through as he's promised, the phone will be destroyed anyway so that will get rid of all evidence of any of my phone calls. Doing what Xander wants me to do will also solve the problem of Jessica – although I would have to specify that her phone is destroyed too in order to completely destroy the message trail. In the meantime, I can use this one to ring the number Georges has given me with complete impunity. The Chiaroscuro number.

'Dr McCray. How nice to hear from you!'

It is Xander, but then, Abigail had warned me it might be.

Chapter 29

The queue shuffles along, step by step. I can't quite believe there are so many of them crowded in here on a stifling September afternoon when 2017 is experiencing the biggest heatwave for a decade. So different to a year ago – in so many ways. And how is it that a book on amorality is so popular? Director Anhelm's PR minions have done their job almost too well. I listen patiently to the inscription the woman with the bleached blonde hair and heavy make-up wants in her copy. She is gushing about Dada and how she once met him as a student. She looks too old to have been one of his acolytes, or maybe life has been as hard on her since as it has been on me. I smile and obediently inscribe. The banner above the desk where I am conducting the book signing proclaims, 'We make our own morals'. Director Anhelm came up with that one himself, and of course there is a plug for Ethos underneath. Why wouldn't there be? He has spearheaded the campaign to get Dada's book published with my name even more prominently displayed on it as editor than Dada's as author. Abigail had probably already figured that out when she suggested it to me, but then she would also have known I would have spiralled into another guilt trip if she'd mentioned it, so right until the end it had been my atonement, and now I didn't even mind that she had manipulated me too. It has taken just under a year to produce – a year of my life, so I have given something back – plus it kept my mind off other things admirably. It is kudos for Ethos too, that it is so popular. Even the press have bitten hard, and I am reliably informed I am the subject of a double page spread in one of the nationals tomorrow. The great man and his – potentially – even greater daughter is Ethos' creation – for the moment. But Dada has his moment of glory too. He has proved his exceptional self beyond a shadow of a doubt.

Director Anhelm at least had the grace to add underneath the proclamation, '... but morality is a choice we all make,' attributing it to Dada. It still makes me laugh privately that he has no idea how ironic that statement is. Abigail laughs louder, of course.

The pile of books in front of me is like a barricade but the bookshop has also supplied their own guardian angel in the form of Barry, a retired security guard – now working part-time for holiday pin money – he tells me, anticipating a clash from the pro-life and abortion campaigns after what some called the inflammatory remarks about life and death choices in the pre-release publicity. But I am bomb-proof. Abigail and Director Anhelm have made sure of that too. I am both a stalwart single parent, having chosen against abortion, yet also a staunchly outspoken proponent of freedom of choice. What do I really believe? That is as irrelevant as the anomalies the forensic team identified in Dada's study. It does not affect the outcome and I am fully accepting of the manipulation this time. It is a necessary evil currently. I am a kraken slumbering in the deep. I am an asset awaiting valuation.

I smile and wave indulgently at Romaine and Emma, tucked into the corner near the kids' books. Emma is too young to read. At three months, she can barely gurgle, but they're part of the publicity exercise too. The irony that the amoralist has morals. The twist that turns the quietly afraid woman into the shooting star. That, and what burns inside me like a sacred flame. The knowledge that one day…

***

'I didn't expect it to be you,' I lie.

    'Who did you expect it to be?' Xander's voice is smooth, unsurprised.

    'No one in particular.'

    'Then I am no one. What are you ringing Chiaroscuro about?'

    'I need Chiaroscuro's help.'

    'You understand the conditions if you're provided with help?'

    'That I may have to reciprocate one day?'

    'That you will have to reciprocate one day.'

    'And if I can't?'

    'That isn't an option. Where one choice begins, another ends. Do you still want to proceed?'

    I hesitate, remembering Georges' caution. Once asked, the request cannot be retracted. For good or ill.

    'I don't think I have any choice. But will you… will you also do as you said you would if I do?'

    'What did I say I would do?'

'Destroy the films and the phone. Everything.' My voice cracks with tension.

'I always keep my word.' His voice is soft – almost gentle. Abigail's advice is good. Very good.

'And you'll leave me alone – just let me get on with my life?'

'If that is what you want, you won't hear from Client X ever again.'

'Then I want to proceed.' My words come out fast, forceful. It is done. For good or ill.

'Good.'

'Alexander Parsimon. That is your real name, isn't it?'

'Who told you that?' This time there is surprise, and then amusement in his voice.

'Jessica Morgan.'

'Ah. And who do you need help with?'

'Jessica Morgan.'

He chuckles, rich and ironic. *'Synchronicity. Chiaroscuro will look into your problem, and resolve it.'*

'Will that make me a member of Chiaroscuro?'

'You already are. Do you understand now?'

'What?'

'How stealing can be acceptable?'

'I don't...'

'You are stealing the power Jessica Morgan has over you. You are stealing in order to survive. Bonne chance, Abigail.'

If it hadn't been for the file in the range at Ethos, Client X might never have existed after that. Director Anhlem and his entourage returned triumphantly from their conference the next day. My patient list contracted to lose Client X, Jessica Morgan and Georges Thierone, and expanded to include mostly mild-mannered, untroublesome patients. Poor Jessica's withdrawal looked as if it might be permanent after her accident. Client X and Georges Thierone just melted away and I felt it best to leave it that way, overall. No questions meant no answers to process and I'd had enough answers for the moment. Jenny may have had something to do with the type of clients I was allocated, once I confided in her, but I can't prove that. I learnt how to call them clients, not patients, and to his face, address Director Anhlem as Robert. Privately I couldn't take to him, but it's all about appearances in the Ethos world. We aren't what we seem. We are more, and we are less. Jenny showed me that, with her quietly efficient manoeuvring of people and situations. Looking back, I wonder how much planning went into making sure I had access to the files on myself and everyone else. How much secret knowledge she knew I had to acquire so I could make use of it myself. As the facts fell more into place with every moment recovered from my tremulous memory and every snippet gleaned from the meagre notes I gradually weeded out from Jenny's generous filing cabinets; they described a pattern, but not the rationale for it. I needed more, but Abigail assured me it would come, at the right time. Director Anhelm waited four months, until my condition was too obvious to deny it. Then it came.

'We need to talk, Gaby.' His eyes linger on my thickened waistline. 'We have a high profile and one that upholds certain principles. I'm not sure it's appropriate for you to be working here, in that condition, with no ... '

'Husband? Rather heavy-handed morals, don't you think?'

'Well ... '

'Alright, I have a moralistic question for you too. What is a C/AG review?'

'Where did you hear of that?' Director Anhelm is unnerved. His eyes widen just long enough for me to register he is worried. He should be. I have my own file in my hand. It is one of perhaps a hundred or so I have now identified, all the same. Jenny never did ask for the master keys back. Deliberately, I suspect. I put the file gently on his desk. Or rather, Abigail does. We make a good team these days. 'Ah.'

'Did your son work for you too?'

'My son worked with your father, not me.'

'Then this is his file?'

'It's not an Ethos file.'

'But you aren't surprised it exists?'

'I was nothing to do with their project.'

'Their project? I didn't mention a project. And a C/AG review? What's that?'

'A review of how their project was progressing, I assume. I had nothing to do with it, like I said.'

Something about the way he keeps repeating that makes me think he is glad he had nothing to do with it. But he knew about it. He knew all about it – this project.

'May I talk to your son?'

'No.'

'Why not?'

'He's dead.' His face suddenly closes in on itself. It can't have been a good death.

'Oh.' I wonder if I should voice my commiserations, but hell, his son had dangled me on a string and pumped me full of memory-distorting drugs for over a decade. I can't find sympathy for either of them in me at the moment. 'But you knew all about this project?'

'I knew *of* it. I had nothing to do with it.'

'Tell me about it anyway. And why you have my file in your filing range.'

'Stephen or your father must have put it there because it's not of my making.'

'And the others?'

'Others?'

'There are other files also referring to a C/AG review. My guess is that you probably knew about them too.'

I think of the names. M. Norrish, G. Heland, L. Morton, A. Parsimon, J. Orland-Roper, Openshaw and Williams, amongst the many others. I only actually know two of them – or maybe three at a push – but I imagine they all have something in common – the same thing as me; a project Director Anhelm is glad he wasn't anything to do with, but his son and my father were.

'I don't.' He stares at me, bold-faced. Lying. We both know it. 'Anyway, all that's over with now. Both Stephen and your father are dead.'

'What was *all that*, nevertheless?'

'It wasn't my project.'

'Oh, for God's sake!' Abigail's patience finally snaps. 'So you keep saying, but you do know what it was, so why don't you just tell me? Unless you want me to talk to someone else about it?'

That got him. Who he thought I would talk to, I don't know. I certainly had no idea. The Chiaroscuro number had gone dead after that one and only conversation – as Georges had said it would. As his had too. I merely let Abigail guide me – and guide me, she did.

'It was based around transferrable psychosis. The sleeping Behemoth.' His lips clamp shut. He has spoken the devil's name and now is in mortal fear of it.

Something stirs in me, but I don't quite understand – yet.

'Transferable psychosis?' Psychosis is psychosis. You either suffer from it or you don't. 'You mean group fear? Transferable panic?'

'No, no, no!' He shakes his head. 'Nothing like that. Psychotic tendencies that can be manipulated – off and on. One minute you're fine. The next the psychopath within has control. The sleeping Behemoth. They found ...' His lips pinch so tight they are bloodless.

'What?'

He breathes out. Defeated. Afraid.

'They claimed to have found the switch. The on-off switch. Normal one minute, totally transformed the next.'

'In the people for whom there are files within your records?'

He shrugs. 'I have no idea.'

'You have their files.'

'But not the knowledge that goes with them.'

'You know about me. Am I psychotic one minute and normal the next?'

He spreads his hands and shakes his head.

'None of it was ever proven. Things changed before they got that far. Your father died, and Stephen ... had problems. It was an on-off switch anyway. It would have to be switched on to be effective.'

'So, what am I? Off or on?'

'Off of course! You couldn't possibly work for Ethos if you were an active psychopath.' We stare at each other. Mortal combat has mortally wounded him. 'Not that I'm admitting ...'

'Of course not. And nor if I'm pregnant with no husband?' He opens his mouth to argue but I continue. 'Or is that open to negotiation – if I'm an inactive psychopath, as opposed to an active one?' I can't help laughing at his expression.

'It's not the pregnancy or the husband that matters, it's our image. And you are inactive in anything related to psychopathic intent as far as I am concerned – even if the on-off switch idea were possible. The Behemoth – if it exists, as it possibly does in all of us, maybe – remains sleeping.'

'Are you sure? You are taking a great risk if it's not.'

'Stephen wouldn't have suggested you, if so.'

'Stephen suggested me? I thought he was dead.'

'Before he died. It wasn't that long ago. He thought you might well become our own shooting star, one day, with the right grooming.'

'Indeed,' Abigail agrees on my behalf, even though I demur. 'I *could* be a shooting star given my genes, and what I know.' I watch him watching me. We understand each other, and he understands he was wrong. The risk is great.

'How have you found all this out?' He asks, softly and suddenly. I am taken aback.

'You set me up to find out all of this right from the word go.'

'Me? I tried to steer you away.'

'Like my father would have wanted you to?'

'Yes.' He frowns. 'How…'

'It was in the tail end of your first email to me. The one where you said sorry for not being here when I first arrived.' He frowns again. 'Look if you don't remember. Under your sign off.'

I wait as he trawls through his correspondence and then stops, his mouth slowly drooping at the corners as he reads the sentence below the sign off.

'It was just before …' he pauses. 'He recommended you and then the day before he died, he sent that.' His head droops, a flower head denied rain. 'He was so on my mind when you came… None of it was there for you to find unless you were pointed towards it.'

'But you did. Or your son did. And my clients did too.'

'Oh.' His mouth turns down at the corners. 'I really didn't want you to take them on, you know? It would have been better if you hadn't.'

'No, it wouldn't.' I shake my head. 'The truth is always better to know, even if it is bad.'

'You really are your father's daughter.' He is watching me closely. 'And you are a tribute to him. If nothing else, I am honoured to have the opportunity to help you follow in his footsteps, even though it has led to this.' His top lip is lined with sweat. Little droplets like diamonds in the sunlight streaming in from the side window. I could ask him for anything now and he would agree, because I am my father's daughter and he knows what that means. I think about the manuscript and the promise I made Dada, even as I destroyed him. A tribute – and a bribe.

'In that case, I have an idea to put to you. It's about a book and my future.'

And so it was. I made my case, and it was a good one – to use the pregnancy as the tool to gain publicity for the book. It would position me in the professional world, but it would give me time too; time to cement the bond between my child and I, now I understood. He didn't like it – of course. It undermined his authority to have to agree, but after all Ethos doesn't treat illnesses, it finds ethical solutions to problems, and firing me for being pregnant but unpartnered was certainly not an ethical solution.

Over the months that followed that last conversation with Xander I expanded – both in body as the pregnancy progressed – and in confidence. Yes, I understood stealing now, and the need to survive. There were moments when the outcome seemed not so sure and I feared everything would crumble to dust – when I thought I'd lost my bright blue sky of hope, but it proved to be a false alarm. One that intrigued the doctors but clarified everything even more for me. I had a bad bleed at the end of the first trimester, but a subsequent scan showed my baby holding on tenaciously, if a little small. Healthy, but not quite how the doctors would have expected it to present given my dates. But then, I am not how I appear to present either. I am also both more and less too. I took note of what the doctor said, all the information he gave me from that scan and stored it away. It made sense to me if not to the medical world, and that was all it needed to do for the time being. Appearances are all, if they can be maintained, or manipulated. Another lesson I'd learned at Ethos, and paramount to my child's well-being, in this case.

Whatever else Romaine knew about that fateful day, eleven years ago, she never spoke about it again, and neither did I. It was our pact. Leave the past in the past. And far from destroying me, after a while, knowing the truth about myself tempered me. I am timid, and yet I can be fearsome too. I can be manipulated, and yet I can manipulate others too. I am not the woman who first arrived at Ethos. I have faced my challenges and completed them, however they came to be set. I have survived. My C/AG review may even already be complete; my switch turned on mere days – or maybe – years ago. Who can tell now? I have a feeling I will find out one day, though. Maybe I now have something of the flowing lava Xander's eyes contained within my own. Maybe I have more of the 'everyman' in me, together with everyman's sin. I am more human for being inhuman. It helps to see myself as both Gaby and Abigail, even though I am both and I am neither. They are only two strands of me, twisting together. Maybe there will be more, over time? I have yet to see what they will produce when the weave is complete, but in the meantime, nine months on, and somewhat overdue, I produced a tiny carbon copy of myself. For Romaine, I think Emma is a greater gift than ever I was, and for me, she and Romaine are the greatest gifts I have ever received. Romaine enjoyed the table-turning on Director Anhelm too.

'Never took to the man,' she admitted in a reminiscing moment. 'Bit of a Judas, I always thought. Psychological issues are illnesses, aren't they? Not issues to be solved.'

I didn't think to ask when or how she'd come to that conclusion. Or where she'd remarked on the Ethos tagline from. It seemed irrelevant in the grand scheme of things. I just laughed appreciatively and continued to enjoy the fact that finally life had a kind of peace to it after the turbulence. A flat calm I knew couldn't last, because of the existence of those files, and the names I already knew on them, apart from my own, but for the time being, I relished the time I'd been allowed to make the transition from past to present and prepare.

And so here I am, pen in hand. It is warm in the bookshop. The main door has been propped open but the place is packed, keen to storm my barricade. The bookshelves around me remind me of a fairground, fluttering with brightly coloured book bunting. The titles are perhaps less fair-like. *Killing Spree. Death to Destiny. When You Are Alone.* They have positioned my signing table next to the crime thrillers because they occupy the greatest surface area in the shop. Crime and sex pay, apparently. They hope my book will too. *Fractured Morality – Trading Scruples for Saintliness: An examination of our flawed moral response to an imperfect world,* by *Professor Aaron McCray, edited by Dr Gabriella McCray MBPsS.*

Downstairs, in the basement, the proprietorial coffee shop is churning out coffee and customers with equal abandon. The smell of roasting Arabica makes my stomach gurgle. I could kill for a coffee. I want to giggle. Abigail has such a wicked side to her, revelling in mischief. That side of me can't help laughing even whilst Gaby is shocked and inclined to castigate herself for her misdeeds.

I set my pen down and turn to Barry. 'Is there any chance of a ...' I stop. The woman next in the queue is small and dark, hair swinging glossily over her cheeks. 'Mariah!'

'Hello, superstar!' she is grinning, ear to ear.

'I thought you were going to China?'

'China? Oh no, not for all the tea in... Far too volatile. Power to the people and all that.'

I laugh ironically at the way it's said, given that, for the last three days, the people have been rioting in Tiananmen Square again, but today a shaky detente has been announced between the government and its opposition.

'What are you doing now then?'

'Apart from acquiring my own copy of the hottest thing in the world of "ologists" currently, be that anthropologists or psychologists, I'm still doing what I was doing a year ago.'

'But I thought… Isn't she…'

'Jessica out of action? You would think so, wouldn't you, but the queen left instructions even in the event of – and as she isn't actually dead, just dormant for the time being, her empire operates as per normal.'

Dormant. An interesting word in relation to Jessica Morgan. I want to ask more but daren't. My interest is too keen, too raw to dissemble as mere curiosity. I settle for, 'So, you didn't escape after all?'

'Not entirely, but sometimes negative things work for the positive, even if that seems rather contrary. Order out of chaos – or order within chaos, perhaps. I'm pretty much running the show for the moment.'

'Clouds and silver linings, then?'

Abigail nudges me. *That's your doing.*

'Yes.' Her grin broadens yet more, if that were possible. She hands her copy of my book to me, receipt sticking from it to prove her entitlement to my signature. I take it from her and write, 'To Mariah Norrish, who opened my eyes to what understanding history can do for you…'

She laughs appreciatively at what I have written, even though for her it is upside down, but then, it is all upside down for now.

'I was just going to suggest a break,' I add, glancing doubtfully along the queue. Barry looks discouraging. He clearly doesn't want to have to hold the fort whilst I gossip with an old acquaintance. Unprofessional. Director Anhelm would probably shake his head too, but stuff both of them.

'Oh, I'm sorry. I'm off to Paris shortly. Three-forty flight from Heathrow. Not quite as plush as Jessica's jet this time, but light and shade, light and shade.' I feel a strange tug inside me at her words. Her grin becomes complacent and I am about to allow raw need to overcome caution and ask her why not in Jessica's jet when the fire alarm sounds. The noise is deafening. Now I don't have to bother about placating the queue or Barry or Director Anhelm. Evacuation is in progress before I even push back my chair to stand. Romaine edges through the departing queue, Emma perched on her hip and starting to grizzle. She looks anxious.

'Yours, I hear,' Mariah says, studying Emma. 'In defiance of convention and the boss,' mock-teasing.

I take Emma from Romaine and bury my face in her milky skin. She smells of summer sunshine and wheat fields and I never want to let her go. Romaine and Mariah exchange glances. Romaine steps forward protectively.

'We should go,' she plucks at my sleeve. 'It's probably a drill, but just in case.'

'Yes,' I say to both of them, allowing Barry to part the Red Sea to let us through, three generations fleeing disaster. 'Stay with us,' I call over my shoulder to Mariah. 'We have a lot to catch up on.'

I assume Mariah is directly behind us but when we get outside and I am nursing Emma close to me, trying to shield her from the raucous alarm, Romaine says to me, 'Your friend said sorry she had to go, but she'll be in touch.'

She brushes Emma's cheek and something in me knows now is the time.

It is a false alarm. Probably set off by the heat. Heat breeds fire like pestilence breeds plague. My queue beats me back to the table and I am both heartened by their enthusiasm and daunted by what lies ahead of me. I barely need to find the small note inside the book that has been left on the table in front of where I have been sitting to know what is going to happen next. The book that I have inscribed to Mariah.

'Reciprocation is now due. You'll know who and where. Bonne chance, Abigail.
C.'

C. Chiaroscuro. C/AG review. Norrish, Heland, Morton, Parsimon, Orland-Roper, Openshaw, Williams and McCray. I knew it couldn't just end with Dada's death, whatever Director Anhelm said. Dada wasn't like that. Whatever Dada's project was; whatever he immersed me in so thoroughly that I could beat his skull to a pulp and then put a gun into his mouth, was more than just a project or a reference to some unexplained review in a file. It was more than just an assortment of names, and it was more than just about me. It was chiaroscuro indeed. Light and shade. Life and death. I have stolen power to survive, but the real thief is still out there, waiting to steal it back from me. It seems that moment is now.

We were asleep but one day, we will awake. The Behemoth.
And so it ends, and so it begins…

ABOUT D.B MARTIN

D.B. Martin writes adult psychological thriller fiction and literary fiction as Debrah Martin, as well as YA fiction, featuring a teen detective series, under the pen name of Lily Stuart. She is also a painter and her book on writing and painting and the inspiration behind both, Savage Seas and Sfumato Skies, written under the penname of Debrah Martin contains many of her paintings.

You can find more about her work and sign up for news and updates on forthcoming publications on www.debrahmartin.co.uk.

BOOKS BY THIS AUTHOR:

Writing as D. B. Martin:

PATCHWORK MAN (Book 1) Winner of a B.R.A.G. Medallion

Laurence Juste QC is the perfect barrister; respected, professional, always wins. But Lawrence Juste isn't who he says he is. He's a patchwork man, pieced together from half-truths and lies. Now his past is about to come back and haunt him as the patchwork man begins to unravel.

PATCHWORK PEOPLE (Book 2)

No sooner does Lawrence Juste patch one hole in his fraying life than another appears. No-one is what they appear to be, and there's a certain irony in the fact that only someone even more deceptive than him can help – but they're already dead...

PATCHWORK PIECES (Book 3)

The wheel has turned full circle: the past is the present, the betrayed are the betrayers and the dead in Lawrence's world have resurrected. As his options diminish, the only way out is a lethal form of natural justice for the man for whom law and order were once king.

LADY LAZARUS

When Roseanne Grey jumps to her death on a cold December day, there's no apparent reason why – not even according to her psychiatrist. Detective Sergeant Darwin Grant is told to file the death as a simple suicide, but he's not so sure. There was a lot to know about Roseanne; none of it explicable ...

MIND GAMES

The enviable position of Deputy Director at the elite psychological treatment centre, ETHOS, comes with strings that Gaby McCray would prefer to ignore – until they threaten to compromise more than just her integrity. Can you be both good and evil, doctor and devil, simultaneously? Do you kill, or be killed to protect the answer?

THE BEHEMOTH

The truth behind the secret project psychologist Gaby McCray's eminent but mysterious father initiated lies deep within Gaby but as she comes to terms with who or what she might be as a result, the 'truth' changes once more. The deeper she digs, the more terrifying the prospect of what she has released as the Behemoth rises…

THE FOREVER PROJECT

His nickname of JC ("walks on water") becomes more than just a private joke when Jason Crane's ForEver Project – a means of combining robotics and biochemical engineering to extend life in the terminally ill - becomes more than just a project. He hadn't bargained on being the first test subject for it though – or what it might mean to him as a human, with or without a soul …

Writing as Debrah Martin:

FALLING AWAKE

The story of Mary, Joe and a world populated by love, betrayal and obsession – and what it does to those who live in it. Fantasy or madness? The impossible is only a breath away.

CHAINED MELODIES Winner of a B.R.A.G Medallion

Courage isn't about facing death, it's about loving life – and life isn't always conventional. The unusual story of how two men find not just courage, but self-belief and the true nature of love as one transitions to female and the has to face their prejudices and fears. A different kind of love story. A different kind of life.

Non-fiction books:

WRITE, PUBLISH, PROMOTE

From first idea, through first draft and into print: Debrah teaches creative writing and publishing as well as practices it. Write, Publish, Promote is a distillation of ten years of teaching and writing – "Debrah is an excellent teacher. That first novel is nearer than ever..." say her students.

SAVAGE SEAS AND SFUMATO SKIES

Debrah is an artist as well as a writer. This book describes both oil painting techniques and combines some of her writing – short stories and poetry – with her paintings to demonstrate how to find inspiration through both to prompt creativity. And if you've never painted in oils and want to try – here's how...

Writing as Lily Stuart (YA fiction):

WEBS

Meet Lily: one smart cookie with a bitchy BFF, moody boys and crazy school friends. Life's a breeze by comparison to what happens when her mother starts internet dating with lethal results though. Step up Lily S: Teenage Detective.

MAGPIES

A boy with looks to die for – and Tourette's – tricky BFFs, and and a gang of drug-dealers... THE teenage detective is back and looking for trouble – or trouble is looking for her. It finds her in the form of a childish rhyme, with a deadly hidden meaning.

Printed in Great Britain
by Amazon

17097361R00164